The Myrtlewood Grove

By
Royal LaPlante

BLACK FOREST PRESS
San Diego, California
May 1998
Second Edition

The Myrtlewood Grove

By
Royal LaPlante

PUBLISHED IN THE UNITED STATES OF AMERICA
BY
Black Forest Press
539 Telegraph Canyon Road #521
Chula Vista, CA 91910
(619)656-8048

Disclaimer

This document is an original work of the author. It may include reference to information commonly known or freely available to the general public. Any resemblance to other published information is purely coincidental. The author has in no way attempted to use material not of his own origination. Black Forest Press disclaims any association with or responsibility for the ideas, opionions or facts as expressed by the author of this book.

PRINTING HISTORY
First Printing 1994
Second Printing 1998

ISBN #1-881116-94-8
Printed in the United States of America

Acknowledgments

The author acknowledges the advice
and encouragement of his mother, Margaret LaPlante.
His wife Joanne prepared the manuscript, serving
concurrently as proofreader, editor, and advocate.
The critical advice of fellow writer, Earl Murphy, was
useful in completing the final draft of
The Myrtlewood Grove.

Prologue

The lone figure of a dusky-skinned and long-haired boy scaled the white rocky cliffs, intent on the aerie just beyond his finger tips. A mother screeched angrily as she dove over the head of the young interloper, talons extended, yet somehow not a threat. He touched one egg in the lofty nest, fending off the soaring bird with a retaliatory scream of his own. Chah-al-ah-e smiled in satisfaction and pride as he withdrew to more solid footing. He would have a good story to tell his father, Chat-al-hak-e-ah, village Chief of the Tututni tribe.

Swinging over a deep crevice between two crags, he scrambled to a mossy platform near the top of the promontory; and filling his lungs with fresh ocean air, he purviewed his domain for the day. His deed was suddenly forgotten, and his gaze widened in amazement. A great canoe of the white strangers was passing the Cape; then Chah-al-ah-e was startled anew when the canoe puffed smoke into the wind, and turned toward the shore. He had seen such a craft before, but never so close. The boy left the rugged headland, running for his village to warn his father of the coming of a great smoking canoe.

Chat-al-ah-e thought perhaps he should have alerted his cousins in the Shix village near the white cape, but he did not like Sa-qua-mi. The village Chief was Tututni of course, but he had advocated slaying any strangers in their sleep. He was not a great hunter and noble warrior like his father, who had spoken in tribal council against warring with the whites. Chat-al-hak-e-ah would face the strangers forthright, but only challenge them in battle if they tried to steal Tututni land. Naturally, the Russki could live with the Tututni people, because he had become one of them when he was washed ashore ten winters ago. He had prophesied that other white men would come one day to take their land and had pledged to stand beside his Tututni brothers until the sun came up no more.

The lad dreamed of his father being clothed in honor with the red shirt, and ordering the strangers from their land. He pictured the white men paddling back to the great smoking canoe, obeying his father, and he smiled in imaginary pride at such a sight. Maybe Chat-al-hak-e-ah would become Chief of the Tribal Council.

Entering his small village on the creek, he shouted his news, "Tututni warriors, the great smoking canoe comes! Father, white strangers are here!" The lad faltered briefly as he noticed more warriors around the campfire than lived in his village. Recognizing several of Red-Shirt's men, he repeated his message, and his father rushed out of his lodge carrying a bow and arrow and his trusty old war club. Behind him appeared Sah-mah-ha-e, a nephew of Red-Shirt, the Tututni War Chief. A brief exchange between the father and son followed, during which Sah-mah-ha-e ordered two warriors south and two warriors north to summon all Tututni to the cove "where the gray whales play."

The Chief took his men over the ridge trail to the brushy hill overlooking the cove, not far from the giant rock in the water. As they exited the dense forest, a chorus of "ohs" and "ahs" sounded among the party. The great smoking canoe was lying in the cove, very large and impressive and seemingly filled with men. Two smaller canoes were leaving its sides, similar to the play of calves leaving a cow whale — a scene common to these coastal waters.

Chat-al-hak-e-ah waved his warriors to the beach, signaling and shouting to the men in the canoes, "Go away, white strangers! Do not land on Tututni shores." His band echoed his words, shaking fists at the now milling canoes. Chah-al-ah-e was filled with pride as the white strangers returned to the great smoking canoe, for he saw his father's position as a wise leader vindicated by this success.

The warriors of both villages praised Chat-al-hak-e-ah vociferously, but the Chief silenced them with a hand chop across his foreboding visage. "Look!" he said, "The white strangers bring a big gun to war against us. We must wait for Red-Shirt and Russki to drive these enemies from our land." To his son, he said, "Return to our village and have the women prepare food — much food."

Disappointed at missing the excitement on the beach, Chah-al-ah-e nevertheless obeyed his father with haste, returning two hours later with three younger boys, all laden with baskets of food. As he reached the brushy hill, he saw an impressive panorama of the impending battle.

Before him on the sandy bluff stood the Tututni warriors, facing the giant rock where nine white strangers were encamped on its forested crest, straddling the only approach with their big gun. On three sides of the tidal rock were insurmountable cliffs standing in the roiling waters of the cove, and the rising tide was lapping over the sandy isthmus which connected the beach to the sloping trail.

In the distance the great smoking canoe puffed its way toward the sun, leaving the white strangers and their war weapons on Tututni soil. Such effrontery must be challenged, and Chat-al-hak-e-ah strode forward into the shallows, once again demanding the white men leave Tututni land or his warriors would take their scalps. The intruders talked back in their strange tongue, but did not budge from their position. Sa-qua-mi and his men arrived from the Shix village and lent their voices to the increasing clamor for the white strangers' scalps throughout the night.

As dawn broke the next morning, several young warriors loosed arrows upon the rock, some running to the rock itself to show their outrage and courage. Chat-al-ah-e himself followed suit, only to see his arrow fall short of its target. Panting with excitement as well as exertion, the lad returned to his father's side to watch the arrival of a Tututni war canoe carrying twelve men. Red-Shirt leaped ashore waving a long knife, and letting out a bloodcurdling scream, led his warriors up the rocky slope against the whites. Arrows struck the plank bulwarks of the defenders, wounding two of the defenders as the massed warriors reached the hastily constructed fortification. The big gun fired, killing Red-Shirt and several warriors, and Chah-ah-ah-e ran away up the beach with most of his comrades. A few warriors fought to the death behind the bulwarks, the last attacker's bullet tearing the thumb from a white stranger's hand.

The war party gathered on the beach to prepare for a second attack, when Russki strode forward, laying down his bow and arrow as he approached the rock. Gesturing friendship, he met with the Chief of the white strangers to arrange a truce for the removal of the Tututni dead. He kicked Red-Shirt in contempt, stripping the shirt from the body, and walked away. The disgrace of the former chief was confirmed as his body was deserted on the tidal sands.

In the gathering of warriors up the beach, Russki held the red shirt before him in silence, until another village chief was pushed forward, donning it to the acclaim of his warriors. Chah-al-ah-e listened to Russki tell of his conversation with the white Chief in his strange tongue. The invaders promised to leave when the great smoking canoe returned in fourteen suns.

The boy missed the rest of the story as he was sent on a hunting party to gather food for the growing war party — more Tututni on the beach than Chah-al-ah-e had ever seen. When the great smoking canoe failed to return on time, he raced to the beach to watch Red-Shirt harangue the white strangers, finally waving his long knife and giving a piercing yell to charge. Shots rang out from the rock and the luckless Chief fell mortally wounded, his comrades taking the red shirt but leaving the body where it had fallen.

Soon another village chief donned the red shirt, and his strong voice carried over the sand and water, threatening the whites. Great bonfires were lighted on the beach as the Tututni ate and danced, girding themselves for a third attack at sunrise.

A voice carried through the damp morning air from the scout near the giant rock, "The white strangers have escaped. They are gone from the rock. They run toward the Shix village."

Chah-al-ah-e watched Sa-qua-mi and his warriors move in quick pursuit, giving chase to the fleeing whites while hurrying home to protect their village. He turned his attention to the Tribal Council meeting, only to grow tired of the indecisive bickering over what to do. Many warriors returned to their villages and the war party continued to shrink in numbers. When the great smoking canoe was sighted on the horizon, Red-Shirt took his war canoes down the coast, and the remaining Tututni melted into the forest.

Chah-al-ah-e asked his father why he was so solemn after they had won a victory at Battle Rock. Chat-al-hak-e-ah's answer echoed Russki's prophetic belief, "But the white strangers will come again."

Chapter One

Wisps of coastal fog swirled around the murky ghost of a steamship, gusts of wind creating whitecaps which quartered the prevailing westerly sea. The heavy rain had given way to Oregon mist, but visibility continued to tease the sailors steering her warily toward the Umpqua River bar a scant mile off the bow. The ship moaned as she rolled in the tumultuous sea and shallowing waters of the bar.

A late seasonal storm had forced the Kate Heath, eight days out of San Francisco to sail well offshore, and had delayed anticipated landfall for over sixty hours. With daylight came a clear, but all too brief sighting of the coast line and the Umpqua River bar, The Kate Heath took a new heading and crept forward toward landfall. Scott McClure braced himself against the starboard rail forward of the wheelhouse, holding a rigging line firmly in his right hand. He wore a thick brown flannel jacket over a plaid work shirt and tan corduroy-ribbed pants tucked into his leather boots. He was properly attired for the weather and for the expected landing this morning.

Scott had shaved before coming on deck. His father's straight razor was a reminder of the purpose of his long journey. His brown hair held a tint of red—his father's was red as his mother had told him so many times, and it was cropped short under his wool stocking cap. His deep wide-set eyes under full brows, though normally expressing curiosity, became unfocused as he stood thinking of

1

his travels. He was blessed with strong white teeth, and his pleasant but unremarkable countenance brightened when he smiled. Scott was slim but solid at 5'10" and 168 pounds, looking younger than his twenty-six years. His physical strength was hidden except in his large farmer's hands. A plow had given him a powerful grip, with corded muscles extending through his arms and shoulders. He had "Indian wrestled" and bested men much heavier than he was, well known for his arm-wrestling skill around St. Charles, Missouri.

The moist, cool air was calming to this farmer who was impatient to set two feet on firm soil. The rumble of surf on the beach mixed with the steady beat of the ship's engine. An occasional voice called out a sounding, and more than once spoke a muffled, "Damn weather!" Mate William Tichenor nodded to Scott in passing, as he made his way forward in steady seaman's strides.

Scott's thoughts turned inwards again, as he smiled with amusement at his landlubber's first attempt to stride, or even to shuffle, along the deck of a seagoing vessel. He had tried his sea legs on the second day out of New Orleans, only to stumble with his third step and fall to the railing of the Primrose. Further disgrace befell him as his stomach rejected his tentative breakfast of coffee and hardtack. At least he was hanging over the rail, a position approved by the grinning crew members. While seasickness was controllable and he could now walk a rolling deck, Scott knew that he was no sailor.

He had arrived in New Orleans during the Easter holidays seeking passage to Panama, and had found that the California gold rush had put great demands on passenger berths. Tickets were sold out on Panama-bound ships many days before their posted sailing dates. Prices were high, ticket lines were long, and fights between prospective voyagers were common along the Mississippi levee. Scott had queued up for a ship, foolishly hoping that space would be available for a few passengers. But as commonly expected, the gangway was lifted with nary a man in line moving forward. Hearing the man behind him mutter, "I'll get aboard!"

he followed him with his eyes. The stranger addressed the Purser briefly, bought a ticket, then slipped two more gold coins into the officer's open palm, and walked with him up the crew's gangway a moment before lines were cast off.

Scott mulled over his options at supper in the hotel dining room. His choices appeared his ticket purchased for a ship scheduled in two weeks, or spending an extra $40 to bribe an officer. His thoughts of bribery caused him a twinge of farmer's conscience, but his practical thought won out, Hotel prices are high in New Orleans. It's cheaper to bribe the Purser than wait here for a ship. Two weeks is a long time.

He had unconsciously been eavesdropping on two gentlemen at the next table who were discussing commerce. The Steamship Primrose was carrying a cargo of rum to port and they worried about its security with a potential mob on the docks. Scott was fully alerted when a third man strode to their table and greeted them with a whisper, "She'll dock within the hour and leave for Panama on the morning tide." All three men hurriedly left the room.

Without hesitation, Scott packed his gear, checked out of the hotel, and hired a cab to take him to the levee. A ship was being docked at a well-lighted wharf, as he motioned the driver to stop beside a nearby warehouse. Walking directly to the lowering gangway with canvas bag over his left shoulder and hand case in his right hand, he enjoyed good fortune in finding both the right ship as well as meeting the Purser on the gangway. All passenger berths had been sold out days ago, but Scott's two coins secured a berth in crew quarters.

The Primrose sailed on schedule the next morning, and the excitement of his good luck and lofty venture lasted through the six uneventful days of the voyage. Aside from his seasickness, Scott's only anxiety came as the Primrose lay off the Caribbean beach at Panama, and he thought apprehensively, What a mess! Everyone's trying to be first ashore. Why does the Captain allow his passengers to crowd into those small boats? Oops! There goes one, capsizing in the surf—and everyone's laughing. This mayhem is not very well organized. I'll ferry to shore later.

As he stepped ashore two hours later and planted his feet in the sand, he observed all the beach activity, muttering to himself, "Well, here you are Scott McClure. Where to now?" A steam whistle blew a farewell chord as the Primrose stood out to sea.

Native guides promising an easy overland trip to the Pacific Ocean were everywhere. Scott spotted a Spanish-speaking passenger talking to one of the guides. Reaching a spontaneous decision, he set out after the pair as they reached some agreement and walked up the beach to a campfire surrounded by men. Scott joined the group of twenty-one travelers and three guides.

In the morning, the party headed into the sunrise and through the tropical jungle, with its natural barriers of swamps, wild animals, and unfriendly natives. However, the white man's real peril developed more slowly, as the ague gripped three men in the group. Scott shared his comrades' fear of the fever, and was relieved when the sick men were left behind in a native village with one of the guides to nurse them. He wondered if they would live to see San Francisco.

After seventeen days of hardship and travail, most of which was but a dim memory to Scott, he and his comrades stood on the Pacific beach a few miles southwest of the City of Panama. He soon found that he had endured privation and risk in a jungle crossing only to face the frustration of seemingly interminable waiting for a ship. His funds were rapidly depleted, both by his purchase of a ticket on the steamship Tiburon, and by his delay in Panama when the ship was overdue for twenty-two days.

Scott's patience was further tested as the Tiburon made several ports of call along the Mexico-California coast, before sighting the sunbathed Golden Gate of San Francisco on June 11, 1850. He scrambled forward on the unsteady deck, grasping a rail as he admired the majestic scenery, "My God, California is beautiful," he declared, realizing that he had spoken aloud when a deckhand replied, "She's a land of opportunity, sir. Good luck in finding your fortune here."

Scott smiled at the seaman's assumption that he was a Forty-Niner, and eager to dig for gold. After all, everyone else on board seemed to be headed for the gold fields. As they cruised the gentler bay waters, he looked up the Mate, asking how he might go about finding a ship bound for Portland with a call at the Umpqua River, where he intended to start searching for his father. The Mate smiled wryly as he commented, "So you're not another Forty-Niner? Well, Mr. McClure, passage to Oregon is difficult to find since most ships are provisioning the California gold boom." He paused, thoughtfully adding a warning for the traveler, "San Francisco is a wild city. Watch your valuables and stay out of 'dives,' where the hoodlum element preys on newcomers."

It was advice Scott heeded as he waited patiently for a ship, finding it necessary to work on the docks in order to pay the inflated prices for room and board prevalent in the bustling port. The city's boisterous and often lawless populace did not attract the quiet farmer, nor did the get-rich facade of the gold fields. He often thought, There are too many people, and everyone of them on the move. I like the land, but this city life is stifling. He was not comfortable again until he sailed out of the Golden Gate aboard the Kate Heath in late June.

A loud cry of "There's the spit!" roused Scott from his reverie. A shaft of sunlight pierced the heavy mist to give a fleeting glimpse of the north spit and the choppy water over the river bar, and then vanished as the ship moved forward. Mate Tichenor called, "Steady as she goes!" From his position on the bow, his solid frame seemed to lean forward as if he would lead the ship across the entrance bar to a safe landing. His dark hair and full beard were sprinkled with gray, and resolute dark eyes were set above a strong nose and a wide mouth. His command presence was reinforced by the dark officer's suit with a black bow tie and visored cap. In contrast, his feet were more practically clad in common seaman's boots—he would not change to officer's shoes until the Kate Heath was safely anchored in the river estuary.

A strained voice cried, "Four fathoms," and then more urgently, "Three fathoms." The Mate repeated, "Steady as she goes" as he listened to the surf and the rippling water of the ocean meeting river water over the shallow bar, Tichenor had proven to be an experienced sailor on the voyage north, and now proved his worth as an Umpqua River pilot. An almost audible sigh of relief came from all hands as the ship cleared the bar and took a northerly turning in the mist-shrouded bay.

Scott pondered the likelihood of finding a trace of his father in the Umpqua valley. Sarah McClure had maintained an absolute faith that her husband was alive and would return to her in Missouri. Even though his last letter from Oregon had been delivered in 1829 by a neighbor returning from the St. Charles Post Office, his mother was always hopeful and expectant that word from James McClure would arrive at any moment.

Scott was a curious five-year-old when their neighbor brought that crumpled and water-stained envelope to Sarah. His mother opened the letter and her hands trembled in excitement as she scanned the single page, looking for a clue as to when James McClure might return from Oregon after his two-year absence. Sarah read the letter twice, before turning to her son and saying, "Scott, your father sends his love. He is healthy and employed by a fur company captained by Jedediah Smith. He wrote this letter from a campsite on the Sixes River last summer. Oh, I hope that he will come home soon."

As Scott grew to manhood and worked the family farm, he had doubts about his father being alive; but he never questioned his mother's trust in her husband nor her certainty of his return. Neighbors grew uncomfortable talking with Sarah about her husband, and seldom called at the McClure farm. Scott courted Alice Tidwell, whose parents owned a nearby farm, until she complained about Sarah's "fantasies." They had their first and only argument, and after that incident, they grew apart. When she married a storekeeper in St. Charles, Scott was not surprised but turned morose, and rarely laughed anymore.

In late November 1849 a winter storm brought cold and snow to the St. Louis region. Sarah caught a cold which developed into a fevered hack and finally pneumonia. Scott walked twelve miles to St. Charles for medicine, and when he returned to the farmhouse his mother was unconscious. During the night her labored breathing rattled in her throat as she mumbled incoherently, and her strength continued to wane as the fever ran unchecked all the next day. When it broke during the following night, Sarah awoke and was lucid and coherent for a few minutes.

"Scott, you are the spitting image of your father! Your face is more serious than James,' but when you smile (cough) . . . I see the McClure good nature and lively sense of humor in your eyes. They twinkle, you know. Ah . . . how much I wish he (cough) . . . were here for me to touch. Scott, give me your hand . . . promise me that you will find your father, and (cough) . . . bring him home . . . to me."

A paroxysm of coughing shook her frail body, and hastened Scott to say, "Hush, shhh . . . mother, don't talk . . . shh. I promise to find father . . . you rest now." Sarah smiled and closed her eyes, falling asleep with her hand joined to her son's. She passed away in the early morning hours.

Scott found no incongruity between his deathbed promise to his mother, and his belief that his father was dead. He gave credence to the possibility that his mother was right and James McClure was alive, and he stood firm in his duty to find him or learn of his fate.

He sold the farm and all of his possessions, except for a canvas bag which held his clothing, boots, and five of his favorite books, and a hand case for the family Bible, his father's straight razor, his mother's locket, and a few personal mementos of the McClure farm. His only other possessions were a money belt strapped snugly about his waist under his longjohns, and his best hunting knife sheathed on his belt near his right hand.

Scott regretted selling his musket, a family heirloom, but he planned to travel to Oregon by ship and the musket was not necessary. He would buy a new hunting rifle in Oregon.

He was remembering his trip on foot to St. Louis and the riverboat ride to New Orleans when his attention was called back to the present. "Hard starboard!" shouted Mate Tichenor with urgency, and within moments added, "Steady as she goes." Sounds emanated from the mist ahead of them, most notably the sound of carpenters' hammers and loud but indistinct voices. As the Kate Heath broke free of the fog bank into bright sunlight, Scott could see cargo stacked on the shore and shelters being built above the beach.

****

William Tichenor's job as pilot completed, he turned to Scott. Gesturing to the green forests and river valley, "How do you find Oregon, Mr. McClure?"

"It's primitive, isn't it? The forests grow right down to the shore and the hills are darkly foreboding, but such wilderness has beauty as well. Is there any good farming land here?"

Tichenor smiled with understanding, answering with an advisory manner, "Yes, the Willamette Valley grows everything, but I prefer this coastal land. You should settle here. It's a land of opportunity not unlike California, but with less people."

Looking past Scott, he addressed two other passengers, "Will you gentlemen be settling in Oregon?"

Philip Ritz responded with a dour grimace, "I'm not impressed with this wet and hilly wilderness. I'm going farther inland. Will you join me, Bush?"

Bush Benton nodded and turned to Scott, "Mr. McClure, will you stop here or would you like to join us?"

"Thanks, but I have business here. Good luck in your travels." Tichenor nodded to the men and returned to the bridge. Scott went below to collect his gear as the ship anchored near shore.

Returning topside, he saw Benton and Ritz being ferried to shore in a canoe. Scott waited until the Mate was free, and then walked over to him to ask, "Mr. Tichenor, do you know anybody that was here in 1828, or that might know about Jedediah Smith's fur company?"

"No," came the answer, "most of the people that you see on shore are newcomers. Several of them are survivors of a shipwreck a few days ago on the Umpqua bar—it can be treacherous." He paused and pointed, "I understand this settlement has been named Gardiner. There is a store located up that slope which should be a good place to ask about old-timers. Besides, I've heard Harvey keeps clean rooms—stay there." Stroking his beard in thought, he added, "And maybe there are a few trappers left upriver in Verneau or Fort Umpqua, the former Hudson's Bay Company trading posts."

Scott nodded his thanks, and wished Tichenor good sailing. As he climbed into a dinghy, he heard, "Best of luck, I hope that we meet again."

Unloading his gear on shore, Scott observed his friends Benton and Ritz in conversation with two men. Bush looked up and offered, "Mr. McClure, Monsieur Brobant and his partner have agreed to canoe us to Verneau today. Why don't you come along?"

"Thanks again, gentlemen, but I'm staying here for a couple of days." Turning to Brobant he asked, "Have you ever heard of a trapper named James McClure?"

"Non . . . in the Umpqua Valley? . . . Non . . . you might ask for the old-timer, Buzz Smith, at the store."

Scott nodded to all four men, and walked briskly up to the store. He entered the open door, and hesitated in the dim aisle. The only light came through the window and door behind him, so he let his eyes adjust to the interior. A customer picked up a burlap sack from the floor and turned away from the tall, thin man behind the counter with a "See you next month, Harvey."

Scott stepped aside to let the man pass, and then moved forward with his canvas bag still over his shoulder. "Do you have a room for me?"

Harvey nodded, "Yup, for how long?"

"A day or two maybe, my name's Scott McClure."

"I'm Harvey Masters." As he offered his hand, he said, "Did you come in on the Kate Heath?"

Scott shook hands as he continued, "Yes, I'm from Missouri and I'm looking for my father, James McClure. He was with a fur company at the Umpqua in 1828."

"Hudson's Bay Company?"

"No, he was with Jedediah Smith."

Harvey paused, looking intently at Scott, "Mr. McClure, you know . . . Jedediah Smith's company was massacred by Umpqua Indians . . . only a few trappers escaped."

Scott blanched, thinking aloud, "He may have survived. . . ," and taking a deep breath, "Where did the survivors go, Fort Vancouver?"

"Yes, at least Smith went there. I don't know about anyone else. I just moved to the Umpqua and built this store last month, but everyone has heard about the Jedediah Smith massacre."

Scott stood quietly for a few minutes, and remembering the Frenchman's advice, he asked, "Do you know an old-timer named Buzz Smith?"

With a low chuckle, Harvey replied, "Yup, he's upstairs sleeping off his sixty and some birthday party. He'll be down for supper. . . . He never misses my woman's cooking. You're welcome to join us after I close the store."

"Thank you, sir. I'm looking forward to a home-cooked meal. Which room is mine?" Scott followed the storekeeper to the rear and up the stairs to a small room, simply furnished with a bed and a washstand.

"The outhouse is out back, please lock the door if you need to use it in the night."

"Sure," he said as he dropped his gear on the bed. "I'm going to walk around town today." He followed Harvey downstairs and stepped out the back door, strolling around the store on the path leading to the beach.

He spent several hours walking through the settlement, talking to men at the landing, the building sites, and the tent saloon. Scott was tired when he returned to his room—he had talked more today than he had in years. He lay down on the bed to plan for the next day, and was awakened by a rap on his door.

"Supper's ready, come on down to the kitchen," Harvey announced.

Scott arose and shuffled over to the washstand, where he poured tepid water from a pitcher into the basin. He rinsed his face and hands, ran his fingers through his hair, and dried off on a rag towel hooked to the stand.

Walking downstairs briskly, a fragrant aroma pervaded the hallway. "Chicken," he thought as he entered the lighted kitchen. He hesitated in the doorway, observing a short motherly woman with pink cheeks and gray hair bending over the oven. Seated at the table were Harvey and an old-timer, dickering amicably over the price of three pails of honey.

Harvey nodded to Scott, "Mr. McClure, meet my wife Alma and my friend, Erastus Smith."

The woman smiled, "Mr. McClure, welcome to Gardiner. I understand that you've just arrived from San Francisco?"

"Yes, aboard the Kate Heath. Thanks for sharing your supper with me, Mrs. Masters. And please call me Scott." Turning to Smith, he asked, "Are you Buzz Smith?"

"That's right, Scott. Only Harvey and Alma call me Erastus. When I first came to the Umpqua in 1831, I visited a small Indian village up near Verneau. Squaws were collecting honey from beehives . . . rotten old hemlock stumps . . . on a hillside burn." Reminiscing, Buzz drawled on, "Well those Indians loved their honey just like me, but I figured to show off a mite. I found some cedar shakes and made four beehives. Heh, heh, I had everyone guessing what I was doing, and when I dug out my first colony of bees from one of those stumps . . .well, they thought I was crazy. Anyway, I taught the women how to care for proper hives, but first the Indians had a belly-laugh at my expense and named me 'Bees'. Of course, it sounded like Buzz; and my trapper friends picked it up, saying bzzz, bzzz, bzzz, goes the 'Bees'. Heh, heh . . . the name stuck. Now, another time when I was in Fort Umpqua, an Indian . . ."

Alma interrupted, "Erastus, enough of your tall tales! You let Scott talk, I want to hear all the news from San Francisco. Scott, I hope you like chicken and dumplings. . . . Don't worry, you can eat before I ask all my questions. Harvey, say grace so that we can start."

"Oh Lord, bless this meal and our friends supping with us tonight, Amen!"

Scott had been studying Buzz Smith as he talked, taking a natural liking to his good-natured and friendly manner. Scott envied Smith's easygoing story-telling; and thinking to himself, I can't tell stories about San Francisco. I don't know what Alma wants to hear.

Conversation stopped as everyone enjoyed the meal. Scott managed a, "Fine cooking, ma'am, I haven't eaten a better meal," between mouthfuls.

Buzz echoed the compliment while swallowing food, "Alma, you're a wond . . .", and everyone chuckled as he choked a little and tried to finish swallowing. As he caught his breath, his ruddy face darkened further, and his Adam's Apple jiggled under his short gray beard. His reddened scalp tinted his thinning gray hair and wrinkles stood out momentarily on his face.

He continued unabashed, "Harvey, how come you're not fat? If I ate Alma's cooking regularly . . . why I'd swell up . . . Alma, can I have seconds?"

"I won't be able to get into my buckskins tomorrow." He demonstrated his imaginary plight by standing up, stretching his white shirt and denim trousers and loosening his leather belt. "I was 5'6" and 130 pounds when I sat down and now I'm 5'4" and 150 pounds." His lean muscular frame denied his jocular claim as he sat down and resumed eating. Scott thought that he was mighty fit for his age.

After two pieces of wild-blackberry pie, Scott's cup was refilled with coffee, and he was called upon to answer Alma's questions about San Francisco. He acquitted himself well, as he recounted his trip from St. Charles to Gardiner. His companions listened to every word, smiling and laughing at his anecdotes. Scott became so comfortable with his new friends that he talked about himself and his family as he never had done before.

The wall clock struck twelve times before Scott, somewhat embarrassed, said, "It's late and I'm keeping you up."

Alma quickly responded, "Not at all! We all thank you. News from the outside is a treasure, and we're happy to make a new friend."

As they stood up around the table, Scott asked, "Buzz, are you acquainted with any trappers who were here in 1828?"

"No . . . well, yah . . . a friend of Alex McLeod still lives up around Fort Vancouver. Harvey told me that your father was with Jedediah Smith's party, and my friend, Abner Dundee, worked for the Hudson's Bay Company party which returned to the lower Umpqua a month after the massacre. McLeod was known and respected by the Indians, and he recovered horses, beaver pelts and camp gear for Smith. Now, I understand that Smith was along and wanted a little revenge, but McLeod followed the Hudson's Bay Company policy of protecting property rights without killing Indians."

"What became of Jedediah Smith?"

"Well, I heard the company bought him out and he left Oregon. You know . . . there might be someone left at Verneau or Fort Umpqua who was around in 1828. You might ask around."

"How can I get to Verneau? I reckon that's the place to start searching."

Buzz answered, "Well, you're welcome to canoe upriver with me tomorrow. I'll be leaving mid-morning."

"Thanks, I'll pay you the going price."

"Well . . . the only pay I'll take is in work. Heh, heh, you can paddle. Good night, folks."

Scott thanked Alma for dinner and said his good night as he went upstairs to his room.

****

Buzz stored his own gear in the bow of the canoe, and packed Scott's toward the shore end. With a doubting look, he queried, "Have you handled a canoe before?"

"Yes, but not since I was a boy playing 'Injuns' on the Missouri River. Don't worry Buzz, I'll earn my passage."

Scott stepped gingerly into the canoe and sat down on the aft board seat. He saw clear skies to the east, but the bay was partially covered with fog. The Kate Heath had lifted anchor and was steaming slowly into a light mist.

As Buzz pushed off from shore and took the forward seat, he mused, "Well . . . I hope that ship has a good pilot. He's as eager to get to sea as you are to reach Verneau. Course, I reckon the bar will be clear of fog in half an hour. Say, Scott, there's sloughs and marshes all around the bay, so I'll guide us out from shore and then head upriver."

Scott followed Smith's lead, paddling lightly until he saw and felt the flow of the river. Without comment, he dug his paddle into the water with real force and the canoe leaped forward. He concentrated on maintaining a balanced stroke, but he did take notice of cabins along the river.

"How many settlers are in the valley?" he asked.

"A couple of hundred people down river from the rapids at Verneau. Kinda hard to keep track this past year. Lots more when you cross over to the Willamette, and Portland's a real city."

"Do you do any farming? . . . besides being an apiarist?"

"Apy-who? What's that big word?"

"Apiarist, a beekeeper . . ." Scott chuckled, "My mother taught me at home. She must have done a good job."

"Ah . . . I knew that word . . . apiarist, but I wondered if you did. You're pretty good with that paddle, too."

Following a few minutes of silence, the canoe rounded a bend in the river, and Buzz spoke again, "Scott, see that river yonder?" Pointing to the north shore where a small river joined the Umpqua, he continued, "If you pull up on that flat east of Smiths River, I'll show you where Jedediah Smith's party was camped when the Indians attacked them."

Scott and Buzz tramped over the grassy meadow for an hour. His young companion's face developed a disappointed look, and the old-timer muttered, "Nary a sign after twenty years, but this spot is where fourteen men are buried." Scott merely grunted and headed back to the canoe.

They were quiet for the next hour as Scott propelled the canoe upriver. When his shoulders tightened and his stroke shortened, Buzz joined him in paddling, and the canoe moved over the surface with speed and grace. A little before noon, Scott saw a small cluster of houses on the north shore.

Buzz announced, "Welcome to Verneau! Those rapids we've been hearing are just upstream. The river's a lot tougher to travel above Verneau, although it's still the fastest passage to Fort Umpqua. The trail is slow traveling and hard work. Give me a canoe anytime."

"Where do we land . . . at the dock?"

"Nah, go past those older buildings to that cedar snag. My cabin is just beyond . . . kind of tucked into a small cove. Mr. Scott has a donation claim covering much of Verneau. There's talk of building a real town by that dock . . . and naming it Scottsburg."

Moments later they paddled around the point and Scott spotted a small log cabin above the river bank. As they glided through a quiet eddy in the cove, he saw a stretch of sandy beach. He rested his paddle athwart the canoe and let Buzz ease the small canoe to a landing.

The men unloaded the canoe, hoisted it atop the low bank, and walked to the cabin with their gear. Scott noted that weather-beaten logs formed a square box, with notched ends securing the corners. Mud and grass chinking was stuffed in cracks between the stripped logs. The roof was made of cedar shakes covered by a thick layer of gray-green moss; and its slope was shallow, suggesting limited headroom within. The Old-Timer opened the plank door and stepped into the single room. Scott paused as he ducked his head under the roof edge, and found Buzz was busy with flint and dried moss in the fireplace. As a small flame kindled and grew brighter, Scott could see the crude interior and simple furnishings. To the left of the door stood a small table and two stools—solid blocks of wood cut from the trunk of a Douglas fir. Between the table and fireplace were three small shelves pegged to the wall— bare except for a tin of coffee and two cans marked BEANS.

The fireplace was fashioned from rocks and some form of mortar, and an iron pot hung from a chain hoist next to the firebox. In the corner sat an old shipping crate containing several pieces of cookware.

Along the back wall, a bunk formed from poles and leather straps sat a few inches over the plank floor, and was covered with a matted bearskin. Buzz put his rifle in a rack situated directly over this bed. He threw his gear onto the floor between a pile of traps and a stack of firewood opposite the fireplace. A leather-bound chest rested in the front corner beneath three pegs designed to hang coats, like the tattered buckskin jacket draped over the last peg.

A hand-crafted wooden rocking chair sat before the fireplace, the only concession to comfort in a utilitarian room. Scott rocked the chair with his hand and murmured, "A fine piece of workmanship, Buzz! It's a solid piece of furniture . . . light colored and heavy. But it isn't oak, is it?"

"No, it's myrtlewood and came from down the coast a ways. A friend spent the winter trapping along the Coquille River with an Indian band, and carved the eighteen pieces of this rocker from a single myrtlewood log given to him by the Chief."

"How long have you owned it?"

"Well . . . let's see . . . I bought this cabin in the spring of '32 from a Hudson's Bay Trapper, and my friend gave the rocker to me on my birthday three summers later . . . '35."

"And you've lived here ever since?"

"Yah . . . well . . . I did spend one winter trapping on the Suislaw River north of here, but otherwise I've lived here. Used to be Indians camped around this flat, but not this past year."

Buzz added a couple of logs to the glowing fire and asked Scott, "Say, you are staying with me, aren't you? It's not much; but we can fix a bed on the floor, and I'll introduce you to all the old-timers at the post."

"Thanks, I'd appreciate both favors. I'll need to buy a rifle if I'm going to help fill your meatshed out back. Looking at your wall larder, I reckon we'd better go to the store. Can I treat you to dinner?"

"You bet! And I'll stand for a drink at the bar. We may have to do some serious dickering for a good rifle." Taking his gun from the rack, he continued, "Let's walk to the post and get some vittles."

The two men moved briskly along a faint path through the trees for a minute before emerging into an open field. Buzz pointed to seven beehives bordering the glade. "Those hives are mine. Honey is a cash crop in these parts. With the fur market all but gone, my bees are about the only thing that keeps me here. It's too civilized around here for an old-timer like me."

The path widened as they approached the older log buildings which they had seen from the river. "The Hudson's Bay Company was here for over twenty years, but they left in '46. This large building was the fur warehouse for the post. The storekeeper uses it now, and I've traded a few furs with him. The smaller building next door is the hotel . . . actually it's a saloon with food, and bunks in the loft." Buzz turned toward the store, and suggested, "I'll order supplies now. Why don't you look the settlement over?

The house by the dock is Mr. Scott's, and he should know if any old-timers are around. We can meet in the bar."

Scott walked to the house and the dock, visiting with men stacking timber on the shore. None of them recognized James McClure's name, and the only old-timer in the settlement seemed to be Buzz Smith. Continuing along the river-front he passed several log cabins, stopping to visit when he found people at home. He returned to the saloon after two hours, opening the door to hear the sound of Buzz 's voice. The old timer was in the middle of a yarn about a huge brown bear which he had killed outside his cabin. He smiled at Scott without pausing in his narration, and signaled to the bartender for another glass. He continued his tale as he filled the glass from a whiskey bottle on the table. Pushing it toward Scott, he ended his story with a flourish, ". . . skinned the critter right on my doorstep, and it still keeps me warm at night."

"Pull up a chair, Scott! I've asked folks around here if they've heard of your daddy, James McClure, but nary a soul has."

He continued to his cronies, "Do you know of anyone who was here in 1828? . . . knows about the Jedediah Smith Fur Company?"

Everyone shook their heads to the contrary. Buzz changed the subject, "I'm looking for a good rifle. That young clerk at the store was too serious. He wouldn't haggle at all."

The bartender replied, "New rifles cost a lot, but I have one of the best new breech-loading models available today. A hunter left his 1848 Sharps and eighty-three paper cartridges with me to settle his hotel and bar bill. You can have the gun and cartridges for . . . say $75."

Buzz bargained good-naturedly for half an hour before asking to see the rifle. He glanced at it, passing it to Scott with a "Should I give this scoundrel $40 for this gun?"

Scott inspected the weapon carefully and smilingly replied, "Buzz, $40 may be a little high."

The bartender guffawed, "I might consider $60, if you've got gold coin."

Buzz laughed heartily and continued haggling. When the bottle was empty, he concluded a deal for $55 with the whiskey thrown in. Scott paid the bartender in gold as agreed, and commented ruefully, "Good thing I'm staying with you or the bar would likely repossess this rifle. I'm about broke."

"Buzz, Scott, I need fresh venison. The deer seem to have moved into the high country with warm weather. Can you hunt for me?"

Both men nodded readily and had a drink on the house as they made a deal. After eating a trout dinner in the bar, they returned to the cabin with their rifles and supplies just as darkness fell. They turned into their beds immediately, planning an early start in the morning.

****

Buzz signaled to Scott from the nearby hillock, and Scott counted silently to three as he shot the big stag in the meadow 200 feet ahead. An echo sounded as Buzz fell a doe in the same meadow. The remaining deer melted into the forest in a flitter of movement and light. They had tracked the herd since early light and after two hours had overtaken it high above the Umpqua.

As they dressed out their kill, Buzz complained, "Well, now comes the hard work. We have to tote this meat over five miles back to the post."

Scott joked, "Ah . . . you're getting old, Buzz. A little walk will do us good."

"Well, my head's still working. Heh, heh, you can carry your meat and I'll carry mine. Heh, heh, why'd you think I gave you such a big target?"

"Why, Old-Timer, I think you doubted my rifle . . . or maybe my aim?"

Buzz laughed, "Call me an old-timer if you want, but last one to the cabin buys drinks." Both men set off at a hurried pace down the mountain.

Their friendship grew during the ensuing days as Scott learned to use both his head and his youth before he could win any race against the Old-Timer.

They hunted and fished for two weeks until there was no market left in Verneau. Scott continued to question strangers about his father, but nobody was able to help him. Buzz and his friends were equally unsuccessful, and Harvey Masters sent a similar message from Gardiner.

One evening the two men sat before the fire, relaxing after dinner. "Well, Scott McClure, as much as I enjoy your company, it's time for you to go up to Fort Umpqua . . . maybe even Vancouver." Rocking on, he added reluctantly, "Tomorrow morning?" As Scott nodded, Buzz offered, "I'll go with you to Fort Umpqua . . . heh, heh, you can paddle."

"Thanks, do we portage around the rapids?"

"Well, I expect that's best. Although the rainy season can be rough, the Umpqua is fairly quiet in the summer. Shouldn't take us more than a day to reach Fort Umpqua."

The two men sat in companionable silence, thinking their own thoughts, until the fire died down; when room light fell away, they turned in for the night.

****

Scott kept a steady rhythm to his stroke during the first hour on the river, and Buzz had added a light stroke when they encountered shallow riffles. When the river passed through a narrow cut in the hills, both men pulled against the stronger current. Buzz fidgeted in his seat, his paddle across his knees. "Damn coffee! Let's take a break when we hit calmer water. Maybe that beach on the south side over there."

"Sure, Buzz. I see the spot you want."

Scott paddled for a couple of minutes, moving swiftly up the shallow river channel. Seeing smooth water toward the beach, he barked, "We'll go in to shore here," and he pulled hard toward the right riverbank.

Buzz was caught unawares, but yelled, "Wait a second . . . watch that ripple . . . a rock . . ." The canoe went broadside over a submerged boulder and Scott overcompensated in the tilting canoe and fell overboard, capsizing the boat in swift if shallow water. As he went under the water, he rolled with the current, and his head brushed a second boulder before he surfaced. He found himself holding his paddle with both hands, as he struggled to stand in chest deep water. With a lurch and a kick toward the gravelly beach a few feet away, he reached the shallows. Buzz was pushing the capsized canoe ahead of him toward the beach, and Scott grabbed it. Together they righted it and walked through knee-deep water to shore. Scott stumbled briefly on the rocky bottom.

"Are you all right, Scott? There's blood on your cheek."

"It's nothing, but my stupid mistake could have been disastrous. How are you?"

Buzz looked over the soaked gear, and replied, "I'm in one piece, but our rifles are in the river. Let's get our gear high and dry before we search the river bed for them."

Scott stripped to his breeches saying, "You hold the canoe steady, while I stay in the water and get our rifles."

Placing the canoe back in the water, Scott held on to the boat's side as Buzz paddled slowly ahead. As they neared the submerged boulder, Scott stepped on one of the rifles. He hunched down in the current, ducked his head under water, and reached down for the rifle; bringing the Sharps overhead as he surfaced, and staggered downstream. Buzz stayed with him, taking the gun from Scott and paddling upstream at the same time.

Scott held on to the bow and steadied his footing just as Buzz shouted, "There's my rifle . . . in a little deeper water, Scott . . . be careful of those rocks."

He spotted the rifle; and taking a deep breath, he pushed away from the canoe and dove to the bottom. The current swept him downstream before he found the rifle. He came up for air, and Buzz towed him upstream over the gun again. On this second attempt he retrieved the rifle, handing it to Buzz as he rested his chin on the canoe's side.

"I saw my shot at the bottom where my gun lay. Are you up to one more dive?"

"All right, let's go . . . damn, it is cold in this river."

Buzz moved Scott over the shot pouch, and Scott was able to pick it up with his foot, bringing it up to his hand and tossing it in the canoe. Buzz paddled to the beach and left his partner to secure the canoe as he hurried into the brush near a deadfall. A few moments later he was back with a handful of wood slivers and moss, and he motioned to Scott to gather wood for a fire. With fingers trembling from the cold, Buzz made a fire hole in the soil and lined it with rocks. By the time he had used his flint to spark a small flame, Scott had gathered an armful of dry tree limbs to feed the fire.

"We'll camp here today and dry our gear. Is your blanket dry enough to keep you warm?"

Scott pulled it over his shoulders and with teeth chattering, answered, "It's damp, but warmer than anything else of mine. You'd better get out of those buckskins and wrap up in your blanket."

"Right! Throw another hunk of wood on the fire. Why did I pick the south side of the river? The sun seldom reaches this beach."

Both men huddled over the fire soaking up its heat until they stopped shaking. Then they scavenged more wood and made a simple drying frame near the fire. Buzz worried over his buckskins on the rock, until his impatience won out; and he slipped them on still damp.

"They'll dry on me faster than on this woodpile. Besides I want my blanket dry by tonight." He rearranged it over the rack before going back to the river.

"I'd better catch our dinner or all we'll eat are sodden biscuits."

Scott tended the fire and dried the gear, cleaning both rifles as the afternoon progressed. Buzz had lost the percussion caps for his 1841 Harpers' Ferry muzzleloader, and Scott's gear was damp. He loaded his Sharps with the driest cartridge available as Buzz returned with three trout.

"Where are the salmon when they're needed? Ah well, I expect that these trout will do for one night." And true to his word, trout, biscuits, and a capful of huckleberries quieted their rumbling stomachs and fueled their tired muscles.

In the morning, a sharp "Ah-choo!" brought attention to Scott's sniffling condition. "Stoke that fire, Buzz. I've got a chill."

"I'll have the coffee ready in a few minutes. Stay wrapped in your blanket until it's ready. There's no hurry . . . it's just an hour or two to Fort Umpqua."

That coffee did the trick, he thought, as he helped Buzz stow their now-dry gear in the canoe. The sun was shining in the river valley as they launched their boat into the shallows off the beach campsite. Scott insisted that he continue paddling; and his partner acquiesced, adding his paddle through the rougher currents.

The August air warmed perceptibly as the sun rose higher in the clear blue sky. Scott sneezed again and remarked, "Where will we camp in Fort Umpqua?"

"I figure to pull in next to the old Hudson's Bay Company post on Elk Creek. There's a good campsite in a cottonwood grove nearby."

As they swung around a bend in the river, Scott saw several smoke columns drifting up through the trees a half mile ahead.

"Would that be Fort Umpqua over there?"

"Hmmm . . . must be a band of Umpquas . . . probably catching and smoking salmon."

As they drew nearer, Buzz continued quietly, "Hmmm . . . quite a large village . . . lots of families in this band . . . shouldn't bother us. . . ." After a short pause, he added, "But keep on paddling, we're not prepared to meet Indians . . . no firepower or trade goods."

The Indians fishing along the riverbank gazed at them curiously, and finally two small boys waved to them. Both Buzz and Scott waved back, but kept their pace and stayed in the middle of the river.

"It's been a few years since the Umpquas attacked an armed party of white men around here."

Buzz chuckled, "Of course we hardly qualify as a party . . . or armed for that matter. You keep paddling and watch ahead . . . maybe there's another band hereabouts. I'll keep an eye on this bunch."

The partners relaxed as the village dwindled from sight and they had the river to themselves again. After an hour of steady travel, Buzz commented, "This stretch of river ahead of us is pretty rough. Stay alert. We'll be at Fort Umpqua in ten minutes."

Both men were sweating as they cleared the white water and traveled upriver. "Now that smoke ahead is Fort Umpqua, and Elk River lies between the post on the left and the new settlement on the right. The trail to the Willamette goes up Elk Creek to the northeast and through a pass in the Calapooya mountains."

Buzz reminisced, "This whole country was wilderness when I came through here in 1831. Look at all those new settlers across the creek. None of them were here two years ago when I traveled up to Winchester."

"Why, Buzz, you sound downright sentimental. There's still a lot of wild country here in Oregon."

"Well, that's so. I just miss the old days, I guess. Pull into those cottonwoods on the left just beyond the post buildings, and we'll make a snug camp."

By noon both partners were hungry and eager to visit the post. They set off through the cottonwoods on a faint trail. They passed a dilapidated pair of log cabins with doors hanging askew and roofs caving in.

"These cabins have been empty since the Company moved out in 1846. The post buildings are still in good condition though," Buzz said as he surveyed the three major buildings set on eighty acres. Two bastions still stood erect, although the stockade showed signs of neglect.

Scott coughed as they walked up to the store entrance, and said in a raspy voice, "Right now I'd like a good meal. Can we eat?"

"You sound like the devil. Is your throat really that bad?"

"Ah, it's just a cold. Dinner will make me feel better," Scott said as he followed his friend into the post dining hall.

Buzz visited with friends at the post, while Scott rode across the creek with two men who lived in the new settlement. Their dinghy kept his feet dry on the short trip; Elk River looked too deep to ford easily. No one had heard of James McClure in the settlement, although a hostler at the stables told him that one of his mule skinners had trapped the Umpqua valley in the 1820's. Curly Lambeau was working on a mule train due back in two or three days.

As Scott returned to the creek, he saw Buzz waiting for him in the canoe.

"I thought you might like a ride to our camp. You need to stay dry and warm if you're going to get rid of that cold. Did you have any luck visiting with those settlers?"

"Not much, do you know a trapper named Curly Lambeau?"

Buzz brightened, recollecting, "I've known Curly for years . . . heh, heh, he's as bald as can be . . . he was in this country when I arrived. We've been passable friends since we did a little trapping together in the winter of '36. He'll help if he can."

"I'm not feeling very well . . . maybe I'll rest awhile."

Scott turned into his blanket as soon as Buzz had a fire kindled and the coffee perking. He coughed a few times before falling asleep, and his forehead soon glistened with sweat. A slight trembling quieted as he fell into a deep slumber. His partner woke him at dusk, and insisted that he eat fish soup that he had brewed. Scott drank what was given him without expression and promptly fell asleep.

"At least he isn't coughing," muttered his friend.

Scott awoke coughing however, and seeing Buzz sitting by the fire studying him in the early morning light, he hacked out "Good mor . . . (cough) . . . ning . . . (cough) I feel terrible."

The Old-Timer agreed, "I thought so, that cough's reaching for your lungs and you're fevered. There's a doctor across the creek in the settlement and you're going to visit him now, while you are still able to walk."

Scott started to argue, but coughed instead and silently nodded. A cup of hot coffee soothed his throat some, but did little for his chesty cough. He stumbled to his feet and followed Buzz to the canoe and across the creek.

Head hanging, Scott shuffled after Buzz up to a small frame cottage with a solid wood door and a latticed glass window. On the wall next to the door was a sign, marked Dr. Wells, M.D. Buzz rapped sharply on the door. It was opened almost immediately by an attractive young lady in a gingham dress. Looking first at Buzz and then at his sick companion, she introduced herself, "I'm Mrs. Wells. Are you here to see the doctor?"

Scott nodded, coughing, and swayed against his partner.

"My, that has a nasty sound. Come in and sit down. My husband will be right in."

Buzz introduced himself and his friend, explaining the circumstances of his illness. Mrs. Wells was very sympathetic, but somewhat puzzled, "There isn't much illness around here in the summer months."

"Well, ma'am . . . Scott here has just arrived in Gardiner last month. Maybe he's not used to Oregon, or maybe the river's too cold for him." The Old-Timer's eyes were twinkling, but his friend missed the humor as he began drowsing in his chair.

A stout young man in a white jacket entered the room tweaking his full black mustache. Dr. Wells addressed his wife, "I overheard Mr. McClure's problem, my dear." He took Scott's wrist in his right hand and felt his forehead with his left hand. Scott continued drowsing, so that Dr. Wells needed Buzz' help to put him on the bed in the next room.

"I'll examine Mr. McClure and dress him for bed." He hesitated, "Your friend has walking pneumonia. It's a good thing that you convinced him to come here as early as you did."

"Thanks, Doc. It came on kinda fast. When can I come back to visit?"

"Let him sleep the night through. Tomorrow morning will be fine."

The Old-Timer returned the next morning to find his partner still unconscious.

"He's pretty sick," the doctor told him. "Can you sit with him today while my wife and I meet a friend?"

Buzz agreed reluctantly, more than a little nervous at taking on this nursing task. Although Scott's eyes fluttered open on occasion, and he rambled incoherently about his mother, he didn't recover full consciousness that day.

Mrs. Wells returned after lunch to relieve Buzz. "My husband is helping our friend collect her baggage at the freight yards. The mule train came in a day early."

"Was my friend, Curly Lambeau, working on that train?"

"Yes, I believe he's going back to the Willamette valley for another shipment in the morning."

"Well, I'd better go down and say hello to him now. I'll be back in the morning," and he added as he left, "Thank you, ma'am."

Scott awakened the next morning as Dr. Wells felt his cool brow. "Well, sir, I believe the worst is over. My wife has a bowl of chicken soup for you."

Mrs. Wells hand-fed him the soup, and he fell asleep while eating it. When he awoke that evening, she had a finely chopped beef stew ready for him.

"Mr. McClure, you need to eat and regain your strength," she advised; but Scott didn't need any encouragement, he was famished and ate with gusto.

"Your friend, Mr. Smith, was by to visit this morning, but I told him to return tomorrow. You can vis . . ." She smiled to herself as she stopped talking to her sleeping patient. "Good," she murmured, "he's resting."

Scott slowly opened his eyes and saw small white and yellow wildflowers on the dresser at the foot of his bed. He remembered that he was at the Wells house and thought it very nice of Mrs. Wells to have such pretty flowers in his room.

Movement in the corner of his eye caught Scott's attention and he turned with a small smile expecting to see Mrs. Wells. His eyes widened a little in surprise as he gazed into the lovely green eyes of a young woman, a girl actually. Her smile widened over perfect white teeth, her face becoming animated with humor. She tossed her long brown hair over her shoulder and stood up to curtsy. "How are you, Mr. Scott Addis McClure? I'm your substitute nurse, Melissa Anne Nelson."

Scott continued to study her pretty features and girlish figure until she blushed, and drawled, "You can say hello, can't you?"

He reddened and stammered, "You're . . . uh . . . hello." He thought her beautiful; but in his confused state, couldn't make his tongue utter anything intelligible . . . let alone flattering. In the end he gave up trying and relaxed, smiling serenely as he fell asleep again.

Melissa's heart was pounding as she sat down and regained control of her emotions. "What a nice smile . . . what an ingenuous man," she thought. "I wonder if I looked mature enough."

On her sixteenth birthday last month, Melissa had asked her father to stop calling her Missy. After all she wasn't a child anymore; next month she would be teaching school in Marysville as well as keeping house for her father.

Bemused, she whispered, "I'm a woman!"

In the morning, Scott awoke to the sound of muted voices outside his bedroom door. The door opened slowly, ". . . asleep, but you can sit with him until he wakes up." He recognized her voice and thought to himself, well, it wasn't a dream. Let's see, her name is . . . Melissa.

His reverie was broken by the Old-Timer's, "Well, you're awake and smiling. By God, I'm glad to . . ."

Scott broke in, trying to look around his friend, "Is she coming in?"

"Heh . . . heh . . . looks like you're snakebit for sure. You must be feeling better if a pretty girl is more welcome than your old partner." Buzz chuckled as he added, "She's fetching your breakfast. You're a lucky fella to have two attractive nurses."

A puzzled look flitted across Scott's face, before he grinned and said, "Ah, Buzz, Mrs. Wells is a married woman, and she doesn't . . ."

". . . Count! Well, Scott my boy, you're gone! No use talking business with you this morning."

Mrs. Wells entered the room with a loaded breakfast tray. Scott's smile faded and she quipped mischievously, "Don't worry, Scott, Melissa is bringing coffee for you and your friend."

Scott laughed weakly and moaned, "Enough . . . enough."

Mrs. Wells nodded to Scott, "I'm glad you're better. Now you need to eat and regain your strength. Bon Appetit!"

Scott dug into his eggs and hash with relish.

After a few moments a sobered Buzz related, "Curly Lambeau was in town while you were ill. He didn't know your father. Although he arrived in the valley in 1825, he spent most of 1828 on the South Umpqua. He heard about the Jedediah Smith party's tragedy, but never talked to any of the survivors. He did offer to ask around on his Willamette trip. He'll be back in ten-twelve days.

"By the way, Curly and I got to swapping yarns about the old days, and we decided to trap fur this winter down on the Coquille."

"Down south? Are the Indians friendly?"

"Yes to both questions. Curly can't leave until October, so I figured you and me should partner on a couple of hunting trips. Both the post and the butcher will buy meat from us, and Dr. Wells asked us to take him along on our first hunt."

"Good morning, gentlemen. Coffee is served."

Buzz greeted Melissa with, "You'll have a cup also, young lady. Ah yes, you've brought three cups."

"It isn't every day that I meet an Old-Timer full of tall tales. I want to hear about Indians and fur trading." Melissa sat down and glanced at Scott, saying, "A good appetite is a sure sign of recovery. You'll be on your feet in no time."

Jokingly Buzz offered, "Scott tells me that with two pretty nurses to tend him, he's in no hurry." Glancing at Scott, he urged, "Speak up, lad, here's your chance."

Before Scott could speak, Melissa chimed in, "Yes, Scott, what have you got to say? And don't you dare fall asleep with that silly grin on your face."

Not to be outdone by his visitors, he replied, "Last night an angel visited me and today everyone is deviling me." With a serious note, he added, "I'm in debt to all of you. Thanks for taking care of me."

The seeds of profound friendship were planted that morning among the three visitors to the Wells home. And Buzz entertained his two friends with a story about a 300 pound sturgeon which he caught in the Columbia River. He was still pulling the big fish in as Scott drifted off into gentle slumber.

During the ensuing week, Melissa visited Scott daily, taking long walks with him as he recovered at the Wells home. Buzz traveled to Verneau for three days, and returned to Fort Umpqua with two pails of honey to sell at the post store. He brought a smaller coffee tin full of honey to Scott, who was sitting outside in the sunshine.

"I thought maybe you'd like to give this treat to Mrs. Wells."

"Thanks, Buzz. I've paid my bill, but I owe them much more. Taking Dr. Wells hunting is one thing, but a tin of honey for Mrs.

Wells is just the right gift for her nursing care. You know, if you stay with me, I bet you get invited to supper."

"Well, I'll bring the Wells a salmon I caught earlier today in the creek. We can ask Dr. Wells when we can go on the hunting trip."

"Come on, let's pick up that salmon before we return to the house; I need the exercise, and I can return a couple of things to our camp."

****

The three hunters left Fort Umpqua on Saturday morning heading up Elk Creek for better than an hour. Buzz had a contract for both venison and bear with his butcher friend, and he had promised Melissa a pheasant during the Wells supper earlier in the week. Their route turned northwesterly up a mountain game trail.

"There's a meadow with a small lake north of this mountain where we can set up camp. Take us . . . maybe two hours. . . ," glancing at a puffing Dr. Wells, Buzz went on ". . . you up to it, Scott?"

Catching his intent, Scott replied, "Let's rest for a few minutes. I can use a drink of water."

As they sat quietly enjoying the forest solitude, Scott saw several deer grazing along the canyon slope opposite the men. He touched Dr. Wells' shoulder and pointed. As Dr. Wells raised his rifle, Buzz whispered, "Those animals are like mountain goats. We'd play hell toting them off that rocky wall. You want to try it, Doc?"

Dr. Wells smiled and lowered his gun, "Where is that meadow of yours, Old-Timer?"

The men trudged up the trail through a verdant forest of canopied firs until the slope gradually fell away and they started downhill. After less than a mile they emerged into a grassy meadow sprinkled with wildflowers. "We'll work our way across to that shelf above the lake. There's a spring where the mosquitoes won't pester us much."

Buzz talked about the hunt planned for the next day, relating a story about a twelve-point buck that he bagged in the meadow a few years back. When he picked up his rifle and set off to scout in the remaining daylight, Scott and Dr. Wells continued a quiet conversation on the merits of Oregon. Dr. Wells was quiet for awhile, starting to speak two or three times before voicing a personal concern. "Scott, you've been seeing a great deal of Melissa. Mrs. Wells and I think you're a fine young man, but Melissa is very young. She just turned sixteen this summer, and she's very impressionable. I feel responsible for her while she's visiting here . . . kind of like an uncle . . . you know what I mean? . . ."

"Don't worry, Dr. Wells, I wouldn't hurt Melissa for anything. We're good friends, and I respect her." Scott felt less embarrassed than resentful at his friend's remarks, but recognized the good intention. He thought to himself, "I didn't realize she was so young. I wonder what she thinks of me? . . . what am I doing . . . I can't get involved now." His actions over the following days were affected by the conversation, as he saw little of Melissa before she returned to Marysville in mid-September. He managed a farewell talk with her the afternoon before she departed, but she was rather distant in her own manner as they said good-bye.

The partners completed their last hunting contract with their butcher friend just before Buzz and Curly left camp for the Coquille. Scott remained at the campsite for several days, saying his good-byes to friends and waiting for the next mule train north to the Willamette. One frosty morning in October, Scott broke camp and walked to the freight yards with all his belongings packed on his back, and carrying his rifle. Buzz had told him to seek out Fort Vancouver and Scott was eager to pursue his quest.

Chapter Two

Scott sat quietly in his room, staring out his window at the busy riverfront just a block down Mill Street from his boarding house. Visibility was uncertain on this rainy and gray November afternoon, but he was enjoying a restful break following his two-week trek to Portland. He had arrived two days ago, wringing wet, and considered himself fortunate in finding comfortable lodgings. Mrs. Sloan was a widow who owned a clean establishment and charged modest prices, even if she seemed an old grouch. At least he had his privacy, and he was only a few miles from his destination. I'll need better weather to travel to Fort Vancouver, across the Columbia River, and I'll need to find work if I'm going to stay here for awhile, he thought to himself.

Portland was a bustling city, and even on this stormy day, people with packages were scurrying through the streets, like squirrels preparing for the winter months. Saloons along Dock Street were busy, although Scott could see only the two corner bars from his window. A street south had several businesses, including a general store. He'd been told by Mrs. Sloan that a "rough element" hung out along the riverfront, but "nary a hoodlum" was allowed in her house. She looked warily at Scott as if his credibility was in question, but said nothing. She actually smiled after he had taken his father's razor to his stubble and had trimmed his hair.

His trip from Fort Umpqua had been tedious until he had reached Marysville. His traveling companions had selected to bivouac overnight north of town. He had found the Nelson home late in the afternoon, and when Melissa answered his knock looking

33

as beautiful as he remembered her, romantic feelings befuddled his thinking. She was pleased to see him, flushing lightly as they renewed their acquaintance, but not as tongue-tied as her visitor. He relaxed after her father came home and welcomed Scott, seeming to know a lot about him. The Nelsons were hospitable at dinner and invited him to spend the night, but Scott declined, explaining his travel arrangements. He was in a gay mood returning to camp late that night, and maintained good spirits on the rest of the trip down the Willamette to Portland.

Broken clouds drifted overhead as the rain stopped, and Scott decided to stretch his legs. As he left the house, he elected to go uphill and away from the docks. He hoped that a small hilltop at the end of Mill Street would offer a panoramic view of the city and the river. He checked his long strides well short of the summit as the rain returned. Heading back toward the boarding house, he observed a sudden commotion outside the two saloons at the foot of the hill. Five men were having a loud argument in the middle of Mill Street. As Scott mounted the steps to the porch, he heard clearly, "No, I won't buy you a drink, leave me be!" Scott turned to see one of the antagonists pick up a board in the street and swing it at a husky man who dodged the blow. Scott acted in sympathy without a conscious decision, running into the street, and calling out, "What's going on?" All four assailants had surrounded their intended victim, grappling with him. Scott's powerful hands seized two men by their upper arms, tightening his grip unmercifully as he pulled them away from the attack. Without their restraint, the stranger pushed the ringleader into the mud and parried a knife blade with his left forearm. Scott threw both culprits whom he held, into the man with the knife and stood shoulder to shoulder with the dark-haired stranger. The four men backed down the street muttering oaths but leaving the scene to the young men.

"Friend, are you ever strong! You saved me from a real beating and I thank you. I'm Sam Olson," he said, shaking Scott's hand.

"I'm Scott McClure. Are you hurt? I see blood on your coat sleeve." The dark peacoat was slashed in the left arm and his new friend's dark eyes watered in pain. He was somewhat disheveled in appearance, since he wore no cap and his wet black hair straggled down his face.

"No problem with this nick, but those toughs live near me on Dock Street. Now that's a problem."

Scott hesitated for a moment as he saw Mrs. Sloan looking out the dining room window. "Come with me and I'll clean you up." Mrs. Sloan frowned as Scott opened the door, and started, "Mr. McClure, I don't . . ."

He interrupted quickly and inserted, "Mrs. Sloan, this is my friend, Sam Olson. He's bleeding and needs help."

"It's a pleasure to meet a lady such as yourself, ma'am. I told Scott that it was too much of an imposition on your household to tramp in here all wet and muddy. My apologies for dirtying your fine carpet."

Expecting a harsh response, Scott was dumbfounded as Mrs. Sloan smiled coyly and bubbled, "Welcome to my home, Mr. Olson. You're not any bother . . . I can bandage your arm myself. . . . I'm a bit of a nurse, you know." Turning to his handsome friend, he saw that Sam's jaunty smile and charming manner had captivated Mrs. Sloan. He followed the patient and his "nurse" into the kitchen, and waited by the warm stove as Mrs. Sloan washed and dressed the small wound on Sam's arm. Before the newcomer left the room, he was Mrs. Sloan's new border; and soon Scott was walking with Sam to pick up his gear and pay for his former lodgings. Mrs. Sloan had instructed Scott, "And you take care of this poor boy . . . he's too sensitive to live around bullies. You can see that he's a gentleman."

Scott's sense of humor surfaced as they walked down Mill Street, "Mrs. Sloan thinks I make a good bodyguard for a gentleman. Ha, ha, I'm still trying to figure out who was the bully and who was the victim."

"Come on, Scott, old buddy, you and I may know the real Sam Olson, but Mrs. Sloan sees me as a 'son'."

Laughing, Scott parodied his friend's tone, "Well, Sam, old buddy, do 'we' have enough money to settle your lodging bill?"

"Why of course! . . . Mrs. Sloan slipped me a gold coin on account, and I'll pay her back as soon as I find a job."

Scott paused for a moment on Dock Street and pointed north along the riverfront. "I dare you to come with me to that sawmill and ask for work. I'm short of funds too, and we both need winter jobs."

Hesitantly, Sam followed Scott toward the mill site and sputtered, "Uh . . . my arm's sore . . . probably no job for a gentleman, anyway. . . ."

"Hah, Sam, old buddy, put up or shut up!"

He led his friend up to a bent-over, husky figure, who was working alone, struggling to load a wagon with lumber. Pulling Sam forward, he asked, "Mister, is there any work to be had in this mill?"

A middle-aged man turned a probing glance on Scott, and then on Sam, introducing himself, "I'm Jack Smith." He extended a callused worker's hand to each man, before continuing, "This is my mill. Yes, I can use two good workers, but I can't abide men with California gold on their minds. Are you willing to stick around this winter?"

Scott answered quickly for both men, "Yes, Mr. Smith, we'll be here for awhile. We live up the street at Mrs. Sloan's boarding house."

The mill owner's expression relaxed, "If you're living at Mrs. Sloan's, that's a fine reference in itself. Call me Jack. Are you ready to work now? I have to get another order out this afternoon."

Scott agreed for both men and started stacking lumber on the wagon while Sam moved to the other side of the platform with Jack to haul more lumber from a storage shed. Neither man had inquired about wages, but they knew what millworkers were earn-ing, and they trusted their new boss.

The partners returned to Mrs. Sloan's house with Sam's be-longings well after dark. Mrs. Sloan met them at the door. "I was worried about you. Is everything all right?"

With his charming smile in place, Sam told her, "I found work at Smith's mill for Scott and me. We helped Jack for a couple of hours."

Beaming with approval, she said, "Oh Sam, should you be working with that arm? You look tired and hungry. Come into the kitchen, I've saved dinner for . . . both of you."

Scott elbowed his friend, whispering lightly, "Thanks for din-ner, Sam . . . and for finding me a job." His voice was sarcastic but Sam took it straight-faced and replied aloud, "Stick with me partner, and I'll take care of you."

As their friendship grew, Sam learned of his partner's quest for his father. When the mill closed for the Christmas holidays, Sam insisted that he accompany Scott to Fort Vancouver the day after Mrs. Sloan's yuletide banquet. With pay in their pockets, the two men set out shopping on the day before Christmas. Scott asked a blunt question, "Have you repaid Mrs. Sloan the loan?"

With mock indignity, Sam declared, "I'm a gentleman who keeps his word. And now my doubting friend, let's have a drink on me before we do our shopping. I'm going to buy a Sharps rifle just like yours from the gunsmith on Dock Street."

After one round, Scott left his partner in the tavern visiting with friends; and set forth shopping for presents. Sam had taken a shine to Scott's hunting knife one evening when they were visit-ing in his room. He found a knife similar to his own and bought it for Sam, and in the same store he purchased a tinderbox for Buzz. He would tuck it away in his gear until he saw him next year. In the bakery, he bought a box of San Francisco candy for Mrs. Sloan. Buying a gift for Melissa was difficult because he wasn't sure that he could send it to her and doubly so when he considered propriety and Dr. Wells' advice. A stroke of good fortune simplified his dilemma. He met one of his traveling companions who had made the trek north with him. As they visited, Scott learned that the man was heading south after Christmas. An offer to take a message to his friends in Marysville was eagerly accepted. Scott remembered a silver chain with a gold nugget which he had seen in one store's jewelry case, and returned with his former associate to purchase it. Entrusting his gift to Melissa with his companion, he walked back to his room to wrap his gifts for Sam and Mrs. Sloan.

****

As they followed Jack Smith's directions north to the Columbia River boat landing, Sam talked volubly about the delicious duck dinner which Mrs. Sloan had served yesterday and the tremendous presents that he had received—and given. Scott agreeably accepted his friend's exuberance, and didn't need to speak very often to hold up his end of the conversation. He appreciated the pocket watch given to him by Sam, and Mrs. Sloan was touched to receive their gifts, particularly pleased with Sam's crystal jam jar. By the time the partners were in sight of the Columbia, both men needed their breath for the hike to the landing.

They secured passage across the river on a freight barge, a bateau transporting a handful of passengers and two crates with Boston markings to Vancouver. Scott chatted with members of the crew as they rowed across the river, and found a French-Indian trapper who knew Abner Dundee. The half-breed pointed out a log cabin upriver from the wharf which they were approaching, and identified it as the Dundee home. Scott could see a road winding past several houses near the cabin. He rejoined Sam in the bow and shared the news, suddenly impatient to step ashore as the barge docked. Scott set off at a brisk pace with Sam close beside him, heading east along a road well traveled by horse and wagon. They walked on the shoulder of the road to avoid deep mud and sloppy puddles, but keeping good balance required short steps and a slower pace. Scott kept looking ahead, searching for a glimpse of the log cabin, but houses on both sides of the road obscured his vision. The farther they walked from the post; the fewer houses they could see, and the forest thickened perceptibly. Sam grabbed Scott's arm and pointed to a path going toward the river. "Will this trail lead us to Dundee's house?"

Scott nodded and they turned down the gentle slope until they could see a log cabin, and beyond it, the river. "I believe that's Abner Dundee's place ahead. He's isolated out here . . . must like his privacy." He approached the cabin making noise intentionally, and called out, "Hello, the house . . . anybody home?"

After a moment the door opened and a squaw with a dusky and wrinkled face stepped onto the doorsill. "Abner no here . . . fishing . . . there!" she said in broken English, as she pointed to a small dinghy visible offshore. A man was fishing in the eddied waters upstream a hundred feet from a boat slip.

"May I wait here?" Scott asked, pointing to the landing. The squaw gave an unconcerned grunt and nodded as she went inside and closed the door.

"I'm going to the post and find us a pair of bunks for tonight. Meet me at the dining hall when you've talked to Dundee."

Scott nodded and the two men went their own ways. It was chilly, but not raining, so he settled atop a stump to wait for the trapper. Evidently Scott was visible from the river, because the man in the dinghy pulled in his fishing line and rowed to the landing. Scott arose and went to the slip to help pull the boat out of the water. Scott saw an old-timer who could have passed as a double for Buzz. His craggy and wrinkled face showed his age, but his brown eyes were clear and alert. Long dark hair was streaked with gray, and showed a deeply receding hairline when he removed his cap. He secured the dinghy with a rope; and straightening as much as his stooped frame would permit, he said, "Thanks, I'm Abner Dundee. You looking for me?"

"Glad to meet you, Mr. Dundee. My name is Scott McClure . . . and yes, I'd like to talk with you."

"Good! Let's go up to the house and have my woman fix us coffee. You come over from Portland today?"

"Yes, I'm working at the Smith sawmill for the winter months. . . ," he trailed off as they entered the cabin.

"Daisy, meet Scott McClure . . . bring us some coffee. . . ." Both men hung up their jackets and caps before sitting at the table. "McClure is a good Scottish name. I came over from Edinburgh to work for the Hudson's Bay Company in 1811, and I've been here since Fort Vancouver was established in 1825. There were a few McClures who worked for the Company. Any of them your kinfolk?"

"No, my father worked for Jedediah Smith's party which was attacked by Indians on the Umpqua River. Mother received a letter from my father in 1829. Do you know anything about the fate of James McClure?"

Abner stared into his coffee as he stirred in sugar, recalling an unpleasant memory, as Scott fidgeted in his chair. He looked at Scott soberly, "You must know that the party was massacred. Only four survivors made it to Fort Vancouver and your father wasn't one of them. Do you know the whole story of Smith's company?"

Scott was saddened by the credibility expressed in Dundee's pronouncement, and felt a strong desire to hear the old Scot's story. He nodded for Abner to continue.

"Jedediah Smith was a young man who explored trails from Salt Lake City to San Diego. He had more courage than common sense, but he was an adventurer and a leader of men. Smith told me himself that the Spanish chased him out of San Diego in 1826, and the Mojaves killed ten of his men on the Colorado the next year. His Oregon party was made up of the Colorado survivors and a bunch of recruits whom he enlisted in Salt Lake City. When did your daddy come west, Scott?"

"He left St. Louis in the spring of 1827. Mother received a letter from Independence saying he was going westward to California."

Abner considered the date, and mused, "He must have joined Smith at Salt Lake City in 1827 and gone to California. The Jedediah Smith Company gathered 300 horses, trade goods, supplies enough for eighteen men, and left Sacramento in the spring of 1828. They traveled up the coast of California and Oregon, trapping furs and trading with Indians. Their horses were heavily laden by the time they reached the Umpqua, and they camped for several days on a flat where Smiths River flows into the Umpqua. That's the spot where we buried fourteen men in October of '28."

Scott commented, "I heard McLeod's men helped Smith recover property. Were you with that party?"

"Yes, Smith was with us when we buried his men—what was left of them. We found a few personal items which helped identify bodies. I don't read or write, so Smith read for me. That's how I know your daddy is dead, Scott. I found a letter addressed to Sarah McClure of St. Charles, Missouri. It was one of four letters that Smith asked me to give to the next American ship that arrived at Fort Vancouver. I did my solemn duty after Smith left the Columbia River and headed south. I'm glad that your mother received that last letter."

"Thanks, Abner. It's been hard, not knowing my father's fate. I appreciate you answering my questions."

"You are welcome, lad. Can you stay for supper?"

"No thank you, I must meet a friend at the post, but first I extend greetings from Erastus Smith. Buzz is the friend who sent me to you because he couldn't answer my questions. He and Curly Lambeau are trapping along the Coquille this winter."

Abner's toothless smile broadened, "Ah, two old comrades that I haven't seen in many years. Does Buzz still keep his beehives at Verneau?"

"Yes, his honey is popular along the Umpqua River. Thanks again Abner, and good-bye," Scott said as he stood and put on his jacket. He waved to Abner from the edge of the clearing and hurried along the darkening path.

Scott felt oddly relieved, his quest was over and he had fulfilled his promise to his mother.

He thought of his good friends in Oregon, Sam Olson, the old-timer Buzz Smith, and of course, Melissa—she was in his thoughts often. Buzz liked trapping and Sam wanted to prospect for gold, but Scott knew that furs were passe and getting rich quick was a foolish dream. Yet, it might be fun to look for gold—but not in California. He liked Oregon and believed hard work would produce a just reward. He would talk to Sam about building a stake for next summer—maybe they could work together on some project.

Scott arrived at Fort Vancouver at dusk and had to ask directions twice before he located the dining hall. He entered and looked for Sam, but did not see him. After searching the neighboring buildings, he approached a man who seemed to be in charge of the dining hall. He queried, "Could you help me? I seem to have lost my friend, Sam Olson."

"Are you his partner?" At Scott's affirming nod, the man answered, "Sam went down to the boat landing with some men that he met. Whiskey and cards were mentioned, I believe. By the way, you men have bunks in the dormitory tonight, but we lock up at ten o'clock."

"Thank you, we'll be in before ten," Scott agreed. He thought that he'd better move fast before Sam got into trouble. Jack Smith had warned them about the hangouts on this side of the river. He hurried through the dark toward the lights at the landing.

Approaching the tavern door slowly, he scanned the porch and sides of the building, seeing no one. However, he heard the clamorous din from within the bar, and entered the room cautiously, moving to his left and placing his back against the wall. Sam sat at a card table across the room, with a half-filled whiskey glass in his hand. Scott drifted along the wall to the left of the door, his rifle trailing behind him as he held the barrel firmly in his left hand. Sam didn't see him as Scott positioned himself behind Sam's right shoulder, and took time to study the men at the table. The man across the table won the stud poker hand and raked in the gold and silver coins.

Sam's stack of coins grew smaller as he lost another pot. The first cards were dealt face down to the players, and the second cards came face up. As Sam lifted the corner of his whole card, a harmless-looking older man behind Sam signaled to the winning gambler opposite him. Scott thought for a moment about how to stop this rigged game, and then quietly gripped the shoulder of the man who had signaled, and turned him to the wall. Scott's menacing look silenced the man. He held him there effortlessly as the next hand was dealt.

Scott thought, probably the first time this evening that Sam's the only person who knows his whole card. He returned the crooked gambler's flat stare as the betting escalated. Sam's coins went into the pot and then he placed his rifle on the table as collateral to call the last raise. As his three sevens beat the two pair, aces over tens, Sam hollered, "My luck's back . . . wahoo!" and gathered in his winnings. Scott released his grip and stepped forward. "Sam, pick up your winnings, we're late for supper." Sam staggered a little as he got to his feet; and with a silly grin on his face, began to pick up his coins. The gambler threatened, "You're not leaving with my money, Olson. Sit down and play cards."

A couple of toughs moved toward them as Scott repeated, "Put the money away, Sam."

The gambler rose from his chair as the two toughs drew billy clubs. Scott moved suddenly, seizing the first man's hand holding the club and twisting. The assailant howled as a bone snapped and fell backwards, out of the fight. Scott brought the butt of the rifle into his right hand; and smoothly continued the motion, meeting the charging man's face with a "thwack" heard around the room. Following through, the business end of the rifle was shoved under the crooked gambler's nose, with Scott's finger resting on the trigger. The irate gambler blanched and showed Scott his palms, all bluster gone. Sam walked to the door, swinging his rifle up to cover the now-silent crowd. "Come along, Scott. No one needs to be shot tonight." Scott slid out the door and stepped aside on the porch, letting his eyes adjust to the darkness. "Now Sam . . . watch your step . . . move uphill about fifteen steps and cover me."

Three loggers started toward the door, not wanting any part of this fight. Scott's voice was clear and cool as he ordered, "Stay away from the door, friends." They obeyed quickly, and Scott followed his partner up the slope until they stood together. Scott advised, "We'd better move out of here before anyone gets ahead of us. I don't want this affair to end up in a shooting either."

The men trotted up the hill away from the river. Slowing to a walk at the post entrance, they slipped into the dining hall and relaxed.

"Thanks, Scott old buddy. They were a rough bunch, but I showed them how to play stud poker."

Scott threw up his hands and exclaimed, "But they rigged the game. Don't you have any sense at all?"

Sam grinned in his good-natured way and offered his friend a drink, "I picked up this pint of whiskey off the table. Care for a swig?" Scott nodded, laughing with his irrepressible friend and thinking that it was a good thing that they were leaving tomorrow. It might not be healthy for them to stay north of the Columbia.

Lying in their bunks that evening, Scott related Abner's news to Sam, ending with a probing comment, "I like Oregon. How about you?"

"It's all right, but we ought to go to California and dig gold right out of the ground. We could be rich, Scott old buddy!" Sam bubbled on, extolling the virtues of California gold. We're partners, Scott. What do you say? Will you go to California with me?"

Scott responded slowly, "We're partners, but I won't go back to San Francisco. Isn't there gold in Oregon? We need to outfit ourselves for an Oregon gold prospecting project, not a California dream. We'll talk more about it tomorrow. Good night!" He rolled over ad drifted into sleep with the background of Sam's rambling voice in the night.

During the ensuing months, both partners worked industriously to earn funds for their venture. Scott insisted on acting as treasurer and holding their money in his room. He doled out spending money like a miser, denying either of them any luxuries. On Sundays and holidays, they went into the hills on hunting trips. The markets of Portland were eager to buy their meat, so that extra money trickled into their treasury. Their heavy work schedule left little time for leisure activities.

When Scott received a letter from Melissa in April inviting him to visit Marysville, he found himself too busy. She thanked him for writing to her and for giving her a Christmas gift. She would wear the chain and nugget the next time they met. Scott hoped that he would be able to visit Melissa during the summer. "I'm sure not going to California," he vowed to himself.

****

They were hunting east of Portland one day in early May, when Sam hit a big buck with a seemingly impossible shot. The echoes of his rifle fire were still sounding as he ran down the hillside, across the creek, and into the meadow where the deer lay. As Scott neared the site at a more leisurely pace, he found Sam arguing vehemently with a bearded older man, whose countenance reflected patience as well as conviction.

"It's my animal. I shot this deer," the newcomer declared with certainty.

Sam's volatile retort was prompt, "It's mine! I shot it cleanly, you . . ."

"Sam!" Scott rescued his friend from exploding anger and further indiscretion by asking, "What's the argument? And tell me in a calm voice so that I can understand."

As Sam took a deep breath, his mature and courteous adversary stepped forward. "I'm J. M. Kirkpatrick, presently of Portland."

Scott offered his hand to Kirkpatrick as he said, "I'm Scott McClure, and my partner is Sam Olson." Sam turned away from Kirkpatrick, refusing to shake hands.

The man explained, "I was thirty feet away . . . over there . . . and went for a head shot. Your partner was almost 300 feet away . . . across the creek. Look at the deer . . . it's obvious that my shot killed it."

Scott pulled Sam over to the carcass and they examined it with scrupulous care. A bullet had entered near the left eye and exited through the right ear. A second bullet had slashed through the rump leaving a bloody groove ten inches in length. Scott looked at his friend and waited patiently. After a prolonged pause, Sam admitted, "I reckon that rump shot is mine . . . not a killing shot . . . it's yours." He turned away without any apology and traipsed across the meadow, following a game trail through the trees. Scott nodded to Kirkpatrick and followed his partner.

"He was an arrogant bastard. That's why I won't shake hands with him." Sam's frown turned to a smile, "You saw that I hit that deer from 300 feet." Scott wisely kept his own counsel.

As summer neared, Scott had more daylight hours to spend on the docks. He wanted to sail to Gardiner, but Sam kept harping on San Francisco . . . and gold. Scott thought that their partnership would break up if a compromise couldn't be found. He was determined to stay on the Oregon coast, wanting no part of the 49er gold fever.

Scott had run across J. M. Kirkpatrick on one of his walks, and they had exchanged pleasantries. He felt a little guilty of being friendly to his partner's foe, but found no fault with Kirkpatrick. When the man sought him out in early June to offer him a position in the "Settlement Company," he declined because Sam wouldn't accept Captain Kirkpatrick even if gold was mentioned. Scott later heard that the company had sailed on June 4 aboard the Sea Gull, bound for Cape Blanco on the southern Oregon coast. The ship was captained by William Tichenor. Scott regretted missing his old friend from the Kate Heath, but he thought he might see him on his return voyage to Portland.

Sam threatened to leave for San Francisco repeatedly as June's rainy weather changed into July's sunny days. Scott convinced him to wait until Captain Tichenor returned, suggesting there might be gold on the Oregon coast. The evening of July 2nd Scott heard that Kirkpatrick's party had been massacred at Port Orford. Tichenor had reported the event upon his arrival in Portland that day.

The next afternoon Scott left work and hurried down to the steamer dock seeking Captain Tichenor. He found the familiar figure in the ship chandlery, greeting him effusively, "Captain Tichenor, I've been looking for you. Do you have a moment to talk to me?" Taking a breath, he continued, "Are you in port for long? . . . You remember me? . . . My name . . ."

". . . is Scott McClure!" Tichenor interposed. Smiling at Scott, he added, "and I'm glad to see you also Mr. McClure. How can I help you?"

"J. M. Kirkpatrick, God rest his soul, offered me a position in his fated company. Is it true that his party was massacred?"

Captain Tichenor answered Scott's questions slowly, relating his story of Port Orford and the men left on Battle Rock. The Sea Gull had sailed to San Francisco and Tichenor was delayed for several days on legal matters. He stopped at Port Orford on his return trip. Finding debris from the battle and a dead Indian, but none of his men, he sailed on to Portland to report that all of his men were lost. "But I'm more determined than ever to establish a settlement on my 'Donation Claim' at Port Orford, and I'm recruiting a company of good men to sail with me next week."

"Is there gold in Port Orford? My partner and I want to prospect for gold, but we are willing to work with your company at the settlement. Sam Olson and I are good workers, and we can fight if we need to."

"You and your friend are invited to a meeting on my ship, the Sea Gull, on July 6th at nine o'clock in the morning. I can guarantee you passage to Port Orford if you join me."

****

The partners arrived on the Sea Gull early and Scott introduced his friend to Captain Tichenor. Talk of gold in Oregon exhilarated Sam, and he became an outspoken proponent for the venture. The meeting adjourned shortly after most of the men agreed to join the Tichenor party. Several men chose Scott's option of paying for their passage rather than joining the settlement company. Captain Tichenor accepted everyone who agreed to sail on July 9th to Port Orford.

Scott and Sam were assigned a small cabin in the forecastle fitted with eight bunks. They went below and tagged a pair; Scott chose the upper and Sam took the lower. Scott went aft to visit with Tichenor while Sam talked to other passengers on deck.

The Captain smiled as Scott approached and shared good news, "Scott, Kirkpatrick and his party escaped from Battle Rock and are recovering at Fort Umpqua. Most of them sustained minor injuries, but two of them were wounded seriously enough to require Dr. Wells' medical care. I feel like a load has been lifted from my shoulders."

Scott shook hands vigorously with his friend, and exclaimed, "Congratulations, what glad tidings you bring! I'll share it with our comrades. They'll feel more secure when we land at Port Orford."

He joined Sam and his companions at the gangway, repeating the story of the survival of Kirkpatrick and his men. Scott expressed confidence in the safety of the company in landing at Port Orford next week. One young man asked, "Will it be safe to leave the settlement and prospect for gold?"

Sam responded, "My partner and I plan to prospect for gold whether the Indians are there or not."

Scott suggested, "Two or three men prospecting together in Indian country is common sense, at least until we have an understanding with the Indians."

Turning to Sam, he asked, "Captain Tichenor will allow us to move aboard ship with our outfits tomorrow. Shall we do our buying this afternoon, partner?"

"Yes, and our celebrating tonight, old buddy!"

The partners had prepared a long list of supplies and equipment needed for their prospecting venture, and they each had another list of personal items needed in the wilderness of the Oregon coast. Scott managed their affairs efficiently, saying his goodbyes and writing a lengthy letter to Melissa while Sam celebrated with his friends. They stayed on ship all day on July 8th, eager to sail and watchful of their outfits with so many men moving about the ship. Scott heard several complaints of theft before they sailed the next day.

After they cleared the Columbia River bar, Captain Tichenor found Scott in his favorite spot on the forward starboard rail. "Mr. McClure, have the men reported instances of theft to you?"

"Yes, sir. Eight men talked to me yesterday before we sailed. Do you want their names? I assumed they had talked to you."

"No, Scott. One of my crew overheard your name mentioned by the passengers and passed it on to me."

Scott frowned, "Good Lord, Captain, do they think that I stole from them?"

"No, not at all, Scott. They look to you as a steady experienced hand. I believe they expect you to straighten out the problem. I wanted to tell you that I will support you if you find the culprit."

"I'm not a policeman. Where would I start?"

Captain Tichenor finished by saying, "See John Larsen, and talk to the men, both passengers and crew. They trust you to protect them . . . more than me it seems. Sam has told quite a few tales of your fighting prowess and your strength."

Scott chuckled at his last comment, but agreed, "My old buddy Sam has a gift of gab. Very well, Captain, I'll try. Where is John Larsen?"

Captain Tichenor signaled to a tall, gangly young man who was watching them. John Larsen had a homely but pleasant face with scandic features and deepset eyes. He was clean-shaven, with unruly blond hair and heavy eyebrows. His seagoing ancestry was evidenced in his steady walk over the rolling deck. Scott recognized him as one of the men who had talked to him about paying passage rather than joining the company. He admired the man's huge hands and powerful grip as they shook hands.

The Captain wished them well and went about his business.

Scott started by saying, "The Captain has asked me to investigate some thievery aboard ship in Portland. Several men told me that they were missing valuables, but none had any idea who the thief was. Do you know anything that could solve this mystery?"

John replied, "When we talked that day we moved aboard the Sea Gull, you and Sam mentioned that you were staying aboard to watch your gear. I was impressed that you were an experienced hand, so I decided to guard my cabin also. Eight of us were assigned to a cabin next to the Captain's. The third cabin aft was being used by the ship's officers. Of course you know that we didn't lose a single item in the fore and aft sections. Only the men in the hold were robbed."

As he paused, Scott asked, "How many men lost valuables?"

"I understand eleven passengers were robbed, but there are probably more men who are afraid to complain. I'm sure they'll talk to you if they'll talk to anyone."

Scott interjected, "Whoa! Why would they talk to me?"

"Sam told everyone that you single-handedly took on a saloon full of crooked gamblers to save his life and his winnings. Those toughs were so scared of you, that you didn't have to raise your voice or fire a shot. Did you really break a man's arm with one hand?"

Scott shook his head in exasperation, giving an oblique answer, "Sam tells a tall tale. I was the most frightened man in that saloon."

John chuckled and then volunteered, "I saw two incidents that day that made me suspicious, but I don't want to accuse anyone without proof."

"What you saw, John, is factual and needs to be said publicly, but what you suspect will be kept in confidence. Will you tell me everything?"

"Yes. I saw a big stranger with dark hair and full beard visiting on deck and in the hold. I thought that he was another passenger, except he came aboard at noon empty-handed. That caught my attention. At dusk he left with a small duffel bag. I suspect that the missing valuables were in that bag."

Scott mused, "I recollect that fellow . . . friendly sort . . . looked like he could handle himself in a fight. . . . I've wondered why I hadn't seen him today. Did you hear his name?"

"He was called Dutch by one of the passengers. They were obviously acquainted, although they didn't come aboard together. This man's name is Tom Burton but I think of him as Weasel, because he's small, shifty, and rat-faced. I'm a little biased in suspecting him to be a thief. That's all I know."

Scott spent the next two days talking to every man on the ship, including Weasel and finally Captain Tichenor.

"Sir, John Larsen's facts were correct and I agree with his suspicions, but I've no proof that Weasel and Dutch are the culprits. If I share my belief with the victims, Weasel could be beaten or killed. The feeling is running strong in the company for justice— or revenge. The latter might be preferable since the valuables don't appear to be on ship and can't be recovered."

"Scott, a sea captain doesn't need *proof,* as a judge might, but he does have to be convinced, to be certain. Fairness and justice are key factors in being a good captain." He paused for a moment, shrugged his shoulders, and asked, "Do you have a suggestion? I told you that if you were sure, I would support your decision. This matter should be concluded before landfall, so that trust and good fellowship are possible in Port Orford."

"Have I your permission to search Weasel's belongings and threaten him? If I can't get a confession of theft, I'll declare him innocent and blame Dutch."

"Yes, I'll stay on watch until you return. If anyone objects to your methods, send him to me."

John was given the task of taking Weasel to his bunk, and Sam was instructed to bring all the victims to the hold. Several other passengers were in their bunks when the group gathered around Weasel's bunk. Scott explained the situation in stern language, turning a menacing look on the thief as he clenched and unclenched his hands. "Why did you steal from these men, Tom Burton?"

The men muttered angry oaths and moved forward threateningly. John Larsen made a ferocious face and leaned down toward the thief, proving himself a good judge of men when Weasel broke and cried, "Please don't! No . . . Dutch made me . . . owed him money . . . don't hurt me . . . please?" Angry victims cursed him but Scott stepped forward before violence could occur. "We will take this thief to the Captain for judgment."

John and Sam escorted the cringing scoundrel on deck to stand before the Captain. Scott announced, "Captain, we have here Tom Burton, a confessed thief. The men he robbed have agreed to bring him before you for judgment."

"Mr. McClure, is he the only guilty man?"

"No, his accomplice, Dutch, is not aboard ship."

The Captain stared at the thief, "Well, do you have anything to say for yourself, Tom Burton?"

Weasel shook his head from side to side and looked around, "I'm sorry shipmates, I'll pay you back. Mercy, fellows. Please, Captain!"

Captain Tichenor proclaimed without hesitation, "Tom Burton, you will pay every wronged man just compensation from your own goods this day. You will spend the rest of the voyage confined to the brig. Bosun! Take charge of the prisoner and carry out my orders."

The skipper watched the men go below, before turning to Scott with a comment, "Well done, Scott! Will the passengers leave Weasel alone if he's in the brig? Actually, it's just a dark storage room where we keep hawser and chain."

"Yes, the men seemed to accept your judgment as fair and just. You've got a good company of men sailing with you."

****

Fair weather prevailed for the next two days, and the deck was crowded with men enjoying the warming sun. After land was sighted on July 14th, the men became excited with anticipation of landing. Cape Blanco was clearly visible from several miles at sea, its white bluff, green-timbered shoulders, and ten small islets becoming distinguishable as the Sea Gull cruised slowly southeasterly. Captain Tichenor stood amidst the men on deck, pointing out landmarks with a sort of parental pride. It was obvious that the Port Orford settlement was close to his heart.

Finally he pointed to the Orford Heads, behind which lay the small harbor that was their destination. The Sea Gull rounded the headland, sailing alee of the grand promontory and its adjacent rocky cove, before dropping anchor in a second cove. A sandy bluff rose over a quiet beach north of the ship. The surf was still and the gulls' cries overhead could be heard. Sailors pointed out Battle Rock, which was situated beyond a break in the beach a few hundred feet east of their anchorage.

The bosun shouted, "Whales to the southeast! I count five grays, Captain."

John Larsen climbed on the railing and asked, "What are they doing, bosun?"

"Just playing, sir, they come north in the summer from California heading for Alaska. We often see them at sea when we're sailing within sight of land, although this pod of grays is kind of late."

Sam was studying the shoreline as everyone else watched the whales. He called out, "Captain, there are Indians over there," pointing beyond Battle Rock to a low sand hill. Three figures were standing and watching the ship, but made no hostile move. Soon they turned and walked into the woods.

Scott, Sam and John volunteered to scout the area around the landing site as the company landed supplies and equipment. Each man carried his rifle and a knife, plus powder and shot and some hardtack. Besides guarding against Indians, Scott was to survey the donation claim for defensive positions and a townsite. They returned before dark to help establish a night guard on the bluff above the beach.

The next day John was asked to build a small dock at the edge of the cove, and since he was a fisherman by trade, he consented without hesitation. Scott and Sam decided to follow the direction the Indians had taken, and explore the coastal beaches to the south.

They agreed to stay within sight of each other at all times, a difficult task in the forest. Their progress was so slow that when they found a trail leading toward the beach, they descended to the water's edge. Port Orford was about two miles west of their position as they turned away and walked along the beach. Soon they came to a modest creek flowing across the sand and into the surf.

The smell of smoke and a faint sound of voices drifted out of the small valley between two forested ridges. They advanced along the creek stealthily, stopping as they neared a small pool in the creek. Scott stepped forward around a giant cedar tree and came face-to-face with an Indian boy. Momentarily surprised, Scott raised his right hand, palm forward, and said, "Hello!" loud enough for Sam to hear. The lad's eyes were wide from both fright and curiosity.

Pointing to himself with fingers to his heart, he said, "I am Scott . . ." and paused before repeating, ". . . Scott . . . Scott . . ." He pointed to the boy, touching the Indian's chest, "Who are you?" The Indian youngster was startled anew as Sam came into sight with rifle at a ready position, but he stood his position, watching Scott.

Scott was patient and calmly repeated his question using signs. He pointed to his partner and named him, "Sam . . . Sam . . ." Finally the boy nodded and answered, "Chah-al-ah-e."

Sam spoke out, "Sounds like his name is Charlie." Pointing to the boy, he repeated, "Charlie," pointing to himself, "Sam," and pointing to his partner, "Scott." The Indian lad pronounced all three names dutifully, and when four other Indians stepped out of the forest upstream, the boy gestured that all five were together, as "Tututni." Scott explained to a puzzled Sam, "Charlie and his friends are Tututni, the tribe which attacked Kirkpatrick's party. They appear to be friendly now. Well, Sam old buddy, we can't outrun them, so let's make friends."

He signed to the men that he was friendly and spoke his name. The boy talked volubly to his friends for some time, until each man put his hand to his heart and gave his name. Sam responded in due time, even though the partners were unable to decipher the sounds in Indian names. Everyone seemed to understand this act of friendship.

The boy signaled for them to follow him, and with perhaps a little reluctance, the men gave the same gesture as they turned upstream. Walking single-file along a well-traveled forest path, they entered a clearing with nine lodges situated along the creek. The Indians stood quietly by their lodges as Charlie spoke respectfully to a red-shirted man standing before the large middle lodge.

Red-Shirt stepped forward smiling and saying his name, "Chat-al-hak-e-ah," and holding his hand up, palm forward. Charlie repeated the man's name to the partners, gesturing that he was chief of this band of the Tututni. Scott understood the boy's message immediately, but not until Red-Shirt put his arm around Charlie's shoulder, was it clear that they were father and son. Now each individual in the band stepped forward with introductions, showing friendly intent. Scott counted seven men, nine women, and nine children. Charlie named two men who were not present, evidently on a hunting trip. Scott and Sam struggled with the language barrier as they visited with the men of the village, and stayed for a meal at dusk. They thanked their hosts and returned to the settlement down a moonlit beach.

Scott pondered the significance of the Indians' behavior, "I'm thankful for their friendship. Do you suppose that breaking bread has a universal meaning? Perhaps we need to return the favor one of these days. You know, give them a gift or a side of venison."

Sam agreed, "You were calmer than I felt. I was afraid we'd make a mistake and have a fight on our hands. But I'm glad that we have friends so that we can travel around this country without fearing attack. Did you see that gravel bar in the creek above the village?"

"Yes, are you thinking that it's a prospecting site?" Sam nodded and Scott continued, "We'd better keep that idea to ourselves."

"I can keep my mouth shut if gold is the subject. What do we report to the rest of the men?"

"Exactly what happened today, but remember that these Indians are Tututni and probably were fighting at Battle Rock. We'll give a complete and factual report, but no gold talk."

The men in the settlement were relieved to hear of friendly Indians, but surprisingly to Scott, no one else seemed interested in meeting the Indians or visiting their village. Everyone was busy building the settlement. John Larsen enlisted the partners in finishing the dock, and they helped him fall and split three Port Orford cedars. He was crafting three boats with his own hands and tools which he had brought with him from Long Island, New York. The company was buying a dinghy and Captain Tichenor had ordered a small skiff, but the big boat was his own fishing trawler. John's explanation was, "I can fish with the company dinghy and make a living this year, but as new settlers arrive, I'll need a stout boat for the big catches which I can make offshore."

****

One day as they were carrying lumber down to the dock, John called from the top of the bluff, "Scott, there's an Indian lad in the settlement. He must be asking for you." Scott and Sam rushed up the hill to a crowd of men gathered around Charlie. The boy looked like he was ready to run off. Scott greeted the Indian with a smile, "Charlie, welcome to Port Orford!" Sam chimed in with, "Hello, Charlie!" Scott then insisted that each man present his own name and smile at the boy. As the friendly introductions concluded, Charlie handed Scott a brace of quail that he was carrying, obviously a gift. Scott asked Sam to take the game to the camp cook, while he and John showed Charlie their boatbuilding project. The boy spent the rest of the day watching the men work, and he offered several suggestions in a guttural dialect which none of them understood. They took Charlie to dinner in the dining hall, where curious white men studied the boy. Most of them followed Scott's friendly pattern of introducing themselves to the Indian. After dinner Scott walked with Charlie down the beach for a mile before saying good-bye. He was ensuring that no incident occurred near the settlement.

One Sunday when everyone was visiting after church services, Scott and Sam packed a duffel bag with twenty-nine gifts for Charlie's band and hiked down the beach toward the village. Three Indians were fishing in the surf and greeted the partners with a wave, joining them with their catch of several salmon. Talking and signing along the path, the Indians wanted to know what was in the bag. Scott teased them with the contents, indicating the Chief, "Chat-al-hak-e-ah," must see the gifts first.

Work stopped in the village as the men entered the clearing. His Indian friends chattered to their families until all eyes were on the duffel bag. Scott greeted Red-Shirt with a long harangue on friendship and on Charlie's gift of game-birds, jiggling the somewhat noisy bag in mystery. The Indians loved a game and played it straight-faced. Custom dictated that their guest should finish his discourse without interruption. When Scott stopped his monologue, running out of breath, Charlie could wait no longer. He pointed to the duffel bag, and then to himself, expectantly. Scott laughed and drew a blanket from the bag, spreading it over the grass. He beckoned Charlie's mother forward indicating it was her present, and asking in sign if he might use it for the gift-giving. She was pleased and nodded eagerly in agreement. Scott gave Sam the bag to empty onto the blanket after he had presented Red-shirt a prized steel hatchet. He grinned at his eager young friend, and gave him an equally valuable hunting knife. The Indians oohed and aahed at the valuable gifts, watching Sam with unabated interest.

Sam displayed his wares, gesturing to the chief that he was to give each member of his band one gift. Red-Shirt beamed with pride as he called forward each man, each squaw, and then each child to pick out a gift. When everyone had chosen, there was a bracelet and a fishing line with a steel hook left on the blanket. Sam signed that they belonged to Red-Shirt. It pleased all of the Indians that their chief was so honored in the ceremony and the partners were given seashell necklaces as a thank you memento. They sat and enjoyed the friendly interplay, trying to learn the names of their friends as well as a few words of the Tututni language. The Indians treated them to a festive clambake, one which took most of the day for the women to prepare. Steam pits lined with hot boulders were filled with freshly dug clams, covered with green foliage and a reed-like net, and then water was sprinkled over it for an hour.

Scott found the clams to be delicious in their now-open shells, and the grilled salmon and cod were almost more than he could eat. He and Sam were presented a special delicacy which was tasty but different. They couldn't understand what it was, and at Sam's quizzical expression, Scott said, "Don't ask me what it is. I have this feeling we don't want to know."

They walked down the beach on the way home, laughing at Scott's remark on the unknown delicacy. He was right as they found out when Charlie took them to the carcass of a stag and graphically explained that they had eaten its testicles, commonly known by frontiersmen as Rocky Mountain oysters.

The weeks passed quickly into September as the townsite was developed. The partners had been welcome visitors in the Indian village, and had received Red-Shirt's permission to pan for gold along the creek. They began planning an immediate prospecting venture, when the U.S. Army arrived on September 14th to establish Fort Orford. Stories of hostilities with Indians were commonplace along the Oregon coast, and the Tututni, or Rogues as they were known by the Army, were being nicknamed the "Rascals" for their continued harassment of settlers.

With the troops came more settlers, including women and children. Scott and Sam were needed to hunt game as food supplies became short. Scott accepted the task willingly, and though Sam was reluctant to delay his quest for gold, he acceded to his partner's sense of civic responsibility. They would go prospecting next month.

Chapter Three

The advent of families to Port Orford altered the social life of the community. Church attendance blossomed and rough language in public all but disappeared. Civilization was coming to town.

An outdoor salmon bake held on the fort's parade ground included dancing, even if only six women were available to dance with 160 men. Sam danced and charmed all the ladies, without offending their husbands. Scott was impressed. He had danced with each lady, albeit a little clumsily, early in the party. His preference was watching the people enjoy themselves, visiting with acquaintances, and meeting newcomers. The partners had returned last evening from a successful hunt up the Elk River, northeast of Port Orford. Sam had contrived to be back in time for the party, hiring five men to help them transport the meat from seven deer and a bear. The partners had washed their best outfits after midnight so that their clothes would be clean and dry for this social event of the year.

As the afternoon mist closed around the gala, Scott helped build five large fires. They needed both light and heat if the dancing was to continue into the evening. He was standing near the most westerly fire by himself, warming his hands, when a stranger carried an armload of dried branches out of the woods. He dropped them near the fire and remarked, "You have a grand fire burning. Mind if I join you?"

"I'd welcome your company. My name is Scott McClure," he replied, extending his hand.

"I know. You brought in quite a load of meat for the town last night," the man commented as he limped perceptibly toward Scott and shook hands. He explained, "I work at the store. I'm George Hermann from Philadelphia." Pointing to one of the dancing women, he continued, "You danced with my wife Mary earlier in the party."

"Of course, she mentioned you and a four-year-old daughter. Have you found a place for your family to live yet?"

"We're living in the back of the store temporarily. As you've seen, I have a leg that slows me down a little, and I prefer a house in town. Where are you from, Scott?"

"St. Charles, Missouri, although I spent last winter working in Portland."

The two men conversed for some time in getting acquainted. George Hermann impressed Scott as a solid citizen and a good family man. His character and intellect stood out in this group, even if his physical stature was unimpressive. His body was short and stocky. His face was framed with dark curly hair, trimmed neatly around his head and neck, and the beard was squared at the throat. Altogether his features were regular and unremarkable. Scott thought to himself, "George Hermann may not look imposing, but he'll be a sound member of our community. I like him."

Mary Hermann joined the men at the fire, breathing heavily from a vigorous reel. George reintroduced her to Scott, and said to the man who came forward to ask her for a dance, "Friend, this is my dance with my wife, and we're going to sit it out."

Mary added quickly, "But you have the next dance, sir."

The man smiled and nodded, "I'll be back ma'am."

Turning to her husband, she asked, "Can we stay awhile longer, George?"

"I'm comfortable watching all you dancers. There's no hurry if you're enjoying the party."

Scott listened as they chatted about the people whom they had met in Port Orford. Mary seemed to be the motherly type although he guessed she was his age. Her buxom figure was sturdy, yet graceful, as proven in her dancing. Her hair was light brown, its strands curled at the ends just below her ears. Her face was pretty with freckles on her small nose, and her blue eyes smiled in consonance with her lips, combining to give her a friendly and caring visage.

"I wish you could dance, dear. That Indian woman over there is sitting out again. It seems most men are avoiding her." Glancing at Scott with a twinkle in her eye, she added, "Have you danced with her, Mr. McClure?"

"Yes, ma'am. But I believe it's time to ask her again," he admitted ruefully.

He crossed the field leisurely, and as he approached the woman, a lithe older man in buckskins spoke to her. Scott hesitated, saying, "Ma'am, could I? . . ." and paused as she looked up at him. The man turned and smiled, "Pardon, Monsieur. You wish to dance with my wife Sally?"

"Yes, I hope that I'm not too late for this square dance."

"Non! Jacques Dubois is a gentleman tonight. I will wait for the next dance."

"I'm Scott McClure. Mrs. Dubois, may I have the honor of another dance?"

He nodded to her husband as he escorted Sally Dubois onto the parade ground.

"Thank you, Mr. McClure. I saw you talking to my friends, the Hermanns. Have you known them long?" Sally spoke English better than her husband, and danced as gracefully as Mary.

"No, I just met them. I've been hunting for several days. When did you folks arrive?"

"We came down the coast trail from the Coquille valley just last week. Jacques heard there was logging work here."

They separated as they entered the coterie of dancers and formed squares. Scott thought Sally looked very Indian and Jacques looked very French, and together they made a strange couple for Port Orford. He wondered if they knew Buzz Smith. He'd ask later, after this dance, but Sam claimed Sally at the break so he returned to George and their fire.

****

Early the next morning Scott and Sam headed north on their final hunting trip. Scott was interested in exploring the Sixes River where Jedediah Smith's Campsite #9 had been located. They returned to the Elk River, crossing it at a ford they had used before, and then turned west, traveling on the higher ground until they were on the heights above Cape Blanco and could see much of the Oregon coastline. Although the sky was overcast and the misty air was cool, visibility was good from their panoramic view. They could see a steamship bearing in toward Port Orford from the south. Sam complained, "That ship is probably carrying more settlers. We'd best move on before all the gold is gone." He was still sure that his fortune was buried in the ground just waiting for him to find

To the northeast, Scott could see the estuary of the Sixes River a scant mile away. Smoke rising from the grassy tidal land indicated an Indian village. Sam pointed upriver to a second smoke cluster. His voice tightened as he essayed, "At least two villages . . . must be a lot of Indians . . ."

"You're right, Sam. Charlie informed me that the Shix was a much bigger village than the Port Orford's. We can't hunt the Sixes River without making friends with the Indians who live there. Are you ready to meet them?"

"I suppose so. You lead the way and I'll cover you. I just hope these Indians are as friendly as Charlie and his daddy."

The two men descended a slope covered with windblown coastal firs, and halted on a small knoll above the river. Sandy beaches reached upriver from the monoliths standing in the ocean and guarding the river entrance. Over 100 acres of grassy lea stretched out before them, divided into three parcels by twin channels of the Sixes River. A village of thirty-forty lodges was situated on the south flat, with smoke rising from the dwellings. Across from the village, several people were working along the shore of a sizable island. The north channel was deserted, where a narrow flat of land was bordered by timbered hills.

"What a beautiful site for a village. Do you think your father camped here in 1828?"

"No, the Smith party camped upriver along the coastal trail. Traveling through here would be difficult. Besides, this village has been here for ages."

Scott nodded toward the downriver edge of the village where several Indians were fishing with traps along the shore. He reflected, "Perhaps we should approach those fishermen rather than walk directly into the village. What do you think, Sam?"

"Sounds reasonable. Our options will be better in case they're unfriendly. Let's get moving!"

Scott led off down the slope and across the marshy meadow. Studying the scene he spotted five men knee deep in the river, an old man with a knife in his hand standing on the low bank, and two men in a drifting canoe offshore. Several gutted salmon lay behind the old man, obviously their generous catch for the day. The men in the canoe gesticulated excitedly when they espied the white men approaching.

As the old man spun to face the strangers, the partners stopped about twenty feet short of the river. Scott repeated his successful technique of greeting Indians. With his right hand held up, palm forward, he smiled and said, "Hello!" The old Indian just stared at him as the other Indians joined him on the river bank. Scott and Sam signed their peaceful intentions in unison.

The old man unhurriedly stepped forward two paces and spoke in the familiar Tututni language. Scott caught the terms "Shix" and "Quah-to-mah" as he gestured toward the land around them.

With a respectful tone, Scott responded, "Chief Sixes, I am Scott. . . ," and pointed to himself, repeated, ". . . Scott." Placing his hand on Sam's shoulder, he continued, "My friend is . . . Sam."

Chief Sixes turned his head toward his tribesmen and spoke to them. Scott listened and guessed at what the Indians were saying. "I think this band is named the 'Quah-to-mah' and the Sixes valley is their tribal land. He seems to have understood our names, and while he's not unfriendly, we are interlopers. This is their territory."

Chief Sixes addressed Scott at length, finally smiling as each Indian stepped forward to give his name. A score of men had come from the lodges during these introductions. Scott and Sam repeated their names and gave their standard hand salute. The newly arrived Indians replied in kind. The men now opened a lane in deference to a short stocky Indian who was younger than Chief Sixes. Scott's surmise that he was Chief of this band was confirmed when Chief Sixes stepped aside respectfully and spoke to him. He then turned to the partners and introduced "Sa-qua-mi" as his Chief.

The white men showed respect by introducing themselves. In a deliberate and unprovocative manner, each hunter removed a steel knife from his pack. Scott stepped forward, gingerly extending the handle of the knife to Chief Sa-qua-mi. The Chief took the knife, and as Scott signed that it was a gift, Sam gave a knife to Chief Sixes. Both Indians beamed with pride and pleasure as they showed their new possessions to their envious friends. The white men were welcomed into the village to share a meal of roasted salmon. During their visit Sa-qua-mi gave them permission to hunt upriver. Chief Sixes offered to guide them past the band's smaller village. Scott understood that the lower Sixes was off-limits and accepted the tribal offer with grace. He and Sam would respect their new friends' territorial claim.

Chief Sixes led the hunting party over a well-worn trail to the other Quah-to-mah village in less than an hour. Scott speculated, "Jedediah Smith must have camped here in 1828. He stayed on the south side of the Sixes, but my father never mentioned an Indian village. I wonder if those lodges across the river are temporary?"

Sam agreed, "It appears the coastal trail crosses this ford. I can't see any other possibility for a campsite. Let's follow Chief Sixes across the river."

They forded the shallow river to lodges on the north side, where several deer carcasses were hanging from trees behind the village. The squaws were dressing the game and drying the venison for winter stores. The Subchief introduced the white men and talked with a wrinkled old man for several minutes. The oldster nodded repeatedly at Chief Sixes and gestured upriver, evidently agreeing that the white men could hunt east of the village. On the trail again, Chief Sixes conveyed the idea that his 'uncle' would tell other Indian hunters about them.

Soon the open valley narrowed into a cut between two ridged hills. The rocky face of a cliff on the south side was not traversable. The trail followed the river around the north bluff quickly deteriorated into a single lane of gravel and shale running about twenty feet above the river's rushing waters. The footing remained uncertain for 250 feet before the trail widened once again. Scott thought, I wouldn't care to walk this path on a stormy night. They continued for another mile before they came to a small rivulet cascading down its rocky course, before flowing into the Sixes River. They jumped the creek and under a screen of stately firs, descended the slope of a small knoll. The valley widened at the bend of the river, forming a large flat into which the hunters emerged.

To Scott's left was a brushy gully reaching upwards to a fir-covered bench, and to his right was a grassy lea bordered by blackberry vines and the river. Spreading before them was a flat, spotted with fir copses between small meadows. And as a centerpiece for this beautiful park-like setting, stood a grove of magnificent myrtlewood trees. Remembering a conversation with Buzz Smith last summer, Scott estimated the 'granddaddy' of the trees at over 200 years of age, its dark trunk and luxuriant foliage prominent in the verdant background.

Chief Sixes spoke in guttural tones, signing repetitiously that the valley was theirs.

Scott exclaimed, "I believe that he means that this land is a gift to us from the Quah-to-mahs. Not only can we hunt, but we can settle here."

Sam queried in anticipation, "Can we prospect for gold along this river too? Maybe we'll have time to pan while we're hunting."

Scott nodded, picturing a farm setting laid over this flat. His partner might dream of gold, but a home near the myrtlewood grove would be more satisfying to him. As their friendly guide returned down river, the two partners acted on their separate ideas. Sam took a shovel and pan down to the river to seek his fortune in gold. Scott paced off a cabin site. He then wrote out a claim which he buried in a tin can next to a solitary cedar on the corner of the 'cabin'.

****

Over the next week Scott bagged five deer, and Sam panned every gravel bar and sand beach around the flat. He was disappointed, in concluding, "There's no gold here. Let's go to Charlie's village on Hubbard Creek. Do we have enough venison to fill the store's order?"

Scott nodded. "Maybe the Indians will help us over the river ford with these carcasses. We can a save several hours if we cut back to four loads of meat, and give them the rest of the venison."

Chief Sixes' uncle cheerfully accepted Scott's offer, and his hunters assisted the partners across both the Sixes and the Elk rivers. They camped that night on the south side of the Elk, and toted their meat into Port Orford the next afternoon.

George Hermann greeted Scott upon his arrival at the store, "Welcome back! Can you hang that venison haunch in the back room for me?"

"Sure, George, Sam's bringing the rest of your order. He talked two men into carrying it from Garrison Lake." After completing his task, he took a deep breath, "Whew! It feels good to be back. Anything new happening in town?"

"Captain Tichenor sailed into port with more supplies and a few settlers, including two families. Oh yes, John Larsen agreed to build a house for me after he fills all of his fish orders. And I have your supply order ready in the corner over there. Are you going prospecting soon?"

"Sam and I are leaving tomorrow, but we'll be back, off and on, during the winter."

"Well, Mary's hoping that you and Sam will have supper with us tonight, and tell us about your hunt." George chuckled, and continued, "She has a letter for you from Portland which Captain Tichenor delivered . . . a lady's handwriting . . . Mary's itching to question you. You're on the spot, my friend. Do you like pot roast, mashed potatoes and gravy well enough to attend the inquisition?"

Scott grinned broadly. "You mean that I'll be fed a grand meal, but then I must satisfy the cook's curiosity." He laughed, and added, "Thanks, George, Sam and I accept your invitation. We need to pack our gear for tomorrow and bathe before making a social call. Is six o'clock a good time?"

George replied, "Yes, you can read your letter before eating. And you're welcome to sleep in this storeroom with your gear overnight." Turning toward the front door, he raised his voice and called to Sam and his companions, "Bring that meat back here, Sam!"

Scott helped Sam hang the meat, and then said, "We're eating at the Hermann's tonight. George has our supplies. Settle with him and start packing. I'm going to see John, and I'll be back within the hour."

"Tell John that he's invited to supper tonight. Mary asked him to come earlier in the week. I'll help Sam while you're gone."

The three bachelors arrived at Hermann's door promptly at six o'clock, and were met by George before they could knock. "Living in the back of this store has one small disadvantage, or advantage as the case may be. We can hear everyone that walks by the door. Come in, friends." Over his shoulder, he called, "It's our guests, dear!"

Mary greeted them in the kitchen and introduced their daughter, Angela, to Sam and Scott. Sam thanked her for the invitation as George talked to John about the new house. Scott sat on his heels and asked the shy youngster, "Do you like Port Orford? Have you found any little girl to be your friend? Are you Mama's helper?" Angela watched Scott with her eyes big and round, but said nothing. With Mary and Sam watching him, he wondered if he looked as foolish as he felt. Trying to talk to a four-year-old child was an uncommon experience for Scott.

"Have you seen any Indians?" Angela nodded vigorously, as Scott continued, "Were they nice men?" When Angela shook her head, Scott asked, "Why weren't they nice?"

Angela spoke shyly. "The soldier-man said they were dirty rascals. What's a rascal?"

"That's a person who lies and cheats. Some Indians the soldier knows are probably bad men, but I know many good Indians. One of my friends is Chief Chat-al-hak-e-ah. He gave me this shell necklace." Scott took it from his pocket and offered it to Angela, "Would you like it?"

Angela looked at her mother, who nodded, and took the necklace. "Thank you, Mr. McClure. Do you really know an Indian Chief? He must be a nice man if he gave you a present."

Mary laughed, helping her daughter put the string of shells around her neck. "Scott, you've made a conquest. Angela seldom talks to strangers."

"I'm not a stranger, am I, Angela? I'm Uncle Scott."

Mary laughed in approval, handing Scott a letter and kidding him, "You must charm all the girls, Scott. Here's a letter from your lady friend in Portland."

"Actually, Melissa lives in Marysville," Scott responded in good nature. "Do I get to read my mail in peace?" he asked rhetorically, as he opened the letter.

His thoughts drifted back to last year's convalescence at the Wells house, and his visit to the Nelson home a few weeks later. He missed Melissa's company and regretted being unable to visit her last spring. As he focused on the neat schoolmarm's handwriting, he perused both sides of the single page carefully. Leaning back in his chair and staring at the kitchen wall, he mused as to how her letters touched him in a warming way.

Scott became aware of the lack of talking in the room, and looked around to find everyone watching him expectantly.

Sam broke into his reverie, "Mary's too polite to ask, but I'm not. What's the news from Marysville? How are Melissa and her father?"

"Melissa is fine and she is teaching again this winter — she enjoys the children. Her father has been ill with pneumonia and hasn't been able to work for weeks. She saw our friend Buzz Smith in Elkton—that's the new name for Fort Umpqua. Buzz is trapping again this year with Curly Lambeau, but Melissa says that he's getting too old to traipse around the country. As I recall, she said the same thing last year to Buzz and he just laughed. She says Portland is a big city with thousands of new settlers arriving this past summer. Aside from her meeting with Captain Tichenor and visiting with him, that's all there is." Scott concluded his summary, put the letter in his pocket, and changed the subject.

"Have Sam tell you about the Quah-to-mahs and our friend Chief Sixes. Er . . . actually he is a subchief . . . but a good man in the Shix village."

The conversation was lively during the meal, with Sam entertaining their hosts with tales of his adventures in Oregon. His stories of the partnership seemed more credible, particularly when Scott corrected exaggerations inherent to Sam's monologue.

Scott questioned Mary about Port Orford activities until she had brought the partners up to date on developments. One item which disturbed him, was the military commander's comments to the effect that all Indians were renegades and not to be trusted.

"How can that officer be so righteous about Indians? He's only been at Fort Orford for a month. Has he talked to the local chiefs?" Scott asked emotionally.

George answered, "I know that you and Sam have Indian friends, but most settlers don't like any Indian. They have no respect for them. Several men have suggested that the Army Commander chase them off 'our' land. Most people don't want Indian neighbors and refuse to recognize them as human beings. I'm sorry, Scott, you are only one voice of rationality in a chorus of bigotry. I don't think the white man and the Indian can live together in this region with the existing feelings."

"I realize the Indians are fighting for their land. There should be room for all of us, but you may be right that no middle ground is possible. Sam and I will fight if we are attacked. Battle Rock is still a vivid memory. I just hope the soldiers use common sense in carrying out their orders." Scott paused, and smilingly concluded, "This conversation is entirely too serious. I guess philosophical considerations can wait for another day. Thank you, Mary . . . and you too, George, for the fine supper. John, if Sam and I can help you build the Hermann house, get word to us through Charlie. We'll be prospecting near his village on Hubbard Creek. Good night!"

****

The partners were walking down the beach before daylight, on their way to Hubbard Creek and those gravel bars which Sam had identified for their winter prospecting project.

They were greeted warmly by their friends in the village, but Chief Chat-al-hak-e-ah hesitated before introducing a tall young stranger to Scott and Sam. The newcomer remained stoic as the Chief gave his name as "Sah-mah-ha-e" and pointed to "Scott" and "Sam," signing that they were friends.

Sam repeated his own name, "Sam . . . you're Sammy," he said to the young Indian. He smiled in genuine pleasure at meeting someone with his name, and the stranger repeated both names. The partners hoped they had found a new friend. After Sammy departed, Scott asked Charlie who he was and what he was doing here. Charlie pointed south and indicated that Sammy was from another band of the Tututni. The language barrier hindered any detailed explanation, but Scott experienced a moment of clairvoyance. He stopped questioning the boy and pulled Sam aside to share his feeling.

"Sammy and Charlie were at Battle Rock with most of the Tututni on this coast. I bet Sammy was talking to the Chief about fighting the settlers. We're a paradox to these Indians — we're both friends and white men. They don't know how to take us. I don't feel threatened, do you?"

Sam looked around and replied, "No, I'm sure we're safe in this village, but we'd better watch ourselves with other Indians. The Chief has assigned us space beyond the last lodge. I think we're getting help to build a shelter."

Charlie waved to the partners and ran upstream to their campsite with most of the Indians following more slowly. Everyone worked on a sheltered lean-to, which was made of fir boughs interlaced with a log lashed between two stout cedars. The partners furnished the canvas sailcloth which fronted the shelter and served as a door. Scott thanked the Indians as they finished the lean-to and returned to their other chores. Sam helped Scott secure the interior and pack their gear, then eagerly went to the gravel bar with his shovel and pan. He had an hour of daylight left, and Scott had agreed to prepare supper.

"Eureka!" Sam screamed as he ran to the fire where Scott was cooking stew. With excited tones, he added, "Isn't that what that Greek yelled when he found gold? Look at this pan!" Sam extended a pan of sandy water toward Scott and fingered several bright specks of gold. "Tomorrow morning will prove us to be rich men. I'm going to be ready at first light."

Scott laughed happily, "At least it's a relief to see more than sand in your pan. This is a good place to spend the winter. Eat up, partner. Finding gold is often easier work than digging it out of the ground."

After supper, Sam cleaned out his pan in the firelight. There were seventeen flecks of gold in his hand. He put them in an empty coffee tin, calling it their treasure chest. Both men had a fitful sleep, arising early and organizing their work schedule before dawn.

They worked without rest until the light failed, cutting cedar planks from a downed tree. Their Indian friends helped them trim the lumber, but wanted nothing to do with digging in the river. They had no interest in gold treasure.

Scott warmed the leftover stew and opened a package of fruit bread which Mary had given them. Thus they celebrated their good fortune and wearily crawled between their blankets.

On the third morning, their sluice was in place beside the creek, and they began working their claim. Scott dug pails of creek sand and soil from behind a small diversion they had built along the bank. He washed a loose conglomerate in the sluice until the gold flecks could be extracted. His operation was simple and effective, but most importantly, he did not stand in the flowing water of the creek.

Sam panned pockets of sand in the middle of the gravel bar, where he found an occasional nugget as well as dust. Here the water was cold and it was necessary for the partners to switch jobs hourly. At the end of the day, Sam put all of the day's gold in their 'safe', and they estimated its value at five dollars. Sam had a disappointed expression on his face, but Scott cheerfully predicted, "We should wash several hundred dollars out of Hubbard Creek this winter. Your idea will pay off handsomely!"

The miners lost track of time as they toiled long hours on their claim. Days flowed into weeks as their coffee tin filled with the valuable gold dust. Both men had found a few nuggets in the early days of panning, and they put them aside as mementos. The claim was still producing dust, but they hadn't found a real nugget in several days. Charlie was a big help, keeping their lean-to watertight and bringing them fish and game from time to time. Often he joined them for dinner and practiced his English, which was improving rapidly.

****

One afternoon he called from the far side of the village, "Scott . . . Sam . . . John and Jacques . . . here . . ." Scott espied his friends entering the village, and waved them to the campsite. Since Charlie was guiding the white men, the village Indians were unalarmed. In fact several people waved and greeted the men who replied in kind. The village had a happy and congenial atmosphere.

John Larsen looked over the mining operation and said, "Those prospectors on the beach were right. There is gold in that creek. Are you doing well?"

Sam glanced at Scott, silent understanding in their exchange. Grinning he announced, "Eureka, we have found it!"

Laughing, Scott added, "What my partner means is that we have a producing gold placer claim, but we aren't rich yet. However we can afford supplies . . . we are a bit short. What did you bring us?"

John shook his head and replied, "Sorry my friends, no supplies. Mary and Sally sent freshly baked bread which Jacques and I will help you eat this evening. Plus an invitation to Christmas dinner in the new Hermann home."

Sam accepted energetically, "The house is finished? Wow! We'd welcome the visit as well as home cooking." Frowning he asked his partner, "Can we leave our claim, Scott?"

"Sure, we'll take our gold to George and pick up needed supplies. We need a break, and Charlie will watch our claim for a few days. John, our calendar isn't up to date . . . which day is Christmas?"

Jacques laughed with his friends. "Monsieurs, tomorrow is Noel . . . how you say 'eve' . . . plenty of time to help John and me . . . ah . . . buy a thing for the new house."

"Can Jacques and I help you dig gold this afternoon? We've never done it before. It sounds exciting—is it?"

Scott laughed and made an offer, "All the gold dust which we mine today, goes toward a housewarming gift tomorrow. But beware, we don't allow any malingering on this job!"

At supper that evening, John ate ravenously, commenting to his friends, "That was hard work. I'll take fishing any day. How did we do, Sam?"

"Your work certainly made a difference. Today's take is by far our largest . . . maybe $15. What shall we buy the Hermanns?"

"A friend is holding a large mirror for me until I return tomorrow. The price of $22 is high, but not many homes in Port Orford have a beautiful piece like this one. Can we?"

"Say no more, John. Sam and I will make up whatever difference in cash that is needed. But I don't want to show gold dust. We have some gold and silver coins which would attract a lot less attention. Do we have enough cash amongst us?"

John nodded understandingly, and all four men poled their cash, a total of $24. "Buy Angela a doll from all of us, and bring a bottle of spirits for our festive dinner party," Scott suggested. "We'll go to town in the morning with our can of gold and turn it over to George."

The next day started as ordinary, with the trip into town and ordering supplies at the store consuming the morning hours. They took George aside in private and handed him the tin of gold dust. Scott urged, "Please be careful, George. We don't want miners running all over Hubbard Creek. We're enjoying being the only miners at the village."

George understood Scott's rationale for privacy, and agreed readily to keep their secret. He told them that they had $600 in credit after deducting the supply orders and giving them a few coins as spending money. He concluded with, "That's mighty fine wages for two months work. No wonder you're keeping your claim secret."

As they visited with the townspeople, both partners remained noncommittal on the subject of gold. They grew smug in believing that their behavior was normal — just friendly and natural. Scott was shocked when John caught him late in the afternoon with an exclamation, "I never told!" He took a deep breath, and continued, "Everyone in town is talking about your 'silence'. The gossip is that you've struck it rich. I guess you can't keep a secret in a small town."

"Can we stay with you tonight on your boat? I'll find Sam and we'll sneak aboard after dark. I'm sure that we'll be better off not talking anymore."

Scott found Sam at the sutler's store at the Fort. A prospector acquaintance was asking Sam, "Didn't I see you and your friends coming out of Hubbard Creek this morning?" The other men gave Sam another glass of whiskey and continued the verbal attack with a harangue of direct questions.

Scott wrested Sam from the crowd with physical force, telling a grand falsehood, "Come on Sam, we have to get back to our camp on the Elk River. Let's go!"

It took a full hour to shake the following gold-miners and slip aboard John's boat. They ate a quick meal and doused the cabin light as they crawled into their bunks. John sat in the wheelhouse and kept watch for an hour. When the town was quiet, he turned in also.

Christmas day was cold and blustery as Scott and Sam walked a roundabout path to Hermanns' place. They arrived early and George laughed in greeting them, "News travels fast, my friends. How did you find your way here without a crowd on your trail?"

Scott laughed and turned to Mary as she came into the parlor, "I'm sorry, Mary. We're early, but at least safe and sound. John and the Dubois will be along later."

"George has told me about all the rumors flying, but you have to give me the true story. Are you rich or not?"

"Sam will tell you a good tale, but I'll tell you we're not rich. Our claim is producing gold dust, but I believe we have passed the peak. However, we don't dare leave while we're doing so well. There might be a big pocket still to be found." Changing the subject, he asked, "May I have paper and pen? I want to write a Christmas letter to Melissa." He thought that he would give everyone gold nuggets as presents, and had wrapped his best find in a package for her. She could add it to her necklace from last Christmas.

He completed his letter as the remaining guests arrived with three wrapped presents. Angela loved the brightly dressed rag doll and the adults knew that the bottle of wine was for dinner. It had required John and Jacques both to carry the third present, and Mary had difficulty keeping her eyes away from it.

Scott teased, "Yes, Mary. That's for you . . . and George. Would you rather open it after dinner?"

"Stop it, Scott!" Sally rejoined. "You're embarrassing Mary." She turned to her friend and told her, "It's from all of us for your new home. Go ahead and open it, Mary."

John chimed in, "We all panned for the gold to pay for it on the Hubbard Creek Claim. I brought my tools with me to help George uncrate it."

As the burlap covering the frame was lifted, Mary saw her reflection and tears welled in her eyes, somehow matching her tremulous smile. "What a precious gift. It's beautiful . . . I know just where to hang it."

George smiled at his friends in appreciation adding, "Thank you, my wife is seldom so excited about receiving a gift."

"I have my tools, George. Shall we finish? Where will it go, Mary?" John followed Mary's pointing finger to the parlor wall opposite the front window, and had the mirror attached to that spot in a few minutes, "How does that look? Good enough?"

Christmas day was exemplary, with good cheer, good food, and good friends abounding. Walking with fully-laden packs on the beach that evening, Sam spoke their common thought, "What a wonderful holiday! George's saying of the Grace was eloquent . . . it made up for our missing Christmas Eve services." They were in a gay mood as they reached Hubbard Creek.

****

In the lingering grayness of dusk, they saw twenty-some men nonchalantly waiting on the beach. As the men gathered around the partners, a gaggle of comments filled the air, "You didn't fool us!" "The Indians stopped us from going up the creek." "Is it a big strike?" and "Merry Christmas!" The latter statement quieted the crowd.

Scott responded, "And to you, sir, many more Christmas Days like today." He saw men, reasonable Christians, who were seeking help. "Our placer claim is decent, but not a big strike. We are located next to the Indian village, and you are not welcome there. I am willing to talk to the Chief for you if you will stay away from his people. You can prospect here or go above the village."

The men agreed readily and when Scott spoke to Chat-al-hak-e-ah, the Chief nodded reluctantly. Both men recognized that he had no other choice if he was to avoid fighting. Scott guided the gold miners to several claim sites well away from the village, while Sam worked theirs. The partners knew that one of them must always be present on the claim or at the village, in order to forestall trouble. And as winter passed into spring, their presence maintained peace along the creek. Minor pockets of gold kept the miners on Hubbard Creek, but it also kept them happy with their claims. Theft was not a problem during the winter of 1851-1852, and Scott thanked God for letting him keep his word to his Indian friends.

Scott and Sam worked harder than ever, but produced less gold dust each week. They worked the sand and gravel for over 200 feet along the creek with almost no gains. Most of their success was directly connected to the original gravel bar which had been petering out since March. They decided to dig deeper into the bar in hopes of unearthing more of the precious metal, but by early May their hopes were dashed. Ten days of strenuous digging had produced less than an ounce of gold. Their claim was played out.

The Port Orfords moved to the South Fork of Hubbard Creek, about a mile away, allowing the increasing number of prospectors to work the village site itself. The partners agreed to sell their claim and equipment to three newcomers for $100 cash and promptly packed their personal gear and left Hubbard Creek. Scott thought to himself, Well, so much for mining . . . no more for me . . . Sam still believes . . . maybe next year.

****

A ship was anchored in the harbor as the men walked into Port Orford. Scott recognized Captain Tichenor and sent Sam with their gold dust to George, while he strode to the beach to greet his friend.

Tichenor waved when he saw Scott, and shouted, "Hello, old friend! Come and meet my family."

Scott was impressed with the handsome family introduced to him on the landing. Mrs. Tichenor was pleasant, appearing to be a proper lady. Jake was a quiet boy nearing manhood, but not at all prepossessing like his father. The older daughter, Anne, favored her mother in looks and in manners. Scott guessed that she was fifteen years of age, and thought her manner friendly but reserved. Ellen was bright and precocious, stating clearly, "I'm four years old. I'm learning to read!" She was the one child that resembled her father and sparked an interest in Scott. He thought, this girl has more character and personality than anyone else in the family, including the Captain.

Captain Tichenor asked Scott, "Can you help me with this personal luggage? My family will be staying with the Winsors' until I build a house. There seems to be a lot of strangers in town."

"You're right, Captain. I've been out of town for several weeks and I don't recognize most of these people. Did they come in on your ship?" Scott asked as the men carted the luggage up the street.

Tichenor grunted a response, "No, they must have come down the coast trail. Mother, what have you packed in this valise? It's damnably heavy!"

"You needn't curse, William. I brought the family silver service. We had to carry some nice things with us for our home in Port Orford."

"Thanks, Scott, you can leave our luggage on the Winsors' porch. Jake and I can take it to our rooms later. Please come for a visit after we're settled."

Scott said his good-byes and walked on to the store. In the next block, he could see Sam walking with friends to the Fort. George welcomed him warmly, taking him to the storeroom before handing him a moneybelt. "Sam told me to hold your reserve until fall, but he split your earnings for the winter. Your share is $161 after paying outstanding supply bills. He told me that you sold your claim and are going to celebrate."

"He's celebrating already, I do believe. For me, I just want a break in this mining routine. Sam and I are going separate ways this summer, but we've agreed to meet here in August for another venture. He plans to prospect the headwaters of Hubbard Creek while I'm visiting the Umpqua valley and Buzz Smith."

"And maybe Marysville? Yes, Mary has a letter for you from Melissa. Did you know that my wife has exchanged letters with your friend? Mary's a born matchmaker, and you will have to come to dinner tonight so that she can practice on you. Sam told me that he has other plans."

Picking up his gear, Scott laughed quietly as he accepted, "Of course, I'm hungry for Mary's cooking. Do you have a good bottle of wine in the store?" Scott bought an expensive Spanish red wine over George's objection, and added a sack of hard candy for Angela.

"Does the hotel up the street take boarders?"

"Yes, Mrs. Knapp and her son Louie will give you a good room with meals. Tell them that I sent you. 'Grandma' Knapp is quite a character."

When Scott entered the hotel lobby, he introduced himself to Mrs. Knapp as a good friend of George Hermann.

"Glory be, Mr. McClure, I know all about you. You're a rich gold miner, and a friend of the Tichenors as well as the Hermanns."

"Whoa! There aren't any rich miners in Port Orford, let alone me. But I am proud to say that I'm friends with many good people in this town."

A young man entered the lobby, and Mrs. Knapp introduced them to each other, "Mr. McClure meet my son, Louie. He's the hotelkeeper in this family."

"Call me Scott, folks. I'm pleased to meet both of you. Have you been in Port Orford long?"

As he chatted with the Knapps, he could see the "Grandma" title was deserved. She was gray-haired and of small stature, with dark-rimmed spectacles for her eyes. The son had a very youthful look and seemed frail even though his movements were quick and strong. To strangers, they looked more like grandma-grandson related, rather than mother-son. Louie showed him to his room overlooking the street, and gave him a key.

"Meals are at 7, 12, and 5 o'clock, although mother will save you a plate if you give her notice that you'll be late."

"Tell your mother that I'm dining with the Hermanns tonight, but I'll look forward to eating here tomorrow morning."

Leaving his hotel, he strolled south down the street, exchanging greetings with people he recognized. From the bluff over the harbor, he could see John Larsen's boat far to the southwest. "Probably staying out tonight to catch the early morning tide," he muttered to himself. He would do some visiting in town before he headed north to the Umpqua.

Meandering past Battle Rock as dusk prevailed, he turned north, ending up before the Hermanns front door. Mary opened it before Scott could knock.

"I've been watching you for half an hour. How are you, Scott? Aside from looking lost, you seem healthy enough."

"I'm fine, Mary. I think that I've forgotten how to relax. The placer claim took all of our time this winter. You're looking well. Living in your own house must agree with you."

A small voice said shyly, "Hello, Uncle Scott!" Angela held up her arms and Scott picked her up, hugging her for a moment. "Thank you for the candy."

Glancing at Mary with a lifted eyebrow, he replied, "You are welcome, Angela. When did your daddy give it to you?"

"A little while ago. He came home to tell Mama to fix dinner for you."

Mary laughed, "Ha, ha, there are no secrets in this family," and as Scott blushed a light red, she added, "You have a standing invitation, Scott Addis McClure You're just like family!"

As he lowered Angela to the floor, he chided Mary, "You've been corresponding with Melissa. No one else has ever used my full name. How is she?"

"She's fine, although her father's health hasn't improved over the winter." Mary paused and mischievously added, "I bet that she'd welcome a visit from you. Here's your letter. Have a chair, and we'll leave you alone to read it. Come along, Angela."

Scott read and reread the letter. Melissa's concern for her father fairly leapt out of her written words. She asked him to visit Marysville and he made up his mind immediately. He would take the next ship to Portland. Maybe he could secure passage with Captain Tichenor.

As he sat musing over his changed plans, George entered the house, surmising correctly, "Mary's right, you're going to Marysville."

Scott threw up his hands in mock surrender. No response was necessary, his intentions were known.

After supper the friends sat in the parlor and visited. While Mary tucked Angela in bed for the night, Scott asked George, "When is Captain Tichenor leaving for Portland with his ship?"

"The day after tomorrow. He's unloading furniture for the hotel and equipment for the Army tomorrow. Besides, he's in no hurry now that his family has moved to Port Orford. Is one day enough for you to finish your business?"

Scott thought for a moment, and replied, "Yes, I need to see Sam. He can take care of the partnership. And John should return with fresh fish at midday. I'll talk to Captain Tichenor in the morning. Anything I can bring you from Portland?"

Mary heard Scott's offer as she returned to the parlor, and asked, "Could you bring me some material for a child's dress? Everything that the store displays is for adults — mostly men. Angela needs a pair of shoes, also." She looked plaintively at Scott, and added, "If it's too much trouble, she can get by."

"I'll have Melissa help me find what you need, but I'll need Angela's foot size. Can you write it down for me?"

As they chatted about Port Orford activities through the evening, Scott reflected on how quickly the town was developing into a community since the families had arrived. Mary told him that there was talk of a school next fall. There were eight children of school age in town.

The next morning Scott joined the Knapps for breakfast and informed them of his plans to visit the Willamette and Umpqua valleys. Louie told him that Captain Tichenor would be coming to the hotel with a load of furniture at about 9 o'clock, so Scott had another cup of coffee and conversed with the young man until Tichenor's party arrived. He arranged passage to Portland, agreeing to report aboard the ship at 8 o'clock in the morning. The rest of the day was spent in completing chores and visiting with friends around town. John, Sam, and Scott had drinks and ate supper at the sutler's store on post. They would all go their separate routes the next day.

Chapter Four

As the Portland waterfront came into view upriver, Scott searched for familiar landmarks. New construction was everywhere in the growing city. The bustle of Portland was quite a change from the uneventful trip north. It seemed that the only familiar factors in the city were docking at the same wharf as the previous year, and the ships' chandlery nearby.

Scott strolled up Dock Street past a new warehouse which was on the site of Jack Smith's sawmill, and then walked up Mill Street to the boarding house. A man answered his knock, and Scott introduced himself, inquiring for Mrs. Sloan.

"Pleased to meet you, Mr. McClure. I'm Reuben Avery. My wife and I bought this place from Mrs. Sloan in March. She returned to her family in Boston last month."

Hesitating a moment, Scott replied, "I'm sorry that I missed her. Do you know what happened to the Smith sawmill on Dock Street?"

"Never heard of it, Mr. McClure. Probably before my time. Are you staying in town?"

"No, I'm just passing through Portland on my way to Marysville. Thanks for your time, Mr. Avery."

Scott thought to himself, how much this city reminds me of San Francisco, growing and changing every day. I don't like cities very much. I'd better move on, and find an inn on the road south of Portland.

He set a steady pace through the streets, following a familiar route south toward Oregon City. After leaving the confining atmosphere of the city's streets and buildings, he relaxed a little, enjoying the greenery and the quiet of the valley. He saw a freight wagon ahead of him, and from the deep ruts left in the muddy road, Scott guessed it must be heavily laden. Two large drafthorses were pulling the wagon until it abruptly jolted to a stop in a mudhole. As he approached the scene, he noted that the wagon wheels were mired axle-deep in the gumbo mud. The lone teamster had jumped down and was standing before the horses, coaxing them to pull together. However, the slick footing diminished the team's power and no movement was forthcoming.

Scott walked wide of the wagon and the mudhole, staying on firm soil as he drew abreast of the horses. The teamster cursed in a mixture of German and English at his dilemma, and then plodded through the mud to stand beside Scott. His stout body suggested strength as well as a good appetite. The stranger's round face was red behind a dark beard, and his head was covered by a green alpenhut. Leather pants and boots were both covered with mud.

"Mein Gott! Ich bin ein esel, how did I get into this mess? There are three anvils and eight barrels of nails in the cargo bed. I can't unload it." His accent and his appearance identified him as German, although his fluency and vocabulary were excellent. A smile replaced his frown as he took a deep breath, and spoke to Scott, "My name is Kurt Gerbrunn, and I'm on my way home to Salem. Are you looking for work, perhaps?"

"I'm Scott McClure of Port Orford. I'll be glad to give you a hand." He pondered the situation for a minute, before continuing, "If you have enough rope in the wagon, we could unchain the team from the wagon tongue and run rope lines to their harnesses . . . say over there." He pointed to a graveled section of roadway some thirty feet ahead.

"There's new half-inch rope in the wagon. Your idea sounds good to me." Kurt went aboard his wagon, found two coils of rope, and threw them to Scott. He climbed over the driver's seat onto the tongue and unchained the horses, leading them to solid ground.

Meanwhile, Scott had placed his gear on a dry stump, and laid out the two ropes. "Mister Gerbrunn, if you'll tie the ropes to the horses' harnesses, I'll secure their other ends to these couplings."

"*Danke.* Yell when you're clear of the wagon." Kurt waited for Scott's signal and then urged his team forward, the wagon rising slowly from the sump until it stood on firm ground again. Scott jumped on the wagon seat and set the brake, while his new friend rehooked the team to the wagon.

"*Ach!* Driving a heavy wagon along this road is a two-man job. But my helper ran off to California when I paid him last week. Would you consider working for me—at least until we reach Salem?"

"I'm headed south to Marysville and would appreciate the ride, but pay isn't necessary. Do you live in Salem?"

"Yes, but for less than two years. My family arrived just before the city changed its name to Salem." Gerbrunn paused, reflecting aloud, "My father worked as a coachman for a rich landowner in our village near Wuerzburg. When the Graf died, he willed my father a year's wages. We came to America twenty years ago on that money. I was a lad then, but a good worker while my father was building his freight business in Harrisburg. After he died in 1848, I packed up my wife and two sons and our equipment, and we crossed the entire width of the United States to Oregon. I even brought eight milk cows. It took us two years to reach the Willamette valley, and I settled in Salem because of the university. Johann and Uwe will study there when they grow up. Maybe they'll be doctors or lawyers. Not an old teamster like their father."

As Kurt finished his family history, Scott asked several questions about the Oregon Trail. Over a campfire outside of Oregon city, Scott talked about his family and his trip to Oregon. Descriptions of Port Orford and the Tututni Indians were interesting enough to the teamster; but when Scott mentioned his gold claim, Kurt's refreshed curiosity prolonged the dialogue well into the night.

Driving into Oregon City early in the morning, the freighter stopped at a general store. Kurt insisted that Scott was on his pay-roll after they completed the arduous task of unloading several crates. Two days later they drove into the Gerbrunn freight yards in Salem. Scott worked for his friend, making deliveries to Salem and to farms nearby. He slept on the office cot and ate supper with the Gerbrunn family. One Sunday Kurt loaned Scott a dun gelding to ride to Marysville. His plans to visit the Nelsons were dashed when he found that Melissa had accompanied her father to Portland. The Nelsons' neighbor told Scott that they had been gone two weeks and should return soon.

****

During the next week, Scott was preoccupied on the job, fretting until Kurt told him to take a day off and visit his friends. Astride the same horse, which he now called Salem, he rode to Marysville on Friday morning. He found Richard Nelson sunning on his front porch, and as he approached his friend, he noted his gaunt appearance and listless manner. He had aged considerably during his illness. Scott dismounted and tied his horse's reins to a picket fence, calling out, "Hello, Richard, you look comfortable in the sun."

"Like hell I am! Don't ever get sick, Scott, the doctors will kill you. Sit down and visit for a spell; Melissa's gone shopping. We heard that you came visiting on Sunday. I've been to another doctor in Portland, without any relief for my lungs."

Scott sympathized, "It's terrible to feel your strength waning, let alone your well-being. How long have you been ill?"

"Too damn long, my friend. I haven't worked since last September, and not likely to now that my boss has sold his sawmill. The new owner won't even talk to me—he's got his own crew.

Thank goodness Melissa is well and enjoys her teaching job. Her salary has kept our larder filled."

"Have you considered working in a mill office? Captain Tichenor was impressed with your experience and know-how when he talked to you and Melissa last year. In fact there might be a job in Port Orford which would suit you. Good men are in demand."

Richard sounded despondent as he replied, "I'm under doctor's care. Besides Melissa is well-thought of in her school and has promised to return in the fall." He smiled slowly and said, "Let's drop this depressing subject. Tell me about your gold mine. Are you rich yet?"

Scott laughed and described his winter activities until he saw Melissa come walking down the lane. He met her at the gate and took her packages, greeting her with a, "Hello, Melissa." She leaned forward and kissed him on his cheek, speaking softly, "We've missed you, Scott. I'm happy to see you. Please come in the house."

Putting the packages on the kitchen table, he took her hand and inquired, "How are you holding up with your father's illness? Is there anything I can do?"

"Father needs encouragement . . . he's so depressed. Visiting with him would help, but could you take him for a walk? A beer wouldn't hurt him, and he might see some of his cronies at the tavern."

"Agreed, but why don't I take you both to supper at the hotel restaurant. You can help me to shop for Mary Hermann along the way. May I put my horse in the back yard?"

The walk was invigorating even with the late afternoon sun, and the trio chatted incessantly during their evening out. Scott stayed overnight, going fishing with Richard at first dawn. When it clouded over they returned to the house before a rainshower fell, and Scott talked about Port Orford and his friends. He excused himself after lunch. He had promised to return Salem so that the Gerbrunns could attend a Sunday church social.

"I have a drayage job next week. When I finish that work with Kurt Gerbrunn, I'm heading south to see Buzz. Can I visit again on next Saturday?" The Nelsons agreed and stood on the porch as Scott rode away. He waved as the lane veered away, and then set Salem at a gallop. He had a lot of miles to cover before darkness fell.

****

During the busy week that followed, Kurt and Scott dickered over livestock. Kurt had complained about the expense of keeping horses and cows in the freight yard in town. When Scott expressed interest in buying his 'surplus', the stock increased dramatically in value. The two friends had maintained jocular repartees on the sale of the animals. Inge Gerbrunn had cooked a schnitzel supper just for Scott, and Kurt had broken out a bottle of schnapps after the apfelstrudel dessert.

"Now that I have softened you up with a fine meal, maybe we can deal on wages and horses. I will sell you Salem for the wages which you have earned." As Scott hesitated, Kurt added, "Salem and Prince . . . he's a good pack animal . . . that's fair."

Laughing, Scott kidded, "More than fair. What's the catch? . . . No, don't answer, just name a price for that milk cow that I want."

"Another fair price? . . . I'll take fifty dollars for all three cows which you want. You can't take a single cow; they need company to be happy in Sixes. We can rope the animals in a line so that you can ride Salem and lead the others. It's a long way to Port Orford."

Scott left Saturday morning later than he had anticipated, and arrived in Marysville late in the day. Melissa was curious about his 'herd' of animals, and amused by Scott's handling techniques. She joked that it was a long way to Port Orford. He was going to hear that phrase many times during the next few weeks.

From Prince's packsaddle came a large cured ham to be used for the Sunday meal, and Scott insisted that Melissa shop with him for yams and fresh rolls. Richard went along to buy a few bottles of ale for the festive occasion. At dinner on Sunday, Scott noticed that Melissa was wearing the silver chain with two gold nuggets. They smiled in remembrance of her promise to wear his gift when they next met. Scott left Marysville feeling happy and ready to take on the next challenge—trailing his stock to Scottsburg.

****

After a few hours of travel, the animals learned Scott's routine and steady progress was made. Scott was thankful that he was vigilant, after he passed three seedy strangers who took an inordinate interest in his horses. He kept his eye and his gun trained on all three men until they were out of sight. Following such occasions, he used caution in varying his route and his speed of travel. His goal was to travel alone and fast until he reached Scottsburg. Six days later he was on a high road between Elkton and Scottsburg, when he passed five unsavory characters riding horses eastward. He completed his evasion technique before he checked his backtrail. The five men were trotting along his tracks about a mile back. He put the cows at their fastest gait down the trail, slowing down at dark, but not stopping.

He reached Buzz's cabin about four o'clock in the morning, and called out, "Hello the cabin! Are you asleep Old-Timer?"

"Well pardner, how could I answer you if I was asleep. I heard you coming down the trail ten minutes ago. What are you dragging behind you?" Buzz chuckled, and added, "You're a sight for these old eyes, Scott McClure."

"I have some stock which a band of cutthroats covet. Help me unsaddle and store my gear. I'm going right back up the trail toward Elkton, and challenge those yahoos."

As they worked quickly and quietly, Buzz queried softly, "How many men are in that bunch?"

"I passed five men on horses . . . didn't recognize any of them . . . half expected them to jump me as we passed . . . narrow enough road." Scott laughed, "Maybe I looked as tough to them as they did to me. I've been moving fast and could stand a bath, shave, and haircut."

Buzz had his rifle in hand as he closed his cabin door, and asked, "Well, how will you handle this affair? I'll back your play."

"I heard them behind me on the road about two hours ago. Maybe they've stopped until daylight, but I doubt it. I've got this feeling that they're close behind—maybe a mile or two. There is no way they are going to stay behind me. They can head east or face my rifle. I'm going right up the middle of the road, and I want you to follow me on the left. When we hear them, you move farther left, off the road, and drift above them. You stay quiet until you're needed. Let them think I'm alone. If there's trouble, I'll hold the road from the north side somewhere below your position."

"Scott, I don't plan to waste lead. With five to two odds, every shot counts in a shooting affair. It would help if you could stall until daylight."

Scott estimated they had come over two miles before he heard sounds of horses on the road ahead. In the shadows of a false dawn, he saw a small rise ahead which had a deadfall of timber to its left side. Pointing at it, he whispered to his partner, "That's my spot." Buzz nodded and melded into the forest. Scott thought, The Old-Timer hasn't lost his touch. If I can't see or hear him, this gang certainly won't. He stopped in the middle of the road and laid the barrel of his cocked rifle in the crook of his left arm, intent on being immobile and almost invisible in the semidarkness. He wanted to surprise the badmen and to stall for good light. Scott wasn't very confident that this bunch would leave him be.

Scott's worry was soon confirmed as voices wafted down the road, carrying pieces of conversation on the moist morning air.

He heard a plethora of disjointed sentences, "That dun gelding is mine." "I'll kill that son of a bitch. . . ." ". . . have a high old time in . . ." "His packsaddle was full of supplies." and finally as they were in full sight of Scott, "We should have killed the bastard up on the pass. Hell, we had him five to one. Let's get him. . . ." The speaker trailed off as he saw his intended victim standing in the road ahead of him.

Scott thought, Well there's no doubt about their intentions. I'm sure Buzz heard them too. Aloud, he projected his voice firmly, challenging the gang, "That's far enough. You men turn around and head out for Elkton."

As the first horse moved toward Scott, he raised his rifle barrel in line with the rider. The horse backed into the others, and all of them milled around as the men muttered to each other in low tones which Scott couldn't understand. Unbeknownst to Scott one man in the rear dismounted, rifle in hand, and prepared to shoot Scott when the other riders cleared a line of fire. As he aimed his rifle in Scott's direction, a shot rang out from the hillside and the man collapsed in a heap. Riders were pulling rifles from their saddle straps as Scott shot the first rider out of the saddle. Scott moved behind the deadfall, and as he reloaded, shouted at the riders, "Drop your rifles and raise your hands before more of you die!" He repeated his order angrily, and three rifles hit the ground, a cocked weapon firing into the air.

"You on the paint horse, dismount and face away from me," Scott directed. After the rider complied, he added, "Pick up each rifle and discharge it at the sky. I expect to hear four shots." The rider gingerly picked up the rifles and fired them. When finished, he held up his hands.

Scott walked up to the horses, looking each man over carefully, and stated his feelings, "You're a rotten bunch and don't deserve to live. If I ever see you in this territory again, I'll kill you. Head east and keep going. Now put your partners on their horses, take your empty rifles and ride out of here."

One wounded man was able to mount with help, but the fifth man had to be stretched over the saddle and held there as the men galloped up the road. Buzz showed himself as the men rode by, and kept his rifle trained on them until they were out of sight. He waved to Scott to follow, as he strode up the road several hundred feet and stopped to sit on a stump.

"Well, I can't hear their horses so I reckon they've gone, but let's sit here for an hour to make sure they don't backtrack. We can hear and see them if they get courage. Your shot hit a shoulder, and the man'll probably live. Was my target alive or not?"

Scott shook his head, "He was breathing but I doubt that he'll make it to Elkton. Thanks, you saved my life with that shot."

"Well, the way they talked coming down the road, they didn't respect life too much. You know, if you were a greenhorn you'd be dead. They were an ornery bunch, but I'm glad you let them keep their rifles. After we let them go, we don't need Indians killing them for us. White men have to stick together with Indians making such a fuss this summer."

By mid-morning it became obvious that the gang was not returning, and the two friends walked leisurely back to Scottsburg. Asked about his last two winters trapping, Buzz complained, "The country's changing, with settlers underfoot everywhere we went. There was almost no market for the few furs that we did trap, so we broke up this spring—Curly went to Vancouver. Why, I made more cash money with my apiary . . . heh, heh . . . remember that fancy word? I'm at loose ends now."

"Would you consider coming to the Sixes River with me?" Scott described his dream for the Myrtlewood Grove Ranch, and then explained his partnership with Sam Olson. He concluded, "Sam is a good friend and we work well together on prospecting ventures, but he's not interested in the Sixes River as a ranch." Scott offered his opinion, "I think you'd like the valley and its solitude. The Indians are friendly and not many white men have seen the upper valley. Hunting and fishing are excellent. In fact, we can sell game in town—it's a cash crop."

"Well, I'll think some on your offer. Scottsburg is filling up with settlers. Can't get any peace and quiet here at all. Which reminds me that we'd best report our little argument to Mr. Scott. He's still sort of the law hereabouts."

The town founder had accepted their story as factual, remarking that several petty thefts had been reported while the gang was in the settlement. "People were glad to see them go. No one will fault you for defending yourself."

Scott nodded and asked, "Can I leave my stock at your farm for a few days? I've been traveling at too fast a pace for them—particularly the horses need to be grain fed."

"Yes, I can handle your animals. Would you consider it a fair trade if I keep the milk? My milk cows are sort of dry right now." The men consummated the deal amicably and spent the afternoon driving the stock to the farm and visiting in the old post tavern.

Rocking before a warming fire, Buzz was pleasantly surprised when Scott gave him presents from two Christmases—a tinderbox and a gold nugget.

The Old-Timer hesitated as he accepted the gifts, struggling to express himself clearly, "Thank you, Scott. You're like family to me—a son I never had. I'd like to partner with you on the Sixes River, but I don't hold with this gold business between you and Sam Olson. Nothing against your partnership, but I don't want any part of gold digging. That all right with you?"

"Yes, it certainly is! I promised to meet Sam in September and set up a prospecting venture. You and I need to get to Sixes and build a log cabin before I leave. I have a friend in Port Orford who may have time to help us. Shall we canoe to Gardiner tomorrow? I'm eager to see Harvey and Alma Masters."

Buzz quipped laughingly, "Only if you'll paddle . . . and stay out of the water."

Gardiner had grown considerably in two years, a major sawmill operation to the north of its bustling waterfront. Two ships were docked at separate wharfs, unloading supplies. Buzz steered his canoe to a familiar landing south of the steamships and secured it on the beach.

Walking up the busy street to Masters' store-hotel, Scott saw prosperity reflected in businesses along the way and in hammering sounds of new construction. There were a dozen people shopping in Masters' when the two men entered the door. Harvey finished serving a customer, smiling broadly as he recognized his visitors. He greeted them effusively, and leaving his clerk in charge, led them to the kitchen to meet Alma. After another warm welcome, Scott asked Harvey, "Shouldn't you be tending to your customers? You seem quite busy."

"Yes, although my clerk is a good man. Summer business requires a second clerk once in awhile." Reaching into the cupboard, Harvey offered, "Here's a key to the only room I have left. I'll put a second cot in it later. How long can you stay?"

"Only over night, folks. We are celebrating Buzz's birthday with you a couple of days early."

Alma interjected, "In that case we'll have time to visit after supper. Be here at six o'clock. Can I fix anything special for your birthday, Erastus?"

As Buzz shrugged his shoulders, Scott spoke up, "Chicken and dumplings would suit us fine, Alma—just like my last supper with you. Don't worry, we'll be on time."

When coffee was served after the meal, Scott told the Masters that Buzz was selling his Scottsburg cabin and joining him on the Sixes River. He elaborated on his ranch. "Actually a lot of work in needed to make it a real ranch. It won't be a paying proposition for a few years, and I'll have to work other jobs for cash money."

Harvey and Alma were happy to see their aging friend partner with Scott, knowing the affection which existed between them. Harvey kidded, "Erastus, where will I buy my honey when you're gone?"

His little joke led to a serious discussion on selling the cabin and the beehives. Harvey suggested that Erastus talk to one of his customers who might be interested in buying him out.

The three men went together in the morning, looking for a French-Canadian old-timer, known only as Anton. They found their prospect standing beside an open fire on the beach, trading stories with friends.

A deal was struck within the hour, in which Buzz received $20 cash from Anton and $20 cash advance on the honey from Harvey, a plowshare, two axes and a rifle.

After collecting the items of payment and the cash, the partners bid farewell to the Masters and set off to Scottsburg. The new owner wanted possession in three days and there was a lot of work to be accomplished before they could leave for the Sixes River and Port Orford.

The French-Canadian Anton arrived two days later and helped the partners pack up and move their belongings to Mr. Scott's landing. The Old-Timer's friends pitched in and transported everything across the river in their bateau. Stock had to be ferried to the south shore one animal at a time, so that it was dusk before the transfer was completed. Scott stayed with the stock in their overnight camp, while Buzz was the guest of honor at a going-away party in the old post tavern. Anton brought Buzz across the river late that night, and Scott was surprised to see four beehives in his old canoe.

As he handed them to Scott, Anton said, "I have no use for empty beehives. My friend here wants them, don't you, Buzz?"

The Old-Timer mumbled agreement and staggered past the fire to his blankets. It had been a good party and he had been toasted roundly by his friends. Scott thought, we may not leave early in the morning after all. Buzz is going to need food in his stomach before he can travel. I'm glad that he enjoyed his party.

****

The small caravan followed the river until the valley widened, and then set a course cross country to intercept a south-bound coastal trail. Prince was laden with the myrtlewood rocker, the beehives, and food supplies on his packsaddle, while Salem carried their personal gear astride Scott's riding saddle. The Old-Timer scouted ahead for the easier route, while Scott led the stock in his wake. After a week of steady travel, the caravan was within sight of the smaller Quah-to-mah village on the Sixes River. Buzz reported that it was deserted, so the partners swung upriver to the myrtlewood grove. They stowed their gear in the crude lean-to and Scott covered it with canvas. They tied the cows to firs in the pasture, allowing slack enough in their ropes to graze.

"I hope there aren't any predators out this afternoon—animal or human. We have to visit the Shix village today, so they'll know you're with me. We can make good time riding Prince and Salem. Are you carrying your sack of sugar candy with you?"

"Yes, I hope these Indians like it as well as the Umpquas do."

"I expect they will. Think of our visit as being neighborly, just paying respects to friends along the river."

As they neared the Indian village, Scott cautioned, "We'd better take care as we enter this river flat, the Quah-to-mahs might mistake our horses for game. Besides we don't want to surprise our friends up ahead."

They emerged into the village a few minutes later with noticeable excitement from the women and children. Casting his glance over the surrounding areas, Scott remarked, "The young men appear to be absent. Chief Sixes is down on that bank, fishing with a few older men." He pointed to his Indian friend, and expressed his growing concern, "Keep loose, Buzz, there's something wrong here."

Chief Sixes strode forward to the center of the village and greeted the white men. At his direction, they dismounted and Scott introduced his partner, and Buzz presented him with the bag of sugar candy. A wide smile creased the Indian's craggy face as he held up his gift, pleased at the simple respect paid him. In turn he invited the two white men to fish with him along the river. Their Indian friend evaded, often ignored, questions related to the tribe's young men, and they were not invited to stay for a meal. Chief Sixes gave them each a salmon and ushered them out of the village.

Scott speculated, "We made the Indians very nervous. They weren't unfriendly, but we weren't exactly welcome either. Chief Sa-qua-mi and his young men are probably up to no good. We need to check with my friends in Port Orford about Indian trouble along the coast."

Back at their campsite, Buzz fixed up the lean-to for sleeping, while Scott cooked a salmon for supper. Planning aloud, Scott said, "We'll make a brush and rope corral tomorrow for the cows. You can bag that small buck which was in the grove at dusk, and I'll repack our gear for a trip to Port Orford in the afternoon. Have you seen any critters that would bother the cows?"

Buzz shook his head, asking, "Are we staying overnight in town?"

"Yes, in a hotel. Mrs. Knapp makes a mighty fine breakfast. We'll give our other salmon to Mary Hermann and invite ourselves to supper, then see George to trade venison for supplies. You'll like my friends. They're solid citizens. After we leave town, we should visit the Port Orfords Indian village so that you can meet Chat-ah-hak-e-ah and his son Charlie, my other Indian friends."

Completing their camp chores at noon, the partners saddled their horses and made a hurried trip to Port Orford. When no one was home at the Hermann house, they rode over to the store. George called to Scott from the storeroom door, "When did you get back? Bring that carcass back here. We can use it today." He shook hands with Scott and with his distinctive limp, walked over to the Old-Timer, greeting him, "You must be Buzz Smith, Scott's good friend and partner. Welcome to Port Orford."

"Thanks, George. I've heard a lot about you and your family. Your store seems busy today."

"Buzz, it's not my store, but I do manage it for a businessman in town. And yes, we are very busy this summer. There's lots of newcomers in town."

Scott returned from hanging the carcass in the storeroom, and handed George the salmon. "We stopped by the house with this fish, but Mary wasn't home."

"She was in the store with Angela a few minutes ago. I'll take care of it. Of course you're both invited for supper tonight, and bring John along—his boat's in the harbor."

"Thanks George. We were counting on Mary's cooking. We'll need these supplies in the morning," Scott said as he handed George his list.

After checking in with the Knapps, they put their gear in their room and stabled the horses. The partners enjoyed a pleasant afternoon seeing the town and visiting with people, ending up on the town dock where John Larsen was mending nets. They went aboard his boat to have a drink, and when Buzz praised the handcrafted fishing boat, John poured another round. Fortified with good rye, Buzz launched into his giant sturgeon story and entertained his friends for the next hour.

After a short stop at the hotel, the trio walked to Hermanns. George answered their knock and ushered them into the parlor where Angela and Jacques Dubois greeted them. Scott shook hands with the logger and got a warm hug from a shy but friendly Angela. While George introduced Buzz to them, Scott went into the kitchen to see the women.

Mary hugged him and said, "Welcome back! Did you have a good trip, Scott?"

Before he could answer her, Sally touched his arm shyly and added, "We're all glad to see you again, Scott."

He responded, "Thank you, ladies. My vacation was fine, but it's good to be home. Having my friend Buzz with me is a bonus."

Mary stared at the package under his arm and asked hopefully, "Did you find time to shop for me in Portland?"

"No," he responded jokingly, "but Melissa and I managed to shop in Marysville. Is six yards of material enough for Angela's dress?"

"Are you teasing me again, Scott? What did you really buy?"

Scott unwrapped the package on the table and showed Mary two pieces of material, saying, "I couldn't decide so I bought both. Actually there's more than six yards here, and of course this pair of shoes."

Fingering the material and then spreading it over the table, she commented, "Both pieces are beautiful. Thank you, I'll make mother and daughter dresses." Glancing sideways at Scott, she added, "In fact, there may be barely enough material for me in my condition. George and I are expecting a child in November."

Scott clapped his hands in joy for the Hermanns and offered, "Congratulations. I hope your health remains good, and the delivery is easy. Do you want a boy or girl?"

"I don't have a preference except that George so wants a son to bear his name. But we will love the child whether it's a boy or girl."

"Well, Mary, the pink material is a gift from Melissa and me. Four dollars is the cost of the print material and the shoes. Now ladies, come out and meet Buzz."

While the women conversed with Buzz, Scott gave his best wishes to George, "It's grand news that Mary shared with me this evening. You'll need to add a room on your house."

"You're right. Angela and George Junior will need to have their own rooms. I'd better talk to John about converting our attic to bedrooms."

Scott guffawed, teasing George, "George Junior, heh? Now you're a prophet as well as a father-to-be."

George grinned good-naturedly, and changed the subject. "Sam was in town last week for supplies. You're to meet him here during the first week in September. He wants to prospect along the Rogue River." He paused and advised, "That area is not safe. The Rogues have been making trouble, living up to their sobriquet—the Rascals." The conversation progressed into the Indian problem and the involvement of local bands. Sally mentioned that she had received hard stares from townspeople after the last Indian raid down on the Rogue River. Jacques' volatile temper was evidenced as he gave his opinion of such people—in French epithets. Mary gently changed the subject to Port Orford social life, and George gave a discourse on the business life of the community. He spent considerable time expounding on the popularity of Port Orchard cedar in the San Francisco market. Tichenor's mill was a booming business, to which Jacques concurred, "Oui, much cedar is for California. Come, Sally." He made it clear that he was needed in the mill to cut all that lumber for San Francisco, and he was off to bed. Scott told of his trip to Portland and his visit with the Nelsons, before the party ended.

Buzz's comment summarized the evening perfectly, "I haven't enjoyed a visit with so many people in a month of Sundays." He complimented Scott, "You choose good friends . . . ha, ha, . . . present company included!"

The partners picked up their supplies from the store and rode out to the South Branch village. Chief Chat-al-hak-e-ah greeted them in friendship. Charlie and the young men were not in the village, and they were not invited to stay as Scott had anticipated. Riding away from the village, Scott quipped, "I guess we'll have to cook our own dinner." And then added soberly, "Maybe we ought to stick close to home this summer."

****

During the ensuing month, the men worked ten hours a day constructing a log cabin. Scott had planned a simple square twenty feet on each side, with a twelve inch log set in a wide trench serving as its base. Smaller fir logs were soon joined together to a height of seven feet, sufficient headroom to satisfy Scott.

He rode into Fort Orford, taking both horses and their packsaddles to carry lumber for the roof framing and the floor. While in town he visited the local woodworker and ordered a door, two glass windows, and a table for pickup the next week. George would find him a cast iron stove and chimney piping and John offered to install the doors and windows. Thank goodness that I bought these animals, he thought as he walked back to the Sixes with his fully-laden horses. He would need to make several trips over the next couple of weeks.

Covering the roof with handcut cedar shakes completed the exterior work on the cabin, and gave the partners time to cut field hay while the weather held. They amassed three haystacks for winter feed, before Scott returned to town to pick up another load of building materials.

Visiting with George, he was given a letter from Sam, who was delayed and would come to the Sixes in mid-September. Scott was pleased with the news, wanting to finish the cabin and clear more land before leaving his ranch.

The partners were busy enough that Buzz decided not to domesticate any bee colonies until next spring. He'd be on his own shortly, working the ranch all winter.

One rainy morning a few days later, a throaty voice helloed the house from the knoll nearby. Scott laid down his tools on the almost-finished floor, saying to Buzz, "That sounds like Sam. I'll go out and meet him." As he stepped out the door and strode across the flat, Sam burst from the forest and called, "Scott, old buddy, are you ever a sight for sore eyes." He gave his friend a bear hug and talked on, "Your cabin looks sound enough. Let's get inside and out of this weather before my cold gets worse. You have any coffee . . . or whiskey for that matter. . . ," Scott chuckled as his friend prattled on irrepressibly. It was good to see that Sam hadn't changed over the summer.

****

The trail around Humbug Mountain was rigorous in comparison to the partners' first day of travel. Charlie had guided them from Port Orford to the mountain near Brush Creek, but had returned to his village yesterday. He had talked against their trip south, citing "bad feelings" between the Indians and white men. Sam insisted that they would be careful and avoid trouble, and Scott acquiesced to Sam's fervor and determination to prospect along the Rogue River. Traveling was easier that afternoon, and before evening they sighted several Indians watching from a hill ahead of them. Smoke was rising from farther down the trail, and Scott surmised, "There's a village on the creek ahead. Should we continue on this route?"

Sam's look brightened as he responded, "Yes! That's Sammy with those Indians."

"You're right, Sam. Besides, it's too late to turn back. Go ahead and greet Sammy—we're close enough."

Sam raised his right hand and called out, "Hello, Sammy. How are you?"

The Indian replied in Tututni somewhat reluctantly, waving them into the village which they were approaching. One of his companions spoke in broken English, "Why you here? . . . this Tututni land." Sammy barked an order which silenced the man, and the group entered the village without fanfare. Scott thought the people looked unfriendly, not a soul greeting them. Sammy led them to the chief's lodge, and all the men waited respectfully. After a few minutes, the chief stepped out of his lodge and addressed Sammy in harsh tones. Their friend heeded his words, and responded at length in a rational voice. The chief shook his head, obviously troubled by Sammy's adamant position, and beckoned to the English-speaking Indian to come forward and translate his greeting to the partners. He invited them to spend the night.

Scott responded to his host, "Thank you, chief, may you live a long and healthy life. Here is a small gift for you." He offered a steel knife holding it by the blade, and thought for a moment that the chief might refuse it, but the man couldn't resist a valuable tool. Both he and Sammy accepted identical honors and even smiled at their guests. An exchange of words between the English-speaking Indian and Sammy resulted in a command from the chief which sent the man storming out of the village. Scott thought to himself, "That fellow will need to be watched, he's definitely unfriendly." Sammy took them to his lodge for a meal, and a sleeping place by his fire.

The next morning Sammy indicated that they should return to Port Orford. He gestured that south was trouble. When they remained adamant that they were going to the Rogue valley, he asked them to wait in the village until he returned, then he spoke to the chief and walked north to the hill above the village. Sam fretted about wasting time, and when the chief signaled they were to leave, he thanked him and led Scott out of the village.

Scott was nervous and said so. "I didn't like leaving the village before Sammy returned." After walking less than a mile, he spoke again, "We're being followed, Sam. Move out a few more paces and look for a spot which is defensible." His partner crested a small rise, and was struck in the leg by an arrow, falling behind an old log. Sam raised his rifle and fired at a target which Scott couldn't see. Dropping to one knee, Scott saw the English-speaking Indian appear on the rise to attack Sam, and shot him through the chest. He reloaded as Sam fired a second time, and then two more Indians crept into view above Sam. Scott shouted and shot the lead attacker. The second man leapt astride his partner, brandishing a knife and striking Sam a wicked blow. Scott feverishly reloaded as the struggle continued, and snapped a shot at the Indian. Wounded, the attacker dropped his knife and rolled into the brush before Scott could fire again.

Sam's voice was weak as he called, "Stay there and cover the flank. There's at least three more of those bastards in the trees. I'm reloading now." He was quiet for a brief moment and then he called again, "There's more of them behind you, Scott."

Scott abandoned his position, and on a dead run, threw himself to the ground near his partner. He couldn't see any movement within his field of vision, so he turned to a coughing Sam, "Are you able to move, Sam?" Blood bubbling from a knife wound in his chest was an obvious answer as Sam gasped out, "No . . . Scott old buddy . . . you run for it . . . I'll hold them. . . ." He punctuated his offer by firing at a shadow in the trees.

"No, Sam. I reckon we'll just stick together. You cover the south trail." Scott crawled behind a stump, pointing his rifle to the north.

An Indian voice called out their names, the sound emanating from the trail in the direction of the village, "Sam, Scott . . . Sammy here." As it was repeated, their friend showed himself and moved forward with three men from his band. He reached the rise and called out guttural and angry words, chastising the attackers. No answer came from the forest. As the men listened alertly, the only sounds came from the wind in the trees and the rattled breathing of Sam Olson. Scott moved closer to his friend to help him, and Sam reached out to grip his hand in friendship. Slowly his strength waned, his grip relaxed, and his breathing ceased. Tears welled in Scott's eyes as he felt the life drain from his friend and partner. His happy-go-lucky spirit would never grace another Oregon campfire.

Scott shook his head to clear it of grief and nostalgia, saying aloud, "God rest your soul, Samuel Anson Olson." To himself he thought, I wonder if an attack is likely with Sammy beside me . . . I guess not. First, I must bury Sam . . . on that crest which overlooks this site, and then I'd better follow Sammy's advice and return to Port Orford. As he actuated his first thought and buried Sam deep in the Oregon soil, two of Sammy's friends picked up the two dead Indians and toted them back toward the village. The other Indian scouted the area, reporting signs of two wounded Indians.

Picking up his partner's rifle and personal belongings, Scott gave the mining gear and supplies to Sammy, who in turn gave it to his friend to take to the village. Sammy gestured for Scott to follow him, and they headed west and finally north, moving to circumvent the village. Scott understood that he couldn't escape retribution if the other Indians caught up with him. He would have to travel beyond Humbug Mountain, the limit of the Cosuttheutens' territory, before he would feel somewhat safe. They had traveled two or three miles, and as the trail passed through a narrow chasm, Sammy halted. He signed that Scott was to continue north on his own, and he would guard the trail overnight.

"I think he expects company pretty soon. He may not be able to delay them until morning. I'd better move fast and far." He thanked Sammy, able to express sadness for the fight between their peoples as well as the resulting deaths.

Emerging from the canyon, he trotted for an hour before darkness fell. He had memorized the route ahead, using Humbug as his reference point. He was able to stumble along his route for a few minutes longer, before he could go no farther. There was a distinct possibility that he would lose direction and wander off the trail. He had to remain ahead of the anticipated pursuit.

Scott ate cold meat and curled up against the roots of a fallen tree, sleeping free of the night breeze for a few hours. When he awoke the clouds had broken and moonshine lighted the landscape. Scott was able to follow the trail at a slow walk, eating pieces of sugar candy and stopping at a small creek to slake his thirst. He would eat his last piece of meat when he had crossed Humbug Mountain.

As daylight brightened the sky, Scott studied the trail ahead. About 500 yards ahead, a ridge intersected his trail, and beyond it nothing was visible. Clear land stretched before him up to the ridge, anyone moving in that area could be seen easily. Without hesitation, Scott ran forward at an energy-consuming lope. He was determined to cross that ridge as soon as possible. He could rest on the other side and watch his backtrail without being seen. It was necessary to alternate his loping gait with a trot as he climbed the ridge. When he crested the ridge, his lungs were gasping for air, and he gratefully slipped into the brush beside the trail, and dropped flat on his stomach. There was no discernible movement on his backtrail as far as he could see.

Breathing more normally after a few moments, he sipped water from his canteen and checked both of the Sharps rifles. He knew Sam's gun was a burden, but he might need its firepower before he reached Port Orford. Studying every foot of the trail south of him, he was not surprised to discover Indians moving in the distance. Scott reasoned with himself, "The Indians are reading my sign along the trail. They must have found where I slept last night, and they'll soon come to where I started to run. They'll speed up their pursuit at that point."

Scott began to ease backward, when he caught a flicker of light to his right. Another group of Indians were circling the flat before him obviously intent on trapping their unseen prey in the open area. He dropped below the skyline and came erect running north with as little noise as possible. Recalling the terrain ahead of him, he realized that neither he nor his pursuers were likely to see each other for the next mile. He mumbled aloud, "They can't overtake me at this pace . . . will have to rest . . . maybe walk every mile or so . . . could throw a rifle away . . . no . . . may have to fight. I'm on Humbug now—will they follow me beyond the mountain?" He popped his last piece of candy into his mouth, and climbed a rigorous slope in the forest, approaching a small clearing on the mountainside. A crashing sound startled him, and his rifle moved automatically into a firing position as he saw a deer bound through the trees and down the hill. Slowing to a walk in his fatigue, he couldn't seem to find the will to run again. But the clamor of voices and thrashing brush came from the direction which the deer had taken. Scott reflected, The Indians ran into that frightened buck, and they'll know that I startled the animal. They are moving after me already. His thoughts induced a newfound burst of energy, and he struck out in panicked flight. He quickly controlled his panic, but did not slow his gait for several

minutes, eventually slipping into his now-familiar jog. He reached
a good observation point and stopped to eat his meat and sip his
remaining water. A shuddering movement in the forest at the foot
of the slope revealed the presence of his pursuers. Scott took deliberate aim at a tree beyond the Indians, and fired a round into
its bole. He saw more movement, and taking Sam's rifle, he fired
a round into a large boulder near the Indians. As the ricochet re-
sounded through the still air, he reloaded both rifles and trotted
quietly north along the trail, hoping to regain his secure lead. The
light meal and the exhilaration of confrontation gave him new
strength as he forced himself to run and run. He could hear his
pursuers even though he couldn't see them. Scott was forced by
perilous footing on the downslope to slow to a walk; he couldn't
afford an accident. As the route eased into a gentle slope, he crossed
Brush Creek and accelerated into a full-out race for the beach somewhere below him. When he was sure that his physical reserves
were playing out, he slowed to a ground-covering jog. The sound
of surf and the presence of windblown scrub firs told Scott that
he had reached the Pacific shore. He stopped atop a twenty foot
sand bluff and turned around, raising Sam's rifle with tired and
trembling fingers.

His adversaries were running toward him less than 200 yards
behind. He fired over their heads and as they dropped to the
ground, he slid down the bluff on his butt. Struggling through the
dry, loose sand to the hard-packed sand at the surf, he began a
stumbling shuffle northwesterly along the beach. Glancing regularly over his shoulder, he espied the Indians standing atop the
bluff. They shook their fists and undoubtedly cursed him from
that vantage point now a half-mile away. Scott continued running
as best he could, relieved to see his pursuers turning back. He
slowed to a walk, reloading Sam's rifle and watching the forest to
his southeast. Alternating running and walking during the next
hour, he soon could discern the gold miners working at Hubbard
Creek. The workers were too busy to notice him as he ran along

the beach, so he fired Sam's rifle into the air to alert them to his presence.

The men clustered about Scott as he told his story, while chewing on biscuits given to him by his prospector friends. When Scott insisted that he was reporting the incident in person, two miners accompanied him to Fort Orford.

Lt. Wyman invited Scott to noon mess and listened to his story as they dined. The officer expressed his sympathy for Sam's death, but did not appear surprised at the Indians' hostility. He conjectured, "You were attacked by the Cosutt-heutens of Brush Creek. I believe that I've met Sah-mah-ha-e, Sammy as you call him. His act was heroic, even for a friend, but you'll probably be looking at him over your rifle sights the next time you meet. Thank you for your promptness in reporting the attack. The U.S. Army can advise travelers going south of this incident." The two men went to Wyman's office to complete the official report.

By the time that Scott's two prospecting friends said farewell to him in front of Knapps' Hotel, it was late afternoon and the town was buzzing with Sam's death and Scott's survival. Grandma Knapp fed Scott a bowl of hot soup and some warmed-up biscuits while he related his story one more time. Louie proffered a glass of brandy to him after the soup, and Scott sipped it as he told of his ordeal on Humbug Mountain. His host helped him to bed, where he collapsed in the deep slumber needed for eventual resuscitation.

Scott awakened slowly, reliving that repetitive nightmare of Sam's death which had dogged his subconscious all night. As he sat up in bed, he found his pillow wet from tears and sweat. His grief and fear had been expurgated during his sleep, and he felt strangely relieved of the emotional burden. The sound of voices in the hallway reached him as he dressed and stretched his cramped muscles.

He opened the door of his room to see George Hermann arguing with the innkeeper. Louie explained quickly, "Everyone has been by the hotel to see you last night or this morning. George wouldn't leave this time without looking in on you. I told him that you were all in one piece—no wounds."

George threw up his hands, justifying his stubbornness, "Mary insisted that I stay until I see you in person. We've heard the stories which have you walking a hundred miles through Indian territory, killing savages with your bare hands, and reaching the fort with three mortal wounds." Seeing the grimace of disbelief pass across Scott's face, George couldn't resist a small jest. "Scott, you're the survivor of an Indian battle and that alone makes you a hero to us townsfolk." More soberly, George expressed his sympathy, "We were shocked to hear of Sam's death. All of his friends will miss his warm friendship and good-natured esprit. Can Mary and I do anything?"

Scott shook his head no, although with a little encouragement he accepted an invitation to breakfast. He would share Sam's final moments on earth with his friends, as well as distribute his personal belongings to them as mementos of a good man and stalwart friend. Afterwards he would take the news to Buzz in the Sixes valley, giving him Sam's Sharps rifle as a remembrance of their mutual friend. Scott was now committed to working his settler's claim all winter, developing his ranch into a paying proposition.

Chapter Five

The southern Oregon coast had experienced fall, with mild temperatures and light rain. Scott and Buzz cleared stumps in their pasture and expanded the corrals to hold additional stock that they planned to acquire in the spring. Scott didn't allow himself much time for thoughts of his disastrous adventure as he slaved long hours on his ranch. Hunting and fishing was the partners' favorite recreation, but even the products of this activity were used to barter for supplies in Port Orford.

In late November, John Larsen returned with Buzz to build a barn. He brought his tools and a load of lumber on the two horses. Combined with several pole size logs and lumber already at Sixes, the barn took shape quickly, giving a look of permanence and stability to the ranch.

The continued mild weather allowed rapid progress in the construction schedule, and John's craftsmanship assured a quality product. But winter finally confronted the trio with a gray and blustery day. They quit early and sat down to a game of stud poker. The partners didn't enjoy gambling for money, but they had modified the betting game. Equal piles of chips were issued to each player, and the game ended when one person had won all the chips. The winner collected a favor, usually the loser doing an unsavory chore. Buzz relished beating Scott and watching him wash dishes and pans, something both men hated to do. John was given the rules and a spirited game lasted well into the evening, with the newcomer winning all the chips.

John laughed and teased his friends, "You both owe me a favor. I wonder what chore that I should have you do. Hmmm . . .

Buzz, you can take me hunting in the morning." The Old-Timer agreed readily, figuring his assignment was easy and fun.

"Scott, you can go fishing with me . . . on my boat of course. You need a trip to town for relaxation."

Scott smiled good-naturedly, replying, "I don't expect to relax on the ocean, riding in a little troller skippered by a wild Norseman. Can you find a calm sea for our fishing trip?"

Two days later, Scott and John led the two horses to town, laden with John's tools and almost 100 pounds of venison. "Does all of this meat go to the store?" John inquired.

"No. I promised a few cuts to the man at the lumber yard, and Louie Knapp bartered five days of board and room at Christmas for a hindquarter of venison. The rest is for you and the Hermanns. Isn't Mary's baby due pretty soon?"

"Yes, it was due last week. George has been fretting all month. Say, I told you that I made a crib for the baby out of cedar. How would you and Buzz like to buy a pad and a blanket for it?"

"Of course, thanks for including us in the gift. Is the trim pink or blue?"

John chuckled as he explained, "George would say blue for a boy, but Mary asked me to wait until the baby arrives before finishing the trim."

When the two friends reached Port Orford, they made their deliveries of meat, ending up at the Hermanns' home. A slightly frazzled George answered the door, announcing proudly that George Junior had arrived two days before. He invited them indoors to see Mary and the baby, who both seemed more interested in sleeping than in visiting. The bachelors were uncomfortable in the nursery atmosphere, and edged toward the door as they chatted with George and Angela.

Scott offered, "Would you like me to hang this side of venison in your woodshed?"

"Thank you, gentlemen. But what's your rush? Can we . . ?" George broke off his comment as the baby began crying, and shrugged his shoulders. "Junior needs me. See you later."

Scott stabled his horses at the hotel, and accompanied John to his boat. His friend had decided to fish the afternoon tide beyond the Orford Heads, and he informed Scott that he could pay off his gambling debt today. "You're getting a real deal—calm seas and half-a-day's work. Here, hold the tiller steady as I rig the sail."

Scott mumbled aloud, "Calm seas—hogwash! This ocean is never calm enough for me. Next thing you know, the wind will act up." Overhearing Scott's pessimism, John laughed and breathed deeply. "Smell that salt air, and listen to the surf. Nothing is more refreshing than setting out to sea."

Trolling through a school of salmon with two lines resulted in a plentiful catch, and as they followed the fish south they neared Humbug Mountain. John finally came about and headed north. His expansive mood was evident as he crowed, "We caught fourteen salmon in that run. Not bad, eh? Hold the tiller again Scott. I'll clean the fish for market." The sail began flapping listlessly in the wind, and a dense gray fog passed over the boat, heading toward land. John straightened up, scanning the seashore for a few seconds and then took the tiller. Scott was unconcerned until he noted their direction had changed westward and the land disappeared behind the fog bank.

"What are you doing, John? Port Orford is there," Scott said, pointing aft of the boat.

"The wind changed and brought fog onto the coast. We'll stay offshore overnight. I'll drop a sea anchor in a few minutes."

Scott queried, "How do you know where we are located? Will a sea anchor hold us off the reefs and rocks all night?"

"Quit worrying. I've done this before. I have a feel for our position. Just hope the wind remains constant during the night."

The men took turns sleeping—napping is a better term. They munched on hardtack and smoked salmon which John kept on board for just such an occasion. They drank water from a five gallon tank built into the cabin. As the dark of night turned lighter, the gray mass still enveloped the boat.

Scott nervously asked, "When will the fog lift? There's less wind now than there was during the night."

John was busy cleaning fish, but he replied patiently, "If the fog doesn't break up by noon, I'll work the boat into the harbor with Norse dead reckoning. I estimate that we are two miles off-shore and a mile south of the Heads."

When there was no change in visibility during the morning hours, John pulled the sea anchor and rigged sail. "I need your eyes and ears, Scott. Sit on the bow and warn me if you see or hear anything forward of us." They sailed a northerly course for fifteen minutes before Scott heard the changing sound of surf on rocks and called out, "I hear . . . and I see the Heads . . . ," pointing off the port bow.

"Yes, I follow you. The fog appears to be breaking up near shore." John brought the fishing boat to starboard as sunshine cleared a lane through the harbor entrance. He laughed as Scott heaved a loud sigh of relief. "We must play poker again, my friend. You make my job so interesting."

Scott waved good-bye to John as he walked up the bluff, proceeding past the fort to the store. George was working today and looked much more relaxed, even with a store full of customers. A clerk filled Scott's small order, and George joined him as he left the store. "Scott, Mary and I want you to be Junior's godfather. Can you come to his baptism on Christmas Eve? And dinner on Christmas day?"

"Of course! I'm very honored. What do I have to do? I'm not of your religion."

"Stand up with us when the priest baptizes Junior. Actually, we're not very good Catholics, but we feel that boy should start his life properly. Will Buzz be able to come also?"

"Yes, the ranch can take care of itself for a couple of days. Which reminds me, would you mail this package to Melissa for me? It's a Christmas greeting and a small myrtlewood deer that I carved last month."

Taking the package, George assured him that it would go out on the next ship to Portland. He returned to his customers, and Scott went to the hotel for lunch and a visit with the Knapps. After eating, he saddled his horses, strapping his supplies on Prince before mounting Salem and riding home to the Sixes.

****

Buzz left for Port Orford two days before Christmas, planning to shop for gifts before the holiday. He would buy for both partners since Scott had to feed the stock on December 24th. Scott would travel to town in time for the baptismal. Buzz would return on Christmas day and Scott would follow the day after. Their interwoven schedule was designed to leave the ranch and livestock unattended only for one day, an acceptable absence to both men.

Scott managed to reach the store before it closed, purchasing a baby outfit as a baptismal gift for Junior and heavy boots as a Christmas present for Buzz. He checked into the hotel, stabled Salem, and walked over to the Hermanns where the priest would baptize Junior. He was the last participant to arrive. The priest was in a hurry and performed the simple ceremony immediately. Mary had prepared sufficient dainty sandwiches and sweets, and Scott never got around to supper. He ate the tiny sandwiches and toasted Junior with George's brandy until Mary chased the partners and John Larsen out of the house. "Begone with your partying. I have to rest if you expect to eat Christmas dinner tomorrow. Good night!" The men retired to the sutler's store on the fort to continue their revelry. Lt. Wyman stopped by to visit, and Scott promptly bought a round. The officer mentioned that the Indians had been quiet since Scott had returned from Humbug. The news pleased him, as he hoped for a quiet winter on the ranch.

Christmas dinner and the gift exchange was enjoyed by all, as a festive aura pervaded the Hermann household. Buzz was surprised when Scott left the house with him, saying, "I'm returning to Sixes with you today."

"Not tomorrow as planned? Are you feeling poorly?"

Scott thought for a moment before answering, "No, I'm well and contented, but I guess that I'm a bit envious of George. He's lucky to have a fine wife like Mary, and two lovely children. I can't explain myself very well, but it makes me feel lonely."

"Well, Scott, maybe it's time that you quit beating around the bush with Melissa. Just ask the girl straight out to marry you. Seems to me that you waste a lot of energy courting her from a distance."

Scott's face reddened as he replied, "Ah Buzz, she's awfully young and not interesting in marrying me. I don't have anything to offer her."

"Well, that's hogwash! I never married so I don't qualify as an expert, but there are a lot more white men, and women, in Oregon these days. In fact, it's getting downright civilized, with families important to settling the territory. George Hermann is typical of the new breed of Westerners. The reason you're envious is because you want the same things. I reckon that I've said more than enough, so I'll shut up. Just you think about it."

Since less than a dozen words had been exchanged on the ride home, it was evident that Scott was thinking, but he was keeping his thoughts to himself.

****

The new year 1853 arrived in flurry of winter weather, a heavy blanket of white snow covering the Sixes valley. The livestock had difficulty in foraging and the partners broke apart a haystack in the meadow. The cold spell continued for three weeks, and a second haystack was consumed before a warm rain melted the snow and thawed the pasture grass.

Buzz shot a large deer which had been grazing with the cows during and after the freeze. He butchered it and the two men delivered it to the Quah-to-mah village. Scott observed that the Indians had not fared well during the colder-than-normal weather, looking gaunt and worn. Two young men were eyeing their horses, Scott noted out of the corner of his eye. Chief Sa-qua-mi smilingly thanked them for the gift, but Scott sensed deceit as he recalled the story of Sa-qua-mi killing a white man named Parrish in similar circumstances. Scott expansively signed good health as he mounted Salem and backed him away from the young Indians. Buzz joined him as they trotted away from the village after saying good-bye.

"Well partner, I do believe that you are learning. Some of those Indians wanted a horsemeat feast. I don't trust Sa-qua-mi a bit. We'd better stick close together on the ranch for the rest of the winter."

In the ensuing weeks, Buzz scouted the trail downriver without any sign of visitors. In late March, he discovered sign of two intruders who had watched the cabin from atop the knoll.

The Old-Timer opined, "If they didn't come into camp openly, they must have been scouting the ranch. They'll be back. I reckon that we'll have to stand watch for a few days."

"I agree. I'll go down to the slide ridge before dawn. You feed the stock and fix food to bring with you at midday. You can stand guard in the afternoon while I do the chores." Buzz nodded and both men turned in for the night.

Light was breaking as Scott nestled between two logs in a pocket of brush. He wrapped the bearskin around him and leaned back against a soft rotting log. The brush enveloped his position except to his front, which afforded him a clear view of the narrow trail crossing the slate face of the steep ridge. He laid the barrel of his rifle on the log in front of him and relaxed. He had a long vigil, and probably for naught. He didn't believe the Indians intended them harm, but being cautious made good sense. The hours went by slowly, with Scott shifting position periodically to keep his blood flowing and his muscles loose.

A small pebble struck the bush to his left. Scott held still, swiveling his eyes before turning his head slightly and leaning forward. Buzz was crouched behind a deadfall thirty feet away, pointing to the top of the ridge. Scott moved his head very slowly to his right and scanned the crest of the ridge. A movement caught his attention and was repeated as a figure dropped behind the skyline. Scott settled back into his position, using a bush to shield his right hand signal to Buzz. They would hold position and see what the Indian intended.

Another Indian stepped around the bend and walked slowly forward, scanning the trail ahead. He looked right at Scott without seeming to see him, as his gaze passed over the brushy position. A second Indian trotted up behind him, speaking loudly enough to be heard over fifty yards away. Both Indians carried bows in ready position, with arrows notched. Scott thought, "Not a very peaceful posture, when Buzz and I are the only 'friends' upriver. I thought I heard the Tututni word for horse. These two men are the same yahoos from the village—the ones who eyed our horses. There's only one way to deal with thieves—actual or intended. Since killing them will only start a war, we'll march them right back to their chief at the end of our rifles." Scott fired a round into the shale behind the Indians, reloaded and stood erect. He told them to stand still in broken Tututni, the threat in his voice carrying the correct message. The second Indian raised his bow to fire at Scott, and it shattered into pieces as Buzz fired a bullet through the grip. The young man cried out in pain as he pulled wood slivers from the palm of his left hand. The other Indian wisely dropped his bow as Scott stepped out, signing both men to lie down on their stomachs. Buzz came up and tied their hands behind their backs with their own bow strings. Throwing the remnants of the weapons in the river.

Scott asked, "Can you handle these two yahoos while I fetch the horses? We need to make our point by marching them right back to Sa-qua-mi before our horses."

"You're right! A show of force will engender respect, and retribution isn't likely if they are delivered alive." He shook the butt of his rifle over the captives' heads, threatening, "I'll crown you yahoos if you move a muscle."

Once out of sight, Scott ran at full tilt along the trail and to the barn. He saddled the horses and returned to Buzz in less than ten minutes. Buzz mounted Prince and motioned for the two Indians to stand and to walk ahead of them. He clicked his breech open and then closed to emphasize his point and the men complied with alacrity.

Their entrance into the village shocked the inhabitants. The grim and foreboding faces of two white friends was frightening in itself, but before their rifle bores trudged two of their toughest young men. The Indians realized that these two white men were formidable enemies, and preferred to have them as friends of the tribe. Scott watched Chief Sa-qua-mi closely, seeing anger in his eyes even though his mouth smiled. Scott concluded to himself, this man is no friend—and never will be. We'll watch our backs around him.

The partners used their rifle barrels to push the two men in front of the Chief. Scott spoke in Tututni, calling them "bad boys"—an ignominious term in Indian vernacular. He softened his rough tones, and placed his rifle butt on his thigh, barrel pointing skyward, as he told the men and women present that friends were welcome in peace, and others were not welcome at all. Not sure of his Tututni words, Scott repeated the message in English, ending his warning with a smile, nodding in respect to the Chief, and backing his horse out of the village. Since they had entered the village without an invitation, the partners were intruders and could not expect custom to protect them from attack. As Buzz trotted by him, Scott turned Salem and matched pace with his friend.

"Well done, Scott! You made your point and we rode out of the village without a fight. I hope this example is the end of any confrontation with the Qua-to-mahs." After they crossed slide ridge, Buzz slid off of Prince and gave the reins to Scott, declaring, "Well, it's my turn to stand watch. Have a bowl of stew ready for me after dark." The men continued to share guard duty for several days, until Chief Sixes approached Scott one morning.

Without any weapons and signing peace, the Indian crossed slide ridge and walked firmly up to his white friend and greeted him. Scott smiled and welcomed Chief Sixes, inviting him to eat with him at the cabin.

Buzz greeted their Indian friend warmly, offering him hot gravy on biscuits and a cup of coffee. He told Scott, "I've eaten already, so I'll just amble up the gully out back and watch the ranch." He remained on the hillside observing the ranch until Scott and Chief Sixes walked across the flat and down the trail. Buzz crossed to the knoll and followed the two men down the trail, being careful to stay out of sight and hearing. As the Indian crossed slide ridge and waved farewell to Scott, Buzz called out, "A right friendly visit!" Scott waited until his partner reached him before explaining, "Our friend told me that the U.S. Army is after Sa-qua-mi and a new chief will probably be chosen. He assured me that the Qua-to mahs are our friends and won't attack us." He reflected on the visit for a few moments, continuing, "I believe him, but I'd better ride to Fort Orford and see Lt. Wyman in the morning. If you'll watch the trail, I'll prepare for the trip. Anything you want me to add to the supply list?"

"Yes, some sugar candy. I miss my sweet honey. By the way, I trust our friend, but he isn't really a chief. I'm not sure that he speaks for all of his band. I'll stay here until dark, and I'll watch tomorrow until you return from town. Make it a quick trip."

Scott reached Port orford without seeing a single soul along the way. After discussing his problem with Lt. Wyman and hearing that Sa-qua-mi was a treacherous devil, he stopped at the store for supplies. George was not working and a young clerk was slow in filling Scott's order. Impatiently, Scott paced in front of the counter until his supplies were packed and he could load them on Prince's packsaddle for the fast ride back to the Sixes valley. He rode up to Buzz as dusk was falling, announcing, "Come along, Buzz. Our friend's story checks out and we need to spend more time working the ranch."

****

A bright spring sun warmed the Myrtlewood Grove ranch on May Day 1853. The partners stood back and admired their winter's work. A soft, thin column of smoke rose from the cabin's blackened stovepipe, a remnant of their midday feast. They'd finished nearly 300 feet of split-cedar fencing for the corral this morning, and celebrated with a meal of venison steak, fried potatoes, and freshly baked biscuits, topped off with an airtight tin of peaches. After eating, they'd walked to the edge of the myrtlewood grove to view their ranch. The log cabin was dwarfed by the stoutly built barn, its rough cut plank walls still showing a raw wood appearance. The corral encompassed the flat adjacent to the barn and the livestock within were munching the last hay from the third stack. Short new grass was growing wherever the sun touched the meadow. The ranch had an air of permanence, earned through the partners' hard work—a labor of love for Scott and Buzz.

Scott announced, "I think it's time to visit Port Orford and see what's happening in the outside world."

Buzz reluctantly disagreed, "I hate to ruin such a good idea, but we'd better visit the Qua-to-mahs village first. I want to see if those Indians are friendly or not. How about taking them that deer that we shot the day before yesterday?"

The partners rode into the village the next morning and greeted familiar faces with a smile and a hand salute. Without hesitation, they went to the central meat rack and hung the deer carcass on it. Chief Sixes hurried over to them, smiling a greeting and thanking them for the meat. Scott noted a good many men were absent from their lodges, but the Indians left in the village were all friendly. Buzz gave their friend a bag of sugar candy as they sat around his lodge's fire and visited. After an hour of conversation in Tututni and English, both parties decided that sign language was easier. Scott turned down an offer to fish with Chief Sixes, but thanked him for his hospitality. Everyone in the village waved good-bye to them as they rode away.

"I was wrong. Our Indian neighbors are friendly again with that yahoo Sa-qua-mi gone. Let's hunt the upper Sixes for a few days. We should take some meat into Port Orford when we go—barter for room and board and maybe a drink or two."

In May of 1853, Port Orford was the business center for the southern Oregon coast. Gold miners, lumberjacks, and soldiers were supplied by local merchants and settlers, who in turn received their goods from ships out of San Francisco and Portland. The threat of Indians did little to deter men seeking their fortunes in gold and timber in the wilderness around the town. The U.S. Army's presence at Fort Orford ensured a safe haven for townspeople, and the garrison was being enlarged so that more troops could patrol the coastline. However, the Army's goal was to control the Indians, not police the civilians, and a rough element developed in the town population, often involving soldiers and sailors on a drinking spree. The Army handled its own miscreants very well, but thievery amongst civilians received little attention. Disagreements between white men were settled on a personal basis with tacit approval by the military authorities.

Scott and Buzz walked through the bustling town, passing a new building which was marked as a tavern because of its volume of noise. A drunken soldier was pushed out of the door, and fell into Buzz, grabbing the Old-Timer. Scott seized the man by his jacket collar and good-naturedly lifted him to his feet. A second soldier yelled, "Hey mister, leave my buddy alone. Are you looking for a fight?"

Scott shook his head and smiled, replying, "Not today, soldier! What's the occasion for celebrating?"

A sergeant grabbed the belligerent soldier by his arm as he interjected, "Good day, Mr. McClure. Don't mind the lad, he's a good Scot like yourself. I'm afraid my men are losing their contest with the sailors from the Columbia. We challenged them to an arm-wrestling tournament, and we're tied in matches. However, no one can beat O'Keefe, their bos'n mate, and the losers must buy a round for the winners."

The belligerent soldier leaned forward and asked, "Are you McClure, the Indian fighter? Say, are you as strong as everyone says? Sarge, maybe he can beat O'Keefe for us."

Looking him over carefully, the sergeant offered, "Can I buy you and your friend a drink and discuss this matter, Mr. McClure?"

Buzz had seen his friend in action and laughingly encouraged him, "Go ahead, Scott. You need the exercise and I can use a drink."

With a broad grin, Scott agreed, "I'll stand with the Army, sergeant, and I'll drink your rye whiskey while you arrange the match. Bring on Mr. O'Keefe!"

Excitement brewed with the announcement of a championship match, best two out of three put-downs, between O'Keefe and McClure. The tavern soon filled with men in a festive mood, all ready to wager on the outcome. Most money was bet on O'Keefe, but many soldiers were loyal to their man McClure.

The sergeant introduced Scott to his adversary, a powerfully-built black Irishman. A look of surprise flashed in those Irish eyes as O'Keefe failed to crush Scott's hand when the men shook. The two men grinned at each other and laughed merrily. It would be a good contest.

The bartender sagely filled all orders before the men sat down at the table and squared off. He was the referee and couldn't serve liquor during the match. As the men flexed their muscles, the room grew still in anticipation and suspense.

Scott mentally practiced a trick that he'd learned in St. Louis, arranging for his eyes to lose focus as the referee shouted, "Go!" His grip tightened simultaneously with his arm and shoulder and with amazing speed, whipped the bigger man's wrist onto the table. The referee choked, "Pin!" almost before he finished, "Go!"

O'Keefe's face reddened in a mixture of surprise, embarrassment, and anger, and as he opened his mouth to object, Scott asked quietly, "And was that a fair move, Mr. O'Keefe?"

His injured pride still showing, the Irishman laughed loudly and agreed, "Fast but fair, my friend. Are you ready for round number two?"

"Not until I buy you a drink. Bartender, bring us rye whiskey," thinking silently to himself, O'Keefe's too worked up for me to beat now. Let him relax and I may be able to overcome his size advantage.

The second round demonstrated strength and endurance, with O'Keefe's size overcoming McClure in twenty-three minutes. Scott congratulated his opponent and immediately set up for the third round, figuring that the Irishman was tired and expecting a rest period. The bartender turned to serve more drinks but Scott pulled him back to the table without comment but with clear intent.

"Go!" instigated a power play by O'Keefe which Scott countered, putting the Irishman on the defensive for several minutes. The advantage shifted back and forth between opponents over the next half hour. Scott thought to himself, perhaps I've underestimated this man's endurance, bigger men usually tire faster than I do. Two successive offensive moves recountered with strength by his opponent, and Scott fell back to a defensive position. He showed power, but was very slow. Perhaps a double-feint followed by an all-out power play will catch him off-balance, Scott thought. When he moved it was with more speed and power than anyone in the room thought possible. The bartender's cry of "Pin!" settled the issue, and soldiers collected their winnings. O'Keefe threw a huge arm over Scott's shoulder and congratulated him, "You're a good man, McClure. If there's ever a fight, I want you on my side. I believe that story of the Indian battle now. You're tougher than hell." The men in the room heard O'Keefe and they too became believers. The rough element looked on Scott McClure as one of their own, with a unique aura of respect and deference.

Buzz brought Scott back to earth with a solid thump on his back and a jingling leather purse, "We won $54 partner, I got two to one odds from those sailors. I knew you had too many tricks to lose an arm-wrestling contest. Come over to the bar, the bartender's buying us a drink."

As the partners walked up to the Hermann house that evening, Angela stopped playing on the doorstep and ran up to Scott and hugged him. "Uncle Scott, did you beat up a bad man? Daddy told mama that you fought for our soldiers. Isn't fighting bad?" The story had preceded him to supper, and Scott had to correct the story for Angela in oversimplistic terms which provided considerable amusement to the enraptured adults.

Mary commented, "Scott, that's a better story than George told me. I wonder what Melissa would say about Uncle Scott's explanation."

"Why is everyone funning me? I just want my sweetheart Angela to understand the real facts." Angela nodded readily and everyone laughed again, and Scott concluded, "Well I won't tell anyone else if that's the reaction I get." His smile belied his words as it was obvious that he was enjoying himself.

John raised the subject of Melissa again, saying, "Mary, tell Scott about the new school teacher Captain Tichenor has hired. Or is it a surprise?"

Mary responded, "Only to Scott. You haven't read Melissa's letter, have you Scott?"

"No, is she coming here? Tell me, Mary."

"It's my turn to tease you, Scott McClure. However, I will be kind. Melissa accepted the position after her father was hired by Winsor to work in Tichenor's mill office. You're quite a salesman, Scott, and sneaky too. Convincing Captain Tichenor to hire the Nelson family without telling me what you were doing."

Scott looked uncomfortable as he replied, "I did mention your name as a reference for Melissa. I wasn't sure Richard Nelson could leave Marysville, but I promised Melissa that I'd help him. However, I want my part in this project to remain between us. Richard is a proud man."

"When you brought me dress material from Marysville, I wrote a letter thanking Melissa and telling her that we needed a teacher.

When I talked to William Tichenor about hiring a teacher for our children, he acquiesced immediately, agreeing to any recommendation which you and I made. He had his foreman write to Richard Nelson. The Nelsons will arrive by ship from Portland in July."

****

After the Dubois and John Larsen had left, George brought up Scott's account at the store. He started his accounting review, by stating, "I've paid the lumberyard and wood worker as you instructed, and your account at the store itself is paid up. I invested $147.63 for you purchasing a bill of sale for four cows on the Floras River. Their condition is in question but the price is good, since I used your money for a man's gold prospecting supplies to get this bill of sale. He has an honest reputation and I trust him. You will have to pay a feed bill to the farmer holding the cows for you."

Scott's silence was assent but George worried that he'd overstepped his authority. "I'm sorry that I didn't discuss this deal with you but there wasn't time. If I made a mistake, I'll stand good for it." Mary's expression became concerned, but she remained silent over the offer.

"No, I agree, George. Your business acumen far exceeds mine. I have to accept risks if the Myrtlewood Grove is to prosper. What's left in my account?"

"A grand sum of $473.16. Remember that your partnership with Sam leaves you the balance. Any questions?"

Scott declined any question on George's report, but posed a different query, "I know you, George, what's on your mind? You could have told me all this anytime. You have something else percolating in that head of yours."

"Well now that you mention it, yes. I believe a freighting business might prove profitable. Your horses and your knowledge of the trail north to the Umpqua are sound assets for such a business venture. My business experience and mercantile connections are equally valuable. We would need a stable in town, and an agent on the Umpqua to start our company. I've laid it out on paper, Scott. I think we could manage with $300 cash, but I only have $70 to invest."

Scott nodded slowly, pondering the proposal for several minutes as George waited nervously for his opinion. "How about establishing a four-way partnership at $70 each, with you, me, Buzz, and John having equal shares. You're the manager in charge of the company assets and our agent in Port Orford. I'll supply the horses and hire the teamsters we'll need. Buzz and John will captain each haul to Gardiner. We'll all share the work and the risk. Oh yes, Buzz and I have a friend in Gardiner, Harvey Masters, who can serve as agent and his hotel can be our northern terminal. Buzz won enough money today to pay his share now, and John can work his share off by building our stable. How does my counterproposal sound to you, George—a four-way partnership?"

George beamed with pleasure as he replied, "Better than my own, Scott. I have details on paper which you should go over. . . ."

Scott stopped him in mid-sentence, "George, you manage the company and don't bother us with details or paperwork. We go forward with trust and faith in each other, and in case of a partner's death, like Sam's, the remaining partners own the company. When that isn't satisfactory to one of us, we'll dissolve the partnership." He offered his hand, adding, "Agreed, George, Buzz?"

The Port Orford and Umpqua Freight Company was thus incorporated with a simple gentlemen's agreement. John Larsen joined the consortium later that evening, and began construction of a stable and office on property behind George's house the next day. Scott stayed in town helping John for five days while Buzz returned to Sixes to work on the ranch.

Scott took the Hermanns to dinner at the hotel with John watching the children. He told George that it was time Mary had a night out and he owed them more than one supper. George gave Scott his bill of sale for the cows, and told him that 200 pounds of supplies had been ordered by the farmer on Floras Creek. "He swapped your feed bill for hauling his supplies, but he wants delivery soon. He has sold several cheese blocks to the store, and my boss agreed to give our company twenty pounds of oats for bringing the cheese back with you. That will start our feed supply in the stable."

Scott chuckled as Mary admired her husband, and he too complimented his work, "George, you're quite a businessman. Keep up the good work!"

****

Five weeks later a group of Coquille settlers landed at Port Orford with farming equipment. John was fishing and Buzz had just returned from Gardiner, so Scott loaded the horses and escorted the five men back to their farms. On his return trip, he stopped at Floras Creek to purchase two cows from a settler who was pulling out. When he reached the Sixes River, he led the livestock into the ranch corral. Buzz hurried across the pasture carrying a string of trout fresh from the river and waved to his friend. Scott went forward to meet him, and Buzz started talking as they neared each other, "The Nelsons' ship came in July 6th—day before yesterday. Some fast talker named Hans Schmidt sailed on the same ship from Portland. He's a shifty looking cuss! He paid a lot of attention to Melissa. She was upset when you didn't meet the ship, but we had a good visit, and I explained your absence. You'd better visit her pronto. She and her dad are at the Knapps' Hotel."

"Will you take care of Prince and the two new cows? I'll clean up and go into town with Salem."

In town, Scott was intercepted by Mary as he left the freight yard, repeating Buzz's message, almost word for word. It seemed as if they had discussed Melissa and him, but such a thought didn't bother him. It would be good to see her again.

Richard Nelson answered the door and greeted Scott warmly, informing him that Melissa was walking with a friend. Scott's spirits darkened at that news, but he suggested, "Let's walk down to the dock and see if my friend, John Larsen, will buy us a beer. If he's fishing today, we can stop by the tavern near the fort."

"Now would that be the infamous drinking spot where you won the arm-wrestling contest against a giant sailor? And won a lot of money gambling?" Richard asked half-jokingly.

Scott laughed and admitted, "Guilty as charged! However, Buzz won the money. Arm-wrestling is a healthier sport than fisticuffs, which was a possibility during that celebration. How's the new job?"

"I start work on Monday. Captain Tichenor has been most helpful to Melissa and me. You know, he speaks highly of you."

"Good! I welcome the good will of the town founder and our leading citizen." He paused as they reached the top of the bluff, and pointed out to sea, "There's John's boat out there." He outlined the area's topography, identifying outstanding landmarks for the newcomer.

The two friends conversed freely as they entered the tavern and sat down. The bartender served them quickly, offering, "Mr. McClure, these drinks are on me. Thanks to you, business has been excellent. Would you be interested in another tournament?" Scott shook his head and thanked the man for his hospitality.

The two men sipped their beer in comradely silence, until Richard spoke hesitantly, "You're kind of famous around here for being strong and tough. When you pointed out Humbug Mountain, you didn't sound as if it was special. Isn't that where you killed several Indians?" When there was no immediate response, he asked, "Is my question out of order?"

"No, it was a sad day for me, but I'll tell you the story," Scott said, as he related his account of Sam Olson's death and the Indian fight south of Humbug. He concluded with a philosophical point, "The white man has disregarded Indians' rights, often treating them like animals. I understand why Indians defend their land

and culture, but they can't win. Personally, in an Indian fight I've killed to protect myself and my property, but I don't like it. So-called Indian fighting is more often an excuse for killing for fun or profit—or both. I think we all share the shame of man killing man, and the equal crime of man abusing man."

Richard contemplated Scott's point, and rephrased its meaning, "You're saying the Indians aren't always bad guys, but we treat them as if they are. Do you mean that we can't live together?"

"Precisely! I don't believe that the local Indians, the Tututni, will be living here ten years from now. We white men will be everywhere."

The two friends continued their dialogue on the way back to the hotel. A husky man with dark hair and beard was exiting the hotel as they approached. Richard greeted him, "Hello, Hans. Is Melissa in her room?" When the man nodded, Richard continued, "Hans, meet our friend Scott McClure. Scott, this is our shipboard companion, Hans Schmidt." The two shook hands, almost begrudgingly, as Scott inquired, "Haven't we met before? In Portland, perhaps?"

Schmidt responded, "No. I'm sure that we haven't. Good night, gentlemen." He hurried off down the street.

Scott paid little attention to the man's abruptness as he anticipated seeing Melissa. Richard called out, "Scott's here, dear," as he opened the door, and his daughter greeted their friend with a smile and a limp handshake. Scott remembered the warm hug that he had received in Marysville and thought, Melissa's cool toward me. Buzz may be right about meeting her ship.

Scott supped with the Nelsons at the hotel, discovering that Melissa was seeing Hans the next day. He arranged a meeting with Melissa on Monday noon, offering to introduce her to people around town.

****

Scott arrived at the hotel promptly at 12 o'clock and found Melissa having a light meal with Hans in the dining room. He sat at the table as the two finished eating and chatting, characterizing himself as a dour Scot. Hans finally excused himself and departed, Melissa commenting, "You weren't very polite to Hans. You could have been more sociable."

Scott was smarting from pangs of jealousy as well as her criticism as he responded, "He's not my friend and I don't like him." He thought Melissa might refuse to accompany him as she glared at him, but she preceded him out the door and they walked around town visiting his friends. Captain Tichenor was at sea, but Mrs. Tichenor proved to be a graceful lady, serving tea and wafers. Visiting the Tichenor family proved to be the prime goal for Melissa and Scott thought he understood her motivation for ignoring his remark about Hans. Not a very flattering reason, Scott thought to himself, I suppose Schmidt doesn't know the right people in town.

As they walked along the street leading to the docks, Hans Schmidt came out of a side street and turned toward them, as a rough-looking and dirty character called out, "Dutch, hey Dutch Schmidt, how is Portland?"

Scott stopped, dead in his tracks, recognition overcoming him. Schmidt backed away from the murderous glare emanating from the usually friendly eyes. Melissa was dumbstruck in looking from one to the other.

"You thieving bastard! You're the petty thief from the Sea Gull—at the Portland wharf. I've a good . . ," Scott was shocked still as Melissa slapped him.

"You rough brute. Keep your insults to yourself. Hans Schmidt is a gentleman."

Dutch had recovered before the gathering crowd, and played the innocent victim by announcing, "Sir, you have mistaken me for another. I just arrived in town last week. If there weren't ladies present, I would challenge you."

"Challenge be damned, Dutch. I know you for the low-life you are, and I'm saying you are a thief and no better than your partner in Portland, Weasel."

Standing now beside Melissa, Dutch again protested his innocence, "I deny your allegations and I'll . . ."

He was interrupted by George Hermann speaking for the crowd. "Scott, you're upset, can you prove your charge?"

The question from George was like a dash of cold water thrown in Scott's face. He calmly looked at each face in the crowd, ending with George's, and stated unequivocally, "This man's a thief, of that I'm sure. I can't prove it in a court of law, but I advise each of you to watch your purse when he's around."

George replied, "My friend, I know your word is good and I believe you. But a man is innocent until proven guilty."

Dutch shouted to the mumbling crowd, "Since when is a killer's word so righteous. He's killed innocent travelers in Scottsburg and peaceful Indians on Humbug. He's not . . ."

"You're a liar as well as a thief, Dutch-friend of Weasel, I saw you leave the Sea Gull with property which wasn't yours, and I heard your partner implicate you as a crook." John Larsen stood before the ashen Dutch and defied him to deny it. Dutch muttered, "You men are in cahoots. I refuse to listen further. Come Melissa," and the two walked hurriedly to the hotel.

Scott addressed George loudly enough so everyone on the street could hear, "Captain Tichenor should be informed of Dutch Schmidt's presence. He passed judgment on his partner, Tom Burton, also known as the Weasel. He can take action if he chooses. John and I had nothing stolen from us." John discussed people's reaction to the allegation as he and Scott walked to the freight yard. Knowing his friend was upset and hurt, John chose not to mention Melissa's behavior with Scott and Dutch.

John suggested, "I believe that Richard Nelson should know that Dutch is a thief and a scoundrel. I'll be glad to tell him if you want me to."

"No, the Nelsons are my friends and Richard should hear it from me. I'll ride out to the mill and tell both him and Winsor— Tichenor's manager."

"Perhaps you should talk to Melissa, and explain your point of view," John added.

Scott was abrupt in answering, "What's there to explain? Dutch is a thief and I said so. The whack she gave me doesn't hurt half as much as the fact that she believes I'm dishonorable and lying. No, I'll tell Richard my story and then return to the ranch. I expect they'll talk to you since Melissa believed that thief."

Scott rode into the Sixes valley still pondering Richard's reception at the mill. Winsor had been convinced the allegation was true because he knew Scott, but Richard expressed doubts, questioning the rivalry between Melissa's two friends and repeating Hans Schmidt's allegation that Scott was a killer, something he had told the Nelsons before. He didn't call me a liar or a killer. I guess he believes that I just made a mistake identifying Dutch, Scott thought. As Scott was to discover at a later date, probably everyone in Port Orford believed Scott and John except the Nelsons. And when Captain Tichenor confirmed their story of convicting Weasel, citizens asked him to charge Dutch with thievery. Tichenor and Lt. Wyman discussed the law, and concluded that a crime in Portland was out of their jurisdiction.

Summer passed into autumn quickly as Scott and Buzz worked long hours on the ranch and the freighting business. Buzz handled all of the hauling contracts, using hired hands. John's fishing enterprise was prospering and Scott insisted on remaining at his ranch. One week in October while John was hauling freight, Scott left Buzz to watch the ranch, and he took a prospecting trip to the river's headwaters and panned for gold. Buzz contended that he was being downright unsociable since the Schmidt incident. When he suggested visiting friends in Port Orford, Scott simply agreed that Buzz should go ahead while he watched the ranch.

****

The old milk cow which Scott had brought from Salem had dried up months before, and when George sent word that beef prices were "sky high," Buzz led it into town in late November and sold it. He brought back a Christmas Dinner invitation from the Hermanns, and made it clear that Scott was going—one way or another. Scott laughed with his partner and agreed to go happily if Buzz would shop for presents on his next trip to Gardiner.

On Christmas Day the weather was wet and blustery. Buzz was all bundled in heavy clothes and impatient to leave for the Hermanns. He'd been cooped up in the cabin with a severe chest cold since he'd returned from Gardiner, and he wasn't going to miss the Hermanns' dinner party. "Mary said that she was going to invite the Nelsons, and I haven't seen Melissa since August."

"All right, my friend. I hope that we don't catch pneumonia. Grab your gifts and let's ride out of here."

Angela opened the door for the men and gave Scott a hug. Junior toddled across the room, closely followed by his mother.

Scott grinned at Mary, "Junior is learning to walk awfully fast. How do you keep up with him?"

"When Angela comes home from school, she takes care of her brother after she does her homework," Mary responded, adding, "and George plays with him in the evening."

Scott asked Angela about school, "Are you a good student? Does your teacher give you lots of homework?"

"Yes, Miss Nelson says that we're all good students. She makes us work hard, but we have fun too. I love my teacher."

Mary added, "Melissa is a fine teacher. All the parents agree with us."

George entered the house carrying several parcels, and echoed his wife, "Everyone likes her. I just hope that we can keep her next year, now that her father isn't working. The mill office was too cold for Richard and his lungs are bothering him. The mill is just too far from the hotel and he can't walk that far."

Buzz inquired, "How are the Nelsons faring without his wages?"

"They haven't confided in me, but Louie Knapp alerted me that they have money problems. That's the reason for my comment. Mary and I would like to help, but Melissa is angry with Mary. She invited the Nelsons for Christmas dinner, but refused to have Dutch Schmidt as a guest in our house. The Nelsons are dining with Schmidt at the hotel."

Buzz gave Scott a questioning look, and then a verbal nudge, "Scott, you're always full of ideas. We need to help our friends." He concluded angrily, "Speak up!"

When the Hermanns nodded in agreement, and looked expectantly at Scott, he reluctantly spoke. "The only way to help a proud man like Richard is to find him a job. George, you need a part-time assistant in the freight office. He could walk from his hotel easily enough. You hire him and pay him whatever is needed for a few hours of work each week." His humor returned as he chuckled and suggested, "Don't mention my name or they'll probably refuse your offer of work."

The Dubois arrived, followed by John Larsen, and Christmas good cheer was epitomized in the now traditional dinner and gift exchange. Scott took Mary aside before he left and gave her a package for Melissa. "It's just a small bear which I carved from myrtlewood. I can't take it to the hotel. I don't trust my temper around Dutch." Mary agreed to deliver it for him the next day, thinking that it wasn't Dutch that he was avoiding.

Buzz had wanted to visit with Melissa while they were in town, but his cough worsened after dinner. Scott not only insisted his partner return to the ranch, but that he take three freight trips to the Umpqua during the winter months. He visited with Richard Nelson whenever they met in the office, and in March he was given a message to see Captain Tichenor down on the dock.

Scott found Tichenor talking to John Larsen on his fishing boat. He greeted his friends warmly, and shook hands with both men. "What can I do for you, Captain Tichenor? I received a message to meet you here."

John answered, "It seems that our Portland thief is at work again. He and his gang are prime suspects in thievery on Hubbard Creek. He and his five friends are prospecting near your played-out claim, and finding plenty of gold dust with a minimum of work. They've been seen up and down the creek bottom, about the same time camps were robbed."

The Captain said, "Unfortunately, there is no proof, only suspicion amongst the prospectors. Dutch beat up the only man who dared call him a thief. Lt. Wyman marched a troop through the area, and his show of force convinced the gang to go elsewhere. One of my sailors overheard Schmidt's men talking about the Sixes River. I thought you should be warned."

"Thanks for the information. I'd better return to the ranch and tell Buzz. John, you're scheduled to take next week's freight run," Scott reminded his partner before he bid the men good-bye.

Buzz wasn't surprised to hear of thievery at Hubbard creek. "I've heard of several petty thefts in Port Orford since Dutch and his friends arrived. It seems that you can find a bad apple in any barrel eventually, and Dutch is ours." He suggested, "We'd better tell Chief Sixes that those yahoos aren't friends of ours. I'm ready to ride to the Shix village when you are. Shall we hunt for a deer first? Our Indian friends may be hungry for venison if their young men are still out of camp."

****

Two days later the partners walked their meat-laden horses down the Sixes River. An Indian lad came running up the trail toward them, talking fast in Tututni, and pointing back to his village. Scott calmed the boy and questioned him slowly for a clear understanding of the problem.

"Buzz, Chief Sixes asks for our help. The men are gone from the village and white men with guns are bothering his people . . .

six men ... could be Dutch's gang ... cut your venison loose and mount up."

Instructing the lad to stay with the meat, Scott directed the Old-Timer to circle south of the village. "I'll ride straight up to the white men and confront them. If it is Dutch's gang, I'll cover him. You come up behind the others, but no shooting if we can avoid it. We don't want to create trouble for the Indians."

Scott checked his rifle as he waited for Buzz to complete his maneuver, and then walked Salem quietly into the village. He recognized Dutch immediately, as the bully pushed his Indian friend away from the door of his lodge. When one of the gang shouted a cry of alarm, Scott jumped his horse forward, stopping abruptly with his rifle lined on Dutch's chest.

"You thieves stand still and drop your rifles—now!" Scott threatened with anger.

"Don't try it, mister! Do as Scott says, drop your rifle," came Buzz's voice from behind to men who had started to move.

Dutch blustered, "Who the hell do you think you are, McClure? We can prospect anywhere we want whether these Indians like it or not. We're within our legal rights."

"Shut up, you low-life thief. You and your miserable partners have been stealing gold dust on Hubbard and getting away with it. You're not welcome in the Sixes valley. You can . . ."

Dutch interrupted in an angry and frustrated tone, "You can't stop us from prospecting."

"I'll put it to you straight out—all of you. Get out of my valley and stay out, or I'll personally deal out the consequences." Scott's cold stare riveted each gang member, ending at Dutch. "Buzz, empty their rifles."

Buzz fired Dutch's rifle and then jammed the bore into the mud, repeating the operation until all of the gang's weapons were nonfunctional. Scott gestured with his rifle for the gang to pick up their rifles and head for Port Orford. The Old-Timer retrieved Prince and helped Scott march them to the Elk River crossing.

After watching them tramp out of sight, Buzz commented, "I doubt if we've seen the last of that crew, but they'll not come back today. We'd better pick up that Indian lad and the venison before we visit with the Quah-to-mahs."

Chapter Six

A fickle spring day had dawned with bright sunlight glancing off the scattered white clouds dancing in the sky above, and Buzz had taken his Sharps upriver to "get out of the cabin." Scott was spreading the last of the winter hay in the corral, when a dark gray thunderhead rolled over the valley, accompanied by torrential rains. Scott moved inside the barn, cleaning stalls while the horses were in town at their freight stable. He was visualizing their next project, creating a water system for drinking, as well as irrigating a vegetable garden behind the cabin.

His reverie was broken by John Larsen's voice calling out, "Hello, the house, anyone home?" By the time that he had rinsed his hands and picked up his rifle, he heard John saying, "Let's get out of this rain and into the cabin. Scott and Buzz must be around, smoke is . . ." Scott heard the cabin door close as he hurried through the downpour to Salem and Prince, taking them into the barn. He returned to the cabin and entered, finding John and Richard Nelson warming their hands above the stove.

"Hello, gentlemen. Welcome to the Myrtlewood Grove, Richard."

From behind her father, Melissa asked, "Am I welcome too, Scott?"

Scott was surprised at her presence but not at a loss for words, "Of course, Melissa. You're always welcome at this ranch. It's good to see you again, but Buzz will be sorry that he missed you. He's hunting upriver. You folks sure picked lousy weather for visiting. Isn't there any school today? Can you stay . . ."

"Whoa!" Melissa said as she laughed merrily, "The first time that we met I couldn't get you to say even a simple hello. Today you are talking nonstop." Holding Scott's gaze, she continued, "I'm glad to see you again, Scott. While I have the courage, I want to apologize for my behavior this past year. I hope we can remain good friends." As Scott smiled and nodded, Melissa laughed nervously, and added, "But let's not discuss 'you-know-who' today."

Richard reminded Scott, "It's Sunday today, or Melissa and I would be working. By the way, Winsor has offered me my old job back next month. I'm feeling better with the winter behind us. I hope that you freighting partners can find a replacement for me. I know George is very busy. Did you know that the Hermanns are considering buying the store?"

Scott exclaimed, "That's good news! I wonder if he needs any help?"

Melissa responded, "Yes, Mary is worried about financing such a venture. We've become close friends, and I can understand her preference for security. With two lovely children like Angela and Junior, I'd feel the same way."

John opened the door to verify that the rain had stopped falling, and offered, "If I can borrow your rifle, Scott, I'll find Buzz while you show Richard and Melissa your ranch. Of course we accept your offer to stay for dinner, what are you serving?"

"Richard and I will catch enough trout to feed us, although I expect you hunters to return with venison."

The visit was enjoyable to all, regardless of the rain showers falling all day. True to Scott's challenge, a feast of trout and venison graced the dinner table. The visitors left before dusk, Melissa and a deer quarter on Prince and Richard riding Salem. John led the way and Scott walked alongside of Prince as far as slide ridge. Buzz had monopolized Melissa's attention all afternoon, but given the opportunity to visit, the two young people were rather quiet as only polite conversation passed between them. As he stood watching them pass from view, Scott thought, What a wonderful day this has been.

****

A short week later, George sent one of the teamsters to the ranch with a message. Since it was the first time that a message had been sent by teamster, Scott concluded that it was urgent, and he joined the man in returning to Port Orford. It was fully dark when they reached town and separated. Scott walked toward the Hermanns' house, thinking, it's a lot faster riding into town instead of walking. I wonder what George needs?

After hugs from Mary and the kids, Scott accepted a late place at the supper table for leftover stew and mince meat pie. "I've got this down to a science, arriving in time for supper. George, you can't believe the kind of skullduggery that a bachelor will commit to eat Mary's home cooking."

George handed Scott a glass of brandy as they sat in the parlor to discuss business. George outlined a special job which was to start Monday, "John should return tomorrow with the horses. You'll have to help Kenneth Hansen stow his cargo after church services."

Scott's natural question was, "Who's Kenneth Hansen? And what am I hauling?"

"Kenneth Hansen is Director of the Providence Colony, a group of people coming to the Coquille River to settle. The company disembarked today from the Columbia and are eager to get to their destination. They have horses, cows, and sheep, all of which are being pastured at the fort. The Army wants them moved immediately, but tomorrow is the Sabbath. Hansen needs a guide as much as he needs a freighter, although your horses will carry a maximum load. I arranged a barter when Hansen informed me that he was short on cash. He has three cows carrying calves, which are unable to travel fast, and he offered them to me. I insisted that he sell you one of his three bulls in the deal. If you get the Colony and its belongings to Coquille before April 30th, you get the bull at half-price as a bonus."

As Mary sat down after tucking the children in bed, Scott agreed. "I'll meet Mr. Hansen tomorrow and set up our freight train to Coquille. Melissa told me that you're thinking about buying the store. Can I be of any help?"

George looked askance at Mary, as he answered tentatively, "I'd like to be my own boss, but Mary's worried about the money. We've agreed to wait until summer before any decision is made."

Scott rode stirrup to stirrup with Kenneth Hansen as they led the Providence Colony on the trail north. John and the Hansen son rode drag with Scott's four animals. John would take them to the ranch and tell Buzz their schedule, before rejoining the train. When they sighted a small band of Quah-to-mahs at their lodges north of the Sixes River, the newcomers became excited. Scott told their leader, "These Indians are not a threat with squaws and children in camp. Besides I'm their friend and neighbor. Wait on this side, while I ride across and talk to them."

Chief Sixes' old uncle was subchief for a hunt. He was friendly, and agreeable to the horses crossing through his village. Scott had Kenneth Hansen present him with a bag of sugar candy when they were introduced. John Larsen caught up with the train before dark, as Scott made camp south of the Floras River.

Tuesday they crossed the Floras and passed the settlement some were calling Bandon, following the Coquille River all that afternoon and the next day before reaching the Colony's destination. On their return trip south the two horses were being ridden, and crossing the Floras was much simpler. Scott pointed to a new cabin and barn, near the river, "When did that new settler move in?"

John had met the man on his last trip, and replied, "The Langlois family has lived here a month or so." Tongue in cheek, he added, "They have several milk cows, but no bull."

"I think my bull may be needed here. Maybe I can barter for stud services."

When they left the Langlois place the next day they were leading a yearling—payment for use of the bull for the month of June.
Scott thought, George has done it again. This bull will pay a handsome dividend. We'll have to figure that factor in determining
shares when we meet next week. He'd better stay in the corral for
security as well as stud service. He hummed a happy tune to himself as they approached the Sixes where he found that the Indians
had returned to their main village.

****

Scott mounted Prince, and led the cow up the Sixes River trail,
while John continued on toward Port Orford. As the valley narrowed at the cut west of slide ridge, Scott was surprised to see
Buzz step onto the trail ahead of him.

"Been waiting for you, or for that trespasser I cut sign on this
morning. If I'm right, we still have two white men somewhere
around our east pasture." The Old-Timer paused, and conjectured,
"Could be Dutch's gang. I figured more men might be coming,
and I could stop them at this bottleneck."

Scott had listened carefully, and trusted Buzz in reading signs
correctly. He dismounted and directed his partner, "Bring the cow
into the flat before you turn her loose. I'm going ahead on foot—
less noise that way." He trotted to the bend of the river and then
sprinted across the loose slate on slide ridge, alternating his pace
to the cascading creek near the ranch. He reached the top of the
knoll and caught his breath until he heard Buzz and the livestock
behind him. He crossed the gully above the cabin and came in
behind the barn, searching it carefully before checking the flat.
His bull was in the corral with three cows, and seemed undisturbed.
Scott checked the cabin, shed, and outhouse before crossing the
pasture to the myrtlewood grove. Buzz soon joined him, and without discussion, Scott mounted Prince behind his partner and they
headed for the east pasture. Buzz stopped the horse as he saw a

man kneeling in the tall grass, dressing out an animal. Scott whispered, "Is that one of our cows or a deer? You circle around him on the horse and I'll search for the second man." He slid off Prince and moved quickly to a copse of trees closer to the kneeling man.

A shot rang out to his left, and Prince squealed in pain. As Scott brought his rifle to bear on the woods ahead, he saw one of Dutch's friends stand and lift his rifle to fire. Scott's sights fell on the man's chest as he squeezed the trigger. His bullet struck true, knocking the ambusher over backwards, rifle falling askew. The butcher in the pasture was running away when a shot from Buzz's rifle knocked his legs out from under him.

Scott moved forward carefully, and finding the ambusher dead, he moved into the pasture looking for the wounded butcher. Passing near the animal carcass, he saw it was one of his cows. Buzz called out, "I've picked this would-be rustler clean of weapons, Scott. He passed out when he saw his own blood."

Buzz hurried back to attend his crippled horse. With his encouragement, Prince hobbled to the barn on three legs, before collapsing on his left side. The Old-Timer cleansed a deep wound in the horse's right shoulder, lamenting his lack of doctoring skills.

Meanwhile Scott had applied a tourniquet above the thief's knee, and then toted him to the barn over his shoulder. He tied the wounded man's hands behind him, and instructed his partner, "Buzz, I'm going to town to fetch help, clobber that rustler if he makes a peep."

Scott set off at a trot down the trail, remembering to watch for the third man in the rustling party. Seeing movement in the distance, he left the trail and worked forward through the trees. He quickly returned to the open trail as he recognized John Larsen riding Salem toward him. Scott waved him forward, calling out, "We've had trouble with Dutch's gang. Buzz and I are all right, but Prince is crippled. I was just coming for your help."

John responded, "I saw one of the gang skulking in the woods this side of Elk River. He took off in the direction of Garrison

Lake when I challenged him. I came right back to tell you. How many of them have you seen?"

"Buzz said that three men were in the valley, but the man you saw left this morning. I killed a man who ambushed Buzz, and the other rustler has a nasty leg wound. I'd like to use Salem to take these two rustlers to Fort Orford. We'll go in tonight and return to Sixes as soon as that new military commander will allow. If we have to stay, I'd appreciate your riding back to attend Prince." Their arrival in town went unnoticed until they drove to the gate at Fort Orford and asked to see the military commander.

The Duty N.C.O. was Scott's Sergeant friend from the arm-wrestling tournament, and he expedited the process for reporting and took charge of the wounded rustler and his dead partner. Scott never did hear the officer's name, but they had a mutual friend in Lt. Wyman. Scott's reputation combined with testimony from his two friends was sufficient to close the case. The wounded rustler would be placed aboard a ship sailing for San Francisco in the morning. The Sergeant escorted his friend to the gate, remarking nervously, "The Army can use your beef, Mr. McClure. How shall the Quartermaster pay you when you bring it in?"

Scott replied, "Good, Sergeant. Have the money paid to George Hermann at the store, when Buzz brings the carcass in tomorrow. Now tell me what else is bothering you?"

"Well, sir, the Commander doesn't want you chasing the third rustler, the fellow who wasn't seen on your ranch. Any questions, sir?"

Scott laid his hand on the Sergeant's shoulder, and responded earnestly, "You are quite clear, my friend. As far as I am concerned the matter is closed. I'll carry it no further."

****

John rode back to the ranch to tend to Prince, while Scott decided that it was early enough to talk to George. A light was visible in Hermann's parlor as he approached the house. He heard voices inside as he knocked on the door, and was surprised to see the Nelsons sitting in the parlor when George invited him in.

Scott stammered, "I didn't mean to intrude, maybe I should ... no ... everyone may as well hear ... not pleasant ... I do have to go home soon."

His incoherence puzzled everyone except George, who sensed trouble and asked, "Did you have trouble on the trip to Coquille? John isn't back yet. Where is he?"

"The trip went fine. John came back to help me with a problem on the ranch." Taking a deep breath, he addressed Melissa, "Please hear me out without interruption." He then related the story of Dutch's gang in the Shix village, his threat to them, and his running the six men out of the valley. His narration shifted to the gun fight in defense of his ranch and his subsequent report to the Army.

George asked the question uppermost in everyone's mind, "Are Buzz and John all right?" When Scott nodded, George continued, "What about your livestock?"

"I lost one cow, and Prince is seriously wounded. He'll never pull a wagon again, George. You'd better forget our freighting runs until we partners can meet next week."

Melissa was shaken by Scott's story, and sympathized, "I'm sorry that you had to shoot that man in self-defense, but I'm happy that you and Buzz are safe. But Hans was not on your Sixes ranch, was he?"

"That is correct, Melissa, and the Army considers the matter closed, only two men were involved."

Richard faced his daughter and posed their dilemma, "Hans will be given an opportunity to explain his involvement with these men, but how can we believe him after he told us those terrible stories about Scott killing an innocent traveler in Scottsburg and murdering Indians at Humbug?"

Scott snorted in rebuttal, but held his tongue as Melissa confessed, "That was why I was angry with you when I arrived in

Port Orford, Scott. I'm ashamed that I could believe you capable of such savagery and deceit. However, Hans telling us a slanted tale of gossip doesn't make him a thief. I've apologized for my behavior, but I won't repeat my error and condemn a friend without hearing him out."

Scott returned to the ranch and prepared a hot meal for Buzz, taking it to the barn where his friend was nursing his faithful horse. He awoke in the morning to a joyful shout from the barn, "Attaboy, Prince, stay on your feet. Hey Scott, come out here. I'm a fair doctor after all."

Dressing quickly, Scott ran to his partner's side, expecting to witness a miracle cure, and hid his disappointment when he saw Prince standing shakily, unable to put weight on his right front leg. Buzz opined, "He'll live, but he'll never be able to work." He looked somewhat belligerently at Scott, as he declared, "We're not going to sell Prince to the butcher. He can be put to pasture here."

Scott laughed happily and agreed, "Anything you say, Old-Timer! But you'd better get some rest, I'll do the chores."

"Not yet, young fellow. I want to show you my beehives. That's how those yahoos snuck into the pasture, I was across the river on Rocky Point digging out my queen bees. We'll have honey this summer."

****

William Tichenor and his daughter Ellen rode into the ranch and found the partners on the river by the myrtlewood grove, fishing for their noon meal. Scott greeted them warmly, "Welcome to our myrtlewood grove, Captain." Helping Ellen dismount, he offered, "Would you like to cook these fish?"

"Yes, thank you. Can I eat one too?" the precocious child replied.

Laughing, he gave her a string of small trout, "Take these fish over to the fire pit and help Buzz grill them." Turning to his other visitor, he suggested, "Let me show you my ranch, Captain. We've got half-an-hour to visit before our picnic dinner."

Walking across the pasture, Tichenor mused, "You have cleared a great deal of land for pasture. Could you board twenty steers for a few weeks? A friend has chartered space on my ship for the cattle. He plans to fatten them here and sell them during the fall and winter. Are you interested?"

"For the summer I can handle them, but they would have to be gone by mid-November. My winter feed is limited or I would increase my own herd. My price will be ten percent of their estimated sale value, or two steers."

"That's fair enough if you agree to take delivery in Port Orford and trail them to your ranch. Furthermore, it'll be your responsibility to bring the steers back one at a time for butchering."

"Agreed. Send a messenger when your ship returns with the cattle. Now let's eat your daughter's cooking."

Buzz complimented Ellen as they ate the fish, "Ellen's a good cook as well as a pretty girl. And she speaks Tututni pretty good."

Ellen showed off her special ability by speaking fluent Tututni. Scott told her, "Ellen, you talk fine English and Tututni. I know Miss Nelson teaches English at school, but where did you learn the Indian language?"

"I just learned it. I play with my Indian friends and talk to them," the little girl replied proudly. Captain Tichenor beamed with satisfaction, approving his daughter's actions and answer. She was obviously her father's favorite child.

****

George had asked the partners in the Port Orford and Umpqua Freight Company to meet on Sunday afternoon, while the children were playing at the Tichenors. Mary cooked dinner after church services and the friends socialized during the meal. The men gathered in the parlor to discuss business, and Mary started washing dishes. George laughed and called out to his wife, "Mary, leave the dishes until later. You can't hear anything from the kitchen."

George gave a lengthy business report on the company, the gist being that each partner had $173 in cash and a quarter-share of the company assets.

Scott complimented him, "Good job, George. We've made a tidy profit during the past year, but with Prince crippled and the ranch prospering, I think we should sell our assets. What do you want to do, John?"

"I agree with your suggestion. I can buy new lines and nets with my money and spend more time fishing. I'm tired of working as a teamster. What do you think, Buzz?"

"Well, my bees and my hunting will keep me busy enough, although I'll go along with any decision that you men make. George?"

"I anticipated dissolution of our freighting partnership, and I have another set of figures for settlement right here. If I keep the stable and corral out back, your three shares are each $244, and mine is $120."

Scott criticized his summary and made a suggestion, "You didn't give yourself a good deal, and where's Harvey Master's share? I propose an amendment to George's fine report. We should send Harvey $25 and a letter of appreciation for serving as our agent, and the three of us will each collect $225. George will receive $152." The proposal was approved and the partnership ended.

After Buzz rode Salem back to the Sixes, Scott walked up to South Branch to visit the Port Orfords. The Indians in the village were pleased to see him, and Charlie greeted him in place of the absent chief. However friendly these people were to him, a change of attitude had occurred which made Scott uncomfortable. He thought, I guess that I'm feeling guilty because the Tututni are suffering and I can't help them. Even Charlie has changed, looking more like a 'Rascal' every time that I see him. I hope that we can remain friends. His mood remained pensive as he returned to town and spent a pleasant evening with the Nelsons.

The next morning he ordered a hand pump and casing for the well being dug on the ranch. He also purchased lumber for a second room on his cabin. The partners would start cutting trees for the walls tomorrow.

****

The summer days were busy as Scott led his bull to Langlois for stud services, the three Colony cows dropped calves, and several additional cows were carrying calves. Prince had assumed the role of watchdog over the cattle as he frolicked in the pasture. Buzz claimed that he was an old cow pony who couldn't quit working, not dissimilar from himself.

Buzz drove four of Tichenor's cattle to town in late August, and picked up a window to finish the bedroom addition to the cabin. He invited the Nelsons to visit the ranch over the weekend now that the addition was completed.

As it turned out, Richard worked with Buzz in finishing the interior of the bedroom while Melissa and Scott played. Father and daughter arrived Friday afternoon in time for a grilled trout cookout in the myrtlewood grove. Melissa laughed gaily as Buzz pampered Prince, feeding him a deboned trout and a biscuit smothered in honey. She quipped, "Who ever heard of a horse eating grilled trout?"

The Old-Timer cackled, retorting, "Missy, you're talking about a member of our family. He's like a pet watchdog. Go on Prince, watch the cattle!" and shooed the horse back into the pasture.

The next morning, Scott told Buzz, "Sleeping in the barn isn't so bad, our guest is cooking breakfast. Mmmm, it sure smells good." Melissa offered to bake a blackberry pie for supper, and naturally Scott refused the simple option of picking berries near the beehives. They went exploring across the river where Buzz said there was a patch of small blackberries growing. During the summer the river was shallow, particularly where it was ten-twenty feet wide.

Scott selected such a crossing broken by several rivulets running through a gravel bar.

"We can jump from island to island, and reach the other bank without getting our feet wet," Scott suggested, demonstrating with a short hop to the first gravel islet.

"Don't you dare leave me alone, Scott Addis McClure. I can't jump that far. A gentleman would carry me to the other side."

Scott leapt back, and with a flourish, bent forward to pick Melissa up, but she stepped around him, saying, "Oh no, it's safer for me to ride piggyback," and climbed on his back. "Giddyup, Scott! And don't you dare drop me in the river," she ordered as he waded across the river in knee deep water. Climbing the bank on the other side, he continued walking.

"Whoa, old horsy! You can let me down now."

Scott teased her, "No, Missy, I like you're hugging me."

Melissa released her hold on his neck and grabbed his ears, twisting lightly until he released her. She slapped the back of his head, and laughed, "That was not a hug. I was just holding on for dear life. You'd know if I gave you a hug."

When they found several berry vines clinging to the ground, they ate as many as they put in their sack. From one point on the hillside, the entire ranch was visible, a vista of yellowing hay, green pasture, and verdant forest. Scott pointed out their fishing hole, commenting, "Buzz and your dad aren't all work. That's them fishing under that myrtlewood tree across from Rocky Point."

Returning by a different route, Melissa walked over a natural log bridge, crossing the river without Scott's assistance. He teased Melissa again, "I made a mistake coming this way. Sure you don't want me to carry you across?" She laughed as they walked through the pasture, slipping her hand into his.

While Melissa cooked supper and Richard finished sanding the bedroom window pane, Scott sought out the absent Buzz. "Sure enough, he's down at his beehives," Scott mumbled to himself. "What's he up to?"

Straightening his back as Scott approached, Buzz asked, "Why aren't you squiring your girl?"

Scott chuckled, shaking his head, "That 'your girl' has a nice sound. I came to see what you're up to, Old-Timer. Why do we need more honey?"

"Well, I milked those Salem cows and while I'm waiting for the cream to separate, I'm gathering honey. How does honey whipped cream over blackberry pie sound to you?"

Sunday night as Scott lay in bed, reliving his memories of the Nelsons' visit, he thought that the sweet dessert which Melissa and Buzz had concocted epitomized the weekend of memorable experiences.

****

As Scott drove the last six head of cattle from Tichenor's herd into Port Orford in late November, he was relieved. One of his seven haystacks had been consumed already, and it wasn't even winter. His bull was at Langlois again, and this time his payment was twenty bushels of oats. With eight calves due before Spring, his herd should grow to twenty head. He might have to sell beef this winter if the weather was severe. He needed more hay if he was going to maintain a larger herd.

He entered the store and greeted George expansively, "How does it feel to be the owner? Are all the papers signed?"

George smiled proudly, trying to look modest and failing. He answered, "I feel great, even if I am under an appalling mortgage burden, and the money which I owe you. I figure it will take me three years to pay off my debts."

Scott reminded him, "You can use the $100 in gold which you're holding for me."

"No, you may need cash for your ranch. You can help me by trading meat, either beef or venison, for your supplies. As long as I can limit my cash outlay locally, I can pay my San Francisco suppliers."

Scott asked, "What's the latest news? Any Indian problems?"

"Yes, several incidents have been reported along the Rogue River, but our local bands have been quiet. Sally Dubois was cursed on the street by a prospector last week. Jacques heard about it and went after the fellow with a loaded rifle. The man was smart enough to leave town before Dubois found him. Jacques was so upset that he couldn't speak a word of English; I do believe he meant to use that rifle." George paused. "There doesn't seem to be a solution to the Indian problem. By the way, your adversary, Dutch Schmidt, is prospecting or whatever at Gold Beach. John Larsen told me that he'd heard Weasel was there too."

"Birds of a feather! As long as they gather at the Rogue, I can't complain. Tell Mary and the children hello. I'm going to the schoolroom and visit Melissa before I head home. Buzz is watching a sick cow—one whose calf isn't due for a few weeks, and won't sleep a wink until I relieve him."

Christmas dinner at the Hermanns had become a tradition for their small group of friends. This year the Nelsons joined the gathering and enjoyed the spiritual warmth of friendship in the Christmas season. Angela was especially pleased that her teacher was present and volunteered to put Junior to bed. Scott was shocked at the haggard and pale countenance of Melissa's father, who ignored his illness and joined in the merriment. Gifts were exchanged, and one present stood out. Mary had sewn a dress from material Scott had purchased in Gardiner, and they gave it jointly to Melissa. She was so pleased that she changed into the new dress and modeled it for her friends. She thanked both of them effusively with a kiss on the cheek.

Scott bantered, "The quilt you made for me is a beautiful gift. I'd better kiss you also." Everyone laughed at Scott's wishful thought, but Melissa good-naturedly offered her cheek for his kiss.

After dinner Scott followed her into the kitchen, "You wash and I'll wipe," he said as he took a dish towel from Mary. When she tactfully left them alone, he asked, "Richard told me that he's too ill to work this winter. How is his health? Can you manage without his salary? I'm being personal, I know, but if I asked your father, I'm afraid that he would be offended."

Melissa stopped washing dishes and met Scott's anxious gaze. She smiled to remove the sting of her response, "You're being nosy, but thank you for asking me. You're right about father's feelings." She paused to organize her thoughts, glancing at the parlor door to ensure their privacy, and continued, "Father couldn't work in Marysville. Did you know that it's called Corvallis now? When you visited after he'd seen that Portland doctor, he'd given up all hope of ever working again. I really believe that he didn't expect to live through the winter. It frightened me more than I can express to see him so despondent. When we both received job offers in Port Orford, I knew that you and Mary had recommended us, but I doubt that father has ever realized how much support that our friends have provided." She laughed before resuming her explanation, "Buzz is our true friend; we can't keep many secrets from each other with him around. For instance, I know that father needed the freight company last winter more than the business needed him. This summer he saved every cent that he could, anticipating that his lungs couldn't take the winter weather. I offered to go to California with him, but he's happy and secure here. That's why we don't move out of the hotel. Grandma Knapp watches out for him when I'm teaching." Melissa paused as tears formed in her eyes, "How is his health? His body is dying, but his spirit is alive and hopeful. What more could I ask for?" Melissa put her head on Scott's shoulder and quietly cried. Scott held her gently but wisely said nothing. She stepped back after a few moments, and smiled wanly at Scott, "Thank you for being my friend."

****

New Year's Day 1855 brought uncommon severity in snow and wind. The safest refuge for wild animals lay in the river bottoms. Deer and coyotes were seen often along the Sixes, and the cattle had to be protected from the canine predators. Three calves were born and Buzz spent his days with them and their mothers. He was very upset when a bull calf died during its third night.

Scott rode Salem around the ranch daily, checking on live-stock and doling out the precious haystack fodder. Prince ran be-side them to chase deer away from the stacks or to drive a stray back into the herd. Scott was invigorated by the desperate condi-tions, being stimulated into an active mode while outside, but ap-preciating the warmth of the cabin in the evening.

Buzz shook him awake early in the morning, "Listen . . . I heard Prince . . . there . . . he's challenging. . . ." Both men dressed quickly and checked their rifles before stepping outside.

Scott heard Prince squeal in pain as Buzz repeated, "He's fight-ing to protect the herd," he broke off as a cougar roared, "My God, he's fighting a big cat." He discharged his rifle in the air to frighten off the predator, as Scott ran toward the noise. Soon the horse was visible, downed on a patch of snow, struggling to rise and defend his charges. A gray-brown shape crossed the snow a hun-dred feet ahead. Scott snapped a hurried shot with no visible ef-fect as the cat disappeared in the woods.

Buzz was kneeling, holding Prince's head to his chest. "He's done for, Scott. The cat hamstrung him and then clawed his throat."

"Do you want me to handle this for you?" Scott asked his grieving friend.

"No, you pack some vittles and bring me shells. I'll take care of my horse." As Scott entered the cabin, a single shot rang out in the night.

Salem, the bull "Francis," and the two calves with their moth-ers were closed in the barn before Scott returned to the pasture and handed Buzz his shells. The Old-Timer was dressing the car-cass stoically, and as Scott approached, stated woefully, "Can't let good horsemeat go to waste, but don't expect me to eat any. We can present it to the Quah-to-mahs as a winter gift."

Scott agreed, "I expect that you're right, Buzz, I know I don't want any either. Let's get on the track of that cat. It'll be daylight in less than an hour."

Buzz followed sign across the pasture without hesitation, but was forced to his hands and knees in the bordering trees, moving forward with all of his senses attuned with nature. As they reached the river bank, he stood erect and told Scott, "You hit the cougar with that one shot so he'll be twice as dangerous—nothing like a wounded cat to challenge the hunter. He entered the creek here, but I need daylight to pick up his sign across the creek." He hesitated and expressed a second opinion, "For that matter he could double back and be stalking us. It makes good sense to wait for daylight. I doubt that he'll go far, bleeding as he is."

The gray overcast held back the daylight until both men grew impatient. Buzz finally made a move, telling his partner, "You cover me as I cross the river and look for sign. I haven't heard any sound from that cougar, but that doesn't mean that he isn't laid up somewhere over there." Buzz waded the shallow stream, signaling blood on an alder sapling growing on the gravel inlet, and then climbed the far bank, waving Scott forward. The two hunters covered each other as they tracked the big cat into the hills for three miles. Full daylight made reading sign easier, and both men sensed that they were very near the still bleeding animal. Scott was leading when he noticed an abnormality in the sign, and as he waved Buzz forward, he mounted a large boulder to better survey the hillside.

"Read that sign, Buzz. Our quarry is acting up. What do you make of it?"

"He simply fell down, quite recently I'd say. Can you see his track from up there?"

"Yes, for maybe eighty feet, then . . . nothing. Maybe he holed up in that cairn of boulders ahead of us. I'll cover you if you'll climb to that small knoll on the left, and you do likewise for me as I move to a spot above the cairn. If he's there, we'll just have to flush him out. He'll be fighting mad."

Both men had stood their positions for several minutes, and Scott was ready to move when he saw the dark stain on the back side of the boulder next to the cat's last sign. He was sure the cougar had been there, but was he still hiding was the question. Scott picked up an agate-sized pebble and threw it into the crevice near the blood stain. A second pebble followed without a re-action, and then Buzz took a hand, firing a round into the rocks. The cougar charged over the edge of the cairn, streaking toward the Old-Timer. Scott was prepared for the move but surprised at the speed of the wounded cougar. His bullet staggered the cat, slow-ing it down so Buzz's shot could kill it. Both men circled their fallen prey warily, before Scott nudged it with his rifle. Buzz stepped in and slit its throat in a single swift motion and immedi-ately stepped back.

"Had a friend over on the Klamath River that almost lost an arm to a 'dead' cougar. I'll be cautious around this cat until his hide hangs on our cabin wall."

Scott nodded vigorously, and added, "I'm glad cougars don't hunt this country very often. One such hunt will last me a life-time. Shall we tote this critter into the Shix village also? Maybe we can convince the squaws to prepare the hide for us. We don't need it on the wall, but we can use it on the bedroom floor."

The week of the cougar hunt remained cold and windy, and the haystacks shrank until only two stacks were left. Scott wor-ried aloud to Buzz, "We have only a bushel of oats for Salem and Francis. There is no reserve. I'm going to town with two cows to sell and try to buy some feed. It'll probably cost plenty in this season, but we'll soon have starving livestock if this weather per-sists. I'll remain at the hotel for a couple of days and fatten Salem up in the hotel stable."

The sun broke through the clouds as Scott neared Port Orford. He hoped that the change was a harbinger of a fair February. By the time he tied the cattle to the cornerpost of the store, people were advancing on George and Scott, eager to buy fresh beef. Only one ship had made port in three weeks, and supplies were low. An Army platoon marched down from the fort and commandeered one head, and his Sergeant friend said, "Thank you, Mr. McClure. The men are hungry for beef. The Quartermaster will pay Mr. Hermann for your cow."

When Scott turned around, the other head was being led into the back storeroom and the outer door was locked. Scott stabled his horse and returned to the store to watch people. Store shelves were being depleted by customers who were allowed to buy five pounds of meat for every five dollars in goods purchased. The shelves were all but bare when the last of the meat was sold.

George didn't have time to talk, so Scott walked around town visiting friends. Louie Knapp told him that John was fishing overnight. Scott found Richard Nelson reading an old newspaper in his room. "Put your coat on, Richard. I'll buy you a beer, and you'll tell me all the latest news."

As they sat in the tavern sipping beer, they overheard a prospector complain that gold claims in the areas were playing out. Richard answered his friend's unasked question, "A lot of gold miners agree with that fellow, but business is still booming and the town is growing. The Army's presence is good money for the town." Changing the subject, Richard suggested, "Why don't you stay over and spend the day with us? Tomorrow's Saturday and Melissa is home."

Scott walked over to the Hermann home after parting with Richard at the hotel. When Mary answered the door, she wasn't surprised to hear Scott begging, "Alms for the poor farmer, ma'am, or better yet, a seat at your supper table." Laughing she replied, "If you will accept an Irish stew, sir, you're invited. Do you realize my husband sold all the beef? The only pieces we have left are scraps of meat and bones—nutritious but probably not delicious."

"Mary Hermann, you can turn scraps into a gourmet's delight. How are the children?" Scott asked as he accepted a cup of coffee and relaxed. Their conversation brought Scott up-to-date on the Hermann family and Port Orford life. George came home after closing the store early, seeking Scott's advice.

"Your arrival with beef today was a boon. I have enough cash on hand to pay the mortgage off and buy a normal supply order from San Francisco, or I can double my order in anticipation of a profitable year. What do you think, Scott?"

Scott glanced at Mary before answering. "Being single, I'd probably gamble for growth and prosperity. But having a family makes a difference. I think that you should reduce your burden of debt. Would it help if I brought you more beef?"

"Yes, I can buy, or barter half the beef for some supplies from my competitors. For example, I know that the sutler's store has flour and sugar." George reluctantly added, "I guess you're right about paying the mortgage off. I know Mary agrees with you."

Thoughtfully, Scott concluded, "If you can be ready the day after tomorrow, I'll bring another cow to you. This time I'll bring it directly into your storeroom. Is there any feed in town?"

"No, the cold weather has eliminated any reserves in town, but there is a bushel or two of oats in my stable. Help yourself."

Angela came home and Junior woke up from his nap, so Uncle Scott entertained the children until supper was ready, and afterwards he told all of them the story of the cougar hunt.

Melissa was waiting for him in the hotel lobby. "Father told me that you were coming to see us, but he went to bed early. You wore him out today with walking, talking, and beer. It was good for him to get out, since the weather was bearable today. Let's take a walk around town before we turn in."

Sunlight blessed the next day as Scott and the Nelsons visited friends. John Larsen joined them for the midday meal, before he returned to the sea. Richard took a nap, allowing Melissa and Scott an opportunity to be alone with each other. When they returned to the hotel, Richard was waiting to say good-bye. "Scott, be sure and give my regards to Buzz. With spring coming maybe I can visit and do some fishing.

Scott responded promptly, "Why wait? The weather's fine, and I need another hand this week. I'm selling another cow tomorrow and Buzz wants to do some hunting. You could watch over our calves and feed the livestock. Why, you might find time to catch a few trout to cook for supper. Would payment in venison be all right?"

Richard smiled broadly, and agreed, "Venison would be fine. Melissa can make a deal with the Knapps for the meat. Let me get my things together." He hesitated, asking his daughter, "You'll be all right without me, won't you, dear?"

"Yes, father, I'll be just fine. You stay as long as you're needed. Maybe I can visit next Saturday overnight if one of you has time to escort me to the ranch." Richard raced upstairs for his clothes and fishing gear.

Scott suggested, "I'll come for you next Saturday morning. You and your father can return together that Sunday. He'll have had enough of us by then."

****

Several days after Scott had taken the Nelsons back to Port Orford, Charlie made his first visit to the ranch. While doing the chores together, Scott carried on a one-sided conversation. His usually garrulous friend was reticent and preoccupied. Scott leaned against the corral fence, and drew his friend out. "Why are you so quiet, Charlie? Is there more trouble for your father?"

Charlie nodded, and answered after a lengthy silence, "White men come . . . shake guns at Chat-al-hak-e-ah . . . big man hit me . . . not good . . . maybe me fight . . ."

Suspecting Dutch's gang, he described the men and their leader. Charlie nodded vigorously, adding a Tututni word which Scott didn't understand. He pantomimed a fifth member until Scott knew that the Weasel was now with the gang.

After Charlie left, Scott fumed in frustration at the injustices committed by his fellow citizens on the local Indians, accepting the fact that he couldn't change the inevitable result. But he could talk to the military commander about Dutch's activities. He could also visit the Port Orfords band at their village on South Branch; his presence might have a salutary effect on their feelings toward white men. He would ride into Port Orford as soon as Buzz returned from hunting.

****

The next day Scott dismounted before the hotel porch, and called to Richard, "How about trading that sunny chair for a shady one in the tavern?" His friend nodded enthusiastically and the two men strolled down the street. Scott noticed that a horse was running down the beach from the direction of Hubbard Creek, and as he recognized the young Tichenor girl, he thought, Ellen's been playing with her Indian friends again.

Richard told Scott that he was working at the mill office parttime, and he was ready for full-time work when business improved. They were near the tavern when the Tichenor girl raced her horse up the street, calling, "Mr. McClure! Mr. McClure!" She pulled her horse in, and took a deep breath, before continuing, "White men killed an Indian in their village. My friends asked for you by name, 'Scott', saying they need help."

"Thank you, Ellen. I'll go to them." He turned to Richard, and bade him, "Go to the fort and tell the Commander. If he isn't on post, tell our Sergeant friend." Scott turned and ran to the hotel, mounted Salem in a bound. Digging his heels into Salem, he raced through town on the trail to the Port Orfords village.

As Salem pranced into the village, Scott sat firmly in the saddle, rifle at ready, as he scanned the lodges. He espied Chat-al-hak-e-ah kneeling beside the lifeless body of Charlie. No white men were in sight as he dismounted beside the Chief, signing grief at his loss. "Dutch" was repeated by several Indians as they pointed to the eastern ridge, encouraging Scott to pursue the murderer. Dutch had departed on a foot trail through the underbrush, so he left Salem in the village and set a fast pace on foot, relinquishing stealth for speed. He recognized the topography, having traveled this route once before, and as he approached a cut in the ridge, he slid into the brush and crawled forward thinking, there should be a deadfall to the right which overlooks that cut in the ridge. If anyone is planning to ambush me, I'll hold the high ground.

From his hidden loft, he watched three of the gang settle into the rocks along the trail. Dutch and Weasel were descending the trail into Hubbard Creek, evidently heading for their claim near the Port Orfords former village site. Scott backtracked a hundred feet and started down a game trail which would bring him to the creek bottom between the murderers and their camp. He saw no point in challenging the three ambushers in the cut.

Scott was standing near a tall cedar when the two men traversed a small clearing by the creek. Scott had planned his strategy carefully, using available cover to his advantage and keeping his adversaries in the open. If necessary, he could shoot three times before they could retreat to the forest. He thought, their best choice is to come straight at me, but surprise is a great confuser. I may not have to shoot at all.

They walked toward him unaware of his presence, and Scott stepped to his right, slammed his breech closed noisily, and growled as menacingly as possible, "Stop right there! Drop your rifles! . . . Drop them or die!" Scott breathed a sigh of partial relief when Weasel panicked and threw his gun aside. "Drop that rifle, Dutch, or use it!" Scott warned, and Schmidt reluctantly complied.

"Schmidt, lay face down and put your hands behind you." Dutch snorted in anger, but did as he was told.

"Weasel, take this rawhide and tie his hands," Scott ordered as he threw a cord to the trembling miscreant.

Dutch mumbled something to Weasel and Scott said, "Shut up, Dutch!" He changed position silently and saw Weasel palm Dutch's knife as he stood erect. Scott was waiting as the small man turned toward Scott's former position, and thwacked him solidly above his ear with the butt of his rifle. The knife fell from his nerveless hand as he collapsed atop Dutch. Scott threw all their weapons in the flowing creek and with the bore of his rifle at Dutch's head, picked up Weasel and threw him aside like a sack of potatoes. He tightened his captive's bonds and effortlessly lifted him to his feet by his coat collar.

"Walk ahead of me downstream and keep your mouth shut. I'm taking you into Fort Orford on a charge of murder."

Dutch ignored Scott's warning, saying loudly, "You can't arrest me. I'm not going with you!" He began running upstream, yelling loudly for his cronies. Scott caught him easily and the murderer felt the kiss of a rifle butt. Scott threw Dutch over his shoulder and started up the steep game trail which he had descended a few minutes before. Slipping noisily on the rough hillside, he managed to reach the top without seeing Dutch's gang. He could hear one of them shout as Weasel was discovered. Working his way along the ridge to his left, he moved quickly, and this time stealthily, toward the Indian village. Twice he paused and listened for pursuit, but heard nothing. When he came to the foot path, he searched the softer soil only to find his footprint was the most recent sign. He hiked Dutch up on his shoulder and trotted down the trail, not an easy task with the murderer's size and dead weight. When he entered the village, he startled the Indians, but they disappeared into the forest as he signed that he was being followed.

Chat-al-hak-e-ah thought Scott had brought Dutch to him for punishment, and when Scott threw Dutch's form over his saddle, a volatile argument ensued. Scott was obdurate before the Chief, the murderer would be judged by the Army at Fort Orford. He rode out of the village with bitter words and feelings behind him. Only their great respect for Charlie's friend stayed the Indians' weapon-filled hands. Scott understood in that perspicacious moment, that he could never return to these people in friendship. They would turn their back on him; he was an outcast without a place in their society.

As he rode the length of Port Orford, people stopped in the streets to follow his route. No man challenged the grim-faced man who stared straight ahead. They had heard of the Indian killing, and recognized Dutch tied across the saddle. Salem was drooping wearily by the time Scott rode through the gate and stopped before the Duty N.C.O.'s office. He cut the rawhide bindings and dropped the semiconscious murderer to the ground before he dismounted himself.

"Lock this man in your guardhouse. The charge is murder," Scott instructed the Corporal on duty. "I'll report to your Commander."

Scott found Richard sitting in the C.O.'s outer office and learned that a detail had been sent to Hubbard Creek to question Schmidt. The Commander called Scott into his office and received his report. He was not enthusiastic about an Indian killing, but he would uphold territorial law and bring the accused to trial.

Scott related the story of Dutch's capture to Richard as they walked the horse to the hotel stable. Even though Scott was relaxed and his face more pleasant, people still gave him a wide berth. Scott thought to himself, am I going to be a pariah to my own people as well? If so, then so be it. I think that I've done the right thing.

John was waiting for them at the hotel stable, and offered, "I'll take care of Salem. Mary and Melissa are preparing supper for us at the Hermanns. Scott, people are talking about the sorry condition of your prisoner."

"He's in a lot better shape than the man he murdered. The Chief wanted vengeance something fierce, but I knew the Army would likely hang him if he took retribution on a white man. I'm no longer welcome in their village, and I suppose that covers you as well."

Richard defended Scott with details of the report which he had overheard, "Dutch's gang was laying an ambush, but Scott fooled them. Five to one odds, and he brought Schmidt out alive."

Scott helped John rub Salem down and then gave his tired horse a bucket of oats. The three men walked to Hermanns shoulder to shoulder, Scott conspicuously carrying his Sharps.

George and William Tichenor cut across an empty lot to meet them in front of the house. Captain Tichenor spoke, "I'm sailing immediately, but I wanted to give you my support. Ellen told me what the Indian children said. Schmidt is a murdering scoundrel, but I doubt if any white man will be convicted for killing an Indian. Good-bye, my friend."

Jacques and Sally were sitting in the parlor as the men entered, and the two cooks left the kitchen when they heard voices. After a hesitant silence, Jacques spoke for the friends gathered in the room, "*Mon ami,* you have my . . . support."

Sally added quickly, "Your sense of justice is right but no white man will be convicted of killing an Indian. There will be more trouble when that killer is freed."

Melissa asked her father, "Are you all right, father? I'm glad that you helped Scott, but you look a little tired."

"Yes, dear! It was quite a day." Everyone was attentive as Richard told the entire story, looking to Scott for confirmation of facts. He had listened carefully to Scott's report at the fort, and since he seemed to savor the limelight, Scott relaxed and let him talk, answering questions after Richard completed his narration.

****

Scott was weeding his garden when John Larsen called out from the knoll, "Good morning, Scott! I see you're doing serious farming today."

"Hello, John. Buzz won last night's poker game. He's hunting while I'm tilling the garden." Scott observed his friend's doleful expression, and concluded, "Your news must be bad. I expect that Dutch Schmidt is free. What happened?"

"Captain Tichenor and Sally Dubois were right. Dutch was found not guilty. He and his gang are celebrating in town and cursing your name. People generally agree with the verdict but a lot of them are pleased that Dutch was taken down a peg or two." John mulled another thought, before venturing, "I think that gang will challenge you by harassing the Quah-to-mahs. If you'll have me, I'd like to hire on for a few days. Maybe I can win another fishing trip out of you."

Scott replied, "Thanks, I can use your help, but I doubt if we'll have time for poker. Go downriver and watch the trail. I'll round up Buzz and we'll meet you there."

The two men trudged across slide ridge and beyond the cut without meeting John. Becoming wary, Scott moved ahead, signaling Buzz to cover him. A shot sounded to the southwest, and Scott broke into a run, crossing the Sixes and heading for a rise in the trail ahead. Buzz moved to his left flank, passing him as Scott slowed to a walk. He conjectured to himself, "If that's John, he must be on high ground to the west. If he'd fire again, I could locate his position." A second shot was fired in answer to his wish. "I was right. I can see him now."

Buzz fired a round in the air as Scott approached the crest of the trail, and two steps later he saw Dutch and his friends spread over the trail, searching for the shooters. Scott emulated his Scottsburg ambush, standing stock still a hundred yards directly before their adversaries. Weasel squealed in fright and dove into the ditch when he beheld Scott's figure in the trail. Buzz fired a round into the ground near one of the men, and the culprit immediately lowered his rifle. Another round from John struck a tree near Weasel, who burrowed deeper into his hole. Scott stared forebodingly at Dutch, until the murderer turned tail and waved his men south. He followed the gang to the Elk, and when they had crossed, he fired one round into the air to emphasize the boundary. They weren't to cross Elk River.

Buzz shadowed the five men into Port Orford with John backing him up, while Scott traveled to the Shix village to explain the shooting. The Indians appeared to be disconcerted, and several young men fled into the brush as Scott greeted them. Chief Sixes was overly nervous at his presence, so Scott bade farewell and headed home, running at full tilt after he was out of sight. The Indians' behavior was unnatural and somehow threatening. He didn't rest until he reached the cut by slide ridge, and here he found a good defensive position to wait for Buzz.

As light faded in the dust of evening, Scott noted movement near the river crossing. He moved toward it and ascertained that it was his partner. He learned that Dutch's gang had gone south with an Army troop which was responding to a report that the Rascals had massacred white people in a settlement north of the Rogue River. The Indian War had begun.

Chapter Seven

From the high-backed crest of slide ridge, Scott and Buzz stood vigil in the weeks to come. One or both men occupied the camouflaged lean-to built beneath the skyline, observing the Indians passing through the country. Scott watched four young men stealthily approach the cut, and drew a bead on the Indian whom Buzz had wounded on the slide ridge trail over two years ago. Chief Sixes appeared suddenly and stopped the men, haranguing them back toward their village. "Well, that was a close call. They were not making a friendly visit," Scott mumbled to himself.

One bright, sunny day Scott saw an Army detachment marching north. At the Sixes crossing, a six-man squad led by Scott's Sergeant friend crossed the river and headed west, while a platoon-sized unit moved directly toward the Shix village. In the distance he caught the flash of reflected light on brass, noting movement which was too distant to identify clearly as soldiers, but Scott surmised that they were a squad from the detachment.

Buzz was coming along the trail by the river to relieve him, as he thought, Lt. Hunter is a Commander who means business. He has surrounded the Indian village and cut off all trails out. The Old-Timer can watch the cut, while I go into the village. Sliding backwards out of his hidden redoubt, he hurried down the east side of the ridge, meeting Buzz at the cut.

"Guard the trail from here. The Army's in the village and I want to talk to Lt. Hunter. Maybe I can help the Qua-to-mahs."

Warily moving ahead as he neared the lodges, Scott was challenged by a sentry. Scott called out, "I'm a friend, Scott McClure. I want to see Lt. Hunter." He passed a trooper from the arm-wres-

171

tling tournament, and was waved into the camp with a casual two-fingered salute and a comradely smile.

Chief Sixes was angry with, and a little frightened by, the Army maneuver. Lt. Hunter was losing his patience as his interpreter repeated a question on the absence of the young men. All three men were glad to see Scott; maybe he could help them communicate. The ensuing hour proved the fallacy of their assumption, when Scott was unable to produce any satisfactory answers.

Lt. Hunter pulled his troopers back to the river crossing. While waiting for his northern squad to catch up, he related the events of the past few weeks to Scott, warning him to watch his "friends." The officer thanked Scott for his assistance as he ordered his detachment back to Fort Orford.

That evening Scott ruminated several aspects of the Indians' problems, recounting the officer's news from the Rogue River and Fort Orford. "The United States Government began establishing reservations for the Umpqua Indians in 1853, displacing them from tribal lands despite their centuries-old claim. There has been some fighting, but basically the Umpquas have accepted their fate as Reservation Indians. The Tututni or Rogues have more gumption and are fighting viciously to drive the white men from their coastal lands. The upper and lower elements of the tribe have joined together, drawing fighting men from the Floras, Sixes, and Port Orford bands."

Buzz commented, "I reckon that's why our Indian friends have been standoffish this past year."

"Yes, it's a wonder that I was allowed to leave the Port Orfords' village with Dutch over my saddle. Charlie's murder illustrated the paradox faced by the Tututni. Their trusted friend is also an American citizen, the heinous crime of murder is punished only if a white man is the victim. The Tututni are called Rascals when they defend their home territory, and choose the preposterous goal of driving settlers from coastal Oregon. It must be discouraging to the Indians when a great victory results in merciless retribution by the Army."

"Where did they ever win a real battle—except for Battle Rock?" Buzz inquired.

"On February 22, 1855 the Indians attacked the Geisel settlement, six miles north of Gold Beach. Winsor's friend, John Geisel, and his neighbors fought unsuccessfully to defend their homes. The Rogues killed twenty-six people and burned all sixty dwellings, the survivors fleeing for their lives. Fort Orford received a report a couple days later—that's when we got rid of Dutch's gang. Regular Army troops and militia responded in force. All of the Indians have fled and are being rounded up now. The government has ordered all Tututni Indians from the Oregon coast, consigning them to the Siletz and Grande Ronde Reservations. I expect the Indians will be gone by summer."

Buzz sighed woefully, "Times are changing, and I'll miss the old ways—even the Indians. I had less trouble with them than I did with most white men. Civilization isn't all that it is cracked up to be."

Scott remembered another item of news, and shared it with his partner. "Captain Tichenor was somewhat of a hero at Whaleshead, south of Gold Beach. He took his ship, the Nelly, almost into the surf, trying, but failing to rescue settlers from an Indian attack. The ship was damaged by wind and waves before it reached deep water safely. Lt. Hunter said that the Captain was deputized by the Indian Agent to hold captured prisoners in the Rogue valley. The Indians are to be moved to reservations this month."

Buzz probed the statement that all Indians would be moved off the coastal lands. "When will the Army move the Indians? What about peaceful men like Chief Sixes? And wives like Sally Dubois?"

Scott just shook his head in confusion. "I don't know how the Army will do it, but I've expected something like this order for years. We'll stand by our friends, but I don't believe that we can protect them very long. The Geisel Massacre has doomed the Tututni tribe."

In the morning Scott worked in the pasture, spreading hay from the last stack. He saddled Salem, explaining to Buzz, "I'm taking Francis to Langlois and barter for some feed—oats if possible. Pasture grass is still short and the feed is about gone. I'll return later in the day. Chief Sixes promised that the young men would leave us alone. I trust him, but I'm not sure about the young men."

Buzz rejoined huffily, "Don't worry about me and the ranch; I been around a long time. You be careful that you don't meet any warlike Indians."

Scott chuckled at the advice, but didn't have any reasonable response except for an affirming nod.

He was returning from Langlois when he encountered Chief Sixes and eight other Indians waiting for him by the Sixes River. His uncle, his son, their three wives, and his two grandchildren were packed and moving. Chief Sixes spoke in deliberate Tututni words, signing to reinforce his request. The Indians wanted to hide in the Sixes backcountry; they wouldn't go to a reservation away from their home.

Scott waved them ahead to the ranch and followed, effacing their tracks so that the falling rain would obliterate any trace of their passage upriver. He and Buzz made a pact with the family that evening in the barn—neither party had seen each other this day. It rained heavily in the night, and in the morning all sign of their presence was gone.

Scott craved more news of the Indian War and rode into Port Orford at midday to find it. George was working alone in the busy store, and invited him to supper as he continued to wait on customers. Putting Salem in the hotel stable with some oats, he sought Richard's company. Grandma Knapp sent him to the tavern where Louie and Richard had gone. He found the bartender entertaining his friends with a story, and sat down to listen to the end. The bartender welcomed him and handed him a beer.

Richard volunteered, "Have you heard the latest news? Captain Tichenor's Indian prisoners were massacred in retribution by the Geisel survivors and their friends. All nineteen of them were dead before the guards knew what had happened—shameful behavior for white men!"

The bartender interjected a comment to Scott, "Mr. McClure, I have a sorry message from the Sergeant. That Indian lad who saved you at Humbug Mountain, Sammy, was one of the prisoners killed."

"Sah-mah-e-ha is dead?" Scott replied in consternation. "When will this bloodshed stop?"

Louie prophesied, "It's over for all of the Indians. Most of them are going to the reservation quietly. However, some are still hiding in the hills, and there is talk that recalcitrants will have a bounty placed on their heads. I hope the government avoids such action as it is not needed. The Tututni spirit is broken."

After a short pause, Louie brightened and continued, "There is good news! The U.S. Post Office will open tomorrow, March 25th. Port Orford is a real city at last. We are supposed to become a voting precinct this fall, and several men are trying to establish our city as a county seat. With the Indians gone, growth will be rapid."

Scott carried that thought with him all afternoon. He needed to discuss business with George after supper. Would it be a good idea to acquire more livestock?

Business conversations were pleasantly delayed as Scott played with Angela and Junior, and the Nelsons arrived with George. Eventually he asked George about the store and discovered that the receipts were falling off. George admitted, "Your advice was good—to pay the mortgage, but I'm still not able to pay you anything on your loan."

"Buzz and I don't need any cash right now. My $100 in gold coins is still yours if you need it."

"Scott, I advise you to use that money to clear title to your property. Your application for a donation claim appears to be hung up in Salem. Maybe your friend Gerbrunn knows a good lawyer who can help you. With the Indians being moved, your valley will attract settlers. Come by the store in the morning and I'll give you the money."

****

By noon the next day, Scott found himself crossing the Floras on Salem, heading for Bandon. As he trotted along the familiar trail, he thought of Melissa and their conversation in the hotel lobby. A warm glow returned to his heart as he remembered her interest in him and his ranch. Salem stumbled and Scott returned to the present. Having taken George's advice literally, he was traveling at a faster pace than his horse could maintain. He slowed to an easier gait for the horse. Two days later he rode into the Gebrunn freight yards in Salem. Kurt dropped everything in greeting his friend, and rode with him to a lawyer. He waxed philosophical as he offered, "Always have a lawyer talk to government clerks. It's the only way to get decent results. John Lee is well-respected in this city; he's a distant relative of Jason Lee, the missionary. Here's his office now."

The lawyer listened carefully to Scott's request to speed up his donation claim application. Lee told Scott and Kurt to wait in his office while he walked to the territorial land office and inquired as to the status of Scott's claim. He was gone for over two hours, but returned with an official document in his hand. Handing the paper to his client, Lee said, "Your application was buried in paperwork, but it was completed and dated properly. I registered the document and as of now, you own the ranch outright. Congratulations."

Scott's wide smile faded a bit as he paid the bill of $25 to the office clerk. Kurt watched his telltale expression and counseled, "Cheer up, Scott. That's the best buy that you'll ever make. When John Lee spent two hours with those government clerks, he saved you two weeks of run-arounds. Lost papers are sometimes never found. Now you can spend a few days with the Gerbrunn family."

Scott smiled again and thanked Kurt, "I appreciate your help today, and I'll accept your hospitality for tonight. Tomorrow I have to return to my ranch." He told Kurt the story of Prince and the cougar, ending his tale with a question, "Do you have a horse to sell me that is as spirited as old Prince? And for less than $75?"

The two men dickered good-naturedly off and on during the evening, while Kurt's older son, Johann, talked about his classes at Willamette University and Mrs. Gerbrunn asked questions about that terrible Indian War. They had been arguing over Salem's double, a three-year-old dun gelding whose white forearm distinguished him from his uncle. Scott finally paid his friend $60 and accepted a bill of sale for Randersacker, or Randy as Scott called him. He had enough cash left to buy a supply of the new cloth cartridges Sharps was manufacturing, and some dress material for Melissa and Mary.

As Scott arrived at the knoll above the cabin, he thought happily, "It's always fun to travel to faraway places, but it's more fun to return home." In a playful mood, he plotted, "I'll fool Buzz with Randy. Let's leave Salem here and see if the Old-Timer can spot the difference." So thinking he walked Randy into the ranch yard and to the barn where Buzz was working. In dismounting he stood before the white forearm and greeted his partner heartily, informing him that the ranch was legally his property. Buzz looked puzzled for a moment, and then beat Scott at his own game.

"Where'd you get this new horse? Heh, heh, are you trying to josh me? Did you forget that Salem always comes to me for a treat?"

Scott laughed, "Ha, ha, you're right. Meet Randy, Salem's nephew. I bought him for you from Kurt Gerbrunn."

"No, he's yours. Salem and I get along fine. Besides, this youngster has taken to you. I'll go fetch Salem; I hear him calling from the knoll. I'm going to take a few fish upriver to Chief Sixes. I'll be back before dark. Leave Randy in the corral if you have visitors, and I'll sneak into the cabin after they leave."

****

One Sunday late in May, the sun shown brightly on the Sixes valley as the Hermanns rode into the ranch on two of the Tichenor horses. It was their first visit to the Myrtlewood Grove and the partners were pleased to see them.

Mary exclaimed, "What a beautiful setting. Look at all the different colors of green. There is the myrtlewood grove that you've spoken about so often."

George was impressed with the layout of the ranch, "You've really built a sturdy and practical farm on this flat. I'd like a tour of the facilities."

Buzz took Angela fishing while Scott carried Junior on his shoulders and showed the Hermanns around.

Mary remarked, "We have joined the Knapps and the Tichenors in hosting a birthday party for Melissa at the hotel. Imagine, she'll be twenty-one years old on June 3rd. All of her students will be attending, and I expect that awful Schmidt person to be there, now that he's back in town." Mary made a face, emphasizing the latter point, and watched Scott.

"Don't worry, Mary. I'll behave myself at the party. Buzz and I know Melissa's birth date, and we're looking forward to celebrating it with her."

The party had become a major social affair in the town, as their school teacher was feted on her twenty-first birthday. Over 200 guests had attended, including Dutch Schmidt. Scott's adversary had attended Melissa, had avoided Scott, and had left the party early. Scott was so cheered by his absence, that he remained until all the other guests had gone hoping to have her to himself, but the hostesses took Melissa into her room. Scott and Richard looked at each other and mutually decided to adjourn to the tavern near the fort.

Richard informed Scott that a part-time Marshal had been hired to keep order in the sometimes wild town. He pointed the man out, and Scott recognized the Marshal as a prospector who was well liked and well respected by townspeople.

They had entered the tavern, and were drinking beer when Dutch Schmidt entered. Seeing Scott, he swaggered to the table, boasting, "I've been authorized to hunt those Rascals who are hiding in the backcountry. I'm going to clean out that Sixes River bunch too."

Scott calmly stated his position, "You mean that you're a miserable bounty hunter. The Shix lodges were burned as soon as the Army moved the band to the Floras village of the Qua-to-mahs. You're welcome to look around the area as long as you stay off my ranch."

Dutch flushed with anger and frustration, threatening, "I'll go where I please to find those Indian friends of yours. You can't stop me from hunting for them on the upper Sixes."

Scott controlled his rising temper, as he countered, "Go anywhere that you please except my ranch. I hold title on the valley from ridge to ridge. Go up Elk River and cross the north ridge if you want to look for Indians in that bleak country. Set a foot on my land and I'll shoot it off."

"We'll see about that, McClure," Schmidt roared as he stormed out the door, heading straight for the fort.

"Sorry for spoiling our beer together, Richard. I'd better spend the summer months guarding my property. Dutch's gang would steal everything in sight if I let them into the Myrtlewood Grove. Tell Melissa that I'll visit her next week. You two should come out for a weekend soon—the fishing's great."

****

The summer passed swiftly as the partners cut hay and harvested their first large crop of vegetables, enough potatoes and onions for the winter. Buzz had taken to riding the trail of the cougar, because he could see the Elk River valley from a high point not far from the cairn where the cougar had hidden. He reported five men hunting the north ridge of Elk River, and he laughed at their attempt, he explained, "They didn't see me so I'm sure Dutch's gang was just too lazy to climb over that ridge. Tomorrow you can check the Sixes crossing for that gang. I wouldn't be surprised if they tried to sneak onto the ranch."

Scott concurred with his partner's guess, and spent the next day in his aerie atop slide ridge. He munched on venison jerky and raw potatoes from his garden, while reading a history book on the Revolutionary War. He was preparing to leave as the sun fell behind the Cape Blanco skyline, when an Indian lad ran up the trail from the derelict Shix village. A shot rang out in front of the racing figure, and he veered north away from the rifleman. The Indian hesitated, and then leaped into the river. Five white men with rifles encircled the hapless youngster, who was wallowing in hip-deep water. Dutch stood on the bank and threw a loop over the Indian's shoulders, dragging his struggling prey onto dry land. As other men began striking their prone captive, Scott fired a round into the air. The gang stopped beating the prisoner and led him away, looking over their shoulders for the invisible rifleman.

Meeting Buzz on the trail, Scott conjectured, "Those yahoos will be drinking their bounty money for a few days. They shouldn't bother us. But I want to check at the fort to make sure that Indian was turned in alive. I don't care for bounty hunters, let alone Dutch Schmidt."

Scott rode Salem to Port Orford, letting his trusty horse follow the familiar trail through the darkness of night to the hotel stable.

After inspecting a battered but live Indian from the Euchre Creek band, Scott left the fort and walked to the fishing dock where he saw a glowing lantern. John Larsen was cleaning his gear and welcomed Scott's company, saying, "If you'll help stow these lines, I'll buy you a beer."

As they climbed the sloping road up the bluff, Scott asked, "How are you doing? Are you selling all of your catch?"

"Fair on both counts! Port Orford appears prosperous, but since the Indians have been tamed, business has quieted down. Gold prospecting has played out in this area, and idle hands have caused the town to be a little wild. I sure wouldn't want that Marshal's job. It seems like prospectors poke fun at him all of the time, and the townspeople don't want him to carry a gun." John halted outside the tavern, stepping aside as two drunken soldiers came out the door.

One trooper guffawed, slurring his observation, "Ho! Ho! It's sure funny the way those miners are joshing the Marshal. But you're right, Corporal, we don't want trouble. Let's go to the sutler's."

John and Scott looked at each other, and as their smiles grew, John suggested, "Shall we go to the Marshal's aid?" However, the two friends sobered quickly after one look at the scene before them. The harassment had turned deadly serious, as three of Dutch's gang pummeled the law officer, pushing him from one to another. The laughter had died as the Marshal fought back, losing all control of the situation. He pushed one of his tormentors against the bar, shouting, "You men are under arrest," as he stumbled backward. The angry culprit at the bar seized a whiskey bottle and struck the Marshal on the jaw, dropping him to the floor.

Scott stepped behind two of the attackers, and grasping their coat collars, lifted them off their feet and forcibly banged their heads together. John grabbed the arm of the man holding the bottle and twisted it behind his back. The bartender provided rope and John bound their hands as Scott helped the injured Marshal to his feet. They escorted the Marshal and his three prisoners to the fort, where military authorities took over the problem. John's observation covered the situation succinctly. "Being a nice guy gets no respect!"

The Sergeant woke them at dawn with a summons from Lt. Hunter, the Acting Commander. Their testimony was needed at a 9 o'clock trial of the three miscreants. Scott and John were offered warm water in a washroom and breakfast in the mess hall before their appearance in court.

The trial lasted twenty minutes. The three men were declared undesirable citizens and banned from the Oregon Coast. The Marshal would escort them to San Francisco in the brig of the steamship which was weighing anchor at 10 o'clock. Summary justice had been meted out.

As they followed the prisoners and their military escort to the dinghy awaiting them at the dock, John observed, "The absence of Dutch and Weasel at the trial was noted by the Marshal and the Commander. I wonder where they were?"

"Avoiding any association with their cohorts, I bet. Lt. Hunter did not care for them before this incident, and might have shipped them out today also." Scott pointed toward a hillock on the beach beyond Battle Rock, and said, "In fact, aren't those two figures walking toward Hubbard Creek the absent crooks?"

The Marshal waited for Scott at the landing, and handed him a badge and a letter, stating, "Mr. McClure, I'm appointing you as Acting Marshal." He quickly stepped into the dinghy and left.

Scott opened the letter as the ship sailed out of the harbor, and grinned wryly, "That son-of-a-gun has resigned, leaving me holding the badge. He's going to stay in San Francisco." After a moment he chuckled quietly, "I'd better give the letter to Lt. Hunter. He can have this problem."

The Commander found a solution immediately. Appealing to John's civic responsibility, he appointed him Acting Marshal for thirty days. The term was extended to last all winter as townspeople endorsed his selection.

****

William Langlois drove his newly-purchased bull into the Sixes ranch corral. He was paying a courtesy visit, as he put it, "To broaden the strain." He spent two nights at the ranch and offered several suggestions for improvement, which Scott found to be good advice. Scott accompanied Langlois down the trail as he departed for his home place. At slide ridge, they stopped and his Floras neighbor offered, "I've got equipment which can broaden this trail into a wagon road. With the Indians gone, a real road can be built along the coast. I can help you with this section next spring if you help me harvest my grain in the summer."

Scott replied, "It's a deal! Buzz and I will start work on a road this winter. We'll see you in the spring."

One day in early December, the partners commenced work on a bridge over the cascading creek west of their cabin. During the previous month, they had cut several fir poles and split them lengthwise. Today they had hauled the split logs to the site, and were building two abutments, actually anchors, one on each side of the creek. They would eventually attach the logs, face-up, to the abutment; forming a bridge surface almost eight feet wide, which would serve man, animal, or horse-drawn wagon. Puffing heavily from moving logs, Buzz rested and asked, "What do you plan to do with all those extra logs down by the river?"

Scott mused, "There must be a way to sell them. Jacques Dubois suggested a log drive in March, when the river is high and logs can be floated downstream. But I'm sure that no ship can enter the Sixes estuary. We'll just have to think about a way to sell logs."

When the men returned to the cabin in the afternoon, they found a gift of two pair of Indian moccasins on the table. Evidently Chief Sixes' family was managing well enough in the backcountry.

After the bridge was completed, Scott rode Randy over the log platform several times, acquainting his steed with the wood surface. Returning to the cabin, he had an idea, and called out, "Hey, Buzz! Come here for a minute," and as the Old-Timer responded, he continued, "Look at this trail. We can widen it to ten feet by cutting out these two old stumps, and maybe three or four firs on the side of the knoll."

"You're right, partner, but if we cut through that thicket of young firs lower down the south side hill, the grade from the bridge to here would be less work for the horses. We can start work on the project after we return from the Hermanns' Christmas party. Tomorrow I want to fetch some game for our annual gift exchange, considering how scarce cash has become this winter. Should we sell a cow to George?"

"No, we'll need to sell beef later in the winter. For now, we have enough credit at the store to buy basic supplies. Our garden produce will help greatly."

****

Christmas morning found the partners suffering cold and blustery weather on the trail to Port Orford. A storm had struck the day before and delayed the men's travel, but they were determined to attend Hermanns' dinner today. As they swam their horses across the rain-swollen Elk River, Scott shouted into the wind, "I'm soaked to the skin and freezing to boot. Let's hurry to the hotel and change clothes."

Buzz nodded and kicked Salem into a gallop matching Randy's pace. They rubbed their horses down in the hotel stable, and then crossed to Knapp's back door. Louie and Grandma met them at the kitchen door and shared a holiday punch as the partners warmed themselves before the stove. They changed clothes and walked over to the Hermanns carrying a hindquarter of venison for Mary.

Scott delivered the game to the meat locker, and entered the back door after knocking lightly. Melissa was alone at the kitchen stove, stirring a pan of gravy.

She smiled and greeted Scott, "Merry Christmas! We were afraid that you might not make it."

Scott washed and dried his hands, and taking her small hands in his broad palms, he answered, "Buzz and I never miss Christmas at Hermanns, and besides, I don't see you often enough as it is." As he leaned forward to kiss her forehead, she tilted her head slightly and his lips met hers. Both appeared a bit startled as their lips parted, but he didn't hesitate in repeating the action with forceful tenderness, drawing her to him in a close embrace. Melissa put her arms around Scott's neck and sighed as he held her.

"You're being very forward, Scott Addis McClure. What do we tell Mary when she finds us kissing in her kitchen?" Melissa asked teasingly.

Scott was too self-conscious to respond in kind, but he didn't release her either. In a confused but determined manner, he proposed, "Melissa dear . . . uh . . . I love you. . . ."

"Yes, Scott? . . ," she encouraged.

Scott shook his head to clear it, and then blurted out, "Will you marry me?" and stood there seemingly dumbstruck by his own words.

Melissa nodded happily and raised her lips to his in a passionate acceptance, breathing, "Yes, of course, darling Scott."

Scott drew a gold locket from his pocket, and offered it to Melissa, "This piece of jewelry was my mother's favorite gift from my father. Will you wear it in place of an engagement ring?"

Melissa responded, "It's beautiful, Scott. I'll always treasure it, but can you give it to me after you ask father for my hand? He will give us his blessing." Scott nodded and she continued, "I'll send him into the kitchen to talk to you." She left the room quickly, disappearing into the parlor.

Richard soon appeared in the kitchen with a large smile and greeted Scott, "My daughter sent me out here to talk to you in private. Have you noticed how quiet it is in the other room? Everyone is waiting. Speak up!"

Scott asked Richard in a serious tone of voice, "May I have your permission to marry Melissa?"

"Of course, my boy! Now go into the other room and satisfy our friends' curiosity," he said as he shook Scott's hand vigorously.

Scott encountered a sea of expectant faces in the parlor, but he had only eyes for Melissa as he walked to her. They embraced and kissed in the still silent gathering. Scott placed his mother's gold locket around Melissa's neck as he repeated his proposal, "Will you marry me, Melissa Anne Nelson?"

At her simple response, "Yes, Scott Addis McClure," congratulations poured out from their friends. The wedding date was set on Melissa's birthday after the school term was completed.

****

The wet and blustery February weather drove Buzz into bed with a cough and unpredictable bouts of fever. He called to Scott who was cooking more potato and venison soup for his invalid partner, "Scott, I think our Indian friends could use some beef. Will you take that crippled yearling to them?"

"Can she walk that far?" Scott inquired, looking into the bedroom to see Buzz nod and cough, before continuing, "I'll go upriver as soon as I feed you, Old-Timer."

Buzz stumbled over the cougar rug and holding the door frame, said, "I can feed myself. You best get going."

Beyond any trail, Scott continued to lead the yearling up the Sixes River. He began to doubt his partner's estimate of the young cow's strength, as it fell again. Scott dismounted and helped the animal stand, thereby missing the appearance of Chief Sixes. He was startled as he turned to find his friend standing by his horse. I'm glad he's not my enemy, was Scott's first thought.

Scott's Tututni vocabulary had shrunk over the past two years, but little talk was needed to give the cow and accept Sixes thanks. He in turn thanked his friend for the gift of the moccasins, and chief Sixes beamed, signing that more would come from his women. Cowhide made good footwear.

On his careful approach to the ranch, Scott saw Salem in the corral and immediately dismounted. He tied Randy behind a screen of trees and with rifle in hand, circled the hillside high above the barn and cabin. He squatted on his heels in the rain for several minutes, finally repeating his move in the direction of the knoll. Their prearranged signal had alerted him to a visitor, but Scott had no clue as to his identity. He thought, "There's no hurry. I'm soaked to the skin already. I'll work past the beehives and cross into the myrtlewoods. If anyone is outside the cabin, I'll spot him." The cabin door opened before he could actuate his plan, and John Larsen stepped out.

Speaking to Buzz over his shoulder, John said, "Scott isn't anywhere to be seen. Where did you say that he'd gone?"

Breathing a sigh of relief that Dutch or some stray Indian hadn't surprised them, Scott walked to the cabin to greet his friend, only to receive equally bad news. Buzz blurted out, "John tells me that Richard collapsed on the hotel porch this morning."

John added, "It's very serious, Scott. Melissa is worried enough that when I offered to fetch you, she sent me right out."

"I'll saddle Salem and we can ride double into town." Scott glanced at Buzz, asking, "Will you be all right?"

"Don't worry about me. I'll ride in tomorrow after I do the chores."

John was puzzled by Buzz's reticence regarding Scott's where-abouts and then Scott's sudden appearance in the yard, and he now wondered about the absent horse. However, he didn't ask any questions, as he recognized that his friends were keeping a secret.

Scott found Melissa sitting at her father's bedside, reading a newspaper to him. He was conscious, but his countenance was pale and gaunt. Scott thought, At least he isn't coughing. Richard saw Scott standing in the doorway and greeted him with a wan smile, and a weak, "Hello, Scott. It's good to see you."

Melissa smiled wearily up at Scott as he put a comforting arm over her shoulders, and kissed her on the forehead.

Richard suggested, "Scott, take Missy for a walk. She's been sitting with me long enough. We can visit after supper." Turning his glance toward his daughter, he told her, "Go ahead. I'll rest until you return."

Melissa was silent as she dressed for the wintry day, and then walked hand-in-hand with Scott down the street toward Battle Rock. Not until they stood together at the bluff's edge looking to the south, did she vocalize her thoughts, "Father's collapse frightened me, Scott. He's a bit better now, but for a moment this morning, I thought that he was dying." Pointing to sea, she continued, "My mother was buried at sea out there, after she died from consumption just three days out of San Francisco. I remember that I cried at the ship's railing until I saw the tears in my father's eyes. It's the only time that I ever saw him cry. He was disconsolate with grief, and I told him that I would take care of him. It made me feel so good to be needed, that I felt guilty for not mourning longer for my mother. Some of that feeling returned this morning when I thought that I would lose him, and I asked John to bring you to me. I realize that being needed and needing another is an emotional give and take, and a solid foundation for love. I fell in love with you when I nursed you in the Wells home—you needed me. But today I needed you, and I'm so happy . . . no . . . secure, and warm with you beside me. Now I'll stop talking if you'll hold me tight."

Scott wrapped his arms around Melissa as they stood motionless above the windswept surf crashing onto the sandy beaches before them. She stirred and raised her face toward his, saying, "Thank you for coming to me." She kissed him lightly on his lips, and added, "We'd better start home before people start talking about us."

"They wouldn't dare talk about their teacher," he laughed. Changing his expression to a leer, he continued, "Besides, we could get married sooner if they found fault with you."

Melissa squeezed his hand and replied with a warm smile, "I'm eager too, but I promised to finish the term." She failed to see Dutch Schmidt wave to her from a nearby store porch, as she teased Scott laughingly. Scott saw Dutch's look of displeasure and grinned to himself as they continued on to the hotel.

Richard was eating Grandma Knapp's soup when they returned, and some color had returned to his cheeks. He had regained some of his humor also, as he teased Melissa, "I see the walk did you a world of good."

"And I see the soup has returned some color to your face as well as spirit to your tongue. How has your cough been?"

Richard answered quickly, "No cough, Missy, but my lungs ache," and hesitating, "I think . . . no, I know . . . I can't work at the mill anymore." With a slight flush from embarrassment, he continued, "I'm not needed in Tichenor's office, and I'm not strong enough to work in the mill itself. I don't know. . . ."

Scott interrupted, "Buzz suggested that you move in with him when we build his new cabin by the beehives. Of course he'll expect you to do your share in building it, so you'll have to spend a few weeks on the ranch this spring. With another hand on the farm next year, we can raise more cattle and plant a bigger vegetable garden."

Richard relaxed, and offered, "I'm a pretty good woodworker and can make furniture. Maybe I'll make a myrtlewood rocking chair like Buzz's."

"Right, and you can make another rocker for Missy and me. Try to sleep now and get your strength back. We'll need you in a week or two." Scott shook hands with Richard on their deal as he left the room.

Melissa joined Scott in the hallway and gave him a big hug and a long kiss. "Thanks for making it so easy for father," she said, and then asked, "Does Buzz know that he's sharing a 'new cabin'?"

Scott chuckled. "He will tomorrow when he gets here. One of us better see him before he talks to Richard. We have selected a cabin site, but I guess that we'd better get to work. We should visit the Hermanns after dinner and see if they have any suggestions."

While Buzz and Melissa were visiting Richard the next afternoon, Scott sat on the front porch enjoying the first really sunny day of the long winter. The streets were muddy and the trees and grass were still moist from recent rain, but the porch was dry and almost warm. Louie Knapp came up the street with a disturbed look on his face, and seeing Scott on the porch, sat down next to him.

Scott inquired as to his frown, "Bad news, Louie? Anything I can do?"

Louie was slow to reply until Buzz stepped onto the porch, and then he spoke in quick and angry tones, "Dutch Schmidt was ranting in the tavern that Melissa was no lady, acting up on the streets with the likes of an Indian-hider like Scott McClure. When he said she was a hussy, I challenged him, but he just laughed at me. I'm ashamed to say that he all but chased me out of the tavern. John Larsen is Marshal, but he's at sea on a fishing trip." Louie took a deep breath, before finishing his tirade, "And to think that I considered him a friend—a scoundrel is what he is."

Scott's facial muscles had tightened as Buzz laid a restraining hand on his friend's arm. Scott's eyes flashed with a wicked gleam, but he heard Louie out before breaking free and marching toward the tavern.

Buzz went inside to retrieve his Sharps and told Louie to keep Melissa at the hotel as he followed after Scott. He was angry with Dutch for his slur on Melissa, but he knew that Scott was more than just angry—he was killing mad. "Scott isn't carrying a weapon. Probably for the best in his mood. I'll tag along and see that Dutch doesn't have a weapon either," he mumbled to himself as he trotted after his partner.

Buzz followed Scott through the door and moved unnoticed against the wall near the end of the bar. Dutch spotted Scott moving toward him in a menacing gait, and standing, he pushed his chair into Scott's path.

"Well, if it isn't that Indian-lover McClure. What are . . . ?" Dutch started to say as Scott slammed the chair against Schmidt's legs, saying nothing, but advancing inexorably. He reached forward and slapped Dutch's face forcefully enough to stagger the man.

The bartender screamed, "Outside, take your fight outside. Please Mr. McClure, Mr. Schmidt, don't wreck my bar. Go outside."

Scott nodded and motioned for Dutch to leave ahead of him. Buzz cut in front of Tom "Weasel" Burton and casually removed a pistol and a knife from Weasel's belt, handing them to the bartender. Without saying a word, he joined the gathering crowd in the muddy street.

Dutch removed his coat and with a humorless smile, he challenged Scott, "You're pretty tough when you have a rifle in your hands. Let's see how well you fight without that Sharps." He shifted his feet and jabbed Scott in the mouth, once, twice, and three times before circling away. Following with a straight right to Scott's forehead, he displayed his experienced boxing skills. When Scott rushed forward to grapple with his adversary, Dutch moved sideways and kicked Scott's legs out from under him, delivering a second kick to his ribs as he rolled in the mud out of harm's way and regained his feet. Dutch laughed confidently as he hit Scott with a flurry of punches and danced away. Scott charged and delivered a backhanded blow which caught Dutch on his nose and drew blood, but Dutch slugged Scott with a powerful right, splitting his lip and stopping his attack. Another sharp right caught Scott on the eye and his vision blurred as he staggered under a series of left jabs and right crosses.

Scott thought, this yahoo knows how to fight even if he is a cheap crook. He didn't see the clubbing blow which knocked him down. Dutch kicked him several times before slipping in the mud to his knees, where Scott hit him on his sore nose with a lucky but off-balance punch. Both men rose and squared off, Dutch beginning to have a worried look as Scott plodded toward him and jabbed his nose again. Scott's battered and bleeding face had taken a beating, but his baleful stare of impending retribution shook Dutch.

He reached into his boot and pulled out a knife, slashing Scott's jacket sleeve and drawing blood from a thin cut. The fight became deadly serious as Scott waved Buzz off, and circled his enemy, waiting for his next move with the blade. Dutch laughed, faked a lunge, and then sliced the air near Scott's face.

With a lightning-like move, Scott's right hand caught Dutch's right wrist as the fisted blade passed. He revealed his powerful grip as he crushed Dutch's flesh between his fingers, and slowly twisted his arm until the knife fell from nerveless fingers. Dutch hit Scott with a frenzy of punches with his free fist, but Scott ignored the blows as he continued to apply pressure. Dutch dropped to his knees, and screamed in agony as wrist bones cracked and Scott brought his knee forward into his jaw. Releasing Dutch's wrist, he backhanded his defenseless opponent across his bloody mouth, several pieces of teeth falling into the mud next to the prone form of Dutch Schmidt.

Buzz interposed, "I think he's had enough, Scott," as his partner raised his fist to strike another blow. Scott relaxed his menacing pose and nodded.

"Bring Weasel along, partner," Scott directed as he reached down, seized the semiconscious Dutch by his collar, and lifted him to his feet. "These yahoos are leaving town today on that ship in the harbor," he stated as he half-carried his stumbling foe down the street and over the bluff to the shoreline.

A dinghy from the ship was drawn up on the sand above the outgoing tide. Scott lifted the hapless Dutch from his feet and dumped him in the small boat. A familiar voice came from his rear, "I'm glad that we only arm-wrestled, old friend. You're a mean son-of-a-gun in a real fight." Bos'n mate O'Keefe stepped forward, and asked, "What shall I do with these lads, Mr. McClure?"

Scott smiled briefly through broken lips as his humor returned. "Where were you when I needed you, my sailor friend?" Pausing for a moment, he continued, "Take these crooks to San Francisco with you. They have money enough for passage in their purses." Turning to Weasel, he threatened, "If I see either of you on the Oregon coast again . . ." His message was convincingly accepted in silence from both men, as O'Keefe rowed them to his ship and out of Port Orford.

The fight crowd swarmed around Scott, offering libation for the victor if he would join them in the tavern. Instead of accepting this attention, he followed Buzz's quiet advice, "The sooner you face Melissa, the easier it will be for you," and walked with his partner up the street. He waved to George as he passed the store and continued on to the hotel, mounting the porch steps with apprehension about Melissa's reaction.

The door opened and Melissa flew into his arms, crying, "Scott darling, what has that terrible man done to you?" and promptly kissed his battered lips. "Oh, I'm sorry, Scott. Did that hurt?"

Scott kissed her back, and teased, "No, Missy, but I'm afraid your lips are bloody too." He said more seriously, "I feel fine now that I've faced you. What you think of me is more important than a few cuts and bruises."

Buzz corrected Melissa's misunderstanding, "Scott won the fight and put Dutch and Weasel on a ship for San Francisco. Good riddance, I say."

Melissa washed his wounds with soapy water and then sealed the abrasions with her father's brandy. Both Richard and Buzz bemoaned the waste of good spirits to no avail, as she used the rest of the bottle on Scott's arm. She hesitated in saying, "I think stitches are needed on this knife wound, or the cut will leave a scar."

"Just bandage it tightly and it'll heal. Any scar will serve as a reminder not to get into another such fight. Besides, Buzz and I have to go home and feed the stock."

But the partners were delayed as the Nelsons and Louie insisted on hearing all the gruesome details of the brawl. When Melissa approved of Dutch's broken arm with an emphatic, "He deserved it!" Scott relaxed and stared lovingly at his wife-to-be. Buzz had to pry him away from their friends so that they could cross the rain-swollen rivers before darkness fell.

****

The following week the weather held and the two men worked energetically in setting a solid foundation for the new cabin. Scott sent Buzz to Port Orford with a cow to sell and a list of building materials needed in the cabin. Richard would return with him if he was strong enough.

Scott fitted and cut niches in logs for the cabin walls while his partner was gone, but he waited until Buzz and Richard returned before proceeding with construction.

During the ensuing weeks, Melissa was a regular visitor and John Larsen came twice to help with the roof and with framing. One day William Langlois arrived with his equipment and two farmer friends. Working long hours on slide ridge resulted in a roadbed stout enough to move the equipment upriver, clearing a road to the ranch yard. The partners' preparation of the bridge and stump clearing on the knoll allowed the rest of the work to be completed quickly.

"Your road will hold a team-and-wagon better than the coast trail does," Langlois commented. "One of these days we'll have a real road up the coast."

"Thanks, William. Send word when your crop is ready for harvest; Buzz and I owe you more than just a little help for all this work."

The wedding was only a couple of weeks off when John Larsen arrived with a wagon loaded with cedar cabinets and off-duty soldiers. The wagon was an early wedding gift from their friends at the fort, and the men had volunteered to help John install his wedding gift. "We bachelors don't understand a woman's needs, according to Mary Hermann. Melissa must have her kitchen cabinets and a wardrobe when she moves in. Have you food enough to feed this crew? Mary sent a batch of fresh bread."

A grateful Scott thought fast and came up with a solution, "We'll have a barbecue in the grove. Buzz and Richard can catch and grill the fish while I butcher a side of venison for steaks. I believe we have enough potatoes to go around. Did you bring a little whiskey along?"

"Of course, you fix the meal and we'll transform your cabin, put your old cupboards in the new cabin, and drink to your marriage."

Later that day after John and his besotted crew had left for town, Scott sat next to the warm fire and admired John's work, "These cupboards look great and smell good too. Too bad Melissa can't see them. When are you going into Port Orford, Richard?"

"I'll ride Salem in next week. I'd have traveled with John's crew, except I'd just be in the way. Mary and Melissa have everything under control. You're having a mighty fancy wedding for a farm boy, Scott."

"Why don't I go with you and look things over, Richard?" Scott offered.

"Because you'll be in the way too, and Melissa told me that my job is to keep you busy and on the ranch. You can't see Melissa before the wedding; she's even staying overnight with the Hermanns on the 2nd. You're an honored guest that day at both the sutler's on post and our favorite tavern. But be careful of free drinks, bachelors hate for the groom to be sober at his wedding."

Scott understood his father-in-law's advice as he kissed his bride on the hotel porch before a cheering crowd of guests. He was confused and befuddled by all the activities of their wedding day, but Melissa was in her element, savoring every minute of the festive occasion. She laughed at Scott's dilemma, and suggested, "Relax darling, and just follow me around. The reception will be over in an hour or two."

Scott knew that he must enjoy his wedding day because all the women told him so. Mary Hermann and Grandma Knapp were very persuasive in assuring him that he was a lucky man and therefore very happy, and even Mrs. Tichenor had a twinkle mixed with a tear in her eye when she congratulated the newlyweds.

Scott asked Buzz for his opinion of the whole affair, and was answered sagely by the Old-Timer, "Of course, you're having a good time. And if you know what's good for you, you'll agree with everything these women say. This day is Melissa's, so you have to be happy." He pointed across the room, and continued, "She's beckoning you now to cut the cake. Go ahead, son. Do your duty."

Scott didn't notice that Buzz and Richard were chuckling at his discomfiture, as he was too busy following Melissa's instructions in holding her hand as she cut the wedding cake. They fed each other the first pieces and Melissa gave him a peck of a kiss as a reward. He whispered to her, "Oh no! That's not a proper kiss." Wrapping his arms around her he kissed her long and hard to the approval of their guests and Melissa herself. She smiled up at her husband with a loving and possessive expression, obviously enjoying the day as much as Scott was supposed to. Mary claimed her for another duty and Scott wandered outside for a breather.

Thinking back on the busy day, he realized he was happy—it was just taking time for it to sink in. Buzz, John, and George had stood up with him, and Mary, Sally, and Angela had served Melissa. It was a grand ceremony, he thought as Richard interrupted his reverie.

"Are you having second thoughts, my boy? When I gave my daughter away it was for keeps."

Scott laughed with his father-in-law as he replied, "I was just thinking . . . I believe all of you have convinced me that I'm having a good time. And anyone as important to me as your Missy has to be a keeper. Let's go back to the party and I'll tell Missy that I won't ever let her go."

When Melissa slipped into Grandma Knapp's room to change clothes, Buzz informed Scott that he and Richard were leaving with the Langlois family. They would pay back some labor for the road construction while they visited. "You can have the ranch all to yourselves for three days, and then we'll be home again. John is suppose to deliver the wedding presents on that day. Remember to feed the livestock," Buzz chuckled as he slapped Scott on the shoulder and left.

Riding double on Randy along the trail to the Myrtlewood Grove, Melissa prattled on, reliving the entire affair. She laughed, "Ha, I know that I'm being a little silly, but I'm so happy and excited that I have to talk. You know that we have to write thank you notes for all of our lovely presents. Mary is keeping a list of who gave what—there were so many. But I remember the Hermanns gave us a set of chinaware, much too expensive, the Tichenors gave us the dinnerware, and the Masters sent us those lovely glasses. I think they discussed their gifts beforehand and Captain Tichenor purchased them in San Francisco. The Langlois family gave us pots and pans, and the Knapps gave us that love seat from my room. The quilt Sally made for us must have taken her over a hundred hours to make—it has such a beautiful Indian design. I don't remember what father and Buzz gave us, except for a three-day honeymoon. Do you remember?"

Melissa paused for a deep breath as Scott answered, "Richard said their presents were in our home and we would recognize them immediately."

"I wonder what's waiting for us? And wasn't it nice of your bartender friend to give us a case of California wine for the reception. I think he felt a little out of place on this side of the bar. Hee-hee, did that sound snobbish?"

Scott laughed, commenting, "You made a friend for life when you kissed him on the cheek and thanked him for attending our wedding. He told me later that he was afraid that you'd blame him for Dutch's gossip in his tavern. He thinks you are the grandest lady on the Oregon Coast, and I agree with him." He kissed her cheek as they rode into the ranch yard.

Chief Sixes and his uncle stood at the door, waiting for the newlyweds. Melissa started in surprise at their presence, but Scott's gentle touch indicated to her that they were friends. Uncle gazed steadily at Melissa for several moments, then cackled and spoke in a rapid burst of Tututni, causing his nephew to smile. Melissa glanced at a smiling Scott, and asked, "What did he say about me? Come now, Scott, tell me!"

With a straight face Scott replied, "Uncle is a mite fanciful in his expression, but I'll agree with him this time."

"Scott, tell me this instant what he said!"

"Well dear, a rough translation is that you are 'ready' to split the blankets with me," Scott said as he burst into laughter. When Melissa joined in the fun, Chief Sixes spoke to Scott.

"He says that humor and beauty are the traits of a good wife. I'll agree with him also. He has a present for us."

Melissa and Scott dismounted and walked to the Indians who were unfolding a deerskin rug adorned with intricate artwork and design. "It's too nice to put on the floor, maybe we could use it as a wall covering in the bedroom," Scott thought aloud, and Melissa nodded in agreement. The two Indians accepted their thanks and turned to walk upriver.

"Where are they going, Scott?" Melissa asked in a puzzled tone, and as realization dawned, she answered her own question, "You're hiding Chief Sixes' family in the valley. Hans guessed right. Who else knows about your friends?"

"Just Buzz, but of course Richard will have to know. Chief Sixes wanted you to see him. He understands that his family is here on your sufferance."

"Oh, Scott, it's not fair to burden me with their lives. Whatever arrangements that you have made with your friends are acceptable to me. But someone will discover our secret eventually. I hope that you will be able to help them when their situation changes."

Scott opened the door and carried his bride across the threshold, closing the door with his heel. There was enough light for the couple to see Buzz's myrtlewood rocker sitting before the fireplace. "Buzz has owned that rocker for over twenty years. It's his personal favorite possession. I'd feel guilty keeping it."

Melissa contradicted Scott, "Buzz gave it to us and he'd be hurt if we didn't accept it. He's giving us its sentimental value as well as a piece of furniture. Buzz and I are good friends, but you two men have a special relationship which transcends friendship. He once told me that you are the son that he never had."

"And he's the father that I never knew. As usual, dear wife, you are right when people's feelings are the issue. Now where is Richard's gift?"

"Looking at these cupboards, Port Orford cedar, aren't they? I can guess what's in the bedroom—a cedar chest." She hurried through the doorway to find that she was correct. "I knew that John was building something with father, but I forgot about it during the past two weeks. Isn't it beautiful, Scott?"

"Yes, and so are you, my dear," Scott murmured as the two lovers gazed into each other's eyes with adoration, their honeymoon before them.

Chapter Eight

A light rain was falling from an overcast sky as Richard and Buzz rode into the Sixes valley three days after the wedding. In the distance they could make out a wagon fording the turbulent river, and finally identified John Larsen and George Hermann working an empty wagon through the rushing water.

Buzz kicked Salem into a gallop, and as an afterthought, called over his shoulder, "Come along, Richard. John knows what he's doing, but we can help Mary and the children across the river." With four horses a somewhat dry Mary and Angela were deposited on the wagon seat on the north side of the Sixes, and the wedding gifts were carefully reloaded.

"What a day to visit the newlyweds. Where did our sunshine go?" John complained.

Buzz laughed as he remounted and reminded his friend, "If it was good weather, John, you'd want to be fishing off the coast." He led the way, calling, "Let's move out. My pants are wet and cold. A warm cabin will sure feel good."

Scott was waiting in the yard for the visitors. "Heard you coming over the bridge. All of you go inside and warm up. I'll take care of the horses."

The men carried the packages inside as Scott did the chores before returning to the cabin. He found the men standing around the stove, watching Melissa and Mary open the packages and put dishes in the new cupboards. Scott said, "Leave the glasses out, Missy. We'll share our last bottle of wine from the wedding with our company." When Mary politely demurred, "We can only stay for a little while, Scott." Melissa responded, "I have a kettle of beef stew and a batch of fresh bread for our meal. Scott can help you return to Port Orford with our horses. Let's have a second wedding party."

"Good idea, daughter. I'll fetch brandy from my cabin after I warm up some."

During the ensuing hours, conversation turned to the capture of Indians along the coast. John mentioned, "Gold prospectors reported seeing three Indians in the hills along the Elk River, and reported it to me as Marshal. I informed the Army authorities, and a patrol was dispatched to bring them in. That was day before yesterday, so I suppose they've captured them by now."

Scott asked, "Are they still sending Tututni stragglers to the Grande Ronde Reservation?"

"Yes, the last group of captives was given an Army 'escort' there. Your Sergeant friend told me that several Rogue River Indians had died from smallpox and measles on the reservation. Their situation is not healthy when they are relocated to those reservations."

Buzz exchanged a meaningful glance with Scott. They would protect Chief Sixes and his family as long as possible.

****

The newlyweds enjoyed an idyllic life during the summer of 1856. Scott showed Melissa the entire Sixes valley from Chief Sixes hideaway to Cape Blanco while Buzz and Richard tended to ranch chores.

Toward the end of August Scott and Buzz rode to Langlois for three days of harvesting the farmer's feed crop of hay and corn. At dinner the first night, William asked, "Have you heard anything about closing Fort Orford?"

Scott responded in a perplexed tone, "No, what have you heard?"

"Just gossip . . . travelers are talking about the fact that since all the Indians are gone, troops aren't needed."

Turning to Buzz, Scott commented, "We'll have to visit Port Orford next week. Army business is important to the town particularly when a county seat is at stake."

Scott and Melissa rode into Port Orford leading two dry cows, one for George and one for the Army. George confirmed the rumor concerning the military post, saying glumly, "The Army will begin pulling out next week for the Umpqua River bar, where Fort Umpqua will be built. The new Fort will take over responsibility for protecting the Oregon Coast. My business will be hurt with the soldiers gone. I foresee tough times coming for Port Orford."

Scott speculated, "I wonder if the Army will keep its commitment for buying beef from me? Our deal may be voided when the troops leave." Turning to Melissa, he decided, "I'll take this cow over to the Fort and see if we still have a deal. I was counting on the Army's cash to tide us over this winter. Why don't you visit Mary and I'll join you later?"

The post was a beehive of activity as Scott entered the gate and asked the Duty NCO for Lt. Hunter. A trooper took charge of the cow, as Scott sat down to wait for the busy officer. His friend joined him later and apologized for the delay, explaining, "I had to dicker with that stubborn Yankee skipper for more reasonable shipping prices. Transporting men and equipment to the Umpqua is going to be expensive. That ship in the harbor will take our forward party to the new site later in the week. I expect to be assigned as the sub-commander and travel with the unit." Flicking his fingers, he continued, "That matter aside, I believe that you wanted to discuss our beef contract. You realize that we won't need any more beef after your delivery today. And we certainly won't ship it at today's prices."

Scott pondered his options, and asked, "Would you honor our contract if delivery is made at Fort Umpqua?"

Lt. Hunter nodded in admiration at Scott's initiative as he replied, "Yes, I can guarantee a onetime purchase of five-ten head as per our agreement, if you'll deliver them on October 15. The Commander likes to buy from local suppliers, but he will acknowledge this obligation." The officer drew a purchase form from his desk, wrote a brief statement, and handed the document to Scott, declaring, "October 15 is your deadline. Present this order form to the senior officer if I'm not on post. Best wishes, Scott."

Scott shook hands on the deal and said, "Thanks, Patrick. I'll see you in Fort Umpqua next month."

At dinner George praised Scott's auspicious practicality, "You chose to follow that money with timely opportunity, Scott. I congratulate you on your energetic approach, but can you deliver on time?"

"Well, George, I can trail twelve steers to the Umpqua beginning next week if we can cut our hay fast enough. That allows three weeks to reach Fort Umpqua."

Melissa offered, "Dad and I can help with the hay crop, and if the weather cooperates, that starting date is reasonable. Can you and Buzz handle twelve steers on the trail?"

"We'll find out, sweetheart. This Army contract may be our last opportunity to realize a cash profit for a few months." Turning to George he asked, "Can you think of any way to sell our logs on the Sixes . . . other than set up a sawmill operation?"

George shook his head, "No, but I'll ask Captain Tichenor about Jacques' idea to float logs downriver to the estuary. I think you're on the right track focusing on farming and timber with both miners and the soldiers leaving our town. Port Orford is going to be a quiet place next year."

****

Scott cursed under his breath at the delay. The partners were six days out of the Sixes, and had been making good time yesterday when one of his steers had wandered into a bog. At noon today the same animal had bolted into a mudflat on the South Fork of the Coos River. When Buzz had pulled the steer onto the river bank, it had suffered a broken leg and couldn't rise from the ground. Buzz had shot and dressed the animal, loading the meat on both horses and hauling them to a store which they had passed three miles back.

He returned well after dark, helloing the campfire from a distance, before approaching the circle of light. Shaking his head, he explained, "Sorry, Scott, I couldn't get any cash for the beef. The best that I could do was barter for a case of Sharps linen cartridges and one hundred pounds of flour, which we can pick up on the way home."

Scott shrugged, and complimented the Old-Timer, "You did well considering our plight. We need cash but that'll come when we reach Fort Umpqua. Your dinner's on the fire. Eat and turn in, I'll take care of the horses and stand first watch on our herd."

The progress remained slow during the next week as minor delays ate up their margin of time.

The small herd stood on the south shore of the Umpqua River on the afternoon of October 11. Buzz suggested, "We'd better swim these steers over in the morning. They look a mite tired."

Scott disagreed, "Those storm clouds to the southwest will likely bring rain tonight. We can't afford to chance a rain storm or a fractious river when we cross. You lead the way, Buzz, and I'll make sure the cattle follow you."

Buzz pushed his favorite steer to the front and drove him into the shallow water before moving Salem into deeper water. The crossing is going smoothly, thought Scott just as a steer floundered in midstream. He swam Randy toward the animal, and sensing the horse's presence, the steer calmly swam to shallow water on the north bank. Scott counted ten steers safely ahead when he heard a bawling sound behind him and turned to see the eleventh steer sink from sight in deep water. He held Randy in check as he surveyed the river's flowing waters, seeing an occasional glimpse of the drowning animal as it tumbled downstream.

Riding up to Buzz, Scott said, "We lost a steer, partner. Randy was ready to go after the stray, but he had more spirit than strength and I held him back. Let's bed the herd down in that patch of grass up ahead. We'll drive into Gardiner tomorrow."

Harvey Masters met them at the edge of town with a message from Lt. Hunter, "He said that the steers must be delivered by October 15 or no deal. There are no ships in port so you'll have to drive them around the harbor toward Umpqua City where Fort Umpqua is being built. It's slow going, Scott, so I'd push those steers hard."

"Thanks for the good advice, Harvey. We'll see you in three days," Scott said as he continued pushing the herd northward.

As expected, their progress was slow for two days, but they managed to arrive a full day early, and were met by a grinning Lt. Hunter. "I'm glad you made it on time, Scott. My Commander insists on abiding by the letter of this contract. That means delivery by the 15th of five healthy steers. Put those first five steers in the corral and come to my office. The least that I can do is pay you in gold coin."

The officer handed Scott the payment, reaching across his desk to shake hands, and empathized with his friend, "I'm sorry that I can't buy your other steers. I can understand your expectations, but my orders were specific. Perhaps your friend Masters can help you sell them. Best of luck, Scott."

When Scott rejoined Buzz and his five leftover steers, he explained, "Patrick did all that he could for us, and we do have enough cash for our immediate needs. Let's return to Gardiner and see if Harvey can help us dispose of our dwindling herd."

They were north of Gardiner the next afternoon, so Buzz rode ahead to see Harvey as Scott continued herding the steers south. He returned before dark, saying, "Harvey is way ahead of us. We're to drive the steers into the corral behind the hotel now, and Alma will feed us supper. He has a couple of potential buyers for the steers coming by in the morning."

After dinner, Harvey described his buyers, "One is a settler on Smiths River who lives about three miles from the Smith Massacre site. Like everyone else around here, he is short of cash.

However, he raises chickens, and he's bringing twenty good laying hens, a rooster, a bag of feed, and of course, their cages. I bartered two steers as a trade, subject to your approval. He's reliable and I trust him to give you healthy, productive fowl." He paused, looking askance at the partners.

"Melissa suggested chickens for the farm last year. I agree with your deal. Does anyone have cash?" Scott asked.

Harvey shook his head no, chuckling as he continued, "I can use one steer, but I want to pay you in seed corn and vegetable seeds left over from last spring. My two burlap bags weigh over 150 pounds; which should be a good deal for you, except for the fact that one of my invoices is dated 1854."

Scott nodded in agreement and wondered aloud, "How are we going to carry all of these supplies back to the Myrtlewood Grove?"

Harvey had the answer, "A friend in town has a small three-year old pinto gelding which his strapping son has outgrown. It should be a fine horse for Melissa, and since he hasn't received a cash offer, he might trade you for two steers. You may have to add a couple of dollars in cash to close the deal. The pinto can carry the seeds and Salem can carry the chickens."

Scott laughed, "And Randy can carry our Coos flour and ammunition. It looks like we will be walking home, Old-Timer."

"Hmm! That's all right for you, since Harvey makes you look good — a thoughtful husband. I bet Melissa will be thrilled, so I won't complain."

Harvey added propitiously, "You'll find these items will grow with your ranch and they are better than cash in that respect. You should prosper during hard times in Port Orford."

****

It was fortunate that Harvey had given them an old piece of sailcloth, since rainfall dogged them on the trip home. Scott covered the chickens at night and kept them near the warm campfire, although several hens looked sickly by the time they reached home. Everyone pitched in to make their poultry project a success. Scott and Buzz built a chicken coop near the garden, while Richard hand-crafted a roost and laying box for the coop. Melissa nursed the hens back to health, and soon eggs were added to their farm diet.

She accepted management of the poultry operation with enthusiastic energy, spending weeks learning to facilitate the incubation of eggs in cold weather. Scott complained about the box of chicks near the kitchen stove but humored her ambition. By Christmas her brood of young chicks outnumbered her layers, but they were growing too fast to stay inside the cabin. Buzz solved her problem when he built a smokehouse behind the coop. By keeping an alder fire going, he got his smoked salmon and Melissa got a warm coop. Even so, three weaker chicks died when a storm brought cool air to the coast.

****

On Christmas Eve Melissa and Scott rode to Port Orford with two chickens which were not laying. They were to be the entree in Mary's Christmas Dinner. The "Egg-Lady," as she was to become known, took a hundred eggs to give as presents to their friends in town. She was going to promote her product, hoping to strike a deal with the store and the hotel to buy her eggs on a regular basis. Like Buzz's honey, eggs would provide another small income to help support the ranch.

Melissa insisted that Scott take a half-dozen eggs to their bartender-friend in the tavern, while she visited with Mrs. Tichenor. He found the tavern empty of customers as he greeted the owner cheerily, "Merry Christmas, Jack! My wife sends you her best wishes and a small gift." Handing him the eggs carefully, he continued, "She's raising chickens now."

"Bless your missus, Scott. She's a fine lady. Can I buy you a beer?"

Scott agreed, "But only if you join me, and tell me the latest news."

The bartender loved to talk and quickly answered in length, "The town seems deserted, what with most miners and soldiers gone. My business is terrible; look around you. A holiday coming and you're my only customer. It's a good thing the mill is operating or the ships wouldn't call at Port Orford. Captain Tichenor told me that the Umpqua River is booming. I may have to move up there if business doesn't get better."

He sipped his beer and changed the subject, "They caught an Indian hiding on Humbug Mountain last week. He was roughed up some going through the old Geisel area, and he might have been killed if that Rogue River Marshal hadn't been so tough. He banged a couple of heads enforcing the law, sounded a little like you."

Jack laughed aloud at his humorous observation and poured another beer. "John Larsen does a fine job here, but he's going to quit before summer. You'd think the town would be peaceful with Fort Orford closed and all the gold taken out, but when times are hard, men take to stealing. John caught a thief earlier in the month, but with no jail, all that he could do was return the stolen knife to the store and ship the crook to San Francisco. He'll be a free man when he lands."

Looking up as the door opened, he called, "Speak of the devil! John Larsen is going to join us in a beer," and poured three glasses full as Scott put some change on the bar.

Scott greeted John, "Merry Christmas, Marshal! Jack tells me that you're still catching crooks."

John chuckled, and replied, "Yes, thanks to you and Lt. Hunter, but I'm quitting in May for sure. Say, where's Melissa? You two newlyweds are never separated."

"Come with me now and say hello. She has a half-dozen eggs for you from her poultry project," Scott rejoined, as the two friends shook the bartender's hand and left the tavern.

George complimented the wives on a fine dinner, and Mary gave credit to Melissa. She told Scott, "Your wife roasted both hens herself, and made the gravy as well. You're lucky to marry such a good cook."

Scott nodded in agreement, "You're right. Our lot has improved on the ranch since Melissa took over the kitchen. Chickens and eggs have improved our fare. Which reminds me, George, Melissa has a deal for you. Missy?"

Melissa spoke in her business tones, "George, my chickens can supply two dozen eggs per week. Better than that when my chicklets come of age. Will you buy them from me?"

"Of course, Melissa, and I have some chicken feed that you can buy from me. It should help both our businesses to work together. The Knapps will appreciate fresh eggs for the hotel. When I get a shipment from Portland, the eggs are sometimes too old for his dining room. Have you any more chickens that you can sell?"

"Not yet. If Scott will put up with my incubating box in the kitchen, we may have a few later in the year."

Scott remarked, "I'm always afraid that I'll step on a chick, but the rewards are great enough. Today's chicken was delicious."

He turned to George and asked about his logging project, "Have you figured how I can sell my timber? I have sixty logs in my way that should be worth something."

Jacques volunteered, "I will help."

George clapped Jacques on the shoulder, "I know, my friend, you want to float them down to the old Shix village." Speaking to Scott he added, "That's not a bad idea. If they were accessible in the estuary, someone might buy them. I'll talk to Captain Tichenor again."

After Christmas, Scott and Buzz cleared land upriver, enlarging their east pasture by fifteen acres. "What do you think, Buzz? Hay or corn?"

The Old-Timer answered promptly, "Hay! We should plant our corn and potatoes below my cabin. Richard and I can keep the deer out of that field. I'm still planning to plant a couple of apple trees down there. That neighbor of Langlois and I will trade bee hives for fruit trees this summer."

Scott ruminated aspects of his pet project, "There must be a way to make money out of these logs. I think that we should form a partnership with Jacques, George, and John, and float all this timber down to the old Shix village. At least we'd be rid of them, and maybe they can be sold. They're in the way on the ranch. I'm going into town and talk to our friends on Saturday. Melissa will enjoy some woman talk and shopping."

Buzz asked, "Does George need any meat for his store?"

"Maybe, but I haven't seen any deer lately, and we've sold all our steers. Healthy cows aren't for sale and neither are chickens. I suppose it would have been prudent to have kept a couple of steers at home to sell to George, but I thought the Army would buy all of them. Ah well, hindsight won't change anything, our cash crop will be limited this next year."

One Saturday in late March, Jacques and a logger friend joined Scott and Richard at the log stockpile east of the ranch, while Buzz rode his horse to the old Shix village to meet John's fishing boat. John, George, and Louie Knapp had crossed the Sixes bar this morning and had set up a log boom on the island opposite the village site. The river was near flood stage with spring rains as the two stockpiles on the ranch were peeved into the rushing water. Jacques and his partner wore cleated boots and leaped onto two sturdy logs for the ride downriver. Dubois was on a lark, showing his skill as a logger.

Scott and Richard followed the loggers downriver on horses. At slide ridge, Richard voiced his first note of optimism, "It's working so far. All but a few logs are going through to John's crew. Look at the crazy Frenchman showing off. He's enjoying his ride."

The two men chose to ford the northern channel to the island, eventually reaching the log boom. Here failure was very evident. The high water and outgoing tide were carrying logs past the boom and out over the river bar faster than John could catch them. The two dinghies were picking up Jacques and his friend as Scott watched from shore. At the end of the log drive only seventeen logs were boomed together, and Scott nodded gloomily as John released them.

Scott addressed his crew, "Thanks, friends, but my idea was just as bad as you told me it was. I'm an amateur at logging and it shows. Someone will figure a way to make money in logging the Sixes — a mill perhaps."

Jacques spoke using his hands enthusiastically, *"Mon ami, je suis* . . . happy . . . glad to help. What fun!"

John agreed, "Jacques is right, Scott. Don't let this flop get you down." He paused, laughing loud and long, "But next time stick to farming." Scott joined in the laughter. His friends were entitled to poke fun at him. John passed a pint of cheap whiskey around as everyone slapped Scott on the back good-naturedly.

John took Scott aside to share a piece of law enforcement news. "Chief Sixes and two companions were seen hunting in the Elk River valley last week. I'm obligated to report the sighting to the Army, but I thought you should know first. The miner who recognized your friend guessed that they moved over the ridge into the upper Sixes." He hesitated in phrasing his question, "What do you think I should do?"

Scott replied soberly, "Your duty, John. Meet me at the ranch in two days, and we'll escort all eight members of the family to Fort Umpqua. Do you think Chief Sixes will be allowed to stay on the coast at the Lower Umpqua Reservation? He's adamant about Grande Ronde and Siletz."

"Eight Indians, you say. That scoundrel Dutch was right for a change. Can Buzz accompany us to help protect them along the coastal trail?"

"Of course, and we'll take a cow along so they'll own something when they reach Fort Umpqua."

John concluded, "That's generous of you, Scott. I'll ask Indian Agent Dart about a written recommendation for his counterpart in Gardiner. Captain Tichenor may be of some help also, both because Dart is his son-in-law and because he's a reputable leader on the coast."

Scott informed Buzz and Richard of the news as they rode home, asking Richard to tell Melissa that he was spending the night with Chief Sixes' family. He passed the cabin, galloping east into the fading light. He searched for two hours in the dark, only to be found by Chief Sixes and taken to his well-hidden lodge.

It was evident that his visit was expected. Chief Sixes rattled on in Tututni, too fast for Scott to translate, but the Indian made his point. He wanted to stay here even though his family had been discovered. He had not harmed the white man in the Elk River valley.

Scott signed a firm "No." He indicated that soldiers would come with guns and chains, if he didn't go voluntarily with Marshal John Larsen. Their lodge was no longer a secret, and Scott could not protect them.

When he departed the next morning, he signed that he would meet them at the ranch tomorrow. Recalling their expressions, he had serious doubts that his power of persuasion was adequate, feeling like he had lost the argument.

The following day John arrived before noon, and looked about the ranch before commenting to Scott, "Do you expect Chief Sixes to come peaceably?"

"I hope so, John. I wore out my welcome in his lodge trying to persuade him that he couldn't stay on the Sixes, but I don't know what he'll do. Put your horse in the barn and give him some oats. Melissa is looking forward to visiting with you. Know any good gossip?"

After a long visit, dinner, and an hour of fishing with Richard, John expressed his doubts, "I guess that Chief Sixes is going to sit tight. I'd better ride to Fort Umpqua."

Scott replied, "Be patient, John. You can stay with us tonight. It's a long two-day ride to Fort Umpqua anyway. Buzz rode upriver an hour ago to see if the Indians are coming or not."

Daylight was fading when Buzz trotted into the ranchyard to greet his worried friends. "Chief Sixes' family will be here in two hours. They are carrying everything they own on their backs. Chief Sixes told me that he didn't 'understand' your ultimatum yesterday. I had to threaten him before he agreed to move."

John queried, "What did you tell him?"

"I suggested that the Army might send each member of his family to a different reservation unless they accompanied the Marshal."

Shaking his head, John commented, "Well, I never heard of such a thing, but I approve of your inventiveness. Shall we wait here?"

Melissa interjected from the doorway, "Shall I cook a kettle of stew for them, Scott?"

"Yes! Thanks, Melissa," and turning to John, "Let's wait in the cabin."

The Indians were settled in the barn before anyone knew they had arrived. Scott greeted them respectfully, moving the horses into the corral. Buzz helped John explain his duty to the Indians, who remained stoical and uncommunicative to the white men. Only Melissa broke through their reserve when she brought them her kettle of stew, and then tended a small cut on the arm of Chief Sixes' granddaughter. The Indians were as friendly and open to her as they were cool toward the men.

Preparing for bed, Melissa asked her husband, "Are you upset because the Indians are angry with you?"

"Yes, I feel as I did the day that I took Dutch out of the Port Orfords' village. I can't 'win' regardless of what I do."

"Perhaps you shouldn't worry so much about being a good guy, and take more satisfaction in doing the right thing. These Indians remind me of my students on occasion. The children weren't always happy with me when I told them what was best for them. Don't try to change what you are, Scott dearest. I love you the way you are."

****

The next morning, Scott packed the Indians' belongings on Pinto and tied a lead rope from its packsaddle to the milk cow. Buzz scouted ahead as John led the walking Indians down the road. Chief Sixes' son led Pinto and Scott brought up the rear. The party encountered no travelers that day, getting only curious glances from settlers along the way. Buzz led them off the trail into a cul-de-sac to spend the night as darkness approached. He explained, "There were a lot of white people in Bandon. I thought we should pass through town at a quieter time."

Scott suggested to John, "Let's leave here at first dawn and move fast in the morning. If we pass Bandon without trouble, we should have another good day."

Just before noon on their third day of travel, Buzz signaled for them to stop. The party rested as he galloped back to explain the situation, "There's a logging operation beside the trail ahead — maybe fifteen men. How do we proceed, John?"

"I'll ride ahead and talk to the foreman so we don't surprise them. Buzz, you ride the ridge above the trail, and stay hidden until our party is in the open. Scott, you ride between the loggers and our Indians. I'll bring up the rear. We won't stop until we're well clear of this Coos Bay marshland."

The loggers had quit working and were crowding the trail when Scott rode Randy down their line. They were forced to step back and stay there as John followed suit, leaving only dirty looks and mumbled curses behind. The foreman was helpful as he sent the men back to work as soon as the party had crossed the creek flowing through their camp. Scott switched places with John, saying, "Good work! Let's hope for easy going all day."

On the last day of travel the party passed through Gardiner and the Umpqua Indian Agent joined them in escorting the Indians to Fort Umpqua. John shared his letter of reference with the Agent and then with Lt. Hunter. Scott gave Chief Sixes a bill of sale for the milk cow, and then a troop of soldiers marched the family toward the Lower Umpqua Indian Reservation. The Indians neither looked at their former friends nor spoke to them, treating them like nonentities as they entered their new world of reservation life.

Scott was depressed by their rejection, and his friends couldn't cheer him up. Even Alma Masters failed to break through his gloom with her supper of chicken and dumplings. It was a long and silent ride home to the Myrtlewood Grove.

Melissa sensed her husband's mood as they embraced in homecoming, and stated her supposition, "Your Indian friends are still unhappy with you." When he nodded morosely, she asked, "Would you do anything differently if you had the chance?"

Shaking his head slowly in thought, Scott spoke, "No. It's as you said before we left, I'll have to be satisfied with doing the right thing. But damn it, that doesn't mean that I have to like it."

Melissa listened to her husband pour out his hurt and frustration late into the evening, consoling his bruised spirit with tenderness and love in their marriage bed.

As spring days lengthened, Scott and Buzz worked long hours plowing land in the west pasture. One April day they stood looking over the cultivated flat downriver from the beehives, and Scott beamed with satisfaction, "The corn and potatoes are growing already, Old-Timer. It feels good to have a crop in the soil."

Buzz smiled, playing devil's advocate, "Not so fast, Scott. By July this field will be parched dry. How are you going to water it?"

"No problem! I'll ask Richard to build a water trough from below our bridge on Cascade Creek, and we'll irrigate our crop. When will you plant your apple trees?"

"Next month is soon enough. You know, the trees won't produce fruit for five years. Apple orchards are slower than corn fields. Do you want Richard and me to buy lumber for the water trough?"

Scott replied, "Yes, I'll help Melissa finish planting the vegetable garden and you men build the trough."

The next morning, Buzz and Richard set off to town, only to return a half hour later. Buzz reported to Scott and Melissa, "We have neighbors, folks. I saw smoke coming from one of the decrepit lodges at Sixes crossing, and three children were playing in the clearing. It looks like a settler and his family, but I didn't go in. I thought that you two should greet them."

Melissa said excitedly, "It'll be nice to have a neighbor to visit. Let's take them a basket of food. We can spare potatoes, venison, and eggs, and maybe we could loan them a cow milk for the children."

Scott doted on his wife's generous mood. "We can give them a little friendly help, but no cow. He can walk up here for milk when his family needs it. Hurry and fix your basket and I'll saddle Pinto for you."

Scott stopped his family a short distance from the lodge, and called out, "Hello the house! We're your neighbors come to call. Anyone home?"

A child's head peeked out of the doorway, and then a tall, gangly man in bib overalls stepped out. His black hair and beard were tousled, and he was barefooted. Scott thought, "Why he's just out of bed, and it's almost ten o'clock."

"Howdy neighbors. I'm Donald Miller and I've staked claim to this land." Drawing his wife to his side, he added, "This is Mary. We have five children running around." A jerky nod came from the nondescript, mousy grey woman.

Scott responded, "Good morning, Mr. and Mrs. Miller. I'm Scott McClure, this is my wife Melissa, my father-in-law Richard Nelson, and my partner Buzz Smith. Welcome to the Sixes valley."

Melissa offered her basket of food to Mary, "We thought you might be able to use this. There's some milk for the children. Our cows are regular, and we have milk for you anytime that you can visit."

Donald Miller asked, "How far away is your place?"

Scott responded, "We're a mile or so beyond that cut up there."

Miller frowned, "That's a far piece for a busy man. You've got nice horses there."

Scott struggled to hide his mixed feelings, laughter and anger, caused by the man's lack of subtlety. He thought, he's not only lazy, but he's an ingrate. I hope that he doesn't visit our ranch.

Aloud he offered, "I'll give you a hand fixing up your home. Call on me anytime."

Miller replied flippantly, "Oh, it's fine, neighbor. I'll build a real house when we get settled."

Scott was exasperated as he waved Richard and Buzz into town with a, "You'd better get into Port Orford and buy your lumber. Melissa and I have chores to do." He bade good-bye to the Millers, and climbed up behind Melissa to gallop Pinto up the trail. At slide ridge he dismounted, apologizing to the overburden horse, "Sorry, Pinto, but I needed to get out of there in a hurry."

Melissa said, "That wasn't a nice thing to say, Scott." Laughing she added, "But so true! I thought that you'd blow up in Mr. Miller's face, but you showed great restraint, my dear."

The spring rains returned and Richard was forced inside the barn to cut and fit pieces of lumber for the irrigation trough. After several days, Melissa commented, "The Sixes is awfully high. I doubt that Mr. Miller can go to town for supplies. Do you suppose that they have anything left to eat?"

Scott's answer was pessimistic. "I don't expect so, with seven mouths to feed. He should be able to fish or hunt, but with Miller, who knows. Perhaps Buzz and I should take some potatoes and milk to the family."

"Please do, Scott, for the children's sake."

When the partners rode into the Miller place, it looked deserted. Nothing seemed changed from their previous visit. Seeing a wisp of smoke rising from the lodge in which the family was living, Scott rode forward, calling out, "Hello the house." The debilitated form of Mary Miller appeared in the doorway, but her desultory manner brightened with purpose as she saw a burlap bag of food across Scott's saddle. Her eyes darted to the cloth-covered pail of milk which Buzz was carrying, and she finally remembered her manners.

"Please come in, Mr. McClure, Mr. Smith. Donald went to town six days ago to look for work and hasn't returned yet. Is that food? Is it for us?"

Scott nodded and carried the bag inside and laid it on the crude table, Buzz following suit. Five small children sat waiting hungrily. Scott thought, The oldest child can't be more than six years, and the baby is crawling. Delivering a child each year would wear on any woman.

He told Buzz, "Try catching a trout or two. I'll cut some wood and stoke up the fire. Mrs. Miller, you cut up a dozen potatoes . . . oh, and these onions that Melissa slipped into the bag. We'll have a wholesome fish stew ready within the hour . . . er, maybe half hour." He didn't think that the children could wait very long for a meal.

Buzz returned with three small trout and fileted out the bones, before cutting the fish meat into small chunks, and dropping the pieces into the kettle. Scott poured milk into the potato water, and Mary dropped in chopped onions. Soon the smell of fish stew overcame the musty odor of the porous dwelling, and the children's eyes seemed to grow larger in anticipation. Only when the mixture thickened and the potato bits softened, did Scott pour helpings for the children. To Mary's credit, she turned away from the kettle to feed her two youngest children. Scott and Buzz took over that task so she could help herself.

Buzz agreed to stay as Scott rode back to Melissa and refilled the bag and the pail. His wife put in their last venison roast, and laughed gaily, "You and Buzz want to go hunting anyway. We'll eat smoked salmon tonight. Saddle Pinto for me, Scott and I'll get some onions out of the root cellar. I'm going to visit Mrs. Miller with you. Maybe I can cheer her up."

Riding back after dark, Scott opined, "We could feed that family everything in our larder and they'd still be hungry. Milk and a cut of venison we can afford to give, but potatoes and onions are part of our diet. We can't afford to support every settler who visits the valley."

Melissa agreed, "I told Mary Miller that her husband could walk up to our ranch for milk anytime, but I know that we'll go broke feeding the Miller family. But I hope that he comes home with some food soon, or you'll have to go into town and find him."

Buzz suggested, "As soon as the river drops, you two youngsters can visit town and talk to people. Richard and I will handle the chores — even the milking."

The following week Melissa made fresh bread and wrapped half of it in an old newspaper; she proposed a trip to Millers and on to town. He carried a pail of milk and followed his wife to the Miller place.

Mrs. Miller met them, and was full of news, "Donald brought food home yesterday. He went back to work in Port Orford." She declared proudly, "He's been appointed town Marshal, a real important job."

As they continued on to Port Orford, Scott related John's pledge that he would quit the Marshal's job in May, "It must be May. John is a man of his word. What do you think of Miller as Marshal?"

Melissa reasoned aloud, "There's not any troublemakers left in the area. What harm can come to him? At least our worry about starving children has been alleviated."

****

The summer passed swiftly and without incident of note. George fretted about poor business conditions, and unpaid bills owed to him by miners who were disappearing from the coast. John visited the Sixes when fishing was slack. Melissa recognized that he was infatuated with her, and finally spoke to Scott about her feelings, ending with a question, "John has been a perfect gentleman, and a good friend to both of us. What should we do?"

Scott suggested, "Nothing. Half the bachelors in Port Orford are smitten to some degree. If John ever offends you, I'll talk to him. What you ought to do is find a good woman for him."

"Now that's the best advice you've given me in a long time. I'll talk to Mary Hermann the next time that I visit Port Orford."

The crop was so bountiful that it took all four of them a month of steady work to harvest it. Donald Miller showed up to help at odd times, asking for his pay in potatoes and onions. Scott insisted that Miller take corn also, telling his neighbor to plant corn in the spring, while Melissa showed Mary Miller how to make corn meal.

Scott sold a wagon load of potatoes and several bags of fresh garden vegetables to George for his store. He bartered three wagon loads of corn to the Langlois farmers a calf and four apple trees. Buzz was ecstatic that his orchard was growing to ten trees, and crowed, "Just you wait Scott, I'll have the sweetest honey and the reddest apples on the coast." He guarded his corner of the ranch like the apple trees were his family. No four legged varmits were going to eat his tender young sprouts.

One morning, Scott was awakened by a shot, and rushed to the orchard to find Buzz dressing out a small doe. Richard said, "Deer will have to learn to stay away from the orchard or suffer their fate." Buzz just smiled and went about his task.

****

Scott was cultivating his corn field with cow manure when Louie Knapp galloped up the road to the ranch. His sudden appearance and downcast countenance indicated bad news, soon verified as Scott found Melissa crying in the yard.

Louie blurted out, "Jacques Dubois was killed this morning in a logging accident. Mother and Mary are with Sally in her home. John asked me to give you this message, 'Hurry, there's going to be trouble at the funeral tomorrow. I need your support.' I think that he's referring to people saying Sally has to leave because she's an Indian. Marshal Miller agreed and told her Indians weren't allowed on the coast. John threw him out of her house, I mean literally picked him up and threw him ten feet. He bounced on his butt in the yard, threatening to arrest John for obstructing the law."

"Tell me the rest as we ride into town, Louie. Where are your father and Buzz, Melissa?"

"They're in the east pasture stacking hay or maybe fishing if they've finished the haying."

Scott went inside the house and fetched his rifle, firing it into the air three times, before catching the horses and saddling them.

Melissa packed a change of clothes for the funeral and brought Scott his shells and knife, "You might need these. Is there anything else that I can get?"

"No, mount up and ride with Louie to the crossing. Buzz and I will catch up shortly." He waited as the two men ran into the yard, panting heavily. "Jacques was killed this morning in a logging accident, and people are harassing Sally. John's called for backup. Richard, I want you to watch the ranch. Keep your rifle handy and stay in the house at night. We'll be a few days. I don't expect trouble here, but Miller is against John, and anything can happen. Come on, Buzz!"

Both men mounted and rode down the road at a gallop, overtaking Melissa and Louie at slide ridge. Scott pushed the horses hard all the way to the Dubois home. Louie offered, "I'll take care of the horses. They'll be in my barn," as Sally's three friends hurried into the house.

Mary Hermann exclaimed, "Am I glad to see you folks. Sally's lying down, but this has been a tragic day. Jacques was killed instantly when he tripped and fell under a falling tree. John suggests a closed casket funeral tomorrow morning. He's building it while George tries to talk sense into townfolks."

Sally emerged from her bedroom and smiling sadly, she said, "Thank you for coming. Jacques would be pleased that his friends honored him." A tear fell from her eye as she spoke softly, "I'm sorry that I'm such a bother. I'm Indian but I've never belonged to a tribe. My father was a half-breed Yakima from the Horse Heaven Hills. My mother was a full-blooded Umpqua from Calapooya Springs, but when they married he worked for Hudson's Bay Company and they lived on trading posts. Jacques had some Cree blood, but we seldom thought about being Indian — we were just people. Can Marshal Miller really force me out of my home?"

"Of course not!" Melissa answered spiritedly, eyes flashing. "No one will bother you while we're here. Sally, we all share your grief for Jacques. He was a fine man."

Scott left Buzz to watch the house while he walked to the mill to find John. As he entered the millyard, he called, "John, where are you?"

"Over here in the lumber shed, Scott. I'm just finishing the casket. Look for yourself, and tell me if we should have a closed casket funeral."

Scott barely recognized the remains of Jacques Dubois, and quickly agreed, "You're right, John. Seal the casket. Can you lock this shed?"

"No, but I'll wire the door shut overnight. It'll keep any animals outside."

As they walked together toward town, John explained the problem and the two men agreed that after the funeral, Sally would be vulnerable to persecution. Bigotry was already evident with some people. John was deep in silent thought, when Scott asked if he could help.

"No, thanks for coming to help, but I need a woman's advice. Would Melissa be offended if I had a very personal conversation with her?" John blushed, but kept talking, "She understands people so well, and I trust her common sense as well as discretion. Perhaps we could take a walk for privacy."

Scott was somewhat taken aback, but could only answer, "I'll ask her and see what she says."

"Thanks, Scott. I'll wait on the porch."

Melissa stepped onto the porch dressed for a walk, and put John at ease immediately. "Let's walk down to the beach. I don't know if I can help you, but I'm a good listener."

John Larsen's light complexion reddened as he struggled to express himself, "Melissa, I think Scott is the luckiest man alive, having you as his wife. You're the model that I hold before me when I think of marriage and family. Women are scarce on the coast and I'm not going to find another Melissa, but I like and respect Sally, and she needs a strong man to take care of her. I think that we would be good for each other, but there's no time to mourn, no time to wait in respect, and no time to court properly. Am I being insensitive and as foolish as I feel?"

"No, John, you are not insensitive. You are a very caring person. You're also innovative in looking at this difficult situation, but I don't have any idea of how Sally feels about you or will feel about your idea. Do you want me to ask her on your behalf?"

John sighed with relief. "Would you, Melissa? Tell her that I will understand if she isn't interested in my proposal. Can we keep this confidential? Of course you can tell Scott if it's necessary."

"No. You can tell Scott if you choose, but I'll keep this conversation and Sally's answer in confidence between the two of you."

Melissa chased the men out of the house, telling them, "Hold a wake for Jacques by having a drink in his memory. I'll stay with Sally; I know that Mary has to fix supper for Angela and Junior." John, George, and Scott complied but Buzz stopped in an empty storefront across the street and continued to guard the house.

After ensuring their privacy, Melissa asked, "Sally are you feeling capable of a very frank conversation with me?"

"Yes, Melissa, I'm fine. You sound very serious."

"I am. A good man will be buried in the morning, and you should have time to mourn him before making any decisions on your life. But I don't believe people will respect your rights and leave you alone. You're aware of the talk, aren't you?"

"Yes, I'm afraid of Marshal Miller. He's such a little man to be filling an important job."

"I'm going to present you with an important option, but it must be in strict confidence. John Larsen is a good man and he can protect you if you are married to him. He likes and respects you and his proposal is honorable, I believe, but it is most unusual. What should I tell John?"

"Why would he want to marry me? He's a white man with a good job fishing. People respect him now, but they won't if I'm his wife. It's too much to ask of him."

"But you're not asking, John is. You can only answer yes or no. Would you like to talk to him?" Sally looked at Melissa for approval as she nodded, being very unsure of herself.

Melissa went to the door and waved in Buzz's general direction. He hurried over to the house, asking "How did you know I was there?"

She chuckled, "You wouldn't leave me here unprotected would you, Erastus Smith? I want to see John Larsen, please."

John knocked on the door within minutes, and entered on Sally's invitation. Melissa stepped outside to give them privacy, and ignored Buzz's "What's going on?" Gazing up at the stars, she drifted into a light reverie, thinking, this role of advisor is almost omnipotent . . . and can be a little addictive. No wonder Scott gets emotional when he acts as a leader or an advisor. The door opening brought her back to reality.

Sally and John were hand in hand, and John spoke softly, in awe of his own words, "Sally said yes, Melissa. We'll be married right after the funeral. I'll ask Captain Tichenor to perform the ceremony."

Buzz recovered from his surprise to advise John, "You'd better keep it quiet until the wedding, or someone will cause a fuss." Buzz grinned as he looked at Melissa, "Scott's fit to be tied, girl. You have him bamboozled with all this secrecy."

The funeral was attended by many of the townspeople, some of their expressions hostile toward the widow. Captain Tichenor read the service and Scott delivered a eulogy. Sally threw a handful of loose soil on the lowered casket and turned away, walking home with her friends.

Marshal Miller was fussing at Buzz with his Sharps rifle in the front yard, while Captain Tichenor performed the marriage ceremony between John and Sally. A half dozen townspeople were in the street urging Miller to do his duty, when John and Sally stepped onto the porch.

John announced, "I'd like all of you to meet my wife, Sally Larsen. We plan to live in Port Orford and hope that our friends will visit us. If you're not our friend, Marshal, you're not welcome."

"Wait a minute, Larsen I have a duty to run every Indian out of town. You're obstructing . . ."

"Be quiet, Miller," Scott ordered in harsh tones, "Only Tututni Indians have been ordered off the coast, and Sally is not Tututni. She's a citizen of this town and you will respect her right, or you'll answer to me. Is that clear, Donald Miller?"

Miller saw the formidable array of citizenry before him, but he looked at Scott's glaring visage the most, and he backed down. When he turned to leave there were no supporters in the street, only passing citizens. Louie Knapp announced, "There's food and drink at the hotel. Let's toast the bride and groom."

"So ended a very unconventional but well-timed marriage day," Scott mumbled to himself. Melissa heard his words and smiled knowingly to herself.

Chapter Nine

Scott and Melissa rode into Port Orford to join the Hermanns in celebrating Junior's fifth birthday, carrying two young chickens for a gift. Junior was a bright youngster with an inordinate interest in animals, particularly Melissa's chicks. Approaching the Hermann house, she expressed a doubt, "I didn't ask Mary if giving chickens to Junior was acceptable to her."

Scott chuckled and responded, "When Junior sees his gift, it won't matter what Mary or George think. They give Junior what he wants."

"He certainly is the apple of his father's eye, a bit spoiled, but he's always smiling and happy."

Scott put the horses and chickens in the barn, after dropping Melissa at the front door. He entered the back door with a light rap. Junior was waiting in the kitchen to greet him with a bright smile, which dimmed as he looked at Scott's empty hands. He said tentatively, "It's my birthday and Momma baked me a big cake." With eyes big in expectation, he confided, "And everybody brought me a present."

Scott hunkered down on his heels and put an arm around Junior, saying conspiratorially, "We brought you a present, but it's a big surprise. Why don't you give Aunt Melissa a hug and ask her about it?"

Junior darted into the parlor and hugged a bewildered Melissa. "Uncle Scott said that you have a surprise for me. He won't tell me what it is."

Angela interjected a very proper answer as she teased her brother, "Georgie, you must wait until your party to open presents."

"No, I don't! Not if Aunt Melissa tells me what it is," Junior replied promptly, charming Melissa with his best smile.

His mother conceded, "You can open one present now, but the rest have to wait."

As Scott returned to the barn for the chickens, Melissa told Junior a story which was a clue to his present. Junior solved the puzzle before the end of the tale, and ran to the kitchen from which cluckings were emanating. Mary rolled her eyes at Melissa in consternation as she followed her son out of the room. He was enthralled with the chickens, and looking at his mother, he rattled on enthusiastically, finally asking, "Look, Momma! Aren't they pretty? Can I keep them Momma . . . please?"

His mother was unable to resist such a hopeful plea, and assented reluctantly, "Yes, Junior, but you have to take care of them."

Junior gave his mother a hug, and over her shoulder, asked, "Uncle Scott, will you help me build a coop for my chickens?"

Looking to John Larsen for his agreement, Scott answered, "Yes, John and I will build a coop after your birthday party. Do you know how to feed your chickens?"

"Yes, Aunt Melissa lets me feed her chickens," Junior replied quickly as everyone chuckled at his confidence and enthusiasm. It appeared that Mary had a farmer to supervise.

"It's clear that Melissa's chickens have captured Junior's attention," George observed. "Let's eat your cake so that you can open your other presents."

Working on the chicken coop later in the day, Scott asked George and John, "How's Miller doing? I haven't seen him or his family since our disagreement."

George replied, "He's still Marshal, but several of us insisted that his salary be lowered. I question the need for a full-time law officer with business being so slow."

John raised a question, "George, is it true that his family has moved into that abandoned miner's shack near Garrison Lake?"

"Yes, he told me that he 'claims' both that cabin and the Sixes farm, but I doubt that he has a legal right to either place. There are a lot of empty houses in town which no one seems to want.

Since he's left Sally and you alone, I haven't paid attention to his comings and goings."

Scott changed the subject, wondering, "Are there any new settlers in the area? It'd be nice to have a friendly neighbor on the Sixes."

George answered, "Several men have passed through town this fall, but no one has stayed. I did hear that three farmers with families have settled in the Coquille valley recently. Oh yes, two miners arrived last month and are prospecting the beach at Hubbard Creek."

"Well, I'll wish them luck. Sam and I had a good winter together and found a little gold, but I've never worked so hard in my life. I'll stick to farming."

John finished the coop as Melissa entered the barn, dressed to ride home. Scott saddled the horses, and George bid farewell, "Good-bye folks, see you at Christmas."

****

When they arrived at the ranch, Buzz and Richard informed them that they could do the chores. The two men had planned an overnight hunt up the old cougar trail, and were leaving at daybreak. Buzz said to the apprehensive Melissa, "Don't worry about Richard, we'll keep a warm campfire in the protection of that cairn up the mountain. We'll return day after tomorrow."

Late in the second day, Melissa called Scott in from the barn, fretting, "Father and Buzz aren't back yet, dear. Will you go after them?"

Scott nodded, recognizing his wife's concern, and dressed for the trail before walking through the east pasture and crossing the river on a fallen snag. He'd gone less than a mile when he saw movement in the forest ahead, and soon identified Buzz and Richard carrying large packs of game meat. Buzz saw him and called,

"Hey, Scott! Get up here. We're looking for a strong back. These bear haunches are a might heavy."

Scott looked at Buzz's pack, and commented, "This is a good-sized load you're carrying, Old-Timer. Are you bringing out the whole animal?"

"Well, Richard and I didn't want to waste any meat. We're carrying the rest of the bear in a sling made out of the bear's hide. If you'll take these packs to the meat shed, we'll go back up the mountain for the rest of our load."

Scott hung his first load of meat in the shed, and told Melissa the hunters were all right, and then returned for the second pack. It was well after dark when all the meat was in the shed and the men were ready to eat supper. Richard was worn out, but happy at their success. He let Buzz tell the story of their adventure.

"Well, we walked right up the mountain two miles or so yesterday, and wasted the morning chasing a big buck and three does. He outsmarted us and got away, so we returned to our trail and went on to the cairn. We dropped our packs in a sheltered spot and traipsed over the ridge toward the Elk River without seeing anything." Buzz paused for dramatic effect, before continuing, "Richard and I were about fifty feet apart when I saw bear sign and stopped. I signaled Richard but he walked right on to the cairn, and then I heard a God-awful scream and a howling roar. . . . I couldn't tell which was Richard and which was the bear, both scared me something fierce. By the time the bear decided to leave our campsite, Richard just up and shoots the varmint right through his snout. Why that Sharps slug tore half the bear's armor-plated skull apart. I had a bead on the animal, but no second shot was necessary. Melissa, your daddy's a crack-shot." He deferred to Richard for his version.

"Melissa, I just looked up and saw that bear at the same time he saw me. We scared each other, but when the bear charged out of that pocket, I shot without thinking. I was just lucky to kill him with that first shot or he would have run right over me."

Buzz countered, "The story sounds better, Richard, if you forget that 'lucky shot' bit, and just say you killed him with one shot. It's the truth. Anyway, we butchered out the prime cuts and started packing out this morning. Scott, were we glad to see you."

Melissa asked, "My goodness, how big was the bear?"

"I reckon that it weighed 700-800 pounds. We brought out 350 pounds of meat. Maybe we should sell some, Scott. Bear meat gets tiresome to my palate in a hurry. I could take the two rear quarters to town and do some dickering. Besides it's a good story to tell my friends at the tavern."

He looked at Richard, and added, "Don't worry, old friend, I'll give you all the credit."

Buzz enjoyed telling his new story and Richard enjoyed the notoriety of a one-shot hunter during the following month. Scott was tired of hearing, and rehearing, the tale, but Melissa loved to watch her father's expression as Buzz related the bear killing. By the time they visited the Hermanns at Christmas, Melissa could tell the story as well as Buzz.

****

Junior had been conscientious in caring for his chickens, so Melissa gave him two more hens and a young rooster for Christmas. As Scott had prophesied at the birthday party, the Hermanns doted on their son, and were supporting his poultry project. Mary had asked to buy more chickens, but Melissa volunteered to help Junior build his brood. The hens would be layers when they matured in a few weeks. Junior was already making a deal to sell eggs to his father for the store.

George expressed the tone of Christmas in 1857 after saying Grace at dinner, "None of us have much money, and business along the coast is bad, but families and friends are gathered together in good health and cheer. What more can we ask for?"

After dinner, George and Scott walked with Junior to the chicken coop, visiting about the townspeople and business conditions. George said, "With a shortage of cash, I can't pay you the money that you loaned me three years ago, but I can afford to pay you in supplies. If you agree, I'll credit your account with what I owe you, and you won't have any bills to worry about this winter."

Scott agreed quickly, "Thanks, George. Crediting our account with your loan repayment will carry us through the year. We can save our cash for an emergency. You know, Melissa and Buzz have earned more cash money for eggs and honey than all our farm produce combined. When do you see a turnaround coming for business in Port Orford?"

"I don't know, my friend. It could be another year or two before conditions improve."

George called to Junior, "Come along, son. Your chickens are doing fine." He affectionately put his arm around Junior's shoulders as they walked across the yard into the house.

****

A wet and windy winter made travel inhospitable, and except for Buzz's biweekly ride to Port Orford to deliver eggs and an occasional side of venison, everyone stayed home. It was family time well spent and enjoyed by all. Richard's lungs stayed clear so that he could bundle up in his raingear and fish almost every day.

When the weather broke in late March, Scott began cultivating his corn field, while Buzz watched his trees and bees. The Old-Timer shot two deer before game learned to stay away from the tender shoots in his orchard.

Melissa walked cheerfully in the bright sunshine to the field, carrying a jug of milk and a basket of sandwiches. Buzz took two sandwiches and returned to his beehives, while Scott wolfed down sandwiches until Melissa exclaimed, "Whoa! Leave one for father and another for me."

Scott laughed, complaining, "I'm a hungry working man, honey. Since when did you start eating two sandwiches?"

With an uppity glance, she retorted, "Since I started eating for two people. Do you want your son to starve?"

"Whoopee!" Scott yelled as he hugged his wife and whirled her in the air. He quickly reversed his action, placing her gently on her feet, and said, "Oops! I better be careful now that you're pregnant."

Now it was Melissa's turn to laugh, "I'm not a china doll, Scott. Your hug was very reassuring to me, even though I know that we both want children."

"When is he due?" Scott queried, also assuming a boy child was growing in Melissa's womb.

"About October 15th. Here comes Buzz with his curiosity showing. You can tell him the good news."

Buzz rejoined, "Good news, Melissa? Are you in a family way?" When she nodded, he slapped Scott lustily on his back, and gave her a kiss on the cheek, a rare demonstration of affection from the Old-Timer. He added exuberantly, "Congratulations! Does Richard know? Can I tell him? I won our bet of a bottle of his brandy if you got pregnant before April 1."

"Shame on you two! Betting on your grandson and godson." Laughing at her good-natured admonishment, she urged, "Go tell Daddy. I'll make a chicken dinner to celebrate."

When Buzz returned from his next trip to Port Orford, he brought news that Sally was expecting, also on October 15th. New life was developing on the Oregon coast even as the economic bust continued to discourage settlers.

The corn was ankle-high when the McClures hosted a joint birthday party for Melissa and Buzz. She had passed her twenty-fourth birthday two weeks before and he admitted to being seventy plus years in July.

Scott had picked a Sunday which he hoped might have sunshine, and then invited everyone within twenty miles to a barbecue picnic in the myrtlewood grove. He had slaughtered a crippled cow in May, and on the morning of the picnic, rigged half a beef over a pit of glowing alder coals, which was supplemented by fourteen salmon which Richard had caught during the previous week.

Buzz helped Melissa prepare an enormous potato salad that filled all of her bowls and pans. Mary brought freshly baked bread and John inveigled Captain Tichenor to bring a small tun of red wine back from California on his last trip. Scott had saved enough milk for the children to drink.

Sunday morning Melissa giggled nervously, commenting, "I hope people come to our party. We have so much food. Do you think this sunny weather will last all day?"

Scott reassured her, "Today is perfect picnic weather. Our friends will come early and stay late. Let's hope that we have enough food." His optimism was well founded as over two hundred people attended with most families bringing a dessert. Food and drink was more than ample, and the honorees received several presents despite the fact that the announcement had said no gifts.

The McClure picnic was the social affair of the year, with Melissa and Sally enjoying their last opportunity to visit with friends for several months. Their traveling days were curtailed as they neared their sixth month of pregnancy.

Melissa drew Sally aside as the Larsens were preparing to leave, and asked, "How are you doing? John told me that no one has bothered you since the wedding. In fact, I saw the Millers talking to you today. But are people really accepting you as John's wife and an expectant mother?"

"People love and respect John just as I do, but most of them barely tolerate me. Of course a few good friends accept me as I am, but people like the Millers are two-faced. Mary Miller drug her husband over to John and me, but his eyes hated me while his lips smiled. I will never trust him." Sally smiled gently as she continued, "Those kind of people don't matter. John is so pleased that we're having a baby that he doesn't see their looks. He thinks well of everyone, but I'm more practical. I just avoid people who don't like me."

Melissa experienced a moment of empathy with her friend, thinking to herself, It must be terrible having to sort out friends from enemies all the time. Aloud she agreed with Sally, "You're right that you can count on your friends. Our children will be age-mates and I hope that they develop a lasting friendship."

****

Angela Hermann and Ellen Tichenor rode to the McClure ranch twice in early August to visit Melissa and help her with her chores. Melissa was grateful for their help, but was concerned for their safety, feeling that eleven year old girls were riding too far from home. She had Scott talk to George and Mary, who were surprised because Angela hadn't told them about the visits, and they stopped them immediately. Although Ellen didn't ride out to the ranch again, she did ride the beach freely with her parents' permission. She was a well-recognized figure as she grew up in Port Orford.

****

After an abundant harvest in the fall, the McClure family waited anxiously for Melissa's time. One night in mid-October she experienced false labor pains, but Buzz had ridden into Port Orford and returned with Mary Hermann before Melissa realized her situation. Mary and Melissa had a fine time visiting for the next three days before the real delivery started after supper, lasting through the night. Richard Erastus McClure screamed his way to attention in the early morning hours of October 17th, a healthy baby boy with reddish hair and blue eyes. Scott was a proud papa, while Richard and Buzz were ecstatic over their grandson and godson, respectively. Melissa was almost forgotten in their celebration, until Scott told them to congratulate the mother.

Mary stayed with Melissa and the baby for two days before asking Buzz to take her home. "You men can take care of Melissa and Ricky. I promised Sally Larsen that I'd help with her delivery. I hope that I'm not too late."

As Buzz discovered on his next egg delivery to the store, Sally had delivered a healthy baby boy on October 23rd. They had agreed to name their son John Larsen Junior, and when the father first saw the towheaded boy with blue eyes, he knew the name fit the child. Sally had suffered through a very difficult labor and was close to death during the hours after her delivery. John sat by her bedside all night offering her his physical and spiritual strength for recovery. When both mother and son were healthy, a relieved John vowed that there would be no more children in the Larsen family.

Scott and John exchanged visits during the following week, admiring each other's healthy son politely, while knowing full well that their own son was someone special — a typical attitude shared by proud fathers.

One day Melissa commented on Ricky's resemblance to Scott, and he beamed a ready reply, "He's going to be a farmer."

"I know, and Little John is going to be a fisherman," Melissa said merrily, adding, "Perhaps the boys might want to be a doctor or a sea captain. Remember, Ricky will have ideas of his own about his life."

Scott teased his wife in response, "Maybe we ought to have a dozen children so we're sure to have at least one farmer in the family."

****

Buzz and Richard delivered a young steer to the store one afternoon in December, and then visited with the Hermanns over supper. They learned that Jack the bartender had moved to Umpqua City, and he had left a bottle of California wine at the store for Melissa. Mary's observation to Richard touched his fatherly pride, "Melissa is such a good person that everyone likes and admires her. That bartender is a casual friend of Scott's, so she treats him as her friend, and he considers her a grand lady."

George concluded, "Well, dear, she is a grand lady. Richard, you raised her right."

He changed the subject, and informed them, "Donald Miller was fired as Marshal yesterday. We just can't afford a full-time Marshal. John volunteered to serve as part-time Marshal for the winter months."

Richard asked, "What is Miller going to do?"

George smiled, and replied, "Be your neighbor. His family is moving back to their Sixes farm."

Buzz harrumphed, "To do what? There's nothing on that 'farm' of his. I suppose Melissa will feel that she has to feed the Miller children all winter. I can't abide his laziness."

Richard had been coughing sporadically for a couple of minutes when Buzz finally noticed his flushed face. He suggested, "You'd better get to bed in the hotel and doctor that cough." Richard smiled wanly and agreed, walking with his friend to their hotel room.

The next morning Richard was feeling better and insisted on riding home before the rain clouds returned. They were both soaked from the waist down when they crossed the Elk and Sixes Rivers on the trip home.

Melissa was anxious about her father's lungs and became doubly concerned when Buzz developed similar symptoms of illness. Two days later, Scott succumbed to the same malady, which Melissa properly diagnosed as influenza. All three men were bedridden for several days and she was alone to do all the chores as well as nurse them and care for the baby.

Donald Miller appeared on the cabin doorsteps a couple of days after Scott had fallen ill. Melissa was pleasantly surprised when he offered to work for food. He was frightened of the fever and kept his distance from her and the cabins, but she had kind thoughts for him as she nursed her menfolks. Scott recovered quickly, displaying a great hunger, and a desire to tend his stock. Melissa refused to let him out of bed until he had eaten and slept around the clock.

He returned from his first foray into the barn with a puzzled look, asking his wife, "Have you seen the two milk cows that were in the barn? One of them has a chewed ear and the other has a black eye; you call her Louise."

"They were there last week, but Mr. Miller may have moved them yesterday, or was it the day before that he worked?" Melissa pondered.

Scott took his Sharps and headed for the east pasture, looking for two strays. Entering the cabin for supper, he explained, "The cows were led downriver, probably by Miller. Rain has obscured the sign, but there is no doubt that they were stolen. I'll ride to Miller's place tomorrow and retrieve them. I wonder what he thinks he's doing?"

The next morning Scott mounted Randersacker and rode into a deserted Miller farm. Cow sign was abundant, and he found where the Miller family and his two cows had trailed north, two or three days ago. Scott rode into town for help, but he was quickly disappointed as he discovered that influenza had brought town life to a stop. George reported that Mary, Angela, and Junior were all ill at home, and John Larsen was bedridden with illness also.

To the question on Miller, George recalled, "He came in here three days ago and said that he was leaving forever. He said that you gave him two cows to pay for working on your ranch while you were all ailing. It was a fanciful tale that he gave me, but no one was in a position to question him. Good riddance, I say!"

Scott laughed ironically, "I guess that I've paid two cows to get rid of Miller as a neighbor. I imagine that he will sell my cows and keep going. I agree, good riddance." He paused in thought, before continuing, "There's no point in chasing after the Millers, but since they've abandoned that old Indian lodge, I think that I'll burn it. Something I should have done before they claimed it."

Scott returned to the Sixes crossing and threw all the trash that littered the Miller place into the dilapidated lodge, and then set fire to it. He watched it burn until the walls collapsed and the gentle drizzle of rain returned, and then rode home.

Melissa was philosophical about the theft, giving Miller credit, "He saved our stock by helping out for a week. Besides, his family is poor, and we'd be feeding them if they lived on their farm."

Scott informed her, "There's a regular epidemic of influenza in the area. How are your two patients coming along?"

"I'm concerned that father hasn't improved. Buzz got up this afternoon and walked around his cabin, and even though he looks ghastly, I believe he's recovering. You look a little pale after your active day. Can you watch our son while I take them dinner?"

Scott replied, "Of course! I'll feed the stock first, and then sit with Ricky. Stay with your father for awhile."

Melissa returned well after dark with a simple report that both men were sleeping soundly.

Scott was awakened by a Sharps periodic firing, recognizing the sound of Buzz's rifle. He shook Melissa awake as he dressed, saying simply, "Buzz needs help."

He fired a round into the air to tell Buzz that they were coming, and then stoked the fire while Melissa checked their sleeping son. They hurried across the flat in a false dawn to find Buzz sitting against the door jamb, cradling his Sharps. He muttered, "Damn fever! I'm too weak. . . . Richard is dying. . . ."

Melissa rushed to her father's bedside, a soft gurgling sound in Richard's throat being accentuated by the still night. A small spasm shook his head as he coughed, awakening him briefly from his coma-like sleep. With tears in her eyes, she gripped his hand and leaned closer to him. In a moment of recognition, he whispered, "Dear Missy . . . cough, cough . . . don't cry. . . . Take care of my grandson . . . and tell . . ." Richard Nelson's breathing ebbed until it stilled altogether, as the sunrise touched the mountaintops of the Sixes valley. Scott held his wife firmly as they mourned her father's passing, finding solace in being together as a family in his final moment of life.

They buried Richard that next morning on a small rise near the myrtlewood grove, just a stone's throw from his favorite fishing spot. Buzz and Richard had selected that site for a family graveyard the previous year. The Old-Timer reaffirmed his wishes, "I'd like to rest right next to Richard when my time comes. This is a pretty spot."

****

After spending a day regaining his strength, and catching up on his work, Scott rode to town with a delivery of eggs. He needed to report his father-in-law's death to the Marshal and the Postmaster. Entering the store he was met by a haggard and pale John Larsen obviously tending business for George.

John exclaimed, "Ah, Scott! You can just about make the funeral if you hurry. George Junior died from influenza yesterday. It's a sad time for our friends. George is terribly broken up over his son's death, and Mary had to get out of her sick bed to arrange the funeral. Perhaps you can help them with their grief, and talk to Angela too. She's confused because her parents are so distraught over Junior's death."

"I'll do what I can, John. Richard died three days ago of the same illness, but Melissa has accepted his death. It must be very difficult for anyone to lose a child, particularly a favorite son like Junior was. His parents adored him."

John sympathized with the McClures' loss, "Richard was a fine man. Give Melissa our condolences. I thought that Melissa might help Mary, but perhaps that's too much for her at this time."

Scott contradicted his friend, "No, Melissa is needed here and she's much better at helping people than you and me. I'll visit with the Hermanns and then bring Melissa to town later in the afternoon."

Scott saw the Hermanns returning home from the cemetery as he rode up to their house. Hitching his horse to the porch railing, he met the family in the street, embracing them without comment. George was stony-faced, his gaze stunned with grief, and while Mary's tears seemed normal, her anxiety for her husband caused her to finger her shawl and shuffle her feet. She was at a loss to help her husband shake his fugue.

"Junior's death is a terrible loss to all of us. He was a bright lad whose memory I'll carry with me forever. I can't find words to express my sorrow at his passing." Nodding to Mary and Angela, he grasped George's elbow and said, "George and I are going to take a walk. Why don't you women rest for awhile?"

Scott led George up the street toward the harbor shoreline, finding neither cooperation nor resistance. He couldn't think of anything to say, so they walked in silence. As they walked down the bluff onto the sandy beach, Scott released his grip and placed his hand on George's shoulder without any visible effect on his friend's trancelike appearance.

"George, Mary and Angela need your strength now. You're a family, and have to help each other overcome your grief," Scott said as he commenced speaking to his friend for several minutes without any response.

He paused, thinking to himself, I'm no good at consoling George. Melissa would know what to say. Maybe I just need to wake him up.

"George!" Scott spoke sternly, "Snap out of it."

He shook his friend by his shoulders until a glint of anger sparked in George's eyes. He shouted, "Leave me alone! I don't need anyone telling me . . .", and ran stumbling up the bluff. Scott followed George home at a short distance, entering the house to find Mary comforting her crying husband.

Scott thought that he'd done a lousy job of counseling George, but Mary smiled sadly at him and said, "Thank you, Scott, George is all right now."

Scott saw Angela listening soberly from her perch on the top step of the stairway, and he remembered John's concern. He climbed the stairs and sat down next to Angela. When he put his arm around her shoulders, she hugged him and sobbed with her whole body, crying mumbled tears.

Scott lost his self-consciousness and crooned a lullaby his mother had sung to him years before. He didn't know the words, and doubted that the tune was on key, but it was comforting to Angela as well as to him.

Face still buried in his shoulder, she sobbed out a muffled confession, "I'm bad . . . so bad . . . I teased Georgie . . . I wasn't a good sister . . . and I can't tell him that . . . I'm sorry." Wrenching sobs shook her body as Scott continued to hold her, and then she blurted out, "No one can love me when I'm so bad."

"Angela, you are a good girl and I love you. And you know that Georgie loved you very much. He always wanted to be with you. Why do you think that you are bad?"

Still sobbing she looked up at Scott trustingly, and answered, "Sometimes I hated Georgie because he was their favorite. It wasn't fair. They always paid attention to everything that he did. But I loved my brother when we were alone, just the two of us together."

"Were you jealous of Georgie because your folks loved him too?"

Angela replied with assurance, "They loved him more."

Scott nodded in agreement, recognizing the child's need for truth, and asked, "Do you think your mother loves you?"

"Yes, but . . ."

"Do you think your father loves you?"

"Not as much as Georgie." Scott waited patiently for her to add, "I guess so, Uncle Scott, but not as much as I love him."

Scott pondered an answer that would satisfy her, but with the paradoxical nature of love, he could only state his belief, "Mary and George are loving parents. Did they love you less because they loved your brother a lot? I don't think so, Angela, but you can be sure that they want your love. They may not show it because they're grieving for Georgie, but they love you. You're part of the Hermann family."

Scott sensed a silence downstairs and was sure that at least part of his conversation with Angela had been overheard. He suggested, "Go tell them that you love them, and everything will be all right."

As Scott slipped out the door, he could hear his friends grieving together as a family.

Scott was exhausted after escorting Melissa to the Hermanns and leaving her, then bringing Pinto back to the ranch. Buzz had played with Ricky for an hour, and then both of them had taken a nap. The Old-Timer was recovering from his bout with influenza very slowly.

Scott teased him, "Taking an afternoon nap! Why it must be your age, partner."

Buzz acceded to Scott's point good-naturedly, "Heh, heh! I expect you're right. I admit that I can't keep up with you anymore. With Richard gone and me slowing down, we may need a hand at harvest time." He dredged up an old memory of their first summer together, "Remember our first hunt at Verneau, or Scottsburg if you like, when we raced back to the cabin with a full load of venison? You couldn't beat me then, but the years are catching up with me. My illness just proved to me that I can't match you in stamina, but I'm just as tough as you are."

****

Scott began construction of a log and earth dam in the draw behind the ranch house. He planned to create a small pool, a reservoir for irrigation as well as a drainage control for the muddy trickle that flowed past the garden in the rainy season.

Three days later, Buzz rode into town to meet Melissa and bring back supplies, while Scott struggled with his dam project. At supper that evening, Melissa related a story of George's aberrant behavior involving fits of temper at home and in the store.

"The day after I arrived at the Hermanns, George moped around the house until Mary suggested that he take a walk. A short time later, we heard a terrible ruckus from their barn, including cracking wood and squealing chickens. By the time Mary and I reached the barn, George had killed all of Junior's hens with his bare hands after destroying their coop. He was contrite and apologetic for losing his temper, without realizing how uncharacteristic his behavior was. A second incident occurred when a delinquent customer picked up a five pound bag of sugar and asked to charge it. George flew into a rage, threatening the man and chasing him out of the store, throwing the bag of sugar after him. He didn't seem disturbed that he had wasted the sugar that the man wanted to buy on credit, although once again he was sorry that he lost his temper."

"People are beginning to avoid him. I don't think he had any customers yesterday, and today Louie Knapp and Buzz were his only visitors. Mary is worried about the business, but George doesn't seem to care."

Melissa frowned as she added, "I told them that we couldn't travel to town for Christmas next week, and I invited them to join us. George ignored my invitation and Mary just shook her head. I told them the invitation was open anytime, but I think we'll spend Christmas day alone."

****

After the new year began, John Larsen walked to Sixes to tell Scott that George was closing the store and going to Gardiner to work for Harvey Masters. "You are to come to town with your horses and pick up what supplies you need for the winter. He said that you still have plenty of credit in your account at the store."

John stayed for supper and slept over in Buzz's cabin. His description of Port Orford was that of a ghost town. Only a handful of families remained in town, and even less people were in the countryside like the McClures.

Scott and John rode into town to the store with all three horses. Scott thought aloud to John as they traveled down the trail, "I'd better get a year's supply of anything George has on hand. Cash is scarce and I believe credit will become nonexistent this winter."

"George said something about paying off his debt to you in supplies. He's still sharp on business practices and loyal to friends, but Junior's death has sapped his spirit. A change of pace may do him a world of good. Mary and Angela will stay in their home and watch the empty store. We can watch after them while George is in Gardiner."

Scott found George to be friendly but uncommunicative when Scott loaded the horses with supplies. He visited Mary briefly to offer any help that the Hermann women needed while George was away.

Mary said, "I'd appreciate eggs and meat, but I'll have to buy on credit."

Scott shook his head, "Melissa will give you eggs and Buzz will provide a side of venison now and again, but I know that neither of them will accept payment. We've been friends too long for you to object to us sharing our food. I just hope that George is able to reopen his store later in the year."

Mary breathed a sigh of relief, and responded, "Thank you, Scott. You are wonderful friends to have in our troubled time, but please don't tell George of our arrangement. His pride might spoil your generosity. He's so unpredictable since Junior's death."

Scott related the news to Melissa and Buzz, who approved his offer enthusiastically, exemplified by Buzz's comment, "I'll take two horses into the Elk River valley and hunt for deer. There's plenty of game in that flat where Chief Sixes was spotted. Whatever I bag will go to John and he can see the Hermanns are taken care of."

Nodding, Scott mentioned, "Good, and John will supply them with fresh fish. What else can we do?"

Melissa volunteered, "We can spare some potatoes and onions. With father gone our needs won't be as great. And I will
visit Mary more often if one of you'll watch the baby."

****

Scott took advantage of unseasonably warm weather in April
to cultivate fields and then plant crops. His dam behind the ranch
house proved valuable in irrigating the vegetable garden as well
as supplying water to the livestock, and the seepage through the
yard was controlled. The only drawback in prosperity resulted from
a sudden hail and rain storm which ruined the first hay cutting.
Scott and Buzz were surprised by the freak storm which hit when
the hay was half cut. John Larsen was called to help tend the wet
cut hay, but the rest of the field had been smashed flat by hail-
stones and was not salvageable.

Scott took the loss in stride, declaring, "Three haystacks are
better than none, and we'll be able to cut hay again in August.
With our smaller herd, a small crop should last us."

Melissa prepared an early supper so that John and Buzz could
cross the swollen rivers in daylight when they rode to town. Scott
asked, "John, can you find time this summer to help me build
another bedroom on this cabin?"

"Of course, as Ricky grows you'll need another room. Can
you and Buzz handle the logs and the foundation?"

Scott nodded in agreement as Melissa shared their news, "We'll
have a second child in November and will need more room."

"Congratulations! Are you hoping for a girl or a boy this time?"

Scott replied, "It doesn't matter, as long as our child is healthy.
Do you have any suggestions for getting the lumber to finish the
room?"

John thought for a moment, coming up with two ideas, "Why
don't we divide the room with a partition wall and make two small
bedrooms?" Seeing approval on his friends' faces, he continued,
"It will take more finished lumber as well as more time. Richard

was always a great help in working with wood, and we'll need someone like him to help us."

Scott felt compelled to tell John, "We don't have $10 in cash in the house. I could barter beef or part of my crop this fall for labor."

"I'll dicker for lumber if you'll give me a steer to barter, and you trade William Langlois corn for labor. He's your friend and a fair wood worker . . . better than any of us."

The summer passed swiftly for the McClure family. Working hard to make ends meet without money was challenging but strengthening. Buzz wasn't able to do much physical labor, but he and Melissa tended the chickens, milked the cows, and weeded the garden. Buzz continued to hunt and fish for the family, supplying the Hermanns and the Larsens with venison as well. The two bedrooms took form quickly and when they were finished the Larsen family were the first guests.

Langlois and a friend helped with finishing the addition, and then returned in early September to help with the harvest, accepting half the corn and potatoes for their work. Langlois' friend sold Buzz five more apple trees for cash, causing the Old-Timer to agonize over the purchase.

"Should I buy them, Scott? We don't have much cash, but . . ."

Scott encouraged his partner, "Your orchard is an important part of our ranch. You're getting a good buy, so go ahead." Looking toward Melissa, he said, "I'm worried about our potato crop. I don't think that we can help Mary this coming winter."

Scott mused over his state of mind for several moments, before confiding to Melissa and Buzz, "I had a weird dream last night. Sometimes I dream and forget about it before I'm fully awake, but this one was like a forewarning of bad tidings, and that eerie feeling has stayed with me."

Melissa asked with a puzzled look, "What was it about?"

"All I remember is being lost in snow and fog . . . seeing frozen carcasses of animals all around me . . . not cows, but not recognizable either. If that's a premonition of a hard winter, our shortage of feed will be a problem."

Buzz made a cogent observation, "Scott, you're not a worrier by nature. Maybe we should listen to your feelings. What can we do?"

"We can reduce the herd, probably selling at a loss to Coquille or Umpqua farmers. Francis is getting old so we'll need to keep that yearling bull, two calves and five milk cows. We can sell the other seven steers and cows for cash. Some of the chickens should be sold too. Whatever money we receive will tide us over another year. This country has to return to prosperity one of these days."

Buzz and Melissa endorsed Scott's plan, recognizing the need for a conservative approach whether Scott's feeling had any meaning or not.

As fortune would have it, a Coquille farmer came to Scott and bought four cows, paying $75 in cash. John found a buyer for one of the steers in Port Orford, so the herd was reduced to a more manageable size of eleven animals. Melissa traded eighteen chickens for three bags of flour in October, commenting afterwards, "We'll have enough eggs for our own use this winter, but we won't have any to sell."

Buzz applauded, "Good! I won't have to make any deliveries. Melissa, you and I will get our honey and egg business going next summer."

****

In late November, Melissa sent Scott through a wild rainstorm to fetch Mary and Angela to the ranch to help deliver her baby. Mary hardly had time to warm her hands before Melissa began her final contractions. Angela proved to be a very reliable assistant, allowing the men to fidget together in the other room. After a baby's cry pierced the cabin, she beckoned to Scott from the bedroom door. Mary offered Scott a long look at the wrinkled little baby, "Welcome your daughter to the world. She's a tiny girl but looks perfectly healthy."

Melissa asked in a shrouded and dreamy voice, "What day is it? What did we decide to name her, Scott? Who does she look like?"

"It's November 26th, and Anne Sarah McClure looks like her mother. She's a darling baby," Scott replied dutifully, telling a little white lie about her looks, because that's what Melissa wanted to hear. "How are you feeling, darling?"

"Tired, but I want to hold my little girl," she replied drowsily, adding with pride a moment later, "Why you're right, Scott, she does look like me."

Mary told the McClures that George was returning by ship any day, and she wanted to be home when he arrived. Working at Harvey Masters' in Gardiner for nine months, he had saved enough money to resupply his store. His letters said that he would open for business in April when his supplies arrived from San Francisco.

Scott took them home the following day, and paid little attention when Salem stumbled on the way home, talking to the horse, "You're getting old, my friend. You'll be back in the warm barn within the hour."

Crossing Elk River, Salem stumbled again, sliding on the gravel bed. Scott pulled on the lead rope to help the horse, when Salem squealed in pain as the 'crack' of a broken bone sounded. Scott spun about in the saddle, knowing full well that he was too late to help. Salem had stepped into a snag and fallen. Tears filled Scott's eyes as he saw the pain and helplessness in the horse's eyes. He hugged Salem's neck firmly as he freed the shattered leg, bone fragments exposed on Salem's twisted shank. Scott removed the saddle and halter. He struggled with his emotions as he brought his Sharps to bear, and then quickly delivered the fatal shot. Scott stood in place, watching the carcass wash down the river; making no effort to change its course to the ocean.

Buzz emerged from the cabin to help with the horses, and seeing Salem's saddle strapped to Pinto's back and the forlorn look
on Scott's face, didn't ask unnecessary questions. At supper that
evening, Scott told the story with full details. The only comment
came from Buzz, "We'll miss our loyal companion. He was slowing down with age, kind of like me. We can get along on the ranch
with two horses working. I don't need a horse. I'm not going anywhere."

The week before Christmas, Scott was checking haystacks in
the east pasture, when he felt a subtle change in the air. The wind
was blowing down the snow-covered mountains east of the ranch.
As it increased in strength a cooling effect developed, until light
snow began to fall in the valley. Within minutes, visibility had
diminished until only the forest bordering the pasture could be
seen, and a white carpet covered the pasture grass.

Scott drove five head of cattle into the corral, where Buzz was
moving milk cows into the barn. They worked together to secure
the livestock.

"Well, Old-Timer, are you up to bringing a wagon of hay into
the yard?"

Buzz laughed at his partner, "No, but if we don't do it now,
we might have to fetch hay through a foot of snow. The wagon's
ready, if you'll hitch Randy to it we can start work." His words
proved to be prophetic as the storm continued unabated through
Christmas day.

Melissa wished her men, "Merry Christmas! I believe we'll
have to eat Christmas dinner without the Hermanns or the Larsens.
No one should be out in this weather, but isn't it beautiful? Just
like White Plains when I was a child. I loved sledding and snow-
ball fights, but as a grown-up, I'll sit by the fire and count my
blessings."

Chapter Ten

The wintry weather ran unabated through mid-February, and the McClures stayed close to home, not seeing another soul for over two months. The children grew steadily, with Ricky walking and starting to talk, saying "Momma" and "Dadda." Anne was becoming cuter each day as her lengthening brown hair turned auburn, accenting the green eyes which she had inherited from her mother. The men welcomed the opportunity to visit with the children, and were actually helpful to Melissa, allowing her to tend her chickens and have a few moments alone each day. Buzz walked Ricky around the yard daily, determined to teach him about the woods and the animals. When the sun finally emerged and brightened the gloomy valley, he took the excited boy to the river to catch his first trout, an adventure to be repeated many times in the years to come.

Just as the hardy winter was dying and spring began to rejuvenate life in the valley, Francis lay down in his stall and refused to budge, regardless of Buzz's nursing. He died the next day and the partners immediately dressed out the bull's carcass. Scott mused aloud, "Francis was a good bull. Hansen guessed that he was ten years old when he came to the Sixes. I wonder how townspeople will like old beef?"

Buzz responded, "I imagine that people will welcome fresh meat, regardless of its age. Salted or tinned beef is usually what the ships bring into port. I hope that you can barter for some sugar in town, since our honey supply will be gone in a couple of weeks."

251

Scott braved high rivers to tote his meat into Port Orford, arriving at the Larsen home without incident. He found George Hermann playing with Little John in the yard as Sally hung her washing on the line. He greeted his good friend with a warm smile and a firm handshake, saying, "Welcome home, George. It's good to see you finally. I'm sorry that we couldn't get together last Christmas."

"Well, old friend, we were all planning on visiting the Myrtlewood Grove, but the weather's been horrible. How's your family?"

"Everyone's healthy, thanks. How about Mary and Angela? And Little John here?"

Sally answered Scott's questions as she joined them, "The Hermanns are all fine and so are we. George plays 'Grandpa' to our son quite often."

George interjected, "Yes, I do. I've reconciled myself to Georgie's death, and I enjoy Little John's company. We're good friends, aren't we, Johnnie?" The boy smiled shyly and entwined his arms around George's knee, before George added, "John is fishing today. Is the meat for him?"

"It's for both of you. I owe John a quarter of beef for his work last summer, but the rest is for you to sell. When will you reopen your store?"

"As soon as Captain Tichenor's ship returns with my merchandise order from San Francisco. However, I can sell your beef without opening my store. Can I credit the proceeds to your account and use the cash to buy more goods for the store?"

Scott agreed readily, "Certainly, and Buzz plans to hunt for game next week. He'll bring whatever he bags to you. And I have a steer to sell you for your grand reopening. Now, can you find Buzz a bag of sugar?"

The two men spent much of the day discussing business and George's work in Gardiner. Port Orford was still a ghost town but George was sure it would grow back into a healthy and busy community. Scott invited the Hermanns to visit the ranch before the store reopened, and when they accepted his offer, he left them the horses to ride and walked home with a five-pound bag of sugar, sharing all the news with Melissa and Buzz.

Both the Hermanns and the Larsens arrived two days later, and were forced to remain overnight as a brisk wind pelted the cabin with mixed rain and hail. After supper, the men retired to Buzz's cabin, while the women and children claimed the more comfortable ranch house. Late the next morning they were preparing to leave when Melissa brought out a surprise for George, seventy eggs which she had been saving for his store reopening. Scott handed George the lead rope for his steer as the party departed downriver.

The McClures missed the grand opening, but John returned their horses and reported on George's big day, "Everyone in the country was there except you folks. Melissa, your fresh eggs were gone within minutes, and the beef sold well also. Mary served coffee and cookies, so I expect that George didn't realize much profit. But everyone wished him well, and he feels good about being back in business. He told me that he'd sent another order off to San Francisco."

John reminded Scott, "Remember our conversation about the Indian wars the other night in Buzz's cabin. I got to thinking about Battle Rock as a historic event and decided that we ought to have a celebration on its ninth anniversary. People are returning to the coast this spring and we could use a good party to get people together and make them feel part of our community."

"That's a grand idea! As Marshal you're a natural choice to organize a festival. Count on us to donate a side of beef for the celebration. Isn't June 9th the anniversary date?"

"Yes! It's the day Kirkpatrick landed his men, but we can use any Sunday between June 9 and June 25, the latter date being the day they escaped and fled north to the Umpqua. Thanks for the beef. I'm supplying fish and George has offered coffee and tea.

We figure everyone can bring a vegetable dish or dessert. I'm sure Louie Knapp will be pleased to sell spirits."

Scott changed the subject, asking his friend, "John, are there any men in town who might be willing to work for a few weeks? Buzz can't do heavy work, and I'm falling behind in my spring planting."

"No. I can't think of anyone, but I'll keep my eyes open. Of course, you know that you can always call on me to help in an emergency," John concluded as he waved good-bye, and set out to hunt as he walked home.

****

Three days of rain kept Scott from his spring planting, until he became exasperated by the delay. Fussing in his corn field one midday, and willing the sun to shine on his efforts, he looked up to see a swarthy stranger standing by the apple orchard watching him. The man was short and wiry, about Scott's age, and dressed in a black seaman's garb which included a stocking cap covering his dark hair. An apparent smile was hidden in his full beard as Scott walked over to him, and his greeting was courteous, "Good morning, sir. My name is Ivan Rokov, and I seek the McClure farm. Are you Mr. McClure?"

Scott shook hands with the stranger as he replied, "Yes, I'm Scott McClure. How can I help you?"

"Mr. Larsen sent me. I look for work," Rokov said with a foreign accent. "Pardon my English, but I am Russian."

Scott smiled at the explanation, commenting, "Your English is quite good, Mr. Rokov. Where did you learn it?"

"I studied English in Petrograd and used it for my job in Sitka." The stranger paused, asking, "Is there work for me here?"

Scott pointed to Melissa standing before the ranch house watching them, and offered, "Come and meet my family, and join us for dinner. My wife will be interested in you and Russia."

Melissa relished this stranger's visit to the valley, soon calling him Ivan as she asked about life in Tsarist Russia. He narrated interesting tales of court life in Petrograd, displaying a fanciful style of story-telling as well as a good knowledge of the English language. As he concluded a funny story about the royal family, and the laughter subsided, Melissa ventured, "You must be an important person to know the Tsar's family so well."

Ivan shook his head, smiling at her assumption, and replied, "No, Mrs. McClure. My father was a servant, a valet as a young man and a teacher when I was a boy." He continued with an account of his years as playmate and student with the Tsar's grandchildren, explaining his talent for foreign languages, he spoke six of them, and the fact that the Tsar knew him by name. These two factors were sufficient grounds to land him a prestigious position as Clerk with the Russian Fur Company in Petrograd.

Scott asked, "How did you come to be in America?"

"Alas, my mentor affronted a Duke, and the Tsar sent him to Sitka. I could not refuse his "offer" for me to accompany him, even though my new position was less important. I'm afraid that my unhappiness with my lot was the reason that he deserted me when the Tsar called him back to court. I was forced to day labor in Sitka, so I stowed away on an American ship bound for San Francisco and the gold fields. And here I am."

After lengthy anecdotes on Russia, Ivan's brief report on his life in Alaska and California stood out as an omission. Scott's probes yielded no new information as the Russian evaded the subject, instead asking questions about the McClures and their Myrtlewood Grove.

Scott hired Ivan to work ten days for five dollars and board, his need for assistance overcoming his misgivings about the man's recent background.

Ivan lacked expertise in farming, but made up for it by plain hard work, which met even Scott's high standard. Buzz accepted

his companionship in his cabin and Melissa approved of his social graces as well as the story-telling. When Scott paid him off
on schedule, he offered to work at harvest, and Melissa rewarded
him with a large package of food for the road.

As Ivan disappeared from view around the knoll, Scott jokingly commented, "He was too good to be true. Maybe we ought
to count the silverware."

****

After delivering eggs and venison to the store, Buzz returned
with news of settlers on the coast. "George told me there were
two families settling in the Elk River valley, and there's an Irish
couple named Hughes settling in the old Shix village. I saw smoke
downriver when I came home, but I thought you folks should greet
new neighbors. I wish you better luck than last time. We certainly
don't need another Miller-type on the Sixes."

Melissa collected the few eggs available and Scott grabbed a
quarter of venison. They rode downriver with anticipation, hopeful for good neighbors. As they entered the former village clearing, they saw a man and woman clearing land near the Indian fishing site. The stranger picked up a rifle from a nearby canvas tent
when he saw them, but soon put it down and waved them forward. Scott approved of his neighbors' caution, although the country was fairly safe since the Indians had left.

The man extended a friendly greeting, his dark countenance
smiling, "Welcome! I'm Patrick Hughes and this is my wife, Jane.
We're from Tyrone County, Ireland by way of Boston. Would you
folks be the McClures, by chance?"

Scott and Melissa introduced themselves, making small talk
about the Irish and the Scots being good neighbors, and then answered questions about the history of the Sixes Indians.

Patrick was a sturdy man with a lot of drive, while Jane was
quiet, deferring to her husband until her curiosity was piqued. Scott

was sure that they were stable people when Patrick proclaimed, "We have eighty acres to work with now, but there's more land around here to use as our family grows."

Scott offered to help the Hughes build their house, and Melissa invited them to Sunday dinner to meet the rest of the McClure family.

****

A casual but busy summer followed the highly successful Battle Rock Celebration. Scott's young bull, Francis Junior, ensured a good calf crop, and Langlois borrowed the animal in payment for helping Scott put up his hay crops.

Jane Hughes bought five chickens and a young rooster from Melissa, demonstrating her sense of humor in promising not to compete for the title of "Egg Lady." Patrick rode Randy when he visited the Coquille valley to buy five milk cows. Then he borrowed Francis Junior, insisting that one of the first calves would go to the McClures. At Scott's suggestion, he made the same deal with Langlois for the following spring. Having an experienced dairyman as a neighbor appealed to Scott as an opportunity to upgrade his knowledge of animal husbandry.

Ricky and Little John played well together, but exhibited signs of an active rivalry. Each wanted to do better than the other. When the Larsens visited the Sixes, Buzz took the boys fishing, and Ricky sulked because his friend caught two trout and he only caught one. Scott had a long talk with his son, but the not-quite two-year-old had difficulty with the concept of sportsmanship. Angela had more success in teaching them to play together, as she employed the no-nonsense attitude of a thirteen-year-old.

She and Ellen Tichenor were maturing into attractive young ladies, with the prettier Ellen earning the sobriquet of "The Belle of Curry Country." Neither of them had any beaus as there was a noteworthy shortage of eligible boys in Port Orford.

****

Scott was splitting firewood before supper one evening, when Ivan Rokov trudged up the road to the cabin, calling out from the knoll, "Am I in time for supper, boss?"

Smiling at the thin and obviously weary Russian, Scott thought, Melissa will have to fatten him up, if he's going to help with harvest. He greeted Ivan warmly, "Welcome back, world traveler! It's good to see you, and yes, Melissa will set another plate at our table just for you."

The dirty dishes sat on that table all evening as Melissa was enthralled with Rokov's tales of his summer along the Willamette. When his journey took him through Corvallis and the old "Bookman Hotel," a puzzled Melissa observed, "Father and I lived in Corvallis when it was called Marysville. There was no Bookman Hotel."

Ivan laughed at his faux pas and revised the facts, "Maybe it was the Workman Hotel. Well, no matter . . ." He concluded the anecdote of Corvallis with humor and more than a little imagination. Even Buzz was impressed by his fanciful turns, enjoying a storyteller who could outdo an Old-Timer like himself. The two men left the house with Buzz telling his famous "bear at Verneau" story to the attentive Russian.

Days ran into weeks as the fall harvest was completed and the three men hunted the country from Floras Creek to Humbug Mountain. Ivan followed Buzz closely when he smoked venison, and made jerky and pemmican for his cabin-partner. The Russian rejected the Indian mixture as barbaric, but ate everything else that the Old-Timer concocted in his smokehouse.

It was Ivan who saved the fearless Richard when he tried to "walk" across the Sixes River at Buzz's fishing hole. The boy explained with a sober demeanor that he was holding his breath as he walked on the bottom, assuring his father that he could reach the other side safely. Ivan suggested that he and Buzz teach the lad to swim.

The men took turns swimming with Richard in the fishing hole, and the boy soon mastered the knack of swimming underwater without fear. However, swimming on the surface was not to be this fall, and the men suspended lessons when the rains filled the river channel. Buzz promised Ricky that they would continue lessons next summer.

John Larsen was visiting with Melissa and the children when the three men returned empty-handed from an upriver hunt. Melissa prepared a light meal as John reported the latest news from back east. There was talk that the southern states would secede if Abraham Lincoln was elected President next week. Scott thought such news was interesting but seemed to lack significance to people on the Oregon coast. However, John felt strongly against slavery and secession, waxing philosophical on these political issues and displaying unusual emotions for the fisherman-marshal. When he ceased his enlightening tirade, the room remained silent for several moments.

As Melissa served the meal, John expounded on the reason for his visit, "A notice came to my office requesting information on the whereabouts of one Ivanovitch Graguri Rokov, wanted by the Russian Consulate in San Francisco. Ivan, there is a reward offered for information about you, but no charge for any crime. What's going on?"

Ivan had sobered noticeably at John's announcement, and was slow in replying. "The Russian bear has a long reach. I thought that I was forgotten by now. My friends, I was caught in a compromising situation with an official's wife, and foolishly fought a no-win duel with the cuckold. I didn't kill him, just sliced his sword arm, but I was confined to quarters for 'Assaulting an Official'. When the man died in an accidental fall from a cliff, a friend told me that I would be charged with murder and locked in the stockade until a ship could return me to Russia for trial. I escaped that night, having an Indian friend row me out to sea to meet an American ship after it left Sitka. Good fortune followed me to

San Francisco, but my luck has been sour this past year. Are you going to arrest me, Marshal?"

"No, but I must send a reply to San Francisco informing the authorities of your presence in Port Orford." John excused himself from the table, "Thank you, Melissa. We'll see you folks at Christmas."

Ivan sat in deep thought as Melissa cleared the table and Scott put the children down for their afternoon nap. Buzz broke the silence with the simple question that was on everyone's mind. "What will you do now, Ivan?"

"I will move farther away from the Tsar's reach. I must go immediately and travel at night through the river ports in case John's notice has been mailed to everyone along the coast. I need a horse," Ivan concluded, as he looked at Scott hopefully.

At Melissa's nod, Scott offered, "You can borrow Pinto, my friend. If you leave now you'll pass through Bandon after dark."

Ivan breathed a sigh of relief. "Thank you, Scott, but perhaps I should buy Pinto. I'm not coming back."

"Leave Pinto at the Gerbrunn Freight Yards in Salem, if possible. Should trouble find you, and you can't leave the horse with Kurt Gerbrunn, consider him a gift." Scott suggested, "If Buzz gives you his jerky and pemmican, you won't have to stop until you're in the Willamette valley. Gather your gear while I saddle Pinto."

Scott filled a saddlebag with oats and Melissa added bread and meat to the sack Buzz filled for Ivan. He rode away from the Myrtlewood Grove on a fully-laden horse, intent on following Scott's advice for traveling the coastal trail. He was determined to avoid contact with people and still reach the Willamette valley in three days.

****

Life on the Sixes settled back into a routine suitable for the winter weather, although both the Hermanns and Larsens traveled to the ranch for Christmas dinner without any problem. John expressed curiosity about Ivan and his flight, pleased that he'd left the area. He told Scott privately, "A U.S. Marshal visited Port Orford last week, but continued on to Portland when I told him Ivan Rokov had moved on. Have you heard from Ivan?"

"No, but I don't expect him to write. If he's as smart as I think, he'll disappear, hopefully somewhere other than Portland. You know, John, I don't know how much of his story to believe, but I'll root for him to avoid any pursuit by the Russians. I'd appreciate hearing any news that you might hear about Ivan."

Winter came and went along the Oregon coast, with little response to Lincoln's election to office and the continued talk of secession. The Larsen family visited while John helped with spring planting. Buzz was excited that several apple trees were in blossom and likely to bear fruit, but Ricky and Little John weren't interested in flowers. They insisted on going fishing, the two friends still intent on besting each other. Little sister Anne followed them everywhere around the house and yard, clapping with approval when first one rival and then the other scored a victory in the contest-like atmosphere. Melissa suspended the rivalry at least two or three times a day, only to have it resurface in their next activity. She gave up the losing cause, and just hoped that they would outgrow their rivalry.

****

The news of the April 12th attack on Fort Sumter arrived by ship from San Francisco in May. John expressed his outrage at the effrontery of the secessionist states declaring a Confederacy as he gave his emotional report to Scott. As an afterthought, he announced that a logger from Langlois named John Sampson had been hired as Marshal and would assume his duties next week. Port Orford had grown enough to afford a full-time law officer once again.

In early July, Buzz decided with inordinate obstinacy that he was going hunting on his seventy-plus birthday. "I'm still fit and able to take care of myself," he stated clearly when Scott suggested that he wasn't as young as he used to be. He added, "Of course, you're welcome to come along if you can keep up with me."

The partners followed Buzz's favorite game trail up the mountain toward the cairn where they had killed the cougar and Richard had shot his bear, the Old-Timer reminiscing all the way. Scott played along, finding enjoyment in reliving the cougar hunt of 1855. Both men knew that their incessant bantering would drive off game, but they were more interested in companionship than in shooting a deer.

Electing to follow an easterly ridge neither had hunted before, they spent the second day traipsing to and fro in dense forest until they reached the valley floor just above Chief Sixes' old camp, his ramshackle lodge still standing, evidence of the Indians' presence along the upper Sixes.

Scott was startled awake by a gunshot the next morning, just before full light. Buzz was standing nonchalantly on the edge of their overnight camp. "You make so much noise, I thought that I'd bag my deer before you start to talk," he essayed, cackling at his own joke. "I shot it and I'll dress it. It's your job to carry the meat back to the ranch."

They returned to the ranch to find the dam's irrigation outlet was plugged, and Melissa was in her garden watering with a bucket. The partners skirted the rear of the barn, going directly to the meat shed. Ricky ran up to his dad to help hang the venison and Scott took time to teach him the simple procedure even though it'd be a few years before he'd be of any real assistance.

His patience was rewarded by a big hug from his son and a kiss from his wife. Melissa offered, "I'll give you a real kiss if you'll fix your darn water system."

Recognizing her frustration, the partners set to work in repairing the outlet immediately; and were cleaning up the tools as they monitored the water flow, when they heard the thundering hoofs of several horses crossing their bridge at Cascade Creek. Soon Lt. Patrick Hunter and four dragoons rode into the ranch yard with a flourish, and a bellowing, "Hello the house!"

Scott stood atop the dam with hands on hips, calling out his reply, "Hello, Lt. Hunter! Since when did infantrymen turn into cavalry?"

Swiveling in his saddle, the officer pointed to his shoulder epaulets and corrected his friend, "Please show proper respect, Scott," Patrick laughed, "It's Captain Hunter now."

Buzz guffawed, teasing their friend, "Well, naturally! Start a war and the Army'll promote anyone. How are you, son?"

"Just fine, Buzz," Patrick answered, and as Melissa stepped out the door, he doffed his kepi, and greeted her, "Good afternoon, Mrs. McClure. You're looking grand, married life agrees with you. Are these your children?"

Melissa smiled her welcome, remembering the charming officer from Fort Orford social events, and greeted him. "It's good to see you again, Patrick, and to hear your Irish blarney. You and your men will stay for supper, won't you?"

"Thank you, Melissa," he responded.

Scott suggested, "Perhaps you should spend the night also. We'd appreciate a good visit and the latest news from back east."

"We accept your hospitality with gratitude. Do you have any oats that I can buy for the horses?"

"You're a guest, Patrick, and your horses will be fed also. Buzz, will you help these men with their horses? I'll show Patrick around the place."

Buzz waved the men and horses into the corral, offering, "Do you men want to sleep in my cabin or the barn tonight?"

Melissa overrode Army tradition by seating enlisted men beside their officer at her supper table, and charmed them by expressing interest in them and their lives at Fort Umpqua. Hunter discovered more personal facts on his men during the meal than he had learned in commanding them for several years. The

McClures understood quickly that the entire garrison was Union, and eager to return to the east coast for action.

After the four troopers had left for Buzz's cabin, Patrick talked of the recent problems that the Indians had been experiencing with measles, looking glumly at Scott as he conveyed bad news, "Chief Sixes and his son died in an epidemic this spring, along with at least twenty other Indians. I visited the reservation to see for myself, and the Indians' condition made me sick to my stomach. The tribes are so badly decimated by the white man's diseases that there is talk of closing Fort Umpqua. Believe me, there is no longer any threat to settlers from the Indians."

Buzz lamented, "Poor devils! Just last night we stayed at Chief Sixes' hideaway while we were upriver hunting. Maybe we could have done more to keep them hidden."

"No, the Army would have arrested them as soon as an official report of sighting was received. I figured that scoundrel, Dutch Schmidt, had reason for his allegation that Scott was hiding Indians, but I ignored him because no one saw anything. Besides, he was such a blackguard that no one could believe anything he said. Oops, sorry Melissa, as I remember, you were his friend."

The silence was heavy as Melissa said nothing, so Scott asked, "What are you doing in Curry County if there are no Indians causing trouble?"

"I'm recruiting a company to fight in Maryland. General Meade is a family friend and has requested my services. There are eleven volunteers from the Umpqua sailing to meet me in Port Orford this week, and young Sampson from Langlois signed up today. I came by to offer you a Sergeant's stripes in my company. I need a good steady man like you, Scott. Will you help defend the Union?"

Scott shook his head, saying, "I agree with your cause, but I'm needed here. Maryland is a long distance away."

Patrick paused for a moment before offering, "Would you reconsider if I could arrange a commission as Second Lieutenant?"

"Thanks, my friend. Five years ago I might have joined you, but I'm older now and have family responsibilities to consider."

Melissa quickly changed the subject, asking the officer, "Is your family in Maryland?"

"Yes, my father is a businessman in Baltimore." He talked about his family and home nostalgically for some time, concluding with the story of his appointment to the U.S. Military Academy at West Point.

The next morning, Buzz arose before daylight and rousted out the enlisted men for a trout fishing expedition at dawn. The troopers proudly presented Melissa their catch, large enough for everyone's breakfast. When the visitors were fed eggs and fried potatoes as well as trout, Melissa was a heroine.

Her comment as the group rode away was doleful, "Those men enjoyed their day on the Myrtlewood Grove, but I feel sad for them. Fun is over for them when they sail for the war."

****

Louie Knapp rode into the yard late in the afternoon. Declining Melissa's invitation to supper, he announced, "You are invited to a farewell party for John Larsen tonight at the hotel. Our friend is now a Sergeant in the U.S. Army and sails tomorrow with Captain Hunter for San Francisco."

Scott was not surprised that John would defend his spirited principles of right, and hurried to accompany Louie back to town. He asked, "Have you rooms for my family overnight?"

"Yes, all of you can stay in the hotel."

Buzz offered, "I'll come back tonight after the party. You folks can watch the ship sail and console Sally and Johnnie before coming home."

People wished John good fortune and toasted his patriotism. Marshal John Sampson administered a great bear hug, requesting, "Take care of my little brother. He's daring and unafraid but he needs to learn caution also."

Mrs. Tichenor presented him with a scarf, a talisman from the ladies of Port Orford.

When Scott saluted his longtime friend with a draught of ale, he cautioned, "Don't try to be a white knight with that scarf, John. Duck while the bullets are flying and come home hale and healthy."

Melissa reported after the party that Sally had been withdrawn and nervous. She found that Mary was worried about her as well. They would have to watch after Sally and Johnnie while John was away.

The next morning a crowd of townspeople stood on the bluff waving good-bye to men leaving for war. It was a festive-solemn moment for Port Orford. The significance of the civil war was brought closer to home with their departure.

****

Fall harvest was accomplished with help from neighbor Hughes, and the hard work seemed to devour the days and the weeks. Melissa announced that she was pregnant again, but as Christmas approached, she experienced illness and abdominal pain which she associated with her unborn baby. This child was giving her a harder time than Ricky or Anne.

The Hermanns brought the Larsens for Christmas dinner, Mary roasting the chickens and babying Melissa into a more comfortable mood for the holiday get-together. Sally shared a letter from John which she had received from San Francisco. He was aboard a troop ship bound for the east coast, and the accompanying news of the war was all bad.

George reported that business was good and Angela was working afternoons in the store. She fairly beamed when her father praised her efforts.

Christmas dinner ended before everyone was through visiting, but the guests had to leave before dark, so Scott declined their offer to wash dishes. He, Buzz, and Ricky handled that chore after sending Melissa to her room to rest. The family settled into the first winter of the Civil War.

Chapter Eleven

As the apple blossoms brightened the Sixes landscape, Scott was reminded that spring planting was as near as Melissa's time. Buzz was elated with the abundance of flowers on his trees, compared to the sparsity of the first blooms the year before. "My bees will go to work and we'll have apples galore this year. Yummy! I can't wait for apple pie with honey-whipped cream."

Rainy weather and Melissa's indispostion during her pregnancy interfered with Scott's cultivation schedule, and he enlisted Patrick Hughes to help finish the spring work when favorable weather finally arrived on the Oregon coast. His neighbor agreed to work at harvest also, and take his payment in corn.

Patrick expressed some concern that prospectors were mining the ocean beaches at the Sixes estuary. "What are my rights? Can they prospect anywhere they want?"

"Yes, as long as they respect your claim boundaries and don't disturb your fields or livestock. The beaches are open for prospecting and miners shouldn't bother your farm. Talk to them, maybe sell them eggs and milk, and there shouldn't be any trouble. If same yahoo causes a problem, John Sampson is a good law officer and will protect your rights."

Scott paused momentarily, suggesting, "You know, Patrick, if miners find gold on the beach, they'll work upriver toward my place. Let me saddle Randy, and I'll take a side of venison to the beach."

Patrick agreed, "Fine, and we can stop by my barn for eggs and milk. I appreciate the advice."

The neighbors' arrival at the prospectors' camp was noticed by one miner on the beach who recognized Scott, shouting his greeting, "Hello, Scott McClure! Long time no see."

Scott grinned at the gray-haired man, responding in a teasing voice, "Bob, what happened to all your red hair?"

The miner laughed, "My youthful days were left behind on Hubbard Creek where you and Sam Olson worked your Indian village claim. You lost a fine partner when the damned Rogues killed him." Bob paused in thought, and then resumed, "I've been working in Placerville, home of the 49ers Gold Rush. I heard from that storekeeper friend of yours that you have a farm up the Sixes River. Is that right?"

"Yes, I'm located three or four miles east of here. This gentleman is Patrick Hughes, who farms right here. We're selling venison, eggs, and milk. Since you're an old comrade, I'll give you a special deal."

"Ha, ha! I'll buy if you don't charge me a high price just for old times sake," Bob teased Scott.

The two farmers made friends on both beaches of the river's estuary, and realized a tidy profit in doing so. Scott estimated, "There are more than thirty men in this area, and everyone is finding gold dust. My old comrade asked about chances on the upper valley, but I didn't encourage him. Sam never found any color around the myrtlewood grove, and I don't care much for people traipsing over my ranch."

"I overheard Bob talking about you. He said that you were tough but fair, and would let prospectors through your farm if they respected your claim boundaries. Sort of what you said earlier."

Scott smiled ruefully, both joking and serious as he said, "Right! Maybe I'll sell supplies upriver before this prospecting mania is over. Buzz and I should hunt deer upriver before the miners move in. With your agreement, I'll ride into Port Orford and visit with the Marshal about our situation here," Scott concluded as Patrick gave an affirmative nod.

While in town, Scott stopped by the Hermanns' home to discuss Melissa's pregnancy with Mary, who was once again going to help with her friend's childbirth. Sally was visiting Mary, and the two women were reading over John's last letter, sent from Baltimore. His company was in training, expecting to enter the fight by summertime. John had been promoted to First Sergeant and had sent home a bank draft, which George was handling for Sally.

She told Scott, "I don't need money, but John worries about us. I just wish that terrible war would end so that he could come home."

Sally's wishful thinking kept Scott silent. He knew that the Civil War was not going to be resolved easily and didn't want to dampen her up-beat spirits.

George John McClure was born on May 4th after a delivery every bit as difficult as the pregnancy had been. When Scott saw his wife's debilitative condition afterwards, he was afraid that she was near death. Mary addressed his concern quickly, "She's fine, Scott, but she needs lots of rest. Her stamina is low but she's a healthy woman."

"She looks so gaunt that it scares me. I don't think that she should have any more children," Scott concluded.

Mary didn't disagree, but advised, "You should discuss your feelings with Melissa when she's fully rested. In the meantime, take your son into the other room and let his mother rest."

Scott sat near the warming stove, rocking his son as he admired the infant's tiny features and blond hair, seeming mesmerized by the physical details as the hour slipped by. Ricky and Anne stumbled out of their beds, sleepy-eyed and yawning, to view their newly-born sibling.

Ricky guessed, "I got a brother."

When Scott nodded smilingly, Anne complained, "I want a sister to play with."

George's fair complexion took on a pink hue as his wee hands flexed, and finally demonstrated his superior lung power. Scott cooed, "Are you hungry, George? Do you want your Momma?"

Ricky exclaimed, "Wow! He can really yell, can't he, Dad?"

Scott laughed and made a fanciful comparison, "You were even louder when you were first born, Ricky. Why, you woke Buzz up in his cabin when you were hungry."

"Shame on you, Scott! Telling your son such a tall tale," Mary admonished. "You were a wonderful baby, Ricky," she added as she relieved Scott of his burden, taking the baby to Melissa.

Scott awoke with a start, still seated in his rocker beside the lukewarm stove. He listened carefully for a disruptive sound, and hearing none, looked in on mother and son. Both were sleeping noisily, and he was comforted to see healthy color back in his wife's cheeks. Settling back in his rocker to drowse some more, Scott was content and pleased with his lot.

****

It was a desultory summer in the Sixes valley. The Civil War disrupted established routines, with war and a minor gold rush lending prosperity to the McClures. Scott wasn't quite sure that it was here to last, but he enjoyed having gold dust and cash in hand again.

Buzz taught Ricky to swim on the surface, but to the boy's chagrin, copycat Anne did it better. Johnnie Larsen laughed at his rival until Anne proved to be a better swimmer than the fisherman's son. The two boys collaborated in rare teamwork to prove their superiority over the little girl by performing tests of strength. Their success was somehow disappointing when Anne simply applauded their feats without contest.

A mature and fifteen-year-old Angela explained to the boys that Anne wasn't competing against them, merely imitating their actions because she admired them. However, rivalry between the boys continued to be secondary to their besting the girl, an attitude which Melissa didn't discourage.

Buzz returned from Port Orford waving a letter in the air excitedly, bursting with news. "Harvey and Alma are coming to visit us. They've sold their store and are retiring. Come on, Scott. Help me clean up my cabin. They'll be here in a day or two."

Every day following that announcement, the Old-Timer rode Randy to Port Orford and then to Cape Blanco, looking for a ship from the north. One day his vigil was rewarded as he sighted his prize off the Cape, and rode into the town to announce its impending arrival. The Masters were pleasantly surprised at Buzz's enthusiasm, but just as eager to visit and share the company of old friends. The Masters said hello to a busy George as Buzz delivered Melissa's invitation to the Hermanns for Sunday dinner. Harvey and Buzz carried on an animated conversation as they walked to the Myrtlewood Grove, Alma clinging perilously to her perch atop Randy. Their stay on the Sixes would be a vacation for the McClures as well.

During a tour of the ranch, Harvey apprised Scott, "Fort Umpqua closed last month. There's been no Indian trouble in years, and the soldiers are needed elsewhere. A hotel keeper named George Mansell bought the whole fort for $200. Why, the Army just plain gave it away. He'll be a rich man; mark my words."

Scott surmised, "It sounds like you sold your store at a good time."

"Yes, I talked to Captain Hunter before he rode south a year ago, and we figured the fort would close this summer. I decided to sell at that time, but fixed my place up some and waited until spring to offer it for sale. The deal went through before the abandonment, but Gardiner is a solid lumber town and the store will survive the business loss of the federal payroll. Umpqua City may not be as fortunate. Several taverns closed before my ship sailed from the harbor." Harvey paused for a moment and commented, "My principal reason for selling was retirement. Alma and I found it difficult to work the long hours that were required to operate the store. When I hired a clerk, my profit margin all but disappeared. Now we need to find a home to enjoy our retirement."

The two men came upon Ricky and Anne swimming in the river under Buzz's watchful eye, and stood quietly basking in the secondhand energy of the children's play.

****

Following Sunday dinner, Harvey offered George a business deal. "I sold my store and its contents, but the new owner didn't want a prepaid order of supplies from San Francisco. I directed the consignment to be delivered in Port Orford, figuring it would be a good deal for you to sell this lot. You could pay me afterwards."

George promptly accepted, "It's a deal! Business is good and you can work with me in the store. When will your order reach port?"

"Next week, I hope. Send word to me when the ship arrives, and I'll help you with the paperwork."

Mary offered, "Why don't you and Alma stay with us while we're doing business together? Our home is large enough, particularly if we're all going to be working."

Melissa and Scott attended the "Grand Sale" at Hermanns' store, buying freely for the coming winter. The Masters had purchased a small house which was alee of the promontory opposite Battle Rock, and protected from much of the prevailing winds. Since George had accepted a position on the Select Committee for the county government, Harvey had agreed to continue working part-time after the sale. Buzz's simple exclamation, "That's great news!" characterized everyone's feelings, as the Masters settled into Port Orford life.

William Langlois offered to include the two Sixes neighbors in a farmers' cooperative for harvesting the fall crops. Patrick declined for both men, "Thanks, but Scott and I have an agreement for fall harvest. I can't stay away from home overnight with Jane expecting soon." It wasn't long after the harvest that Edward Hughes was born.

A bountiful apple crop kept Buzz busy for a few weeks, as he peddled apples and honey to Sixes prospectors as well as townspeople. He inveigled Melissa to make six apple pies and a pail of honey-whipped cream, which he delivered to the beach and sold by the slice to hungry miners. He laughed in telling the story on himself, "I could have made a lot more than $2.50 if I hadn't eaten half a pie."

Christmas dinner at the McClures created a transportation problem, which was resolved by borrowing two horses from the Tichenors, and Scott hauling children's gifts to the Sixes on Christmas Eve. A good deal of excitement was created for Ricky and Anne by the wrapped packages, but Melissa insisted on no touching only looking.

Sally had good news from John in a recent letter. His company was outside of Washington, having seen action twice during the summer. His pride in his unit showed through his writing, even as modesty kept his role in the background. Unfortunately, Union forces were in retreat from General Lee's Army, so war news was generally bad. However, Sally managed to put a good face on the situation regardless of the facts, stating unequivocally, "See how well John's company is doing. He'll soon be able to come home."

****

Cold winds and slashing rains heralded the coming of the new year, and prospecting at the beaches came to a standstill. Somehow it was no surprise for Scott to find three miners in his yard one afternoon, courteously seeking permission to cross his property. Recognizing the men from his old comrade's camp on the beach, he chatted with them about Bob and their beach mining, and fed them supper. After the meal, Buzz invited them to share his cabin for the night, suggesting, "You might camp at an old Indian lodge that's still a decent shelter. I can guide you upriver to the site tomorrow, since I'm hunting in the area."

"Thanks, Buzz. We can use your help. Would you advance credit to us if you bag a deer?" the older miner asked.

Glancing at his partner, Buzz agreed and added, "Yes. I'll advance a little farm produce also, and if you can't pay us in the spring, you can work your debt off during planting time." The Old-Timer was in business with their new neighbors.

Scott returned from a delivery in town a few days later to find the door propped open with a rifle and Melissa patching a nasty gash on Buzz's forehead. From the agitated movement of the patient and the presence of a rifle, Scott surmised correctly that trouble was in the offing.

"If I'd had my Sharps . . . damned thief . . . hurry up, Missy. . . ." Buzz was mumbling as Scott entered the cabin.

Melissa was relieved to see her husband, explaining, "Five miners came through here an hour ago without so much as a hello. Buzz had hung a quarter of venison for his miner customers on the corral rail while he spread hay for the cows inside."

A fidgeting Buzz broke in, "One of those yahoos stole the meat right in front of me, laughing all the time. When I walked up to him and took it back, he whacked me with some kind of club. I heard all of them laughing as they walked upriver. If I'd had my Sharps . . ."

Melissa finished the story, "I heard the arguing voices and stepped outside just as that black Irish wearing a plaid stocking cap hit Buzz with a billy . . . maybe a shillelagh. I ran inside to get a rifle, but the miners left immediately. Buzz is right. They laughed all the way across the east pasture. Perhaps you'd better check the livestock out there while I finish bandaging Buzz's cut."

Scott rode to the edge of his property, accounting for all of his cattle, finally noticing that one of his yearling cows had been running. On closer inspection, he saw that she had a bloody udder and a wound on her neck. Evidently the miners had chased the cow, perhaps trying to milk her. Scott's grim smile was mirthless as he thought, I can imagine Buzz's state of mind if I'm feeling so irate and vengeful over this incident. I hope the Old-Timer can keep a steady hand when we jump those yahoos.

Buzz was alert and eager when Scott returned to the ranch house, advising Melissa, "Keep my old muzzleloader handy and lock the door until we get back."

"You two be careful of those horrible men, and don't take any chances in rousting them out. We can't abide their being our neighbors, but I hope you don't have to shoot anyone," Melissa suggested before she closed and bolted the door.

Buzz led the way eastward, following the plentiful sign left by the party's passage. "They're not far ahead," the Old-Timer told Scott. "They should be in Chief Sixes lodge area now. Will our friendly miners help us or get in our way?"

Scott contemplated his question at length, before shrugging out, "I don't know. We'll find out in a few minutes, I reckon. Can you cross over that ridge and set up above the camp?" When Buzz nodded, Scott concluded, "Good! We'll use our old fight plan. I'll go straight into camp and confront the thieves. Signal me when you're in position."

As Scott advanced slowly, he thought, I'm getting too old for this tomfoolery, and I know that Buzz shouldn't be here. Maybe I should have gone to Marshal Sampson . . . no, he wouldn't be able to solve the real problem. We have to keep bad men out of our valley.

Standing quietly behind a tree, he saw that the thieves had taken over the camp. The old miner was laying outside the fire's heat, holding a hand to his bloody face. The plaid-capped Irishman was pacing before the campfire, cursing the injured miner, while his gang of thugs sat around the stewpot, spearing pieces of meat and potatoes with their hunting knives, wolfing down the food prepared by the former occupants.

Scott slipped into camp behind the leader, but his presence was given away inadvertently by the injured miner who whispered his name.

The pacing culprit whirled about, his right hand hidden behind him, and Scott promptly stepped forward bringing his rifle butt into the man's stomach, doubling him over and exposing the shillelagh in his grip. The farmer delivered a second blow, shattering the crook's jaw and dropping him in a heap. "Look out, McClure," one of the miners yelled as a shot rang out, smashing the upraised knife hand of a second thug. Scott's muzzle was shoved forcefully into the midsection of a third man who dropped his knife and pleaded for mercy. Scott's three friends jumped on the remaining two thugs, pummeling them into submission. When all five men were laying flat on the ground, Scott relaxed somewhat and waved the Old-Timer forward.

Lacking rope proved to be no problem for Scott as he cut one thief's buckskin jacket into narrow strips and tied four pair of hands tightly behind the malefactors' backs. He bandaged the gunshot man's shattered hand with a strip of the man's shirt, and then tied his hands in front of him. One crook raised up to object to the treatment and Buzz cracked his skull lightly with his rifle butt.

Walking downriver, a second lesson was applied by Scott's rifle, before the offenders maintained silence and a steady pace westward. Buzz fired a shot and called out to Melissa before the party reached the corral. She emerged from the house armed and helped guard the prisoners as Scott roped them together by their necks and gave Buzz the lead rope to tie around the saddlehorn. With his partner riding Randy and pulling the string of men, the cavalcade marched into Port Orford at a smart pace, Scott bringing up the rear. Marshal Sampson place all five men in the stout jail, with an admonishment, "My warning wasn't enough I see. Well, Terence, a little prison time for you and your friends may change your ways."

To Scott, Sampson said, "Those prospectors have been causing problems wherever they go. Thanks for not shooting them outright. Maybe the judge will let them enlist in the Union Army. If not, we'll place them in the brig of the next ship to San Francisco. Good riddance either way."

Scott was repairing the irrigation system after the spring planting, when a young man rode into the ranch yard leading a lame Pinto, and a double for Randy. "Oops," Scott corrected himself, "Not a double! She's a mare."

"Hello, Mr. McClure! Remember me? I'm Uwe Gerbrunn. My parents send their greetings."

"Why, Uwe, I wouldn't have recognized you without those horses. You've grown considerably since I last saw you. What's it been, eight years?"

Uwe smiled broadly as the men shook hands, replying, "I was twelve years old when you last visited Salem. You were really interested in Johann's college studies, but I was only a boy in grammar school."

"Is your brother a famous lawyer now? And how are your parents?"

"Yes, Johann works in John Lee's office and I help my father with the freighting business. My parents are doing well. They'll be grandparents soon, as my sister-in-law is expecting in September. Father sent me on this errand as his agent, actually it's a vacation for me." Uwe paused for a breath, pointing to the horses as he continued, "Ivan Rokov left Pinto with us last fall, and though your horse is lame, he'll be good with young children. Dad worked hard to correct Pinto's limping, but a vet told us that his disability is permanent. Anyway, Greta is a replacement, which Rokov bought from us. Father said that you would recognize the bloodlines."

"Thank you, Uwe. We can use both horses on our ranch," Scott admitted. He invited Uwe inside to meet Melissa and his three children, with toddler George grabbing a knee for support and drooling on his pants leg. Melissa was impressed with his good manners and pleased with a small edelweiss pin which he gave her from his parents.

Melissa was attentive to the news of Ivan Rokov, happy to hear that he had escaped his Russian pursuers, and asked a plethora of questions about Salem, the Gerbrunns and the young man himself. Uwe accepted her final comment as a great compliment, as she said, "You remind me of Scott when I first met him."

Both McClures insisted that he stay for a few days, Scott offering, "We'll take you hunting, and maybe our friends will let you pan for gold. We'll make a frontiersman of you before you go home."

Uwe dutifully followed Scott and Buzz on the prescribed activities, never divulging his lack of interest in hunting or prospecting. He accompanied the two men into town, the three Gerbrunn-bred horses making a sterling impression as they pranced down the sunlit street to the store, the modest young man never realizing the gallant figure he struck astride his horse.

George and Angela stood before the store watching their approach, and Scott soon introduced his young friend to both Hermanns. Angela was quietly looking pretty while Uwe was trying to impress her with his worldliness. Scott winked at George, and said, "Can you fill my order for me? Buzz will join us later."

George smiled and followed Scott inside, philosophizing for his old friend, "Suddenly my daughter is a woman. I'm feeling older already. How do you find the Gerbrunn lad?"

"He's a fine young man. I'll vouch for him any day. The entire Gerbrunn family is outstanding."

A blushing Angela interrupted the men with a request of her father, "May I go walking with Mr. Gerbrunn, father? We'll stroll through town." George nodded, as he voiced an aside to Scott, "Mary needs to talk to our daughter about boys." He smiled at his friend, as he concluded, "I bet she did long ago."

Buzz's cabin was only a bed to Uwe over the next week, as he spent his hours in town, usually sparking Angela. Melissa insisted both come to Sunday dinner the day before he was to return home. George and Mary chaperoned them on the trip, but allowed them free time in the myrtlewood grove. The McClures got the impression that George would be relieved when Uwe was gone. Life with a moonstruck daughter was confusing to him.

Uwe and Angela exchanged letters weekly, a situation Scott discovered on his ensuing trip to Port Orford. In fact, he found a letter at the Post Office from Kurt Gerbrunn, asking about their son's interest in Angela. His prompt reply praised Angela and her parents as good friends and fine people. He included a postscript inviting the Gerbrunns to visit the Myrtlewood Grove and to see for themselves. Melissa laughed merrily as she read his letter over his shoulder, "Scott, are you trying to be a matchmaker?" Her husband grinned sheepishly but mailed the letter as written.

Buzz continued to court business with the miners, now nine men, who prospected upriver. He accumulated a little gold dust also, as the prospectors washed color out of the Sixes gravel, but evidently not enough, as some of the miners went back to the beach to work. The Old-Timer's contribution to the family's coffers seemed important to him, a mark of self-esteem and feeling useful. Both Scott and Melissa contrived to acknowledge his participation in ranch affairs.

****

The McClures heard that John's company was in northern Maryland during June, heading for a small town in Pennsylvania named Gettysburg, where "a real battle was shaping up," to quote the Larsen letter. On August 2nd, Hughes brought the news that a fierce battle was being fought at Gettysburg. Scott and Melissa rode directly to the Hermanns to see if any news from John's company had arrived.

Mary was surprised to see the couple, saying, "Sally and Johnnie are coming over. She's so distraught over the Civil War news that I hate for her to be alone. There's no news of individuals yet, only the confusion of a major battle. There may be mail from back east on the ship that made port today. George will come home with all the town gossip shortly, and Harvey will close up the store."

A stilted conversation resulted from the arrival of the Larsens, everyone afraid to hazard any speculation on the war now that John was in the fighting, expressing only platitudes such as "no news is good news."

As he entered the house, George announced the death of John Sampson's brother, "Sampson was killed in the town of Gettysburg. No other notifications came on this ship. You know, Sally, no news is good news."

"I hear that all the time. That battle was over a month ago. Why does it take so long for news to reach here?" Sally complained as she did each time that any news arrived. She harried the Postmaster every day for news, knowing full well the mail from Coos Bay wouldn't be from John.

One of Bob's prospectors brought a message on August 10th that a ship from California was entering port. Buzz stayed with the children again so that Melissa could accompany Scott into town. Once again they found themselves at the Hermanns waiting for George to bring any news from the ship to Sally. When he did walk up to the house, his woebegone expression signaled bad news. Scott experienced one of his cognitive flashes, and just knew that John was dead, but he said nothing of his feeling to the women.

George handed an Army notification letter to Sally, but dreading the worst, she asked George to read it. After mumbling through the preamble, he finally cleared his throat and read, "We regret to inform you that First Lieutenant John Larsen was killed in action at Gettysburg on July 3rd 1863." George paused as the stunned Sally had difficulty grasping her husband's death. She swooned on the sofa and the women took her into the bedroom to console her. George picked up Johnnie and hugged him, knowing the boy didn't feel the same pain as his mother. He was too young to remember much about a father whom he hadn't seen in two years.

Scott picked up the handwritten note which was with the notification, and read, "Dear Mrs. Larsen, I regret the loss of your husband, and write to you in sympathy. John Larsen stood beside his friend and commander, Patrick Hunter, as their company fought Pickett's charge to a standstill. Both men gave their lives for a cause in which they believed, and their sacrifice helped win the battle and perhaps the war. Fully two-thirds of Pickett's rebels were killed and Lee's Army is in retreat. May John rest in peace knowing that he served his country well. Sincerely, Captain Warren Thompson."

George shook his head sadly. "So many young men gone. No one ever wins such a battle, do they?"

"No, but I understand why John had to fight for the Union. Does the name Warren Thompson mean anything to you?"

"No, but he must have known the Larsens and their friends would appreciate hearing about John and Patrick. It's a tribute that you will understand one day, Johnnie," he said to the attentive boy. The tears in Johnnie's eyes were more for his mother's unhappiness than from losing a father in a war far away from Port Orford.

In the week that followed, Sally grew morose and desolate, not able to handle being a widow again. People harassed Sally as an Indian with even stronger and more pointed barbs. She was unable or unwilling to defend herself. George confronted one of her antagonists on the street and was hurt in losing the fight. Marshal Sampson stepped in and settled the issue quickly, supporting Sally's right to be left alone.

One foggy September day, Sally dropped Johnnie at Mary's while she did some shopping. The boy was still there when George came home late in the afternoon, and Mary sent him to look for their friend. After checking her house, George walked to the Marshal's office to seek help. A stranger ran up to Sampson, speaking excitedly, "A woman just jumped off the Orford Heads into the ocean. It looked like Mr. Hermann's Indian friend." George soon found the man to be right as a fisherman pulled Sally Larsen's lifeless body from the sea and brought it to the Marshal.

Harvey Masters volunteered to hike out to the Sixes and notify the McClures of Sally's tragic death. His arrival well after dark astonished the family, but Sally's suicide really stunned her friends. Harvey repeated verbatim a message from Mary to Melissa, "Melissa, please bring Ricky and come to town tonight. I need your help in telling Johnnie about his mother."

The Hermann house was well lit when the party rode up to the front door. Melissa and Ricky dismounted and went indoors, while Harvey walked home and Scott stabled the horses.

Entering through the back door, Scott passed through the kitchen into the parlor. Marshal Sampson immediately said, "Let's read Mrs. Larsen's last will and testament now that Scott's here. I found this single page on her kitchen table with a sealed letter to you two men, a rifle, a ship's compass, and a gold watch. It's sort of a will anyway, not fancy but clear." The Marshal paused, and then commenced reading the short letter, "Dear Son John, I am sorry to leave you alone, but I cannot live in the white man's world without your father. Please forgive me. John would want Scott McClure to have his rifle and George Hermann to have his compass. The gold watch is for you when you grow up. All other property and money should go to the family who raises you. Goodbye dear. Mother."

Marshal Sampson let the words rest with the listeners for several moments, before handing the sealed envelope to George. Scott nodded and George opened the letter and read it aloud. "Dear George and Scott, thank you for your protection and friendship over the years. My last earthly request is for you to place my son in a good home, and to see that he is raised to be a good, strong man like his father. Your friend forever, Sally."

In the ensuing silence, Scott heard the quiet sobs of the women as he and George regarded each other with teary eyes. Marshal Sampson flourished a handkerchief and blew his nose. Scott deferred to George again, who went to his wife's side and implored her support, "Can we raise Johnnie in place of the son that we lost?"

"Of course, George. I believe that is what Sally wanted." Looking to Scott, Mary added, "Does that meet with your approval?"

"Yes, and I agree that Sally would be pleased. If there is ever any need for a change, Melissa and I will open our home to Johnnie."

Life returned to normal after the funeral of Sally Larsen. Mary and Melissa arranged for Johnnie and Ricky to visit regularly, both women believing that the boys' friendship was a palliator for Johnnie's sorrow in losing his parents. And since that tragic night at Hermanns when Sally's letters were read, Ricky had accepted responsibility for cheering his friend, with both boys gaining strength of character from the relationship. One day when Ellen Tichenor visited Angela, she gave the boys an arrowhead which she had found while riding along the beach near Hubbard Creek. The boys' imagination overcame their common sense as they swore blood brothership after cutting their palms with the flint artifact. Mary bandaged their wounds without any reprimand, encouraging their lasting friendship.

****

As fall harvest progressed, Buzz and Melissa teamed up, picking apples and selling them as fruit, in pie form, and as apple butter. Many of the prospectors were leaving the area as fall weather advanced along the coast, but Buzz was ingenious in finding new markets for their products. One evening Scott was teasing Buzz about his apples and honey enterprise, when Melissa intervened, "The last laugh is ours, Buzz. Our receipts for the last month total $104.43, minus the cost of flour and salt."

A finger-pointing Old-Timer, cackled hilariously, and turned the tables on his partner, "That's more than you received for all your produce, young fellow." Scott accepted the razzing from his partner and his wife in gleeful surrender, happy to learn that their orchard could be a good money-maker. Continued prosperity was blessing the Myrtlewood Grove.

Anne turned four a few days after James Hughes was born on
the neighboring farm. She grew prettier every day and her ath-
letic talents remained superior to the boys, who stopped fighting
the inevitable and let her tag along in their games. She also adopted
a mothering attitude with baby George, spending hours caring for
her little brother. Melissa used the free time to work on her poultry project and on Buzz's apple pie production.

As the year drew to a close, the McClures received an unprecedented second letter from Kurt and Inge Gerbrunn, in which
they accepted Scott's offer to visit the Oregon coast and meet Angela and her parents. Scott remarked to Melissa and Buzz, "Kurt
is just old-fashioned enough to inspect his son's love interest."
Kurt concluded the letter stating that the three Gerbrunns would
be in Sixes for the Easter holiday.

Just before Christmas Scott was surprised when Buzz brought
home another Gerbrunn letter with a message from Uwe. The
young man thanked Scott for hosting him and his parents at Easter, and asked for a favor. His request was not articulated very
well and Scott perused the request for ten minutes before he could
make sense out of one paragraph. Scott sat doing a mental exercise to put himself in Uwe's shoes, finally understanding the young
suitor's concern. Melissa heard her husband laugh, and asked,
"What's so funny? Have you figured out what Uwe wants yet?"

"I think so. He's apprehensive about Angela's image of him
when both fathers express criticism of their courtship. He says
that her father treats him like a boy and that his father is domi-
neering; he's right on both counts. He wants me to talk to Angela
on his behalf as 'Uncle Scott'. You know Uwe; the adults don't
scare him half as much as his sweetheart does. Does that sound
familiar?"

Melissa laughed in recalling their own long, and sometimes
rocky, courtship, advising him, "Talk to Angela if you must, but
do so with care. She thinks the world of you, Uncle Scott, but she
also has had a crush on you for years. Part of her attraction to
Uwe is because he resembles you as a young man. Also remem-

ber that matchmakers are notorious for talking when they should be listening."

Scott laughed again, never believing that he would talk too much. He didn't have much to say.

Gathering at Hermanns for Christmas dinner, Scott arrived early enough to invite Angela out for a walk. Angela had always been a pretty girl, but since Uwe had visited, she had fairly blossomed, developing a full figure and a mature look. Her flashing eyes and pert disposition proved that she had passed sweet sixteen and was now an attractive woman.

Strolling along the bluff overlooking the harbor, Scott talked about Uwe's father and his family background. He essayed, "Uwe is worried because Kurt can be very forceful and our young friend is a good son. He wants you to like his parents even if they are critical of your courtship."

"Oh, Uncle Scott, I don't expect Uwe to control his father's attitude any more than I can control mine. Both of our fathers will be sensible if Uwe and I stand together," was Angela's mature response. Obviously, she had been thinking about the Easter visit and had her own point of view.

Remembering his wife's advice, Scott said no more, allowing his young friend to talk freely of her concerns. As Melissa had said, she didn't need advice as much as a friendly listener. Upon their return to the house, Scott murmured to his wife, "You were right as usual, dear."

Christmas dinner and gift exchange were dominated by the five-year-old boys. Johnnie and Ricky ate until they were stuffed and opened a majority of the packages, to the noisy disapproval of brother George, just old enough to complain. Johnnie's resilience following Sally's death was remarkable. Nurtured by the Hermanns' loving care, he was a happy and cheerful child during the holiday season.

Johnnie received one gift from George which was extraordinary. Ellen Tichenor was attending school in San Francisco, and her parents sold the Hermanns two horses, a small gentle gray mare for Johnnie and a black gelding for George. Now both boys could ride and play together when they visited each other. George explained to Scott, "I know Pinto is lame, but Mouse is fourteen years old and won't run far either. The boys are safe enough with these horses."

The McClures returned home that evening in a blustery storm which turned out to be the forerunner of a harsh winter.

Chapter Twelve

Family activities dominated the following weeks as the weather-bound members caught up on inside chores. Buzz reconditioned all four rifles with meticulous attention to detail, and Scott cleaned the barn and meat shed. Melissa began teaching Ricky and Anne the three R's, soon establishing a classroom routine every morning around the dining table. The boy loved to do his sums, quickly mastering arithmetic facts, but he struggled with his phonics. His younger sister was reading a primer in no time, much to Ricky's dismay. However, Melissa was a good teacher, and was quick to praise her son's facility with numbers, a talent which Anne applauded but did not emulate.

Scott rode into Port Orford at the height of a rainstorm to borrow more school books from the town's teacher, and then stopped at the store to order a set of primary textbooks which the teacher had recommended. Mary expressed interest in Melissa's classroom since Johnnie would not attend the Port Orford school until the following autumn. When Scott left town, he was accompanied by the lad, who wasn't too sure that this visit to the ranch was going to be fun or not. He remained at the ranch for six weeks, and after a slow start, soon outperformed both Ricky and Anne in their lessons. Melissa was convinced that Johnnie was bright enough for college when he grew up, and told Scott to mention it to George when he took Johnnie home.

The Gerbrunns wrote to delay their visit because the rainy winter had created swollen rivers and difficult travel. They would arrive during the last week in May.

Scott took time to visit Hughes' expanding dairy farm, noting that Patrick was grazing his cows on over four hundred acres of Sixes River flats. His milk, butter, and cheese were in demand along the coast, and most settlers, including Scott, sold their surplus milk to Hughes for processing.

Scott looked toward the ocean beaches, and remarked, "Patrick, I don't see any prospectors on your beach. Are they all gone?"

Hughes waggled his head to and fro, guessing, "Yes, but only because of bad weather. Bob told me that six of the miners were camping on Hubbard Creek until spring. How many are still upriver from you?"

"Just the first three miners who moved into the Indian lodge a year or so ago. They owe Buzz several days of work, more than I can use. Should I send them over here after I finish spring planting?"

"Thanks, Scott. I'll owe you help at harvest time," Patrick promised as he asked, "Have you heard that we have a new family south of the Langlois place? I heard that he's running a small flock of sheep on his claim. Some folks don't like sheep, but Ireland is famous for its sheep breeding. I wish him well."

Scott recalled another item of news, sharing it with Hughes, "There's a new settler up the Elk River, but I've never met him. Have you?"

"No, but I haven't been to town much this winter. I did hear that he's a bachelor."

Neither man being a talker, they soon ran out of news, so Scott headed home.

The Gerbrunn entourage arrived one sunny afternoon, Uwe impatiently riding ahead of his weary parents. Scott left the corral, waving a greeting as he walked toward them, calling out, "Welcome to the Myrtlewood Grove!"

Melissa came out of the house to meet her guests, followed more slowly by three tousled children, fresh from their naps. Uwe helped his mother dismount, Inge showing the strain of the long trip. Kurt and Scott embraced, unabashedly showing their strong feelings of friendship. Buzz came over from his orchard to say hello, and to announce, "You folks will have more privacy in my cabin. Come along, Uwe, we'll unload your luggage. Your parents can visit for a while."

Kurt looked toward the river, exclaiming, *"Mein Gott!* You have a lovely farm here, my friend. Are those trees your myrtlewoods?"

"Yes, I'll give you a full tour of the valley tomorrow. For now, tell us about your trip." As the adults sat down to converse, the children went outside to play.

Some time later, Uwe and Buzz joined them, but the younger man was unable to sit still and his father gave him a dark glance, filled with irritation. Scott defused a potential argument by telling the son, "Uwe, please ride into Port Orford and invite the Hermanns to supper this evening. Maybe you could accompany them here."

A moment later and Uwe was riding down the trail. Kurt said, "Ach! A lovesick son is hard to live with. What does George Hermann think of this nonsense?"

Scott displayed his true colors in a bantering rejoinder, "He's as contrary as you are, old friend, and you're both wrong. Uwe and Angela may be young but they're not children."

"Aha, friend of my son. He told me that you were sympathetic to his suit. I take it that you disagree with the Hermanns also."

Scott grinned teasingly, "Only George, I haven't heard Mary say a critical word about Uwe. Of course the Hermanns are a good German family and the man makes those decisions."

Kurt laughed uproariously in agreement, "Your argument is without fault, my friend. Melissa, is Scott always so persuasive? Perhaps you should tell me about the Hermann girl."

"Oh no, Kurt, only you men are capable of such judgments," she riposted smartly with a humorous smile. "Angela is a young woman as you will see later. We women will stick together."

Inge concurred with Melissa before her husband could reply, "Listen to Melissa, husband. You may like Uwe's sweetheart." She stood up, and added, "And now I must clean up, if I'm going to meet the Hermanns."

Buzz volunteered to show the Gerbrunns to his cabin, and Scott set out to butcher two chickens for dinner.

The Hermanns arrived before the usual supper hour, obviously under pressure from their daughter to be punctual and gracious. They were settled around the table in casual conversation when Kurt and Inge entered the room. Their nervous son slipped forward hand in hand with Angela and blurted out, "Father, mother, this is Angela."

A doubting Kurt was met by a determined young lady, who passed his outstretched hand to give him a hug and a kiss on the cheek. Stepping back she uttered, "How do you do, Mr. and Mrs. Gerbrunn?" Inge stepped around her dumbfounded husband to give Angela a reassuring squeeze. Silence hung in the air as everyone waited for a reaction from the stolid Kurt.

Slowly a widening grin united with an emphatic nod as Kurt nudged his son with his elbow, and playfully said, "Uwe, why didn't you tell me that you were courting a beautiful woman?"

Angela blushed modestly but held her ground before Uwe's father, introducing her family in a shy but lilting voice, "May I introduce my parents, George and Mary Hermann, and my brother, John Larsen."

George had been amazed at the poise which his daughter had demonstrated in her graceful reception of the Gerbrunns, and beaming with justifiable pride and a rush of paternal love, he greeted the Gerbrunns warmly. Mary touched her daughter's elbow in approval as she stepped forward to meet Kurt and Inge. Only Melissa caught the gesture and understood the import of support Angela had received from her mother.

Three days later Uwe asked George for his daughter's hand in marriage, and was rewarded with a, "If Angela will have you, her mother and I will give our blessing."

A reciprocal supper at the Hermanns served as an engagement party, laying the foundation for an extended family of Gerbrunns and Hermanns. The McClures felt a little out of place in the gathering until Uwe asked Scott to be his best man.

Accepting readily, Scott asked, "When will the wedding take place, Uwe?"

As the young man looked at his fiancee for assistance, Kurt declared, "Before we return to Salem, I hope. Johann hates the freighting business but he's minding the office as a favor to Uwe. Since we're all together, now is the time for a wedding."

The young couple assented so quickly that everyone laughed. George suggested, "If the ceremony is next week, I can treat the newlyweds to a honeymoon trip by ship to Portland. Captain Tichenor is scheduled in port early next week."

"If Melissa doesn't object to her birthdate and wedding anniversary being used, June 3rd will allow us women time to prepare a proper wedding reception at the hotel. The Knapps will be a big help with the food and drink," Mary proposed aloud.

The women all went into the kitchen to discuss the wedding, and Scott recommended a bachelor party for Uwe. It would be a busy few days for the families of the intended, and the McClures didn't want to miss a thing. In fact, Melissa became so involved that she stayed at Hermanns with Inge when the men and children returned to the Sixes farm that evening.

Captain Tichenor's ship arrived a day early but he was accommodating to the Gerbrunn-Hermann wedding plans, staying in port until the afternoon tide late on the third of June. His modest comment was, "I can't miss the wedding of Ellen's good friend. Besides, this June wedding is being celebrated by most of my friends in Port Orford. Louie Knapp says it will be a gala event."

****

Kurt found Scott standing on the hotel porch after the wedding cake had been cut and the reception calmed down. He carried two steins of beer, sudsy and full, offering one to his friend as he toasted the newlyweds, *"Prosit!* To the bride and groom, may they enjoy health and prosperity in their marriage, and raise many grandchildren for Inge and me."

Scott drank lustily to the young couple, nodding cheerfully with the simple blessing.

Kurt lowered his voice in a conspiring tone and admitted, "You were right all along, my friend. Angela is a perfect wife for my son. She . . . they agreed to live with us while we build a house for them next door. I will make Uwe my partner in the freighting business when I set Johann up in his own law office. The Company will remain a family concern. I did promise Angela that Uwe would have a two week vacation every summer to visit her family and friends in Port Orford."

The aging German turned sentimental as they sipped beer together praising his longtime ally, "You've always had my friendship, even when we've disagreed . . . we've done that a few times . . . but add to that relationship, my gratitude for being a host to Inge and me and a special friend to my son. You and yours will always be welcome in our home. Perhaps you and Melissa will find time to come to Salem and see us."

****

Life on the Sixes returned to its pattern of normalcy after the wedding and the departure of the Gerbrunns. The weather turned clear and sunny along the Oregon coast, and the McClure children basked in its summer glow, Ricky exploring the fields and forests of the ranch along trails only a small boy could find. Melissa admonished her son repeatedly for his "disappearances" as he experienced the newly-found independence of a six-year-old boy.

Civil War news had diminished in importance to many Port Orford residents with the loss of John Larsen's company. The great struggle continued to drain the nation's strength in men and money, although the coastal settlements appeared to prosper in contradiction to the eastern United States. During the summer of '64, it became obvious from newly-arrived dispatches that the Union would triumph, probably before the end of the year.

Scott had been selling his steers on a regular basis to the store, occasionally dealing directly with his miner friends. Needing to trim the size of his herd, he sold six cows to the Hughes Dairy Farm in late June. He was returning from delivering the stock when he spotted a wisp of smoke through the trees, coming from the forest behind the barn. He raced Randy into the yard calling out, "Fire! Fire! Melissa! Buzz!" Dismounting on the run, he grabbed a bucket and two burlap sacks and climbed the side of the dam to reach the reservoir. Buzz had been working on tackle inside the barn and hurried to join Scott, picking up a saddle blanket when he saw the smoke. Melissa left two-year-old George with his sister on the cabin stoop, carrying two milk pails to Scott.

"Where is Ricky?" she asked as they carried pails of water and soaked burlap into the forest. Melissa's question was answered as the trio came upon a campfire out of control, Ricky trying to stomp out the spreading flames. Scott threw the contents of one pail on his son's legs to douse his smoldering trousers, and then extinguished the campfire with the remainder of the water as Buzz and Melissa beat out the glowing embers of grass on the downhill side. It took four trips to the reservoir and an hour's work to contain the uphill grass fire. Buzz took the water bucket and his shredded blanket and sat near the blackened forest floor to insure that no sparks were overlooked.

Scott escorted a repentant and pleading Ricky to the meat shed and applied the flat of his palm to his son's bare bottom several times. "We know that you didn't mean to start that grass fire, but Mother told you not to play with fire and she warned you not to hide from Anne and George. Now go tell your mother that you're sorry that you disobeyed her."

That night as they prepared for bed, Melissa said, "I think Ricky learned a valuable lesson today. He's really sorry about the fire accident. That small burn on his ankle and the spanking emphasized its seriousness." Pausing, she fretted, "I was frightened that fire would spread to the house or barn. I think those firs are too close to the buildings. Can't you cut them down and clear off the hillside?"

Scott agreed readily, "I'll start clearing tomorrow. All trees over ten feet tall will come out, right up to that crest two hundred feet above. Buzz and I'll have to figure out a proper use for all the logs."

****

By early August, all of the designated trees had been felled and stripped of branches. When the woodpile grew to almost the size of the house, the men decided to hitch up the horses and move the remaining timber to the east pasture. Eventually they would split the smaller logs and build a holding pen away from the corral proper. The work progressed well until one day Scott attempted to move a tilted log that he'd unhooked from the horses' harness. His satisfaction in solving a minor problem was short-lived, as he experienced a twinge in his back, straightening up with difficulty. Ignoring his discomfort, he finished his work during the next hour as his ever-tightening back muscles became downright painful.

He thought, a hot bath and a comfortable rocking chair will make me feel better, but later when he arose from the chair, shooting pains coursed through his lower back, immobilizing him. Melissa had to call Buzz to help her put Scott to bed. He spent most of his time there for the next week, gratefully accepting Melissa's treatment of heat packs and massage.

With autumn coming soon, they were going to need help, so Buzz took matters into his own hands. He enlisted the miners' help for harvesting the crops, promising a steer to feed their camp on the ocean beach. Bob declared, "Why, Old-Timer, we'd be glad to help our friend Scott regardless of pay, but fresh beef is appreciated. Maybe you ought to hire that fellow who's been helping Hughes. You'll need someone after harvest if Scott's laid up."

Buzz rode to Hughes' farm and located him in a field stacking hay. He explained Scott's problem and asked for a helper.

Patrick commented, "Henri Gaviota is a good worker, but with the haying completed, I had to let him go. He's a Basque shepherd who worked for that sheep rancher near Langlois until his boss sold out. If you hire him, you'll have his family to house. He has a wife, three children, and two sheep dogs."

"Where can I find Gaviota?"

"Look for a shepherd's tent on that sheep ranch near Langlois. Let me know when you start your harvest, and I'll help."

Scott was sitting in his rocking chair on the porch when the entourage led by Buzz walked into the yard. He correctly surmised that the Old-Timer had hired a hand, but he wondered how they were going to feed his family. Scott saw before him a short, wiry man of his own age, with a dark complexion and a pencil-thin moustache. His face was creased by sun wrinkles, attesting to his work outdoors. It took Scott but a simple deduction to conclude that the man was a shepherd.

His wife presented a nondescript appearance, dressed like a Gypsy, but slow-moving and apathetic to her surroundings. Only where her children were concerned, did she emit a spark of life.

The Gaviota family had two boys about Ricky's size, but clearly older. They closely resembled their father in appearance and mother in manner, probably good boys but without much spirit. The third child was a pretty girl of five or six years, who resembled neither parent. She had an olive complexion but fair hair and a vivacious personality, being overtly inquisitive with her glance around the ranch.

Buzz introduced the newcomers, "Scott, meet Henri Gaviota, his wife Maria, and his children, Pablo, Raul, and Lisa. Henri has agreed to work for us until spring when he has a job herding sheep in eastern Oregon. His family will live in my cabin and I'll move in with Ricky and George."

"Welcome to the Sixes valley, Henri. Where are you from?" Scott queried.

"My family comes from the Pyrenees village of Jaca in Spain, but I lived in California for many years before coming here. I am a good worker, Mr. McClure."

"I'm sure that you are, Henri. We have plenty of work on this farm. I hope that you'll find the cabin large enough for your family," Scott concluded as Buzz led them away toward his cabin. The Old-Timer had spring in his step, responding with vigor to the needs of the situation.

After the harvest was completed, Buzz took the horses into Port Orford for supplies. The partners had agreed to double their normal order, and not sell any produce, except for feed corn which Scott owed to Hughes. Patrick was late in picking his feed up, announcing, "My wife delivered a girl last week. We named her Alice."

Melissa came to the door, saying, "Congratulations, Patrick! How is Jane doing?"

"Just fine, Melissa. Do you have a couple of layers that you can sell me? Jane thinks that we need more eggs in our diet."

Melissa agreed promptly, "Of course! I'll put them in a cage for you, and I have a dozen eggs as a gift for your wife."

"Thank you, Melissa. How is your school doing? Buzz tells me that you have six pupils."

Melissa replied, "Very well! It feels good to be teaching again. We have lessons from 9 o'clock until noon, every day except Sunday. Edward is welcome to attend when he's older."

"Yes, Melissa, and thanks. Jane and I have talked about teaching Edward at home, but there's no time and neither of us is a teacher. You're being right neighborly, and we'll accept your offer in two years.

The "Sixes School" was in session all winter long, with Scott helping Melissa establish her classroom routine in their crowded house. His back sprain soon became less painful than managing six children. He was quite happy to walk and to ride without excessive pain, learning to have patience with himself in dealing with the nagging ache which was everpresent. He found that daily stretching exercises limbered his back muscles so that simple labor was possible.

Melissa found that Pablo and Raul, who were nine and seven respectively, had never attended school and didn't care much for this opportunity. Their sister Lisa loved the challenge of learning, although she enjoyed playing and talking as well. Ricky and Anne continued to develop their learning skills under the watchful eye of brother George, who was not really a pupil, but who absorbed data indiscriminately as he sat quietly watching the "big kids" wrestle with numbers and sound out words. And through all this educational milieu, Melissa gloried in refurbishing her pedagogical skills on her captive audience.

Buzz caught a simple cold, which developed into a rasping cough and a fever, seeming to grow worse as Scott's back improved. Melissa worried about Buzz's condition because of his age — over seventy-five years old. To her class' delight, she canceled school early for Christmas vacation, and spent the time nursing the Old-Timer. Marie watched her patient while the McClures spent Christmas day at the Hermanns.

Scott relished hearing recent news from George and Harvey, both of whom knew everything that happened in the County. Gold miners were giving up and moving on. Bob and a few of his friends had said good-bye earlier in the day when Scott had encountered them on the street. The Civil War was still raging back east, and Union forces were inexorably moving to a victory on all fronts. Uwe and Angela were happy newlyweds who wrote sparingly to their parents, and not at all to their friends. Mary reported that they were well and were preparing to move into their newly-built house after the holidays.

Henri proved his worth as a hired hand repeatedly during the winter, saving a cow from the rampaging Sixes River, fixing the roof after a windstorm, and running errands to town. Buzz and Scott were able to recuperate fully before the spring sun shone daily. Upon completion of spring planting, Henri collected his pay, gathered his family and belongings, and headed north to the Umpqua. His new employer had sent word that he would meet him in Scottsburg. Buzz reoccupied his cabin and everyone spread out a bit. The Gaviotas had departed as quickly as they had arrived, leaving little trace of their time on the Sixes.

Melissa commented, "They were culturally different, I guess. Henri did good work, but I never felt close to that family even though we lived together, though I will miss sweet Lisa. I wonder what will become of her?"

The "Sixes School" ended its term in May, shortly after the Gaviota children moved. Ricky and Anne wanted a break and Melissa was pleased with their progress during the winter, but she was mystified as to what George was learning. As a pesky three-year-old he displayed a lively curiosity but seldom talked, satisfied to soak up classroom tidbits like a sponge. Ricky was growing rapidly, but couldn't keep pace with a gangly John Larsen. John had attended Port Orford School all winter and was its star pupil as well as tallest child. Anne was the least changed of the children, somehow making consistency a major character trait.

****

Scott was in town delivering a steer to the store when a ship dropped anchor in the harbor and released word that the war was over. Lee had surrendered on April 9 and rebel soldiers had been sent home to a South that was in shambles. President Lincoln had been shot at Ford's Theater on April 14th and had died the next day. He thought, we're lucky not to be touched by the conflict. It's going to take a while for the country to get back on its feet again. As he visited the townspeople, he found that these sentiments were fairly common amongst the people living on the Oregon coast.

Riding home that afternoon, he found his peaceful reverie turning into a contrary mood, one of his hunches was signaling trouble to his subconscious. "Maybe it's just that big changes are coming with the end of fighting. But I think that we'd better get our house in order, my feelings aren't usually wrong," Scott muttered aloud as he trotted up the Sixes valley road.

Buzz was kept busy during the summer as an unprecedented seven calves bawled their way into life along the peaceful river valley. His gentle care over the ensuing weeks ensured their well-being, but did cause a counterbalancing problem in overstocking the ranch. Scott shared his "trouble hunch" with Buzz and Melissa, which encouraged him to be conservative. The Old-Timer laughingly called his hunches just plain common sense, and agreed that they should sell a few cows while the market was good. Scott led four cows downriver to Hughes, offering the livestock to his neighbor on credit. Patrick invited Scott to accompany him to a meeting of six settlers at Somer's place on Elk River. The newcomers had accumulated a surplus of fir logs as they cleared their land, and discussed how to realize some value from their stockpiles. Scott heard nothing new during the gathering, and declined participation, throwing a wet blanket on Hughes' plans. Riding home to the Sixes, Scott told Patrick about his grand project of gathering logs in the river estuary, and the fiasco that resulted.

"I can't waste energy on logging projects, although I'll be glad to sell timber anytime someone's ready to buy. I concluded in '57 that a sawmill, or a road to Port Orford, was necessary to sell logs. I'll stick to farming, thanks!"

Patrick agreed begrudgingly, "I bow to your experience, my friend. Common sense tells me that you're right, and I should stick to dairy farming. Speaking of which, I'd like to buy your corn harvest next month, at least what you don't need. Is my credit good until spring?"

"Of course, neighbor. I'm hoping for a bountiful crop, and since Buzz and Melissa will be busy gathering apples, I will need your help in harvesting my corn and potatoes. That'll make another good deal for both of us."

Patrick had returned Scott's wagon from hauling his last load of corn, and was observing Melissa's classroom, when three strangers rode into the McClure yard. Their resemblance to one another suggested that they were akin, probably brothers. All three had dark hair and beards, with bulbous lips and deepset brown eyes. Uninvited, the men separated, the well-dressed smiling man dismounting as his brothers rode toward Buzz's cabin.

Melissa acted on instinct, stepping back inside to fetch a gun and confronted the man with her rifle pointed at his feet. "Sir, call your brothers back here immediately. They are not welcome to ride on our ranch."

The smiler started to speak, possibly to offer an explanation, when Melissa discharged the rifle into the ground, spraying gravel into his boots and causing him to jump. A second shot from the apple orchard echoed her round as the two riders came to an abrupt stop and raised their hands.

Patrick stepped out of the house with Buzz's old Hawkins muzzleloader pointed at the midsection of the paling stranger, now without a smile. He raised his hands in a peaceful gesture and stood very still as his brothers joined him. Buzz maintained a prolonged silence with the simple gesture of his Sharps, hearing the thunder of approaching hooves. Scott dismounted on the run, his Sharps pointed at the man before his wife.

Cocking his trigger he poked the barrel into the now-quivering man's stomach, and demanded, "Speak your piece and keep it simple."

Swallowing twice before his tongue would work, the stranger gasped out, "We're friendly men, looking for land to buy. We didn't do anything."

Melissa agreed, "That's right, mister. Just came onto our land uninvited and not welcome."

Scott finished the statement as he lowered his rifle, taking it off cock, "You heard my wife, so saddle up and ride out. Don't ever trespass on this ranch again."

As the men mounted, Patrick added, "Stay out of the Sixes valley. You're not welcome on my dairy farm either."

The well-dressed brother rebutted Hughes, "We'll stay if we like, we bought the Miller place."

"No, you didn't, stranger. Miller never owned it, so you couldn't buy it," Patrick rejoined.

Scott delivered an ultimatum, "You men get out of this valley and stay out. We don't cotton to having ill-mannered louts as neighbors. Keep moving!"

The men glowered but did as they were told, riding downriver at a swift pace. Hughes asked, "May I borrow this rifle, Scott. I'm going to make sure they stay away from my land."

Scott nodded, mounting and riding with his neighbor, following the three men at a distance all the way into Port Orford. When the brothers entered a tavern down the street from the Marshal's office, Scott said, "Watch the street, Patrick. I want to talk to John Sampson."

The Marshal emerged from a cross street and walked toward Scott, asking, "Is there trouble, Scott? You look mean and nasty today."

As Scott explained the confrontation with three strangers, Hughes alerted him, "Scott, those fellows are in the street, mounting up." The horsemen heard the comment, and recognized the law officer standing with their adversaries. Saying nary a word, the brothers turned their horses away, and trotted south onto the beach, heading in the direction of Humbug Mountain.

Patrick rode to the bluff and watched them disappear from view. He shouted, "Good riddance!" as he rode back toward his friends, dismounting and accompanying them inside the Marshal's office.

John explained, "There have been several strangers wandering around the County since the war ended. It seems that Congress has legislation bringing the secessionist states back into the Union — it's called 'Reconstruction'. I hear that many landowners in the South went broke during the war and northern opportunists are buying plantations for the taxes owed. But Oregon shouldn't be affected since we were a pro-union territory."

"Then who were those men?" Scott inquired.

"Reading is the name they used. They claimed to be looking for land to buy, but I never saw any money. Those brothers were a brassy lot, and I wouldn't trust them with the time of day. Tell you what, I'll write the U.S. Marshal in San Francisco with an official request for information on them and a couple of other shady characters in town. In the meantime, Scott, you'd better get back to Melissa before she starts worrying. I'll let you know when I hear something."

As the fall months slipped by unheralded, life went on for the McClure family. Melissa and the children were busy with school daily and Scott had his farm chores, occasionally hunting with Buzz. The fracas with the Reading brothers grew remote until John Sampson paid them a visit, bringing news from San Francisco.

"The Readings are known by the U.S. Marshal's office as roughnecks working for land speculators. However, they don't buy patented land, instead they contest land titles which are in doubt. The Readings are not above pressuring settlers into selling either. My friend suggested that we contact the government land office in Salem if they try anything in Oregon. He also advised caution against getting tough with the Readings unless they break a law. There's moneyed men behind them."

Scott frowned at the latter point, "You'd better tell Hughes also. We've both threatened them with expulsion from the Sixes valley. As far as I know, Miller's old claim is open. But who would want it, unless he is willing to work?"

The Marshal left, heading for the dairy farm downriver, and leaving Scott mumbling to himself about law officers located over five hundred miles away.

When the family traveled to Hermanns for Christmas dinner, Scott's first question of George was, "What do you hear about land thieves these days?"

George knew the root of Scott's agitation was the Readings, so he answered, "Nothing new around here, but have you heard about the 'Carpet- Baggers' in the South?"

Scott shook his head, encouraging George to continue.

"Well, the same kind of people as the Readings are stealing from impoverished rebels down South. They carry carpet bags as they travel, so an eastern newspaper editor has dubbed them carpetbaggers. I wrote Angela the story of Melissa confronting those trespassing Reading brothers, and she answered that Johann Gerbrunn and John Lee want to help if any further problem occurs."

"That's what John Sampson said, George. Go to the lawyers and don't fight the crooks with force. I agree that's good advice . . . as long as they stay off my land," Scott concluded.

George gave one piece of sound advice that stuck in Scott's mind, "Keep enough money available to pay lawyers' fees, even with Johann's kind offer."

Mary called for a change of subject, toasting the Christmas fellowship and wishing everyone a happy new year.

Chapter Thirteen

The mellowing freshets of spring air had enticed apple blossoms to make a scattered appearance in the orchard, as Scott trudged behind Randy and a plow, turning over the wintry soil. Buzz correctly called a spring freshet, "A winter breeze that's lost its oomph, and feels good for a change." He stopped at the end of his furrow near the beehives, and tested his back, stretching muscles until he could finally touch his toes. He decided that he would take advantage of the clear skies to finish his cultivating. His back had been without pain all winter, but Scott knew that with his youth behind him, he had to pace himself.

"Let me finish this plowing, Scott. John Sampson is up at the house waiting for you," Buzz declared as he took over Randy's reins.

Scott found the Marshal sitting in his rocker beside the stove, drinking a cup of coffee as he visited with Melissa.

"Hello, John. I see that you've found the most comfortable spot on the ranch."

"That's right, Scott, and Melissa's coffee is a treat too. I wouldn't have a care in the world if it weren't for those Reading brothers bless their confounded hides! They're back with official-type letters asking about patents on land in the county, including several lots in town. Your place and Miller's old claim got special attention. Their 'employers' are preparing to claim any properties where proof of ownership is lacking."

Scott snapped out his first thought, "Damn it, John! You've seen my patent and you know my taxes are paid. What are these California carpetbaggers trying to do?"

"Calm down, my friend. I told the Readings all of that, plus I ordered them to stay away from here. Of course, I don't have any real authority in such matters. You'd better go to Salem and talk to the land office authorities. You need good legal advice. Doesn't your friend Gerbrunn have a son that's a lawyer?"

"Yes, he a full partner with John Lee, the lawyer who registered my claim for me years ago. You're right, but I'd appreciate it if you'd keep it to yourself while I'm away in Salem."

"Certainly, mum's the word, my friend."

As the Marshal rode out of the yard with a casual salute to his friends, Scott asked his wife, "How would you like to visit Salem? And Corvallis? Buzz can handle things here if Mary will board our children for two weeks."

"Yes! Wait a minute, Scott Addis McClure, you've never asked me to travel with you before. Does this mean that you're worried enough not to leave me behind, or that you're not worried at all?"

Scott laughed mischievously, saying, "Yes," to both of Melissa's questions, "You can figure that out, dear, while I ride into town to see Mary and George." She assumed that his teasing tones indicated that he was confident that their title was secure.

Scott was unsaddling Gerta in the Hermanns' stable when he caught movement in the corner of his eye, and felt a boy's long arms grab him. "Boo!" Johnnie cried, as he was lifted off his feet in a bear hug, "Did I surprise you, Uncle Scott?"

"Yes, Johnnie," Scott answered as he squeezed the boy affectionately, "You certainly are growing tall. It must be Mary's cooking."

Nodding emphatically, the lad agreed, "I'm a good eater too. Mary is cooking a pot roast tonight for supper. Are you going to stay?" Johnnie asked as he skipped backwards through the open kitchen door.

Scott peeked around the doorjamb, and found a smiling Mary anticipating him, "Only Scott McClure would show up at supper time with such a hungry expression. Why, you haven't begged me for a meal in years. I don't know whether to be flattered or angry," she sobered, continuing, "but I know why you're here. George is in the parlor talking to Louie Knapp about the Reading brothers. You go join them, while I finish my cooking. Johnnie, fill the woodbox and leave the men alone for their business."

Louie talked volubly about opportunistic land grabbers, quickly coining Scott's term, "California Carpet-Baggers." He was spokesman for several property owners in Port Orford whose titles were being challenged. Scott listened through supper to his friends gripe aimlessly about the injustice of outsiders meddling in local affairs.

George realized that Scott was sandbagging Louie and him, and with mock exasperation, he asked, "All right, Scott, quit looking superior and tell us how you're going to take care of the Readings."

Scott smiled and joked, "I'd like to ride them out of town on a rail," he paused as his friends nodded eagerly, before concluding, "but John Sampson won't let me. Instead I'm riding to Salem to hire Johann Gerbrunn and John Lee. I know that I own my land, but a good lawyer is needed to deal with California carpet-baggers."

"I want to go with you, Scott," Louie interjected, proffering assistance, "I know some men in the state legislature, and I have enough money available to pay for a lawyer."

"Your help is welcomed, Louie. Can you be packed and ready at sunrise tomorrow?"

"So soon! All right, where shall I meet you? At your ranch?"

"Yes, but eight o'clock is soon enough, and don't tell anyone where you're going. Melissa will feed you breakfast if you like." Scott glanced at Mary and asked, "Can our children stay with you for two weeks, Mary? I'd like Melissa to go with me to Salem."

"Of course, what a wonderful opportunity for her. I wish that I could go. We miss Angela so."

Scott offered, "We can take a message, even a package, to her
if you'll have it ready first thing in the morning. Ricky and Anne
should attend school with Johnnie. Can you talk to the teacher
without the town hearing that we're gone?"

"Yes, of course," Mary agreed absentmindedly as she scurried into her bedroom to prepare a valise of things that Angela
could use. Louie excused himself to pack for the trip, leaving
George and Scott in the parlor with "all-ears" Johnnie.

"Johnnie, you can keep our secret, can't you?"

"Yes, Uncle Scott. Ricky and I are good secret-keepers. Would
you take Angela a picture that I painted of my horse? And tell her
that I miss her a lot."

George shooed the boy to bed with a, "Get your pajamas on,
son. I'll tuck you in when you're ready." Turning to Scott, he offered his support, "Rest assured that I'll back you all the way. When
you say hello to everyone, you might relay a message from me,
'This is a family matter'."

"Thanks, George. Good-bye for now, since we won't see each
other in the morning. I plan to slip in with the children, and out
before anyone sees me."

****

Melissa was excited about traveling overland to the Willamette
valley, selectively recalling the adventuresome aspects of Inge
Gerbrunn's story of her trip south. Her effervescent mood and
lively conversation dimmed noticeably as Scott set a fresh pace
for the trio, reaching Scottsburg before the end of the daylight
hours. Melissa and Louie wearily turned in after supper, but Scott
was intent on gleaning gossip from the men in the bar, one of
them being Anton, the French-Canadian who had bought Buzz's
log cabin. No one had heard of the Reading brothers nor California land speculators in the Umpqua valley. During the ensuing
conversation Anton and another old-timer inquired after Buzz, and
everyone asked about Harvey Masters and his "Missus."

Crossing the Calapooya Pass taxed Melissa's strength and Scott called a halt mid-afternoon at Yarborough's Inn on the Willamette River, located seventy miles south of their destination of Corvallis, where they planned to visit and spend the next night. They had stopped at Elkton in passing, but neither of them had found a familiar face except for the aging Innkeeper, who didn't remember them. Scott hypothesized that his wife's search for old friends in Corvallis was going to disappoint her, but his theory was erroneous, as she talked with former neighbors, grown-up pupils, and a fellow teacher still working at her school. Her former school board chairman, a merchant, and his wife invited the trio to supper. After-dinner conversation proved fruitful to their errand, as their host and Louie discussed legislators, sharing names of mutual acquaintances. The merchant gave Louie a letter of introduction to his nephew, who was a staffer for the legislative leadership. His assistance might prove useful in obtaining support to resolve their problem. Their host told them, "The land office is federally operated, but territorial officials feel more of a proprietary interest in land claims than Washington appointees do. Seek their support before your attorney takes on that bureaucratic land office."

The trip was completed at noon the following day, as the three travelers rode into the Gerbrunn freight yard in Salem. Kurt bellowed a greeting from his office door, *"Wie geht's,* my friends. Welcome to my home." He and Scott exchanged bear hugs and back slapping. Kurt embraced Melissa gently, kissing her cheek, and shook hands with Louie. "Come into the house and see Inge and Angela. They are preparing wurst for dinner — one of your favorites, Scott. How long can you stay?"

"A few days at least, Kurt. We have a problem for Johann and John Lee to solve for us, but we can talk about that later." Scott paused as Angela ran up and hugged him warmly. He told her, "Your folks send love and kisses. Mary had a notion to come along, but she agreed to take care of the children instead. How's married life treating you?"

"Oh, Uncle Scott, we're fine. Uwe and I just moved into our house next door. You can stay in our old room, and Mr. Knapp can have Johann's room. I'm so eager to hear about my family and friends, that I don't know where to start."

Inge joined the reunion, asking questions, and then Uwe returned from a drayage job in town, necessitating repetition of greetings and the story of what they were doing in Salem. A frenetic pace characterized the jumbled conversation at the dinner table so that the import of Angela's announcement was muted but not lost on the McClures. She was pregnant, the baby due to arrive in December.

Uwe inserted, "We plan to ride to Port Orford soon. Maybe we can travel with you on your return trip. Angela's doctor says it's all right."

Louie excused himself to clean up, before seeking out his government contacts, commenting, "I'll butter up old and new acquaintances this afternoon, perhaps buying a drink or two for old times' sake. However, Inge, I promise to be back in time for supper."

Angela helped Melissa unpack her luggage, and recognizing her mother's valise, she blinked large tears from her eyes when she learned it was for her. She admitted to being homesick occasionally, but quickly avowed, "I'm happy here in Salem. Uwe is my true love and a wonderful husband. I just get sentimental about my folks' home and Port Orford every now and then. I'll stop the tears in a moment."

****

Following Kurt through a tour of his wagon house and stables, Scott mentioned that Randersacker was getting old and he might be able to buy a replacement if the legal costs weren't too high, he teased Kurt, "George said to tell Johann that 'This is a family matter', but even a reasonable fee can be expensive for a farmer."

Kurt smiled, but agreed, "Of course, but look at that gelding in the field out back. Johann used to ride him, but he bought his own horse last winter and now Franconia isn't being exercised properly. Look him over and we'll dicker when you have less on your mind. By the way, I have a good milk cow for sale, too. Ha! Ha!"

Scott laughed at his friend's joshing tones, recalling his purchase of milk cows from Kurt years ago, "I already have enough of your cows, but I would like to ride Franconia when you show me around Salem on Sunday."

After a scrumptious supper the men retired to the parlor with their brandies to discuss the legal case before them. Johann deferred to his senior partner, John Lee, to speak for the firm.

"Mr. McClure . . . pardon me, I promised to call you by your given name. Scott, I remember registering your claim several years ago. If you've paid your taxes, I'm sure your papers are in order, and I'll represent you at the land office at no charge. If there is some problem, we'll need to agree on a fee." He nodded to Louie, accepting an earlier offer, "Mr. Knapp, I'll represent you and your clients for a $100 retainer. I'm acquainted with all the men with whom you talked this afternoon, and I'll contact them tomorrow before I go to the land office. Your retainer should cover all of the firm's costs, and I don't anticipate that any additional fee will be necessary."

Johann spoke as his partner completed his comments, "What you gentlemen really want is to rid your community of these brothers. Isn't that right?"

"Absolutely! I'd chase those carpetbaggers back to California if I had a legal leg on which to stand. Is there any way to do it?" said Louie.

John and Johann looked at each other, with the junior partner responding, "We'll explore all avenues for a solution that protects your legal rights . . . and maybe make your adversaries back off. We'll both work on your case tomorrow and see what can be done. Can we meet in our office at four o'clock and review our progress?"

Scott and Louie quickly agreed and the men drifted into political issues, first of the national impact and then local matters. Although the farmer found most political conversations boring, the evening was over before he realized his intense interest in Johann's charming anecdotes of Oregon's leading political figures.

****

Scott and Louie walked into the law offices promptly, and a young law clerk escorted them to Johann's empty office, bringing them a pot of coffee and two cups. It was over an hour later before the lawyers entered, carrying on an animated conversation. Both men displayed confident and pleased expressions.

John Lee spoke briefly, "Your claims were all confirmed as I expected, and your retainer, Mr. Knapp, covered all expenses. You both expressed a desire to discourage carpetbaggers. Johann has set up a proposal to help you, which I endorse, but which he will execute. I'll bid you good evening, gentlemen, and wish you a safe return to Port Orford."

As the Senior Partner left, Johann leaned back in his overstuffed chair and explained, "John has a business dinner, and besides, while he endorses me, he's not crazy about my plan. If you disagree with what I'm about to propose, I'll drop the matter instantly." He paused, checking for both men's understanding, before continuing his detailed description, "Father and Uwe pointed out that our family obligation requires full satisfaction of your wishes, Scott. I have a few days of vacation coming and my wife wants to shop in Portland with her mother, so I am free to accompany your party to Port Orford, and deal with the Reading brothers directly. Louie, your contacts were very helpful in having me appointed as a Special Investigator for the territorial legislature, and with that authority in hand, and a very influential partner at my side, the land office gave me everything that I wanted, including a Deputy U.S. Marshal's badge. I believe that with your local

Marshal's assistance, I can negate any paperwork, official or not, which those men are using. I can lean on them hard enough to send them back to San Francisco."

Looking at the ceiling and smiling, he resumed, "Heh, heh, that's John's concern. I have to bluff, and make it stick, since our firm will represent you if the Californians call our bluff."

"You said our claims are sound, so where is your bluff?" Scott asked.

"The Readings haven't broken any law and have every right to continue seeking developed land that is unpatented. I have no real authority to coerce them into leaving town, but being a fast-talking lawyer from Salem may be enough. Louie's friends in the government don't want California carpetbaggers on the coast, and want me to pursue any wrongdoing aggressively. Do you men accept my offer? Of course there is no fee, my father insists that Scott will need all of his money to buy Franconia."

After Louie nodded, deferring to him, Scott responded, "Thank you, Johann. We accept your generous offer on two conditions. First, we will pay all of your out-of-pocket expenses, and second, you will charge a reasonable fee for any services beyond your proposal."

Johann replied promptly, "Fair enough, can we leave tomorrow? Uwe and Angela will have to travel slowly. Father wants me along to see that they complete the round trip this month. Angela will only have a couple of days to visit her parents, as I have to be back in Salem for a court appearance in nine days."

****

Scott rode a refreshed Franconia, nicknamed Frank, and used his weary old stead, Randy, to pack the party's luggage, including Mary's valise full of gifts from the Gerbrunns. Angela surprised everyone as she proved to be a strong rider, always eager to move forward. Her explanation was simple, "I'm young and healthy, and

I've been riding daily since Kurt gave me this horse." She was the freshest member of the party when they rode up to the Hermanns' front door four days later.

After a joyous but brief homecoming, Uwe offered to care for the horses, and Johann asked George to accompany Scott, Louie, and him to Marshal Sampson's office. He suggested, "I'd like to reach his office without calling undue attention to ourselves. Are the Readings in town?"

George responded affirmatively, "Yes, at least I saw them on the street an hour ago, just before I closed my store. They're living in a plank house behind the jail. Isn't that one of your lots, Louie? Let's cut across the lot ahead and use John's back door. The brothers are probably in the tavern down the street."

A surprised John Sampson readily agreed to the U.S. Marshal/Special Investigator's proposal with relish, and George chortled at the possibilities. Johann recommended, "I'd prefer confronting the rascals right now, and in public, before they know anything about my presence."

John chuckled. "They were in the tavern a few minutes ago. Are twenty-some drinkers public enough for you, Marshal Gerbrunn?" As Sampson led the party down the street, Johann pinned his badge to his lapel, prominent enough to impress even his companions.

The two law officers entered the tavern shoulder to shoulder and walked up to the three brothers who were drinking at the bar. Scott stepped right as he entered, George following while Louie stepped left by prearrangement, with the two travelers' rifles being carried in plain view. The Readings were unaware of the law officers until they were two steps away. The well-dressed brother stuttered recognition, "Well . . . uh . . . Marshal . . . what . . . uh . . . hello . . . ."

Sampson spoke up, his voice carrying to the fascinated spectators in the tavern, "Mr. Reading, I'd like to introduce Deputy United States Marshal Johann Gerbrunn from Salem, who is conducting a special investigation of fraudulent land practices for the territorial legislature. He has shown me his authority, and I will support any action that he orders."

"We haven't committed any crime; we're just looking for land to buy," Reading spewed out, glancing apprehensively at the rifles of McClure and Knapp, and then back to the stern visage of the Federal Marshal.

Johann pontificated officiously, "Mr. McClure and Mr. Knapp traveled to the territorial capitol to seek redress for fraudulent land practices by Californians. Do you deny that you are living in a house near the jail?"

"No, we claimed that property three weeks ago. Here are my papers." Reading's hand shook as he held out an official-looking document.

Johann perused the sheet, reading each phrase and then negating its meaning with what sounded like legal mumbo-jumbo to Scott, but his performance was very impressive to the enthralled audience. Finally, he returned the paper, shaking his head, and declaring, "Worthless paper issued in California. I'll write my colleague in San Francisco about the carpetbagging tactics coming from his city. My records show that Mr. Knapp owns that land. Do you wish to bring charges, Mr. Knapp? Or would rent be sufficient retribution say, a dollar a day?"

Louie responded on cue, "Rent would do nicely, sir."

"And Mr. McClure, you told me that these men trespassed on your Sixes River ranch. Do you wish to file formal charges?"

"Hmmm, I'll think on that, sir. Can I speak to my wife and see you in the morning?"

"That'll be fine, although these men might prefer to settle their differences with you in a cash offer. Now as to this matter of operating a business without a license, and the possible charge of fraudulent intent, I wish to hear your explanation before Marshal Sampson shows me his jail."

Sweating profusely in nervous agitation, the spokesman's voice crackled as he offered, "Sir, I have papers at my place. Allow us the chance to bring them here and prove our innocence."

"Of course, man. Hurry, my time is valuable," Johann declared as righteously as he could manage.

As the Reading brothers scurried out the door, Marshal Sampson offered, "Marshal Gerbrunn, let me buy you a drink. You've come a long way to bring law and justice to our town."

He was interrupted by one of the bystanders who had followed the men out of the tavern, and who now ran back inside, shouting, "Those three crooks are running away. They're riding hell-bent for Humbug, Marshal."

Johann hurried through the door, advancing to the middle of the street and motioning for Louie to give him his rifle. The brothers were over a mile away when the Marshal fired the gun into the air. The riders spurred their horses more vigorously as they raced out of sight down the beach.

A couple of old prospectors summed up everyone's feeling. "Good Riddance! They'd better not show up in this county again."

Scott had trouble keeping a straight face as the party walked back to the Hermanns' house, and broke into gut-wrenching laughter as soon as he was inside the door. He was soon joined by the entire family as George related the events of the confrontation and Johann's heroic performance of his duty.

****

The McClure family rode home late at night, George asleep in his mother's arms and Anne's head resting quietly on her father's shoulder. Ricky was feeling important, riding Randy by himself, and talking excitedly about last weekend's excursion to Hubbard Creek. "Uncle George took us to your gold claim to camp overnight and pan for gold. Anne found an arrowhead where the Indian village used to be, and Johnnie found a gold nugget in the creek. We ate grilled salmon, and slept outdoors, and I've got some gold dust. Can we do it again, Dad?" Anne's silence suggested that she was dozing or that she didn't think it was all that exciting.

Scott acknowledged his son's pleading request, "Maybe when Johnnie visits us next week, we can prospect at Chief Sixes' old lodge. We could hunt for game at the same time. Let's ask Buzz to go along. He's the best hunter."

As they rode across the log bridge, Scott called, "Wake up, Buzz. We're home."

An answer came from the knoll to his left, "Well, of course you are. Anybody could hear you coming a mile away. Hee, hee. . . . It's good to have you younguns home." The Old-Timer walked beside them into the yard, asking, "Did you buy another horse from Kurt?"

"Yes, meet Franconia. He's a younger version of Randy. How have things been on the ranch?"

"Everything is hunky-dory here. We have another bull calf, and this fellow has potential as a stud. There hasn't been a single soul visit the ranch since you left. How was the trip?"

"Successful, partner, the titles are clear and the Readings are on the run. Come on, I'll tell you all about the trip while we groom these horses. They've earned a bag of oats too."

The Gerbrunns' vacation in Port Orford was short and sweet, just as Johann had decided that night in Salem. Angela was resigned to spending only two days with her parents, appearing cheerful and eager to return to Salem. Johnnie had accompanied them to the ranch as they stopped to say good-bye, and Scott allowed the two boys to escort the party north as far as the next farm.

They acted very grown-up when they returned, the morning's independence an experience to savor. Scott accepted their offer to clean out the barn, winking at Buzz who had kept it neat and tidy during their absence. The boys worked up a sweat, and smiled broadly when they received Scott's approval of their job.

While George took his afternoon nap, the other three children went swimming in the river, promising faithfully to be careful. Scott could hear their shrill voices as they cavorted in the cold water. When they grew quiet, he left his corn field and walked to the river bank near the swimming hole. He watched Ricky climb

up the lower face of Rocky Point, turn quickly, and push off forcefully, grabbing his knees as he hit the deeper water of the pool.
Scott thought it was time for him to put some limits on this diving activity.

When Ricky was told to stay off the bluff, he pointed to a
rock ledge about four feet above the pool, seeking permission to
jump from there. Scott nodded, deciding the children understood
his safety concerns, and returned to his chores.

****

The next morning the boys were scavenging lumber, brads,
and rope, intent on building a contraption which piqued Scott's
curiosity. When they carried it off to the swimming hole with Anne
tagging along, Scott gave up on his own work, and followed them.
Looking across the river, Scott observed a diving board taking
shape on the ledge. Ricky called to him, "Dad, will you help us?
This board is too loose. It isn't safe."

Shaking his head in disbelief at the creative energy displayed
by the boys, he corrected the bindings which secured the diving
board to the rock, testing it with his weight. The contraption was
sound, but not flexible, being more of an extension of the ledge
than a spring board.

Ricky, Johnnie and then Anne dove into the pool to demon-
strate its safety. On the spur of the moment, Scott removed his
shoes and used the board to flop into the water, resembling the
play of a whale more than that of a salmon. Anne threw a hand
full of water in his face, precipitating a splashing and dunking
water fight. Scott enjoyed his youth-like exuberance and the youngsters were wildly excited by his playful mood. When he collapsed
on the gravelly shore, his daughter sat down on his stomach and
mischievously shook her hair over his face, spraying him with
water.

The father had run out of energy, but the children had just
begun to play with their new toy at the swimming hole. Scott re-

turned to the house and related the story of the diving board to Melissa and Buzz. He was resting from his workout, when the boys found him again. Ricky asked, "Are you ready to take us gold prospecting, Dad? Remember that you said. . . ."

"That we would prospect and hunt at Sixes' lodge," Scott concluded his promise to his son. "But we can't go camping until Buzz is ready."

Overhearing his name and the opportunity to hunt in the same conversation, Buzz responded promptly from the barn, "What! Hunting with the boys! I'm ready right now!"

Scott threw up his hands, conceding, "All right, we'll leave after chores in the morning, and camp overnight. Everyone pack their gear for the campout, and I'll check it after supper. Remember now, Randy is our packhorse and we all have to hike both ways. Yes, you can go too, Anne."

****

Heavy rains, accompanied by cool fall air, marked the end of summer, and Melissa seized the opportunity to resume her classroom instruction. Ricky groaned at being confined to a classroom all morning, but Anne welcomed the routine. George was silent as he had been the previous school term, until one day the four and a half year old boy responded with an answer for a difficult multiplication problem.

Ricky had asked for a hard problem with big numbers to multiply, prepared to show off his skill at mathematics. Melissa had written on his slate 34x78=, when George's tiny voice had piped up, "Two-tousan, six-hunder, fifty and two!"

Melissa decided his pronunciation might be faulty, but his mental acumen was phenomenal. Ricky and Anne tested their little brother with problem after problem, receiving instantaneous and correct answers, despite frequent mispronunciation. When Melissa slipped in a division problem, George's face clouded in confusion, and he admitted, "I don't know. What is dibisun?"

Melissa explained division, writing the word on a slate, and defining it painstakingly, before giving a few examples. When Anne kept looking toward the clock, Melissa knew that it was time for reading. As she put away the slate, George stated clearly, "Twenty-one!"

"What was that, George?" Melissa asked.

"One-hunder, seventy-six, dibided by eight is twenty-one. You didn't finish the problem, Momma." Several more correct answers convinced Melissa that her prodigy understood mathematical processes innately, but he could become confused by the vocabulary.

She nodded to Anne, who was poised over her open book, to read her story aloud. Ricky followed his sister, reading clearly but without her flourishing style. The last paragraph was saved for George, who read it easily, albeit with fractured pronunciations.

She commended all three students and dismissed school early, seeking out her husband to share her discovery. She hoped that Scott might be able to help her understand George's astounding talents, and how to help him develop them to their fullest potential.

Scott was pleased that George was precocious, but was not as impressed as his schoolteacher wife. However, he did listen to his son recite his lessons after supper and commended the boy for doing well. George asked seriously, "Am I a good boy, Daddy?" Scott hugged his son and reassured him that he would always be special to him.

****

Scott delivered his surplus milk to the Hughes farm one day in late fall, being directed to the beach by Jane. The dairy farmer had a huge bonfire burning, and was busily throwing everything left behind by the departed miners into the flames. Picking up some trash, Scott dropped it in the fire, asking, "Are the miners finally gone, Patrick?

"I hope so, Scott. Since Bob and his friends left the county two years ago, I haven't seen a miner that I liked. I figure that if I clean out the camp and let nature take its course this winter, no one will bother to build another campsite."

Scott laughed with his friend. Patrick finally admitting, "I know that it's wishful thinking. Man's greed is bound to resurface where a little gold can be found. It's worth a try anyway." Scott nodded and helped finish the job, removing all sign of the old mining operation. The blowing surf would eradicate any trace of man during the winter storms.

Over a warming cup of coffee in the Hughes' kitchen, Patrick commented that lumber prices were up because of the California demand. Tichenor's mill was doing well, and hesitatingly he reminded Scott, "Our neighbors are still trying to find a market for their timber. They asked me to bring you to their next meeting. I guess they believe that you are a miracle man. What do you think, Scott? They are our neighbors."

Scott shook his head, but acceded to his friend's gentle pressure. "All right, I'll attend one more meeting to be neighborly, but don't expect me to agree with them."

The Sixes farmers were greeted so enthusiastically by Somer as "good neighbors," that both men left his house agreeing to return the following week. Patrick laughed all the way home, teasing Scott, "I let you answer Somer figuring it was my last meeting, but you couldn't give him a simple no. Where was your fearless 'don't expect me to agree with them' speech?"

But as with previous attempts to sell logs, their friends' efforts failed to produce a workable plan and were abandoned during the next meeting.

****

When Scott returned to his house late at night, he found Buzz dozing in the rocker near the stove, coming awake when the door opened. Answering the question in Scott's countenance, Buzz said softly, "Missy had a miscarriage after supper. I took care of her and I think she'll heal quickly. Did you know she was pregnant?"

"No, how far along was the baby?"

"It wasn't really a baby, maybe two months. I asked if you knew because Missy seemed so worried that you'd be upset. I couldn't figure out what she thought would upset you."

Scott pondered his partner's comments, finally saying, "I didn't think that she should have another baby, but I wasn't against a baby as much as for Missy's health. Thanks, Old-Timer, I'll have to explain myself better to my wife. Why don't you turn in, and I'll sit here and think about it."

Awakening with a start, Scott listened carefully for the sound that had aroused him. He rose and tiptoed to the bedroom door, not wanting to disturb his recuperating wife.

"Scott, darling, come and sit beside me on the bed," Melissa invited in whispering tones. "I heard you snoring in your rocker, and realized that it is near morning. I'm sorry that I didn't share my condition with you, but I thought that I'd surprise you later. You were right though; I think my child-bearing days are over. This pregnancy was like the last one, only much worse. This evening I barely had time to call Buzz before I started bleeding and lost consciousness. Fortunately the children slept through my miscarriage. Buzz was such a good doctor that I even forgot my modesty."

Scott comforted his wife until she talked herself to sleep and then quietly stoked the stove fire and prepared breakfast for the children as the rooster crowed from the chicken coop. Buzz showed up for breakfast, hungry and looking pleased with himself. He asked, "How did Missy spend the night?"

"Fine, thank you, Buzz. She complimented your doctoring skills. Now, how about displaying your teaching skills with the children in your cabin. Keep them there until noon, and I'll have a meal ready for all of us then."

Melissa recovered quickly, although Scott insisted that she stay indoors and take daily naps. School was held, but the men often took the children to Buzz's cabin for part of their lessons.

****

A revitalized Old-Timer announced that he was going out the old cougar trail and bring back game for their empty meat shed. Scott suggested, "Don't try to tote the deer home. Hang the carcass on a tree and come back for me. I'll carry it out."

Buzz snorted derisively, "Do you think that I'm an old woman? I can take care of myself." Chin thrust forward, the indignant Old-Timer marched across the pasture at a swift pace, not slowing an iota until he was out of Scott's sight.

Scott was so busy all day that he didn't give Buzz's hunting another thought until Melissa called him for supper, asking in a worried voice, "Have you seen Buzz yet? He should have returned by now."

"Don't worry, dear. He's probably carrying a deer down the trail to prove he's still young and strong. I'll go meet him after supper, and give him a hand. He'll appreciate my help by the time that he reaches the bottom of that trail."

It was well after dark when Scott topped the ridge about a half mile from the cairn, if he remembered right. He had fired his rifle three times with no response, and had concluded that Buzz was in serious trouble if he couldn't return fire. Since his partner always camped in the same place at the cairn, he continued moving toward it as he listened for any sound that would identify his partner or a four-legged predator skulking in the area.

Rifle ready, he slipped sideways into the half cave under the domed rock, remembering his father-in-law's surprise at finding a bear there ahead of him. But no creature was present this night as Scott felt the floor with his foot as he searched the shadows with his eyes. His foot brushed a canvas bundle, and Scott felt it to confirm it was Buzz's pack.

Throwing caution aside, Scott propped his rifle against the rock wall and gathered bits of wood for a fire, soon tindering a flame in the tiny pile of twigs and shavings. However, it gave him the light necessary to search for pieces of wood, and the fire grew until he found a small cache of fire wood stored in a crevice. Soon the cave was warm and bright, rays of light spreading into the night, serving as his recall beacon. Scott stepped into the open calling Buzz's name, and firing another round into the sky. Echoes of his voice and the shot rang together through the clear night air, mixed confusingly with the faint sound of his own name.

"Scott . . . Scott . . . Scott . . ." diminished in consonance with his dying echoes, but Scott recognized Buzz's voice and fixed his eye on a star overhead, proceeding directly across the rocky hillside toward his guiding star. He moved cautiously, but with dispatch, until he reckoned that he'd covered over a hundred yards.

He stopped before a deadfall in the thick forest. Unable to see his star or continue in a straight line, he fired another round and called out.

A reply came from nearby, "Careful, Scott. This pile of deadfall is loose, and I'm trapped by a fallen tree right below that mess. Your best bet is to back up and circle around below me."

"Did you shoot a deer?" Scott asked.

"Yes, he's a few yards downhill. Like you, my first worry has been that some predators might be attracted to that bloody deer. And me trapped here with my rifle out of reach. But I haven't heard a thing since darkness fell."

"Well, Old-Timer, that's the problem. It's awfully quiet up here. Did we startle the wildlife or do we have company that did? Keep your ears open while I'm moving through this brush."

Scott soon found his partner and extricated him from the log-jam, but Buzz couldn't walk on his injured ankle. Gritting his teeth didn't help him stand, but the feeling of the leg convinced him that no bones were broken, not badly anyway.

A coyote yipped at the moon from a nearby ridge, causing Scott to jump. Buzz laughed, "I had the same reaction. If you're going to save our venison, you'd better bring my rifle to me, and dress that carcass. I'll be a lot more comfortable when I have a cave wall behind me."

It was a night-long task to move Buzz and the meat up to the cairn. Buzz fired shots into the false dawn, not trying to hit coyotes but scaring them off. Scott cooked the liver and with a handful of Melissa's biscuits, their appetite was sated and they were ready to travel.

The afternoon sun was well to the west when the partners stumbled to the river bank, an unmasked groan escaping from Buzz's lips. He had walked all the way down the hill, using two empty rifles and one good leg to reach the bottom of the trail.

"Daddy! Buzz! Can I come across the river and help?" Ricky scrambled over the log spanning the river, and looking at Buzz, he asked, "Are you all right? Momma's awful worried about you."

"Well, Ricky, my ankle's killing me, but I'm more worried about your daddy's back."

Scott agreed, "I'm aching, but I know that you are too. Let's get home so Melissa can nurse us back to health. Ricky, run on ahead and tell your mother that we're coming, and then open the meat house and get it ready for this venison."

Within the hour, Buzz sat in the rocker with his injured ankle soaking in a pail of hot water, while Scott lay on his stomach as Melissa kept hot towels on his back. As she massaged his tired muscles with extra pressure, eliciting a groan from her husband, she said, "You had me worried sick. Why didn't you let the coyotes have their feast and come right home?"

Buzz chuckled loudly in the next room and was the object of her next retort, "Don't you laugh, Erastus Elijah Smith. You're just as mentally deficient as my husband is." She slapped Scott on his sore backside, admonishing him, "And don't you dare say a word in defense of either of you. I suppose that Ricky and I will have to ride into Port Orford and invite the Hermanns and Masters for Christmas dinner. You two 'hunters' won't be able to move for at least a week."

Both men were hobbling about by Christmas day and loosened up considerably when George opened a bottle of California wine. Melissa shook her head charitably, giving up finally, "If I'd known the curative power of wine, George, these men could have been working all week."

A second bottle was served with dinner, priming Buzz to entertain the gathering with a story which stretched the audience's imagination far enough to draw a look of incredibility from Scott. Buzz laughed and revised his last passage to embrace a more reasonable truth, a technique which he had learned from Ivan Rokov. The Old-Timer's eyes dampened a little as he concluded, "And that's the story of my last hunt!"

Chapter Fourteen

Slamming the door closed against the howling storm, Scott leaned against it as his coat and hat dripped on the floor. Smiling at Anne and George seated at the table, he teased them, "Aren't you glad that you have school today and don't have to get all wet?"

Anne rebutted, "It's not funny, Daddy. Why does Ricky get a vacation when George and I have to stay in school? Even Edward has the winter months off."

Melissa corrected her daughter, "Ricky is going to school with Johnnie in Port Orford. He'll come home when the rain stops and the rivers go down. And you know Edward's father won't bring him back until spring. He's awfully young to be a pupil anyway."

Offering a treat to her housebound students, Melissa said, "Let's have Daddy tell us a story about his childhood in St. Charles, Missouri. Do you want to hear about Grandma McClure again?"

"Yes! Yes! Daddy, tell us a story!" the children implored in chorus, always receptive to storytime in preference to school lessons.

Scott embroidered his tales with the geography and history of his experiences, since his children had no personal memories of their parents' families. Scott's goal was to pass along a piece of their family heritage as well as entertain his children. One time George had asked naively if Grandpa Nelson had been as old as Buzz, and was greatly mystified that he was younger, but had died a 'long time ago'. At such times, Scott doubted his ability as a teacher as well as a storyteller, but Melissa encouraged him with an intuitive comprehension that his sharing with his children was a bonding agent for their personal values. She knew that he was being a good father.

Three days of fair sky in February allowed the river level to drop to a point where the McClures felt comfortable riding into town to fetch Ricky and some needed supplies. Leaving Melissa at the Hermanns' house, Scott rode to the store and chatted with Harvey Masters as he bought supplies. George was attending a county meeting on land development and the maintenance of records and deeds, which Louie Knapp had requested.

The front door opened and Marshal Sampson entered, greeting Scott, "Good day, my friend. I saw your horse outside and stopped by to say hello. How are things on the Sixes?"

"We're all healthy, John, but I am glad to see sunlight again. What's new in town?"

Sampson smiled cheerily, "Nothing, I'm happy to say. My colleague in San Francisco reported that the Readings passed through town on the way to the gold fields, and Captain Tichenor told me that Port Orford cedar is in demand. The mill is shipping all it can cut to California. Oh yes, and I received a greeting from Johann Gerbrunn at Christmas, thanking me for doing my job and wishing me a happy new year. He's a fine gentleman."

"Yes, my friend Kurt raised two fine young sons. I hope that I can do as well with my children."

The Marshal hesitated, remembering a disagreeable piece of gossip, "It's not any of my business, but your boy has had a running fight this past month with the Tucker lad. Just 'boys will be boys' fighting, but I know that his teacher has talked to the Hermanns."

Scott frowned, "It's not like Ricky to be a bully."

John laughed, "He's hardly being a bully, when Billy Tucker is a year older and considerably bigger."

"Thanks, John, I'll talk to my son."

When he reached the Hermanns', he found the women talking about Ricky's unusual behavior. Mary explained, "He's a good student and no trouble at all in school, or at home, but he's fought

Billy Tucker on the way home from school four times in the last two weeks. And Bill seems like a nice boy when he plays with Johnnie. I don't know what's going on."

Melissa suggested, "I need to talk to his teacher anyway, why don't I ask for her opinion?" She shook her head at her husband, "No, Scott, you don't need to come with me to school. That might blow Ricky's problem out of proportion. You can talk to him privately after dinner."

Scott agreed readily, and asked Mary, "Who are the Tuckers?"

"They are a new family in town. He's a logger working for the Tichenor mill. They live in one of Louie Knapp's houses over by the fort."

Ricky came home with his mother, seemingly without a care in the world and gave his father a big hug, rattling on about school and playing with Johnnie. Looking around he asked Mary, "Where's Johnnie? In the barn?"

"No, he went to the store with Billy. He'll be back for dinner."

Ricky's face clouded over with dismay and anger as he went to his bedroom with a sulking expression. Scott exchanged glances with his wife, and asked, "Did I see jealousy in my son? What did his teacher have to say?"

"Just what we saw this moment. Ricky has a proprietary attitude toward Johnnie. This new boy is Johnnie's size and it's natural that they've become friends, but our son picks a fight with Billy whenever the two big boys play together."

Scott concluded, "And so Ricky takes a thrashing every time that he has a jealous fit."

Melissa shook her head, responding, "No. My real concern is that Ricky is being a bully. His teacher says that he's tenacious and single-minded enough to win his fights. Billy is big and strong for a child, but not a fighter. She thinks Mr. Tucker is angrier with his son for losing than for fighting. The father is a 'roughneck' logger who's probably fought a few times himself."

Scott joined his son in the bedroom, closing the door and declaring, "You and I need to talk, young man. Did you hear what your mother and I were saying just now?"

"Yes, Daddy, and I'll be good. Are you going to spank me?"

"No, but I expect you to tell me the truth. Why have you been fighting with Billy?"

The boy gulped back a sob, and answered, "He's bigger than me."

"That doesn't excuse meanness and bullying. Tell me Ricky, is Billy a nice boy?"

Ricky was taken aback by the question, but said truthfully, "He's all right, but he's always trying to play with Johnnie and Johnnie's my friend."

"Well, son, Johnnie may have any friends that he wants. It's not a matter for you to decide. Being mean to Billy is not right, and it won't make Johnnie like you any more than he does now."

Tears streaming down his young face, the bay sputtered, "It's not fair! Johnnie was my friend first."

Scott's reply was gentle, "Perhaps you should be friends with Billy, and then all three of you could play together."

Between sobs, the boy replied, "Billy doesn't like me."

Scott smiled, suggesting, "Isn't that your fault? If you pick on him and make him unhappy, why should he like you? How should you behave if you want to be friends?"

"Be nice to him? Maybe play with him? How can I do that, Daddy?"

Scott offered, "Your mother and I will help you. We'll all go over to the Tucker house. You need to apologize to Billy and ask him to be your friend. For now you'd better dry your tears and we'll go downstairs for dinner."

In the late afternoon, as the sawmill workers were going home, the McClures walked over to the Tucker house. Ricky was not eager to face his adversary, but he was sticking with tenacity to his parents' directive, prepared to apologize to Billy.

A solidly built dark-haired boy watched them approach from his swing, hanging from a tree at the side of the house. He said tentatively, "Hello, Ricky "

Ricky responded courteously, "Hello, Billy. This is my mother and my father."

Billy stepped forward as Scott reached out to shake hands, the boy responding slowly, "Do you want to see my Dad?" He looked beyond the McClures, down the street, and said, "He's coming home from work now."

Melissa squeezed Scott's hand lightly, reminding him to set an example for the boys, forcing a smile to his lips, which was met in turn by a hospitable greeting from Billy's father, "Hello, you'd be the McClures, Ricky's parents. Come into my home and my wife will fix coffee for us."

Shaking the huge man's hand, Scott felt his considerable strength and concluded that being friendly with Tucker made good sense. The man's dark Welsh face bore several small scars, remnants of fistfighting Scott surmised. Emulating Scott's amiable example for the boys, Tucker demonstrated his concern for his son's problem and his willingness to help him solve it.

Mrs. Tucker was a full-sized woman with a broad face, almost homely until she smiled, transforming it to a warm and attractive visage. After introductions and greetings were exchanged, and they were seated around the kitchen table with coffee before them, Scott announced, "My son has something that he wants to say to Billy."

Ricky stood up and spoke clearly, "I'm sorry, Billy, for being mean to you. I'd like to be your friend." He thought for a moment and brightened, inviting Billy to his favorite event, "Maybe you'd like to go prospecting on the Sixes with Johnnie and me this summer. Dad promised to take us as soon as the river goes down."

"Golly Ricky, I heard that you found gold and arrowheads, and killed a deer. Gee, Dad, could I go with Ricky?"

"Only if you two boys shake hands and agree to be friends," Mr. Tucker wisely counseled, as the boys solemnly shook hands and went outdoors to get better acquainted. Tucker continued, "That solution deserves a beer. What do you say, Mr. McClure?" Scott grinned and drank his new friend's beer, celebrating another significant moment of parenthood.

****

One spring afternoon, Buzz took the boys to the top of slide ridge, showing them where he and their father had protected the valley from Indians and bad men. He reminisced about the old days, and though Ricky soon tired of his stories, George remained attentive as his imagination kept pace with the Old-Timer's.

George slipped away to the redoubt several times over the following days, his absence going unnoticed as Scott worked on his spring planting. When Melissa realized what he was doing, she and Scott had a long talk with their son. They agreed that he could "play" in his hideaway as long as he told Melissa where he was going, didn't walk on the shale slope, and didn't go beyond the ridge.

Scott had plowed a new patch of ground near his potatoes; and was putting in a crop of beans, when Melissa interrupted his work. "George said that he was going to his 'hideaway' and he's late coming back. Can you look for him now?"

"All right, let me finish planting this furrow, and I'll ride down there. Do you want to go with me?"

Melissa agreed, "Yes, I'll saddle Gerta and Frank, and wait for you at the house." With Ricky and Anne off somewhere with Buzz, they could take their time except that Melissa was fidgeting over George's whereabouts.

Calling to George at the foot of slide ridge produced no answering hail, so the couple continued through the cut downriver. As they rounded the corner they could see their son sitting in the brush near the Sixes crossing. They spurred their horses, Scott searching the area before them as they trotted forward, but Melissa paying attention only to her son.

George waved when he saw them but stayed seated on the ground, petting a golden bundle of fur. As Scott rode up to his son, a dog rose up on his haunches and snarled defiance, barking until George laid a hand on his head. The cocker spaniel stood on three legs, blood matting his right ear and neck as well as his injured right front leg. Scott dismounted and knelt by his son, reaching out his hand only to be snapped at by the dog.

"Be careful, Daddy. He's scared because a bad man clubbed him and left him behind. I think the bad man was a prospector. I hid until he was gone and then came down to help the dog. Can I keep him, Daddy? Please? I'll take care of him. He won't be a bother, I promise."

Melissa acquiesced without hesitation, worried that Scott might say no, instructing her son, "Yes, George, but he'll be yours to take care of, and he'll have to live in the barn with the other animals. Now, can you pick him up and hold him so Daddy can lift both of you into the saddle?"

As Scott hoisted the boy and his dog atop the horse, he noticed a puncture wound on George's thumb and asked, "Why is your thumb bleeding? Did your dog bite you?"

"Yes, but he didn't mean to. It was my fault; I hurt his leg and he was scared."

Scott agreed, "Scared animals sometimes bite. Do you think he's all right now? And what are you going to call your dog, George?"

"He looks like that cougar rug of yours, Dad. I'll name him 'Cougar' — is that a good name?" George asked seriously. He smiled smugly when both of his parents nodded affirmatively.

Buzz's veterinarian's skills helped Cougar recover from his wounds, as the dog accepted the Old-Timer's ministrations at their first meeting. Tender care and regular meals allowed for quick healing, and other members of the family soon petted him. He seemed to understand that he had been adopted and his playful disposition evidenced itself.

However, when he mischievously chased a calf around the corral one morning, he was caught by the scruff of the neck and admonished by Scott. Recognizing Cougar's reaction in an analogy to human terms, Scott thought, "Cougar doesn't know whether to obey me or to bite me. Let's see if he's learned a lesson."

He released the dog, saying, "Come with me, Cougar," and the dog followed him out of the corral. He ordered, "Stay!" and bent down to scratch the cocker's ears, getting a tail wag in response.

George came running out of Melissa's classroom, and breathlessly asked, "Was Cougar a bad dog, Daddy?"

"Well, he did a bad thing, George. It's up to you to teach him to guard the cows not chase them. I think that he's a smart dog and will learn fast."

****

On the last Sunday in May, the Hermanns and the Masters visited the Myrtlewood Grove to celebrate birthdays. George called the turn when he said, "We never pay any attention to Scott's birthday on the Ides of March, but we look after our youngest, Melissa, in June, and our eldest, Buzz, in July. Happy birthday all!"

Alma spoke up teasingly, "Is this your eightieth, Erastus?"

Buzz laughed out his answer, "Ha, ha, it must be, Alma. Either last year or this one, depending on whether you believe my uncle or my aunt. It seems a long time ago anyway."

George outlined his vacation plans after their picnic beside the river. "We leave tomorrow by ship for Portland, and Uwe will meet us at the dock with a wagon. Our return passage is due in port here on June 25th. That should give Mary and me plenty of time to spoil our granddaughter. Harvey has agreed to tend our store while we're away."

Alma laughed, joshing her husband, "Poor Harvey, he never has time to fish since he retired, he's so busy working."

Harvey retorted, "You wouldn't want me around the house all the time anyway." Speaking to the Hermanns, he added, "You folks enjoy your trip and don't worry about business."

The McClures rode into Port Orford to see the Hermanns off, making a gala event of the ship's sailing. Mary was still waving when the ship steamed around the Orford Heads, disappearing from sight.

Scott suggested having Billy Tucker visit the ranch while Johnnie was away. Ricky asked, "Can we take Billy prospecting at Sixes' lodge, Daddy?"

He agreed good-naturedly as Ricky ran up to the Tucker house to ask Billy. Mrs. Tucker packed a change of clothes for her son and smiled at Billy's excitement, volunteering, "Don't hesitate to put my son to work on the farm chores. He can help earn his keep. Would it be fitting for us to pick him up next Sunday?"

Melissa replied, "Oh, he can stay longer than that. But why don't you come for dinner and a good visit? The Hermann horses need exercise and Harvey Masters will loan them to you for the ride out."

"Thank you, I'm sure my husband would appreciate seeing your ranch after all that we've heard about it. We'll be there at noon," Mrs. Tucker replied as she kissed her son good-bye and said, "You be a good boy, Billy."

****

With Melissa urging him to clear the brush from the hillside behind the barn, Scott had plenty of work for the industrious boys. They were cooperative and helpful, anticipating their prospecting trip. At the same time, Scott cleaned up the dam and pool with its clogged irrigation ducts. The whole family pitched in the second morning, so that everyone could enjoy a picnic in the myrtlewoods and a swim in the river. Billy was getting his taste of a farmer's life.

The next day the boys were treated to a prospecting-hunting overnight campout. Both Ricky and Billy found gold nuggets, and Ricky found an arrowhead which he gave to his friend. Buzz shot a deer as they arrived at Sixes' lodge, so the party had venison and trout for supper, the boys feeling like frontiersmen.

The boys were fast friends by the time the Tuckers arrived on Sunday. Billy's mother brought freshly-baked loaves of bread and his father produced a bag of cookies from the Masters. "Harvey said his missus was in a baking mood yesterday and thought of our children," Mr. Tucker remarked.

After spending a pleasant day together in the sun, the Tuckers invited Ricky to stay with Billy sometime. The boys decided that Ricky should return with Billy's family, and Mr. Tucker reluctantly agreed to take them prospecting on Hubbard Creek.

****

Patrick Hughes was helping Scott stack cut hay in the east pasture when a distraught Buzz rode up to them. Seldom-seen tears glistened in the Old-Timer's eyes as his voice broke in announcing, "Alma died of a heart attack this morning. I'm riding in to stay with Harvey and help with the store."

"Oh, Buzz, I'm sorry. Tell Harvey that we'll be with him as soon as possible," Scott said.

As Buzz rode away, slouched dispiritedly in his saddle, Scott waggled his head in grief. "It's hard to believe that Alma's gone. We'll all miss her. She's an old friend to me, but much more than that to Buzz. They were very close."

Patrick offered to finish the haying, allowing Scott to pack up his family and ride to Port Orford. After paying their respects to Harvey at his home, Melissa relieved Buzz in the store, and Scott took Anne and George with him as he arranged Alma's funeral. Ricky was with his mother when Scott returned to close the store. The next day a sympathetic Louie Knapp watched the store, while the family attended burial services at the cemetery.

The ranch seemed lifeless without Buzz at the supper table, as he stayed with Harvey to help his friend in the store until the Hermanns returned from Salem. Even after he returned to his place in the family, the summer was tainted by the Old-timer's tenuous glimpse of his own mortality.

****

George, Mary and Johnnie lined the rail of the steamship as she rounded the Orford Heads and anchored in the harbor. The McClure children's frantic waving infected the adults and they joined the exuberant exchange of signaled greetings. As they stepped ashore amid welcoming hugs, Mary chattered on about Angela and her daughter, all the while searching for a missing face. Melissa sadly informed their friends of Alma's passing, and its depressing effect on Harvey and Buzz.

George and Mary went directly to the store to console their friends, while the McClures hauled the luggage and Johnnie to their house. Melissa started a fire in the kitchen stove and brewed a pot of coffee, while preparing a light meal from her picnic basket. Johnnie announced that he was starving, so the children ate and went into the yard to play.

As the adults sat down to eat, George made an astute observation, "Harvey appears stable, and even showed a little of his old humor, but Buzz seems a little out of sorts — awfully quiet. I didn't realize that his feelings for Alma were so strong."

Scott reminisced on his arrival in Gardiner years before, "I remember my impression in the Masters' kitchen during that first supper which I shared with them. Alma called him Erastus like it was a special name, and Buzz responded like she was a special person."

Melissa changed the subject, asking Mary, "Tell us all the news from Salem. Is your granddaughter as pretty as her mother?"

Mary answered affirmatively, "Of course, she's an absolute charmer, and we succumbed immediately, spoiling her with attention. Angela informed us that a little brother is due in January. We thought that her second pregnancy was a little too soon, but she and Uwe are happy and healthy, so George didn't say anything. Ha, ha, I raised an objection and Angela put me in my place gently and lovingly, but firmly. I have a strong-willed daughter. Even Kurt backs off when she states her mind."

George laughed merrily at his wife's story, adding, "I'm the only member of either family that Angela never contradicts. I'm blessed by a daughter who honors her father, and Kurt Gerbrunn is just plain envious — much to my delight."

Mary handed Scott a well-wrapped bottle of brandy, a gift from Kurt, and she gave Melissa an edelweiss pin from Inge, matching the one which Uwe had given her four years before.

Their continuing conversation caused the afternoon to pass swiftly, and the McClures departed as Oregon mist closed around the town. They rode home cautiously through thick fog, and as often happened at the sheltered Myrtlewood Grove, rode into sunlight as they skirted slide ridge.

****

Early the next morning, Patrick Hughes trotted into the mist-covered ranchyard, riding directly to Scott who was milking cows in the barn. His excitement raised the pitch of his voice a notch as he cried, "There's a shipwreck on the coast near Elk River. Somer is seeking volunteers to help save the passengers and crew if she sinks. I offered to round you up."

As his neighbor drew a much-needed breath, Scott told him, "See Melissa for a cup of coffee and wait for me." Scott quickly saddled Frank and took the milk pail to his wife, who handed him a sack of bread and meat, with the advice, "You two men should eat as you ride. You'll need your strength if you're going to be of any help to those poor people."

The men gratefully ate the food as they rode slowly through the dense fog, yesterday's coastal front laying against the shoreline all night. As the men were to discover from Somer on the ocean beach near Elk River, a Captain new to the Oregon coast had mistaken Cape Blanco for the Orford Heads in the impenetrable fog and had run aground on the sandy beach south of the point. The sea was relatively calm, and with the tide coming in, the ship should be able to free itself of its sand cradle. All the passengers had disembarked and were walking to Port Orford. A dozen men remained on shore watching the crew lighten the ship by stacking cargo on the shore.

George Hermann rode up the beach toward the mate in charge of the cargo, and seeing Scott, he waved him forward. Scott overheard part of George's conversation with the mate, ". . . bring the Port Orford cargo ashore and my partner and I will deliver it to your customers in town. Now where is it?"

The mate nodded slowly, seemingly in no hurry, and pointed to a dune ahead. "That score of parcels is yours when you sign for it, Mr. Hermann. In fact I wish that you could take all of it, but this lot is bound for Gold Beach."

Smiling at George conspiratorially, the mate commented, "Of course, as damaged goods and on the beach, the skipper might sell cheap, and my crew wouldn't have to worry about reloading anything."

The always enterprising George took his cue from the talkative if slow moving mate, and waded to a dinghy which carried him twenty feet to the steamship. After a brief conversation, Scott saw money pass from George to the Captain and his friend received a sheaf of papers, obviously the bill of lading. When George returned to the cargo, he passed two silver dollars quietly to the mate, saying, "For a 'finder's fee', mate."

George and Patrick remained on the scene as Scott worked the three horses all morning in filling the store's back room with goods. His friend could sort out and deliver cargo consigned to merchants in town, but Scott was eager to see what George had bought "sight-unseen" from the Captain.

When he rode north from Garrison Lake near noon the fog bank retreated to sea, exposing the steamship successfully backing out of the surf, apparently none the worse for wear. Scott returned the horses to his friends, commenting, "I'm glad that ship is all right. Not much harm done, and you may make a little profit on your 'salvage' deal. What's listed on the bill of lading?"

George smiled broadly, answering, "Supplies just like my order that came in today, but twice as much for half the cost. We should make 300-400 percent profit on that cargo, partner."

Scott laughed at his friend's business calculations, saying, "You can pay Patrick and me for the use of our horses, but the profit is all yours. Of course I'll take a gift of some of that wine which I packed to your store."

"Thanks, Scott, but I'm serious about your being a partner. However, we can talk about that after we look over the parcels. Do you want to come with me now and pretend it's Christmas?"

Patrick took the invitation to include him so all three men wasted the afternoon in George's back room, opening parcel after parcel until none were left wrapped. Taking Scott's lead, Patrick went home with wine and credit at the Hermann store. What had started as a tragedy, ended with a cheerful bonus, a situation common to the salvage crews along the rugged Oregon coast. Mariners were constantly lobbying the government for a light house at Cape Blanco and Scott was certain that it would be installed soon.

****

The harvest of corn and potatoes was bountiful, but his bean crop was a complete failure, causing Scott to conclude, "This must not be bean country. I'll plant more potatoes next spring. They always grow well in this soil."

Scott suggested a deer hunt to Buzz the morning of first frost, and after a little coaxing, the Old-Timer agreed halfheartedly, poking along so slowly that Scott gave up the hunt without finding any game. However, Buzz was cheerful at supper that night, suggesting they try again when he felt better.

The Christmas holidays came up on the McClure family with good health and a day or two of clear skies. The children followed the family custom of opening a few presents at home and carrying one or two to open at the Hermanns'. Scott had saved a bottle of wine to share with Captain Tichenor, who was home from the sea for Christmas. Scott and Melissa called at the Tichenor home to toast the holiday season, and even the proper Mrs. Tichenor joined in the festive rite, sipping a taste of spirits. The McClures asked about Ellen, who was attending school in San Francisco, and William answered frankly, "Ellen is an attractive young lady and very popular, but she discovered boys and I fear that she prefers San Francisco to Port Orford. I'm to be introduced to a 'young man' on my next trip south. Children do grow up, don't they, dear?" He shared a quiet moment of melancholy with his wife, and then asked about the McClure family and the Myrtlewood Grove.

When Scott related Captain Tichenor's news about his daughter, George spoke up, "Angela heard from Ellen after she and Uwe settled into their new house. I forgot to tell you, but my daughter predicted that her friend was a permanent San Franciscan. There's not much to hold young people in Curry County unless they have real roots here. I know Angela is quite happy in Salem."

Buzz spoke in support of the Oregon coastal counties. "There's no place like this country for men who want to be free and independent. City life may be all right for women and children, but give me the frontier any day."

The McClures rode home from the Hermanns' Christmas dinner, beginning a mild and prosperous winter on the Sixes, with fishing, hunting, and tending stock activities which were shared by Scott, Buzz, and the growing Ricky.

Chapter Fifteen

As Port Orford continued its growth as a bustling port town, George Hermann was a name respected throughout the community and along the Oregon coast. People considered him to be a leader, in the likes of Captain Tichenor, John Sampson, and Louie Knapp, seeking his advice as they shopped in his store.

Whenever George showed signs of self-importance, Mary and Scott deflated his egoism, Mary with gentle counsel and Scott with barbed teasing. George accepted their "attitude adjustment" pressure with good common sense, remaining a steady and popular citizen to whom people talked. In this mode, he was not only a leader, but the fount of community news. He seemed to know anything that happened, or was going to happen, in Port Orford.

It was in the latter fashion that George relayed interesting information to Scott during a spring visit to town. Fairly bursting with his news, he told his friend, "William Tichenor is retiring from the sea and settling in his Port Orford home. He said that he needs to tend to his business interests in town."

Scott responded, "That's good news! When's his last voyage?"

"He's sailing tomorrow for Portland, but he claims that his next call at Port Orford will be as a passenger. By the way, Mary says that his wife thinks that it is about time. She'll be happy to have a full-time husband."

Scott chuckled at George's remark as his friend continued, "The Captain wants to see you Scott. Something about his timber business. He didn't tell me anything else."

"Ha, ha," Scott chortled, "You mean to tell me that you don't know something going on in this town?"

George smiled as he responded, "That's right, but I expect a full report after you've spoken to Tichenor."

Scott found his sea captain friend on the port beach, supervising the unloading of cargo from his ship. After an exchange of pleasantries, Scott offered his congratulations and said, "I'll be glad to see you around town. I always enjoy our visits."

Captain Tichenor replied, "Thanks, Scott. We have been friends for a long time, haven't we? That's why I wanted to see you. We get along well, and I want you to be my partner in a logging company. The market for lumber in San Francisco is excellent now, and I'm arranging contracts down there, but I need someone locally to manage the logging operation. I have rights to over two hundred acres of cedar and fir on Hubbard Creek. What do you think of this deal?"

Scott was flattered, commenting, "I appreciate your offer, but why are you using Hubbard timber instead of stands on the Sixes and Elk Rivers?"

"Scott, you know that there are no roads for hauling logs to port. Your friends would like to sell logs but transportation costs have been the bane of your planning. Hubbard Creek trees are right here ready to be cut and loaded on ships. What is your real concern?"

"I guess it's that my farming is pretty much a full-time job, although logging work in the Sixes valley might be possible. Hubbard Creek is just too far away from my Myrtlewood Grove Ranch. I don't see how I can do both jobs."

The Captain thought for a moment before suggesting, "Perhaps you could hire a hand to work your farm. Buzz Smith knows what needs to be done."

Scott nodded and replied, "I'd thought of that possibility, but frankly I like farming more than logging. Thanks, but I have to decline your offer. If you need a good man to run your logging crew, I'd recommend your own man, Tucker. He's reliable and strong, and the other men respect him."

"I agree that he'll make a good crew boss, if I can't convince you to be a working partner. Think it over, and if you change your mind, see me upon my return from this last voyage," Tichenor concluded as he left Scott and walked back to the beach activity.

Scott stood silently in thought as he watched the stevedores working, reaffirming the unequivocal decision to remain a farmer.

****

Cape Blanco weather patterns were unusual during the hot dry summer, with very little coastal fog present, and even less rainfall. Scott shook off a feeling of impending dread which dogged his subconscious, and resolved to enjoy the warm temperatures and pleasant conditions.

Tucker had been promoted to crew boss for Tichenor's logging operations, and when Scott visited his home with Ricky in August, the logger asked for help. "Thanks for recommending me to Captain Tichenor. The extra pay is great, but I'm too busy to take the boys prospecting on Hubbard Creek. Would you fill in for me?"

Scott agreed readily, "Certainly! You can keep your promise to Billy by staying overnight with us since your work is in that area. I'm sure your son will be happy with that arrangement."

During the same time period, the trio of Buzz, George and Cougar were exploring the Sixes valley and the Old-Timer's hunting grounds. Melissa and Anne were amazed at how much work they could accomplish with the menfolk gone.

****

Scott sold a steer to the new butcher in August, and then delivered his last steer to George the following month. He was planning on wintering fourteen cows and his bull, which would constitute a reasonably-sized herd for the feed crop available on the ranch.

He hired a hand sent by Hughes to help at harvest time. After a week of stacking hay in the east pasture, the man asked for his wages and left the valley. Buzz and Melissa worked with Scott to harvest his corn and potatoes, but it was early October before he turned over the soil and declared the job finished.

With fair weather holding, Melissa declared a week-long school holiday, and the family rode into Port Orford to shop and to visit.

A good harvest and a prosperous year should have put Scott in a festive mood, but as he drank beer with Buzz in the tavern, he confessed to the Old-Timer, "I've had one of my 'funny feelings' all summer. I should be happy instead of depressed."

Buzz suggested, "Why don't you join George and me on our hunt tomorrow morning? A break is what you need."

"Thanks, but I promised Melissa that I'd clean out the irrigation system. You know how the pipes get clogged. Where are you heading?"

The Old-Timer chuckled, explaining, "Well, George tells me that Cougar will lead the way. Your son is sure that his dog is smart enough to find a deer for us. We'll cross the river and let fortune decide which trail to follow."

The trio went hunting at dawn and Scott buried himself in the job of cleaning the pond outlets and water pipes. The hours flitted by as he worked in and out of the pond, with Melissa bringing him a cup of coffee and Ricky asking if he and Anne could go swimming. Midday approached before the water ran freely through the irrigation channels.

Scott felt a chill on his wet torso as a breeze swirled through the yard. The air brought him the smell of smoke and a few ashes from the chimney. He lowered himself into the reservoir one last time to check out the pipes, when his senses came to full alert.

There was no fire in the stove, nor smoke and ashes from the chimney.

Scott listened briefly to an alien roar in the wind and searched the sky, seeing smoke instead of the expected haze.

Leaping out of the water, he bellowed, "Fire! Fire! Fire!" as he ran to the house, meeting Melissa at the door. "Get Ricky and Anne from the river pool!" he shouted as he slipped behind his wife to reach for his Sharps rifle and cartridges. Stepping back outside, he raised his rifle skyward and fired three shots as fast as he could reload.

Running to the far corner of the corral, he talked to the nervous livestock inside as he looked around the hill toward his east pasture and hay stacks. He saw livestock running aimlessly between burning haystacks, and then one by one the cows collapsed in the burning grass. He thought, "The fire is using up the air. The cows are suffocating to death rather than being burned." Just then the fire swept up the south hillside in flashes of incandescence, a line of flames moving indomitably forward through the treetops over the "old cougar" trail. Scott thought, Where are Buzz and George?

Shaking that worry from his mind, Scott spun on his heel and dashed to the house, as Ricky yelled in alarm, "What shall I do, Dad?"

Forcing calm and confidence into his voice, Scott instructed his son, "We have to protect the buildings by watering them down. These ashes in the air are live sparks, and can start a new fire anywhere. Get all the buckets that you can find and tie ropes to them — like this." Scott demonstrated what he wanted and then climbed to the roof, shouting, "Now fill them up for me — open the irrigation pipe." Melissa and Anne followed Ricky's lead, and as Scott doused the roof, they threw water on the walls of the house.

The barn provided a greater challenge to the fire fighters, and when it was thoroughly wet, they breathed a sigh of relief.

As the family gathered at the back of the barn, Scott suggested, "We can backfire around the foot of this hill and across the side of the corral. The forest fire is burning southerly toward Elk River, but a change in wind can still pose a threat to the farm."

"Scott, where are Buzz and George?" Melissa asked plaintively, not sure that she wanted to hear his answer.

"Somewhere over there, dear," he replied, pointing in the general direction of the fiery conflagration raging across the river, "but I don't know for sure. For now all we can do is protect our ranch and wait."

They continued to backfire, and to douse the buildings until mid afternoon, when it became clear that the ranch was safe. Scott told Melissa, "I hate to leave you alone, but I have to search for Buzz and George. I expect Patrick will come by when it's safe to leave his dairy farm. Don't let him try to follow me."

Melissa nibbled her lower lip, and cried, "Oh, Scott, is it safe for you to go across the river?"

Scott reassured his family, "It's safe enough. The fire has moved higher onto the ridge, and the lower trail should be cool enough to walk around. I'll be careful."

As he left the corral, Scott ventured into the east pasture to find his dead livestock, six yearling cows and Pinto. His haystacks were ashes laying on the scorched field. It would be spring before cows could graze here again. He noted that the myrtlewoods were untouched and several prominent firs on the north side of the pasture had not burned. The fire appeared to have started upriver and traveled southwesterly. Scott found himself speaking his thoughts aloud, "I hope the fire stops at the ridge. Somer and Unicans are right in its path if it keeps going."

Scott crossed the all-but-dry riverbed and walked into the still smoldering undergrowth of the once verdant forest. Casting about the lower hillside for some clue of the trip, Scott circled continuously until he found himself back at the river's edge. Shrugging, he muttered, "What a mess! I wonder which trail Buzz decided to hunt. Maybe I should climb to the south ridge so I can see something."

As he contemplated the safest route to the still-smoldering crest, the wind shifted momentarily, and a sudden gust amplified the forest fire's thunderous roar. Scott's ears caught another sound amid the oscillating noises; a dog's barking came and went as the air swirled out of the south. He was unable to pinpoint direction, but he recognized Cougar's bark and called out to the dog. As the fickle wind returned to its southerly course, Scott alternated his shouts with whistles. He couldn't hear Cougar, but he hoped that the dog could hear him. Sure enough, a blackened and limping cocker ran down the hillside, much of his hair singed and his paws showing the effects of running on hot ashes.

Barking what seemed a command, Cougar turned and retraced his steps with Scott following closely and voicing words of encouragement, "Take me to George and Buzz, old boy. Come on Cougar, you can do it."

The dog crossed a hillock and dropped out of sight, barking impatiently for Scott to follow him down the slope. Within minutes he reached a small creekbed and turned upstream toward a rocky cul-de-sac, from which a spring originated. Lying in a shallow pool of seeping water was Buzz's still form. Gulping down a spasm of panic, Scott bounded over smoking deadfall and ran to the Old-Timer's side, thinking, where is George? only to find him in the shallow water, covered by his protector.

"Buzz, can you hear me?" Scott asked as he kneeled beside the burned and blistered body of his friend.

"Scott . . . no strength . . . move me . . . George . . . is hurt . . . agh . . ." was his whispered reply.

Scott gently cradled Buzz's chest and stomach in his arms, and moved him a few inches from the pool. The Old-Timer grunted in pain and his limpness attested to his unconscious condition. George's face was out of water and only his hair was burned. Cougar was licking his face, anxious for his master to show signs of life.

George stirred but didn't answer his father's nudging. As water in the slowly-filling pool approached the boy's mouth, Scott gripped his shoulders firmly and inched his face away from the encroaching water. Suddenly George's eyes popped wide open, and he screamed shrilly, eyes rolling in their sockets as he fainted from the pain.

Scott examined his son's torso without finding any serious injury, but when he reached into the pool and touched George's left leg, the boy jerked spasmodically. The leg lay twisted at an odd angle; and a point of broken bone extruded from a laceration in the skin, blood flowing afresh in the wound.

Without hesitation, Scott moved the boy's legs out of the water, and then grimly straightened the left leg as George groaned in unconscious agony. Seizing two nearby branches, he snapped them from the tree and stripped the blackened bark. He bandaged the bleeding wound with strips of his shirt, before fashioning the limbs into splints along the broken leg, which he secured with his and Buzz's leather belts. George could now be carried to safety.

"George . . . how is he?"

Scott turned to Buzz, answering, "He'll make it, Old-Timer, thanks to you. Now let me help you."

"No . . . agh . . . don't . . . no use . . . agh . . ."

Scott looked at the heavily blistered back and head of the man who was like a father to him, and tears filled his eyes. He knew that Buzz was dying, had been dying for several hours, as his stalwart spirit held death at bay until George was safe. Now the light in those old eyes dimmed as he struggled to speak, "Thanks, son . . . take care of . . . our family . . . love . . ."

As the last breath left the body of Erastus Elijah Smith, Scott murmured, "And I love you, Buzz, more than I ever told you. God be with you, Old-Timer."

Scott wept without embarrassment beside his dead friend, until George's tiny voice said, "Don't be sad, Daddy. Buzz told me that

he was dying, but he would stay with me until you came. He said
that he wanted to say good-bye to you firsthand."

Scott stood up and told George, "I think it's time that I took
you home, son. Can you grit your teeth and put your arms around
my neck?"

"Yes, Daddy, but we can't leave Buzz here alone." He hesitated briefly, and ordered Cougar, "Stay here, boy! Stay!" The dog
settled next to the lifeless form of their friend as Scott set off for
the ranch with his son in his arms.

Trudging across the shallow Sixes downriver from where
Patrick Hughes and Ricky were dressing out the dead cows, Scott
traversed the myrtlewood grove and proceeded directly to the
house. Anne was sitting on the doorstep watching for him and
called out, "Momma, Daddy and George are here."

Scott was in the yard when Melissa came running out of the
door, her joyful expression fading as she saw George's leg. Her
son bravely piped up, "I'm all right, Momma, it's just a broken
leg." Melissa smiled wanly as she kissed George on his grimy
cheek.

Looking about, she asked, "Where is Buzz? And Cougar?"

George answered in a grown-up manner, "Buzz was burned
when he saved my life, and he told me that he wouldn't die until
he could say good-bye to Daddy. Cougar's guarding his body until Daddy can go back for him."

Scott interjected, "George will tell you the whole story while
you doctor his broken leg. I'll take Ricky with me to bring Buzz
home." Taking a blanket from Ricky's bed, he left the ranchhouse,
striding east to inform Patrick of the day's events and his plans.

His neighbor sympathized sadly, "I'm sorry to hear that Buzz
died. He was a good man and my friend. You take care of him
and I'll finish butchering these cows."

As Scott and Ricky neared the spring pool, Cougar was waiting patiently for them, tail wagging furiously as Scott praised him
for being a good dog. Ricky turned pale at the grisly sight of Buzz's

burned corpse, but clamped his jaws tight and helped his father wrap the blanket around their deceased friend. The boy searched for Buzz's pack and Sharps, finding both items burned to a cinder and lying on the hillside above the pool. Ricky held the ruined rifle by its barrel as Scott carried his friend across the burn and back to the ranch.

****

Early the next morning, Buzz was laid to rest next to Richard Nelson's grave, in the spot that both men had chosen years before. Dressed in his best clothes and holding his burned old Sharps, he looked peaceful. Patrick returned in time to join the McClures in prayer as they closed the grave.

As they walked up to the cabin, Patrick asked, "And how is the lad this morning? Will his leg heal?"

Melissa wagged her head with some confusion, saying, "He's sleeping soundly and his wound is healing. However, his left leg is shorter than his right leg, and it's twisted a wee bit. George will have a permanent limp, but I thank God that he's alive. Was everything all right at your farm last night?"

"Yes, I'm lucky. In fact I feel a little guilty as I see your losses and can anticipate the terrible damage that Somer and Unicans are experiencing. Smoke was rising from the Elk River valley and moving south. I hope that we can get some rain before long or Port Orford will burn too. It's a demon forest fire, that's for sure."

Scott checked the ranch perimeter for "hot spots," those mounds of live coals hidden in tree trunks and deadfall, which could rekindle the fire. He found and extinguished over a dozen pockets before he was satisfied that the ranch was safe.

He and Patrick filled their meat sheds with the butchered beef, and in the late afternoon, they loaded the remaining meat on their horses. They walked around the forest fire using the ocean beaches to reach Port Orford. The town was engulfed in smoke and flames, houses and shops afire. One of the storekeepers was throwing clothing and bolts of cloth over the bluff onto the beach in an attempt to salvage something from his business.

The two men delivered their meat to the emergency kitchen which had been set up on the beach. The community operation would have to feed the homeless people for several days. Patrick agreed to return the horses, and watch the Sixes valley while Scott stayed in town to help fight the fire.

The Hermann store was seared but still standing as George led a water brigade dousing buildings in the business district. Scott stepped into the firefight without a word and worked through the night as George's store and a few other structures were saved. Not finding his friend as dawn approached, Scott found the Hermann house in ashes, and finally happened on Mary at the Masters' house, which was damaged but standing. He learned that George and Johnnie had gone to Hubbard Creek with the Tichenor crew to fight the fire.

Over a welcome cup of coffee, Scott exchanged news with Mary, offering, "You're welcome to stay with us while repairs are underway. Tell George that I'll be back to help him tomorrow. I have to visit home and see how my George is faring, and I'd better do ranch chores while I'm there. Can Melissa help you in any way?"

Mary shook her head, responding, "I can't think of anything now, but I'll have a list when you return tomorrow. Tell your son to get well."

****

Coastal fog was spreading over the town as Scott walked along the beach on the way home. He thought, Good! The moisture in the air will damper the fire. Better late than never. He increased his stride into the burgeoning dawn. As he crossed into the Sixes valley and strode upriver, the sky lightened perceptibly. He passed through the cut, crossing slide ridge and the log bridge, and on the knoll he emerged into bright sunlight of a new day. Before him lay his emerald myrtlewoods set against the blackened hillsides. Melissa met him in the middle of the yard and they embraced without conversation, both enjoying the beauty of the Myrtlewood Grove as they began another chapter of their life.

Epilogue

The "demon forest fire" of 1868 was responsible for the destruction of large stands of virgin timber in Curry County as well as the town of Port Orford. Pioneer families who settled the area deserve much credit for building the settlement, and then rebuilding it during the decade of the 1870's. Their tenacity and their love of the Cape Blanco coastline was demonstrated as new homes, farms, and businesses were established.

Captain William Tichenor epitomized that pioneer spirit, remaining actively involved in community affairs despite suffering financial losses in the fire. He remarried after his wife died in 1880, and lived in Port Orford until his death in 1887, while visiting his daughter Ellen's family in San Francisco. His favorite child had married a successful lawyer named McGraw, and from that union came eleven children. The "Belle of Curry County" lived out the rest of her long life in San Francisco. Her siblings remained in Port Orford for many years, Anna marrying George Dart, an Indian Agent in the 1850's.

Louie Knapp maintained his hotel business for seventy-five years somewhat of a record for longevity in Port Orford. The bright light kept at night in his seaward hotel window served as a sailor's beacon until the Cape Blanco Lighthouse was activated on December 20, 1870. Knapp was a popular figure with seamen and neighbors alike.

Patrick and Jane Hughes continued to expand their dairy business and their family, farming over two thousand acres of Sixes River land, while Jane delivered four more children. In 1898,

Patrick completed a Victorian mansion for his wife on a rise over-looking the Sixes Estuary. He died in 1901, but the family home remained in use for decades. It was restored as a museum in 1989, and stands today as part of the Cape Blanco State Park.

Port Orford lost its bid for the county seat in those troubled years following the great fire, but remains a hub of activity in the pristine beauty of the Oregon coastline.

To this list of real people and events described in Oregon history books, the reader should add the Tututni Chiefs Chat-al-hak-e-ah and Sa-qua-mi of the Quah-to-mah (commonly referred to as the northern Rogues) of the Hubbard Creek and Sixes River villages. Other Indian characters join Scott McClure, his family, his close friends, and his occasional foes in the author's fictionalized version of the period.

Historical Perspective

The Oregon coast received scant attention from European explorers noted for their adventuresome probes of North America. Its remote location and inhospitable weather combined with a stark seashore and scarcity of harbors to make this coastal area uninviting to most expeditions. It was overlooked by the Russian trading ships sailing to the Tsar's settlement in California, and bypassed by expeditions seeking the Northwest Passage. Yet during the three centuries following the voyages of Columbus, sailors did find and chart the Oregon Coast.

As early as 1543, the Spanish explorer Ferrelo visited southern Oregon (Cape Ferrelo near present-day Brookings was named after him). Ferrelo sailed north and sighted a white cape, leaving it unnamed. Sebastian Vizcaino led three ships along the coast north of Cape Ferrelo in 1603 (Cape Sebastian is named after him). He sent two ships north from Cape Sebastian while he explored nearby. Captain Martin D'Aguilar sighted a prominent white headland jutting into the Pacific, with ten small islands to the south of it, and he named it Cape Blanco de San Sebastian. Cape Blanco is the westernmost promontory of the contiguous United States.

American Robert Gray (1788) and Englishman George Vancouver (1792) sighted Cape Blanco. Gray passed it over as he went north to discover the Columbia River, but Vancouver spent more time on this coastal area, deciding that Cape Orford (after his friend, Earl [George] Orford) was a more suitable name. In the early 1800s, the name Blanco stuck to the cape, and Orford became associated with the port south of Cape Blanco.

Fur traders traversed the coastal rivers of Oregon and recorded geographical routes to the southern coast. The Hudson's Bay Company sent fur companies from Fort Vancouver to the Umpqua River (1826-1846) to trade for beaver and otter pelts, establishing the trading posts of Verneau (Scottsdale) and Fort Umpqua (Elkton). Alexander Roderick McLeod was one H.B.C. captain who visited the Umpqua valley in 1826, and then explored south to the entrance of the Rogue River the following year.

The American fur trader Jedediah Smith travelled north from California with a party of eighteen men and three hundred horses in 1828 trading for furs along the way. His log included references to a lake (Garrison), and "Oregon Camp Site No. 9 South Side of Sixes River" (near Cape Blanco). Smith's party arrived at the Umpqua River with heavily laden horses, and found local Indians unfriendly to white men and covetous of the party's horses and furs. A savage attack ensued by the Umpquas, in which fourteen men in the party were killed, and the horses and furs were taken by the Indians. Jedediah Smith and Richard Leyland escaped to Fort Vancouver, with two other survivors arriving several days later. The coastal rivers were clearly Indian territory in 1828.

However, farming settlements in the Willamette Valley began prospering as the fur industry faded. Routes of travel which were established in the 1820s were used in the 1840s by adventuresome farmers, loggers, and fishermen. Merchant ships found profitable stops at the Umpqua River. Fights between white settlers and Indian tribes were common as tribal lands became sites of trading posts and settlements. The white man was greedy, wanting to own land used by the Indians for centuries. Disrespect for Indian rights prevailed and no compromise was satisfactory or lasting. Western civilization was expanding its roots along the coast of Oregon.

The United States government claimed Oregon Territory through the purchase of the "Louisiana Territory" and by encouraging Americans to settle in the Pacific Northwest. The authorization to a "Donation Claim" allowed settlement of land without consideration of Indian rights, analogous to their nonexistence.

Concurrently, gold was discovered at Sutter's mill in California, and great numbers of Americans arrived to seek their fortunes. Not all of them stayed in San Francisco or the gold camps around Sutter's mill, but turned to Oregon Territory for timber as well as gold.

Captain William Tichenor plied his steamship, Sea Gull, between San Francisco and Portland. His knowledge of the Oregon coast and the Columbia River were exceptional. He was the second Columbia River "Pilot" authorized by Governor Gaines, and his ships sailed into several coastal river ports. As a young man he had served in the Illinois legislature, moving his family to San Francisco where he established his reputation as a merchant and sailor. Sailing as a mate and then a ship's captain, he had been within sight of Cape Blanco and the Port Orford Heads. During one visit he had seen the harbor alee of the Heads, which he envisioned as a donation claim for opening a settlement to develop gold deposits and timber stands.

In May of 1851, Captain William Tichenor was in Portland with the Sea Gull loading cargo for San Francisco. He discussed his plan for a settlement with a friend named Palmer, who introduced him to J. M. Kirkpatrick. Tichenor proposed that Kirkpatrick enlist a party of about ten men to build a post at Port Orford for the purpose of supplying gold miners and loggers who would be attracted to this untouched region. Tichenor expressed belief that local Indians were few in number and not hostile toward whites. Eight men joined Kirkpatrick (captain of the party) on the Sea Gull's voyage south to Port Orford. They were J. H. Egan, John T. Slater, George Ridoubt, T. D. Palmer, Joseph Hussey, James Carigan, Erastus Summers, and Cyrus W. Hedden. The party was meagerly armed, having only seven firearms, one sword, and several knives.

The Sea Gull sailed from Portland on June 4th, clearing the Columbia River bar on June 6th, and anchoring in the protected harbor at Port Orford on the morning of June 9th. Indians came down the hillside onto the beach to menace the white men who were debarking in small boats, conveying in sign language that they were not to land.

In light of the Indian's hostility, Kirkpatrick insisted on taking the ship's cannon ashore. He selected a defensible position on "Battle Rock," a tidal island rock connected to the beach by a steep slope. Battle Rock had cliffs thirty to forty feet high bordering harbor waters, and the cannon commanded the only approach to the party's campsite atop the rock. Bulwarks were set up astride the ridge, and the cannon was in place before Captain Tichenor sailed for San Francisco. He promised to return in fourteen days. As the Sea Gull left the harbor, the Indians repeated their demand that the party leave, threatening to take their scalps.

When dawn broke the next morning, more Indians arrived on the beach, and many arrows were shot at the white men on Battle Rock. No harm was done from that distance, but Kirkpatrick and his men grew alarmed at the Indians' warlike behavior. A canoe carrying twelve Indians came from the south, and a red-shirted chief landed waving a long knife and giving a terrifying yell, as he led his warriors up the rocky slope against the whites. Arrows filled the air, striking the bulwarks and a plank shield held in front of Kirkpatrick and Carigan. Palmer and Ridoubt were wounded by these missiles as the Indians stormed up the ridge to within eight feet of the defenses. The cannon was fired into the Indians, killing Red Shirt and several warriors. Most of the Indians ran away to the beach, but others charged in hand-to-hand fighting behind the bulwarks until all of the remaining Indians were killed. The party dressed its wounds and was preparing for a second attack when a rifle shot tore Ridoubt's thumb off. An Indian stood up from behind a rock and was killed by return fire. More Indians continued to arrive on shore, but Battle Rock was not attacked.

Later in the day, a chief walked down the beach, laying down his bow and arrow as he approached the rock, gesturing friendship. Kirkpatrick met him at the foot of the ridge and agreed that they could remove their dead. This chief was a large man with yellow hair and light skin, who was later identified as the survivor of a wrecked Russian ship. He had been saved by the Indians and had lived with them for a number of years. All of the dead Indians were removed from Battle Rock and the beach, and taken over the hill opposite the battle site — except for the red-shirted chief. The Russian kicked him and stripped the shirt from his body before following his tribesmen over the hill. Kirkpatrick had explained to his new chief that they would leave in fourteen days when the Sea Gull returned for them. The Indians remained in the area during the ensuing days, leaving the party alone even as their numbers increased to over three hundred men.

On the morning of the fifteenth day, the Indians made a second attack on Kirkpatrick's party. A new red-shirted chief made hostile signs, waved a long knife, and gave a piercing scream for the charge. Kirkpatrick and Carigan fired at the chief simultaneously and killed him. The other Indians fell back and regrouped down the beach. A new red-shirt harangued the warriors in a voice which carried over the distance as well as the sound of the surf. Indians continued to arrive and gather on the beach with hostility evidenced in their action.

The beleaguered party was low on ammunition and food, with two members suffering from serious wounds. Facing them were over four hundred Indians dancing around beach fires and gaining strength for a third attack. The party's escape plan proved ingenious, as the men began felling trees and improving fortifications in a ruse to have the Indian lookouts leave the rock and report their activities. When the way was clear, Kirkpatrick's party fled north, continuing their harrowing adventure of narrow escapes, hunger, and weariness, until all nine men reached Scottsburg on the Umpqua River ten days later.

Captain Tichenor had been delayed by legal business in San Francisco, but he returned to Port Orford soon after the battle. He sighted several canoes racing away to the south as he entered the harbor, and from signs of battle on the rock, he concluded that the men had been killed. He sailed on to Portland to report the massacre, later to learn that the men had escaped to safety.

With persistent determination and renewed faith, Tichenor returned to Port Orford on July 14 with a well-armed party of sixty-seven men. A blockhouse and settlement were started, and the U.S. Army established Fort Orford on September 14, 1851, as the most westerly fort of the U.S. Army. The Rogue River Indian War continued for five years, but white settlers overwhelmed the scattered Indian villages and the U.S. Army defeated recalcitrant bands of Indians. After the Geisel Massacre in 1855, all Indians were banned from the Oregon coast and shipped to inland reservations. The establishment of Port Orford opened the settlement of a major section of the Oregon coast.